The *Highway to H*

SINS OF THE FATHERS

J.D. Toepfer

Copyright © 2022 J D Toepfer. All rights reserved. No part of this publication may be used or reproduced in any manner whatsoever without written permission from the publisher, except in the case of brief quotations embodied in critical articles and reviews. All characters appearing in this work are fictitious. Any resemblance to real persons, living or dead, is purely coincidental.

ISBN: 9781737360315

Edited by Emily Marquart

Cover Design and Interior Formatting by Victor Rook

"Beliefs and customs may change, but superstitions never die."
—*Anonymous*

Prologue

June 1737
Bank of the Olt River, Vascea Province within Danubian Principality of Oltenia

Constantin Antonescu raised his cupped hands from the river and savored the cool water as it passed through his calloused fingers and down his parched throat. A long roll of thunder echoed through the trees, and Constantin eyed the sky warily. A steady rain had plagued the Antonescu family for days as they trudged through the rugged and treacherous Carpathian Mountains toward the Olt River. It seemed their bad luck was not about to change.

Constantin filled a container with water and brought it to his wife, Ana, and pregnant daughter, Maricela. As they refreshed themselves, Constantin's grandsons chased each other around the wagon, but Constantin was oblivious to their game. He anxiously watched the gathering storm clouds with weary eyes and then stared at the river. Crossing it was their next obstacle to building a better life for themselves, far from the Vascea province.

The storms had swollen the river, and the current was strong, as evidenced by the floating tree limbs passing quickly in the water. Constantin frowned. Maricela's delicate condition was a significant concern, and he searched the riverbank for the best place to cross. He nervously bit his fingernails and returned to the wagon.

"It is late, and a storm is coming," Constantin declared. His furrowed brow could not hide his concerns about the changing weather. Pointing at the woods, he added, "Andrei. Marius. Fetch sticks for a fire. Quickly, before it begins to rain again."

As his grandsons ran off to collect the firewood, Constantin yelled after them, "But do not go too far into the woods."

Constantin kept a watchful eye on his grandsons as he prepared to start a fire. He had done his best not to alarm his family, but he was sure that someone or something had been following them since they left their village. Each morning he found strange footprints in the mud around their camp. Constantin knew of no animal with three toes and a protruding talon on the end of each digit. The tracks were unmistakable, and the imprints in the Earth were deep. Whatever had made the footprints was of immense size and weight.

Constantin placed an ember in a ball of dried grass and blew it into a flame. Soon, there was a roaring fire, but he could not shake the uncomfortable feeling something was watching him. His eyes surveyed the woods for an intruder, but nothing was there. He breathed out a disguised sigh of relief when his grandsons returned with more wood for their fire. Silently, he counted to be sure all six of his grandsons were in camp, and as Ana prepared dinner under cover of a stand of tall Blue Spruce trees, Constantin pondered their departure from Ramnicu.

The endless warfare that pitted Oltenia and its Wallachian and Transylvanian allies—first against the Turks of the Ottoman Empire, then the Russians, and finally the Hapsburg Monarchy—resulted in constant upheaval. Every village they lived in was caught in the middle of these warring parties, with nowhere to escape the destruction that inevitably came with their arrival. To avoid the endless bloodshed, the family had moved to the remote town of Ramnicu. However, the result was that they found themselves increasingly isolated from the outside world.

The most recent Hapsburg invasion had reduced Ramnicu to nothing more than a fortress outpost. The vibrant trade that once took place there had disappeared, and Constantin soon found that the documents he produced for government officials from his printing press were no longer necessary. While providing for his family was Constantin's primary concern, the other reasons for leaving Ramnicu dominated his thoughts. His jaw tightened as he stared into the flames and renewed his vow to leave behind the superstitions that permeated the lives of his Transylvanian brethren and threatened his family. Forever.

Last fall, when his neighbor's livestock began to disappear, Constantin was confident that it was the work of a predator, such as a wolf. The villagers, however, increasingly believed otherwise. Constantin embraced the Enlightenment ideas that came with the first Hapsburg invasion in 1719, but his friends resisted them.

In retrospect, he should have realized they would grow to view him with suspicion because he had become a printer and had not remained a farmer like themselves. Rather than raise his neighbors' intellect, these innovative ideas only drove them to clutch to their primitive beliefs that much tighter. This superstition meant that what Constantin accepted as pure coincidence was viewed by his friends and the other villagers far more suspiciously.

The whispering amongst the villagers began when his eldest daughter, Maricela, became pregnant for the seventh time. Maricela and her husband Mihail had made Constantin a proud grandfather six times before, all handsome and healthy boys. However, local folklore warned of a horrible fate that would befall Maricela and Mihail's seventh child if it were a boy. Myths and legends predicted the child would be born a Strigoi, a horrible beast that would perish shortly after birth, only to return from the dead to feed on the blood of the living.

Constantin angrily condemned any such talk, but the villagers grew more fearful when other signs associated with the legend began to befall his family. When Ana went to the market, she could hear the whispers behind her: *"Nenorocit"* (poor soul). The older boys began to torment their grandsons because of their red hair, another supposed bad omen. Of course, up until that time, no one had ever discussed, mentioned, or raised any concerns about their hair color. But now, children who had been their friends stopped coming to the Antonescu home, presumably because their parents would no longer permit it.

"Red hair?" Constantin muttered to himself, stoking the fire. "What does that have to do with anything, let alone some curse?"

Unfortunately, tragedy followed shortly thereafter when Mihail disappeared. Days later, a villager came across his body hanging in the woods. Stories spread that Mihail had been seeing an older woman, reported to be living alone deep in the forest. Rumors alleged she was a witch and that Mihail had hanged himself because of a curse she had cast upon him. When a search found no such woman, the townspeople whispered that Mihail was a *Fustangiu* (womanizer) who committed adultery and was so ashamed by his sins that he hung himself out of guilt. They talked about Mihail's immoral life and the fate he suffered as a further example of how the Strigoi curse was descending on the family.

Constantin clenched his fist. He had a theory of his own about what had happened to Mihail, and it was far more disturbing. He believed that Mihail was lured into the woods or forcibly taken there and hung by the villagers. Their message was clear: They wanted the Antonescu family to leave the village immediately. The final outrage was the insinuation from their former friends that Maricela and Mihail's marriage was illegitimate.

"They were married by a priest, and most of them were witnesses." Constantin threw a log in the fire.

A flash of lightning lit up the sky, and a loud clap of thunder startled Constantin. He wiped the coffee he had spilled from his shirt as a steady rain began to fall. The calendar indicated it was almost summer, but Constantin felt a shiver run down his spine and moved closer to the fire. He adjusted the blanket covering his daughter Maricela and gazed down at her with a soft smile and the loving eye of a proud father.

As he sat alone, keeping watch by the fire, Constantin was soon once more lost in his thoughts.

Yes, he had broken with tradition by allowing Maricela to decide whom she would marry. He'd also refused to seek a blessing for their union from Count von Bethlen, the regional administrator, because Constantin considered him no better than a common thief. His friends had even praised his courage in doing so. Back then, it would have been laughable to question the legitimacy of his daughter's marriage. Now, her virtue was all the village seemed to discuss.

Looking up at the heavens, Constantin questioned, "God, is my family paying the price for my sins? Did my pride lead us to this?"

They had left the village three weeks ago, the reputation of Constantin's daughter in tatters and the name Antonescu forever disgraced. All this misery so that his former friends could justify their fears and irrational beliefs.

As they had departed, he could not help but notice the garlic braids hanging from the homes as protection against *'The Antonescu Curse.'* Constantin's daughter stood tall to maintain her dignity as their cart went through the village square. But his grandsons sat crying, still mourning the loss of their father, as the only home they had ever known faded from their view.

Constantin tried to comfort his family and assured them he would take care of them. He vowed that, in time, they would have another home. His printing business had raised Constantin's awareness that a much larger world existed, far beyond the remote backwoods where they had been living. He read about growing cities such as Vienna, Paris, and London. He even read about a *'New World'* across an ocean. He admitted to not knowing much about such things, but it gave him hope that there was a place for the Antonescu family. It was just waiting for them to discover it.

Suddenly, Constantin flinched.

"I must have fallen asleep*,"* Constantin moaned groggily.

The rain had ceased, but the clouds still concealed the moon, whose light illuminated the sky in an eerie shade of yellow. Constantin squinted into the darkness, searching for the source of the noise that had jarred him awake. He saw nothing.

Crack!

Constantin quickly turned right and felt a bead of sweat roll down his chest. His heartbeat accelerated, and he jumped to his feet. Someone was coming.

A figure emerged from the tree line and moved toward their camp. The fire had died down, and Constantin could not determine who or what it was in the dim light. He peeked over his shoulder at his sleeping family and grabbed a piece of firewood.

"Who's there?" Constantin asked firmly. "Show yourself!"

The figure came into view, and the firewood fell from Constantin's hand.

"Constantin, don't you recognize me?"

Stunned by what he saw, Constantin stood motionless, his mouth agape. Finally, he asked, "Mihail? How can this be?"

***

Present Day
A deep cave outside the ancient town of NonaKris, Greece

The seemingly dead body floated motionlessly in the pool of foul, stagnant water. Suddenly, a bolt of lightning from a powerful storm struck the ground, sending a wave of energy deep into the bowels of the Earth under the Peloponnesian Mountains. The chamber, once black as the night sky, was now ablaze in a brilliant white light. The electricity surging through the Earth caused an eerie phosphorescent aura to surround the floating figure.

For months, the body lay in suspended animation, unaware of the world beyond its cold, sarcophagus-like cavity, but that was about to change. Despite months of inactivity, day after day, absorbing the dark energy of the sacred water had made the figure more powerful. The natural spring in which it rested was no ordinary pool of water.

The Greek people knew the stream as *Mavroneri* or dark water. But it had a more menacing name in ancient times. This pool's origins lay deep within the planet, in the evil underworld humans call Hell. This cave is where the mythical river Styx began its ascent to the Earth's surface.

The long journey through sulfur-infested caverns poisoned the water and turned it into an acid bath capable of eroding metal. However, absorbing the caustic and toxic elements from the water only made the "being" tougher. During its repose, while the body was still, its mind communicated with the most wrathful of Masters. The planning and preparation of the two evil geniuses were now complete. The long months in seclusion were over; the vile sabbatical at an end.

First, the eyelids snapped open, and the red eyes quickly adjusted to the light. The figure exited the dark water, and its skin instantly dried as it left the pool. Donning the clothes shed months ago, the entity went to a stone staircase carved into the mountain a millennia ago. The thick bedrock made teleportation impossible, so a long climb to the surface would be required.

Step after step, the entity ascends until nearing the entrance, it sees the daylight for the first time in months. Upon exiting the cavern, the figure greets the summer sun with an icy stare. Its clammy skin feels no warmth, and its mind reaches out to another figure. A foreboding message silently echoes across thousands of miles: *"The time has arrived, my friend. Rise, and together, we will set in motion events that will reveal our master's supremacy and ensure his ultimate triumph."*

Instantly, in a cave halfway around the world, a beast conceived by depravity awakens to fulfill a prophecy whose origin extends back as far as the existence of humankind itself.

Chapter 1

Late January, several weeks after Amanda Aitken's death
Jack Aitken's residence in Bristow, VA, thirty miles outside Washington, D.C.

Tick. Tock. Tick. Tock. Tick. Tock.

The ordinarily boisterous Aitken house was eerily quiet as Jack Aitken sat behind the desk in his study, staring at the brass pendulum of the grandfather clock in the corner of the room. He watched it swing back and forth repeatedly.

Jack's attorney, J. William Barrett, stared out the window at the gray winter sky. Attorney Barrett finally broke the silence. "Looks like it may snow."

"I heard a few inches," Jack replied, never taking his eyes off the clock.

Unlike Barrett, he refused to look out the window. Jack knew the black vehicle with detectives from the Virginia State Bureau of Criminal Investigation was parked where it had been for months. Right at his front door. They were only waiting for the call that would allow them to take him into custody for murder.

The two men had maintained a silent vigil all afternoon, expecting a call from the District Attorney's office. The wait was excruciating. What verdict would the Grand Jury hand down? Would Jack be indicted for murder, or would he be a free man?

Jack ran his hand through his graying hair and replayed the morning after Amanda's death in his mind. Although he had called the paramedics immediately, he quickly rose to the top of the suspect list. Jack was the only person in the room when Amanda died. Investigators questioned Jack about his conduct and why the machines were not operating when medical personnel arrived. Jack maintained his silence but finally waived his right to an attorney on one condition: He would only speak to Anne Bishop. Only Anne would understand his irrational, if not downright crazy, explanation of that unfortunate night.

Jack explained to Anne the dilemma that Amanda's request to let her die had laid before him in painstaking detail. He held nothing back, telling Anne everything that had happened, including the attempt by Lucius Rofocale, the demon head of government for the Devil himself, to tempt him by suggesting that he had the power to bring Amanda back from the dead.

Anne took Jack's statement, and while she requested clarification from him on several details, she made no overture to comfort Jack or even send him a subtle message that she understood his predicament. The process was like every police show Jack had seen on television, all by the book.

After finishing his statement, the magnitude of what was happening became very real, and Jack anticipated the police would arrest him. Instead, Jack recalled how the door swung open, and J. William Barrett, impeccably dressed in a black pin-striped suit, swaggered into the room.

"I am the appointed counsel for Mr. Aitken." Barrett pointed toward the door. "Do not say another word, Jack. Get your things. We're leaving."

Jack was stunned but did as instructed. They quickly left the building and arrived at Barrett's Ford Escalade. A legal assistant opened the door, and once inside the vehicle, Barrett handed Jack a piece of paper. "I am sure you have questions, Mr. Aitken."

"I've seen you on television, Mr. Barrett," Jack began. "I cannot afford—"

"There's no fee, Jack."

"What?"

"Look at the document I just gave you."

The writing on the top of the paper indicated it was an invoice, stamped *Paid in Full.*

"You have a very persuasive benefactor who wishes to remain anonymous. I have agreed to their stipulations and taken your case on a strictly confidential basis."

"I don't understand…"

With a broad smile, Attorney Barrett stated, "I have explicit instructions. That means I do not tell you who is paying your bill in exchange for taking your case. Capiche?"

The car pulled out of the parking lot, and Jack sat in the backseat, dumbfounded.

"Let me explain what happens next," Barrett went on. "Ms. Bishop will present her findings to the District Attorney, who will certainly convene a Grand Jury. The Coroner's Office has already appointed a Medical Examiner. They are performing an autopsy on your wife's body as we speak."

At the Grand Jury hearing, the M.E.'s findings were interesting.

Amanda Aitken's injuries, sustained during her kidnapping, were life-threatening and irreversible. She would have never recovered. There is a strong likelihood that Mrs. Aitken was dead already before the life support equipment stopped functioning.

Ring! Ring! Ring!

Jack jumped, jolted back to the present, and Attorney Barrett quickly checked the phone. The look he shot at Jack confirmed it was his contact in the D.A.'s office.

"Talk to me," Barrett answered abruptly. He listened. "I see. Right."

Jack inhaled and bit his fingernail nervously. Barrett put the phone back in his pocket.

"Turn on the television, Jack."

Jack fumbled with the remote and finally found the power button. Standing on the Manassas Courthouse steps in front of a collection of microphones was the District Attorney, dressed in a navy-blue suit with a red tie. His poker face revealed nothing about the Grand Jury's verdict.

"I will make a brief statement and will take no questions now. The Grand Jury has completed its deliberations surrounding the death of Amanda Aitken. Based on the testimony presented by the Medical Examiner, the Prince William County Police, and Mr. Aitken, the Grand Jury has declined to indict Jack Aitken."

The District Attorney continued his statement, but Jack did not hear the rest of it. He slumped in a chair and buried his face in his hands, overcome by relief, not joy.

Barrett placed his hand on Jack's shoulder. "It's over, Jack. You're free and clear."

Jack raised his head. "Thank you, Mr. Barrett. Thank you."

Suddenly, Louis and David burst through the front door.

"Dad!" Louis yelled.

"You're not going to jail!" David stated with glee.

Jack rose from the chair, forced a smile, and embraced his children. However, his mother and father-in-law were noticeably absent. They turned away at the door and walked back to their car. Despite the comfort he found in the arms of his family, Jack could not shake the feeling that even though the authorities had brought no charges against him surrounding Amanda's death, he was far from free and clear.

Over their shoulders, he noticed that the grandfather clock's pendulum had ceased to swing. Jack knew this was not the end.

***

Late March, a little over a month since Jack Aitken's acquittal
Jack Aitken's residence, Bristow, VA

Jack grabbed the brown foliage of what had last year been a patch of daylilies and shoved them in a garbage bag. The events at the burial mound in Culpeper and their aftermath had not allowed him to do his regular fall cleanup, but he found the work relaxing, nonetheless. It was an understatement to say that Jack and his family were relieved by the Grand Jury's acquittal, and Jack was sure who had helped orchestrate it. While he had the best attorney someone else's money could buy, were it not for Anne Bishop, he easily could have found himself accused of murder and facing a lengthy period of incarceration—or even the death penalty.

Jack adjusted the baseball cap on his head. Over the past several weeks, he began to piece together a theory of what had happened.

He suspected that once Anne turned the case over to the District Attorney, she somehow worked behind the scenes to influence the investigation. Jack reasoned that Anne's long-standing relationship with the Coroner's Office might have enabled her to have input into the appointment of a Medical Examiner, someone she knew personally. Then, under the pretext of her investigation, Anne spoke with this "friend" and explained the circumstances surrounding Amanda's injuries and death. Such a conversation could explain why the Medical Examiner strongly suggested Amanda was already dead before the machines stopped functioning.

Then there was his confession to consider. Jack knew his admission of guilt to Anne was on tape. The District Attorney and the Grand Jury saw this tape, yet no questions about Lucius Rofocale ever surfaced. This absurd omission by the authorities could only be possible if Anne did something to the video to ensure that the mention of Lucius Rofocale would not appear. While he was grateful for whatever Anne had done for him, he could not shake the question of why she had done it. Jack had to know.

A week later, he asked her to dinner.

***

April 10th
Giuseppe's Restaurant, Haymarket, VA

Jack arranged for Amanda's parents to stay with the boys. He and Anne agreed to meet at Giuseppe's Restaurant in Haymarket at 7:00 p.m. Jack requested a quiet table in the corner so they might speak privately.

They found they had much in common as they ate dinner, including an avid interest in gardening and American history. Both had degrees in political science and history, but Anne's history degree focused on criminal justice.

Jack gulped down the remnants of his after-dinner drink and used the liquid courage to finally ask, "Anne, what role did you play in the investigation surrounding my wife's death?"

Anne tapped the rim of her glass, trying not to reveal that the question caught her off guard. She hesitated. "Wh-why would you ask me that, Jack?"

Jack persisted. "Did you influence the investigation in any way?"

Anne finished her brandy and paused to steady her nerves while considering Jack's question. The room became eerily quiet until Anne finally broke the awkward moment of silence.

"Jack, will you agree that what we talk about will not be discussed again after tonight?"

He nodded.

"I did my job, both as a detective and as a member of JESU."

The mere mention of the Justice Ecumenical Society United caused Jack to grab the glass in front of him and quickly down the rest of his drink. Even months later, it was disturbing to think of their involvement in the events that occurred last fall.

Anne continued. "I believe you and your family had suffered enough. I did not see why your children should lose their father after their mother's tragic death. I suspect that being autistic, your children have already experienced difficulties coping with what has happened."

"They have," Jack acknowledged.

"I struggled initially with what you told me about Amanda's death, but I was not in the room with you and your wife. Based on what you shared, your actions come with their own punishments. You presented no danger to society; nothing good would come from prosecuting you. I also have my concerns about how JESU treated you. Candidly, this entire affair has left me questioning the organization. I am wrestling with what my role should be with it moving forward."

Before Jack could react, Anne continued. "But what you really want to know is, did I interfere in the investigation in any way? Did I do anything to tip the scales of justice to exonerate you?"

"Did you?" Jack asked with a raised eyebrow.

Anne shifted in her chair, then folded her hands and placed them in her lap.

"The ultimate decision-makers solicited my opinion, and I gave it to them. As for Lucius Rofocale, I did erase your reference to him. It was irrelevant to the investigation. Let us face the facts, Jack. The District Attorney would have thought you were crazy and subjected you to a psychological evaluation that you and I know would have been unwarranted. Frankly, you are probably the sanest man I know right now."

Grateful, Jack leaned forward and whispered, "Thank you, Anne. For everything. I am not sure what to say right now other than I have never really had a lot of friends in my life. I guess I've always believed in quality over quantity. I now consider you among the few friends I have. If you ever need me for anything, I will be there. If there is anything you require, you only need to ask."

Their eyes locked, acknowledging the unbreakable bond they now shared.

"Jack, I know your experience with JESU is not a positive one, but there are principles of the organization that I still believe in, even if I may have lost faith in the society. One of those tenets is tempering justice with mercy. I know you are feeling tested, but I hope you will give faith a chance."

Jack offered his hand. Anne grasped it, cementing their friendship. They got up from the table, and Jack walked Anne to her car. It was a chilly evening, but a bead of sweat rolled down his back. There was one final subject he was reluctant to raise. A wound he knew was likely never to heal, but a sentiment that he felt the need to express. They reached Anne's car.

"Anne, I never had the chance to tell you how sorry I am about Mark."

Anne looked up toward heaven while speaking in a quaking voice. "Jack, you don't owe an apology for that. It will take time for me to process what happened to him and my role in it."

"Me too, Anne." Jack wiped away a tear that was about to fall down his cheek. "Me too."

Anne entered her car, and Jack shut the door. Before she pulled away, he knocked on her window.

"One last thing. I meant to tell you this at dinner. Thank you for hiring my lawyer. I want to reimburse you for that."

Anne shook her head. "I didn't hire your lawyer. An attorney with that background is way out of my price range."

Jack waved as Anne drove away. Shaking his head, he asked aloud, "Well, if she didn't pay for the lawyer, who did?"

***

February 12th, about one year after Amanda Aitken's death
Jack Aitken's residence, Bristow, VA
10.00 p.m.

BAM!

The north wind slammed into the window over the sink, startling Jack back to the present. It had already been a long, frigid winter. While today had been Louis's birthday, a blizzard—according to the local weather channel, the *Storm of the Century*—had been hammering Bristow for hours.

"Winter storm *Lucius.*" Jack shook his head and grumbled, "You can't make this shit up."

Lucius Rofocale had disappeared after Jack rebuffed his offer to resurrect Amanda. Anne had phoned Jack months ago to say that even the chatter among demons gave no clue about his potential whereabouts or what happened to him. There were even whispers in the demon community that he was dead. Jack did not believe that for a second. He feared Lucius was out there, and it was just a question of time until his evil shadow appeared in Jack's doorway.

Jack held the plate for an eternity before finally putting it back on the countertop. The dishwasher was already full, and dirty dishes overflowed from the sink, but Jack did not have the energy to clean them. The blizzard had canceled Louis's party, but no one in the Aitken household had really been in a mood to celebrate. Even a year later, they struggled to adjust to life without Amanda. Louis and David were in bed, and Jack wished he were too, but even sleep would not shelter him from the storm that raged in his soul. The darkness had settled in and would not set him free.

Jack rubbed the stubble on his chin. What was happening to his sons was breaking his heart. Both David and Louis seemed stuck. Their inability, or unwillingness, to discuss what happened to them during their captivity caused both boys to become withdrawn and self-isolating. They struggled to regain their social skills and continued having nightmares about the kidnapping, particularly their captor, Lucius Rofocale. Jack tried to be both father and armchair psychiatrist since no medical professional would have taken the boys seriously if they tried to tell a story about demons and a gate to Hell. Jack hung his head, knowing he was failing at both roles.

Louis, always the more outgoing of the two boys, stopped communicating with his friends. Besides going to work, he stayed in the basement watching television and playing video games. It pained Jack to see him avoid his preferred activities, including seeing movies, bowling and going out to dinner. Making things worse was the reality that Louis was slowly losing the social network he had built in high school. His friends were graduating from college, moving away, getting married, and working full time. Louis was watching the parade of life pass him by, and Jack did not know how to help him regain his place in it.

He shut the kitchen light and headed upstairs. The wind was howling, and Jack was sure he heard it calling Amanda's name. Pausing at the top of the stairs, he stood in the doorway of David's room. The previous summer, David had received a CAR T-cell transplant at Johns Hopkins Hospital in Baltimore to cure his Leukemia and save his life. While the initial results had been favorable, these new cells functioned indiscriminately and killed both healthy and cancerous cells. It left David weak and vulnerable to infection.

David required regular visits to the cancer clinic to receive antibodies and immune-boosting drugs. Jack thanked God that David was alive but could not bring himself to utter the word *remission*. David's condition was still tenuous, and his survival remained uncertain. Superstitious due to the family's past trials, Jack worried that even thinking David was in remission would be like tempting fate.

Jack closed the door to his bedroom and stood at the window, watching the snow piling up outside. A tear ran down his cheek. Shamefully, he reached into his dresser drawer and felt around for a bottle. Jack grimaced at the spicy flavor of the rye whiskey as it hit the back of his throat.

Like his sons, he was having difficulty moving forward. He could not shake his guilt over Amanda's death. His role in it cast a dark shadow over everything, and it was as if they were all paying penance for Jack's sins. The night he had shut off the machines keeping her alive was the beginning of a downward spiral that was now pushing Jack to the brink of personal destruction.

***

March 21st
Dr. Kathleen Colby's office
The First Day of Spring

Jack sat in the waiting room of Dr. Colby's office. While Jack had played a part in foiling both Lucius's and Father Desmond's twisted plans, his friendship with Anne was the only positive he took away from what happened in Culpeper. Anne urged Jack to seek help, but even their friendship could not stop Jack's descent into despair. The time after Amanda's death was brutal, and even the simplest things were a struggle. Jack could not help but ask, *Haven't we had enough?* Even Amanda's family had difficulty accepting her death and the events that led to it. Despite being cleared by the Grand Jury, her family withheld their forgiveness. Jack understood their decision, as he found he could not forgive himself.

He did not get in the way of the relationship between the boys and Amanda's family. Jack knew he needed their help and wanted it for David and Louis's sake. Eventually, a cool but workable relationship developed, with David and Louis's best interests being everyone's primary concern. They coexisted for the boys' sake, and Jack saw signs that the boys were benefiting. Both appeared calmer as new routines, such as Louis's grandparents taking him to and from work, fell into place.

Jack, however, was in free fall. As the family's troubles worsened, so did Jack's drinking. Each night he would drink himself into a stupor. Dinner was often a six-pack of beer consumed after his boys went to sleep. He often found himself waking up in a chair instead of his bed. Sleeping in the room where he and Amanda had lived and loved was difficult. The memories and reminders of Amanda were everywhere.

There was no burying his grief and guilt, and he frequently replayed the night of Amanda's death in his mind. He warred within himself about the decision to turn off the machines. On the one hand, he tried to rationalize it as merciful and what Amanda wanted and needed him to do. At the same time, he vilified himself for euthanizing her in a moment of weakness, taking the easy way out. He could find no middle ground and, as a result, no forgiveness for himself.

Somehow, Jack eventually pushed himself to talk to his therapist, Dr. Kathleen Colby. If nothing else, he hoped to try to soothe his conscience. He walked into Dr. Colby's office, unshaven and disheveled. Jack told her everything that had happened. He even told her about Lucius Rofocale. He held nothing back, including his decision to turn off Amanda's machines. Dr. Colby sat and took notes, but as usual, her facial expression did not betray what she might be thinking.

When Jack finished unburdening himself, she put down her notepad. "Jack, I want you to promise that you will make an appointment to see your physician in the next few days. I will not lie to you. You do not look well at all. You seem exhausted and have lost considerable weight since you were last here."

Making eye contact, she continued. "Promise me you will do this first thing when you go home."

Jack's tired gaze met hers, but he did not speak. He simply nodded.

"First, Jack, please accept my condolences for the death of your wife. I am also deeply sorry to hear about David's illness."

Half-jokingly, Jack asked," So, am I certifiable or what?"

"Jack, I will not give you 'psychobabble' or anything like that. You have quite literally been through the wringer. You have had to face life and death decisions that none of us ever wants to make. After losing the most vital person in your life, you now confront the reality of potentially losing a child. To answer your question, no, I do not think you are certifiable."

Jack lowered his head and sobbed. Through his tears, he pleaded, "How do I live with what I have done? How do I move forward when I honestly am not sure that is what I want?"

"I believe some part of you may not want to move forward, but the Jack I have come to know has a passionate belief in doing the right thing and the inner strength to realize it. I am speaking with a man trying to reconcile the decisions he has had to make to begin the process of putting the pieces of his life back together. Deep down inside, you know the way to honor Amanda's sacrifice is to be there for both of your boys. As a mother myself, if I were in her situation, I would want my husband to dedicate himself to love, protect, and support our children."

"I know you're right, but don't you have an obligation to report to the authorities what I did? I murdered my wife, for God's sake."

"I would report it in a situation where a patient has committed an actual crime and is a danger to others. You are not a murderer. What you did was make a difficult decision to honor the wishes of the woman you loved. She knew what she was asking you to do, and Amanda believed you loved her enough to do what she requested. Even under the worst circumstances, she had the wisdom and courage to know what was best for her children. Many would consider her to be a hero, and rightfully so. However, what you did was equally heroic."

Jack smiled weakly. "Thank you. I really needed to hear that from someone I knew would tell me the truth."

Jack reached down to retie his sneaker. "There is one thing we haven't talked about." Jack hesitated. "What I shared with you about Lucius Rofocale and the Gate to Hell."

Dr. Colby removed her glasses and placed them on her lap. She brushed back her brown hair and exhaled deeply. "If I have learned one thing in the years that I have been a therapist, it is to keep an open mind. Part of my job requires me to determine whether my patient is rational or not. Jack, we have known each other for a long time now. You have never given me a reason to believe you are not of sound state of mind, but I trust you understand that a Gate to Hell and this Lucius business are pushing the boundaries of what I can accept as sane."

"So you don't believe me, then?" Jack asked warily.

"I believe that you believe it is true, Jack."

Dr. Colby paused. "However, I sure hope this was a hallucination from your drinking. Because if it is not, what you have described is horrifying beyond words."

***

Jack made a follow-up appointment and called his physician when he got home. Due to a cancellation, Dr. Hackett had an opening that same afternoon. After performing a complete physical, he sat down with Jack.

"While I gave you a complete physical, just looking at you tells me all I need to know. I will not bullshit you or sugarcoat it. You are in bad shape, my friend."

Jack sat quietly, but inside he was worried.

"You have lost a considerable amount of weight, and regardless of what you might tell me, I know you have a drinking problem. You have a swollen abdomen, spider veins on your cheeks, and jaundice. I have seen it before, and there is no hiding it from me."

Without mentioning Lucius Rofocale or the incident at the burial mound, he shared with Dr. Hackett that he had lost his wife and its significant impact on his family.

"I am truly sorry for your loss, Jack. We need to find a way to help you confront your demons before it is too late."

Suppressing a flinch at the reference to demons, he shared that he had just come from Dr. Colby's office.

"Kathleen is an excellent psychiatrist, Jack," Dr. Hackett added with a tone of relief. "If I have your permission, I will contact her. She and I can discuss your current condition and what we can do together to help you."

"Thank you, Dr. Hackett. I appreciate your concern."

That night, after the boys were asleep and the house was quiet, Jack prepared for his nightly ritual and opened the refrigerator door. As he grabbed a beer bottle, Dr. Colby and Dr. Hackett's warnings started to run through his head. He thought about David and Louis and considered what Amanda would think. Jack knew she would be unhappy with him. Not angry and maybe not even disappointed, but undoubtedly upset that he was putting himself through such suffering. He took a deep breath and put the bottle back.

Jack leaned his head on the refrigerator, shut the door, and spoke softly. "Amanda. That's for you."

Chapter 2

June 21st
Brunswick County Sheriff's Office, Bolivia, NC
4:30 p.m.

Today was officially the first day of summer, but it had felt like summer beginning in early May in coastal North Carolina. The humidity moved in and would stay until November. Sheriff Glenn Hill kept his office door open, trying to catch any hint of movement in the air which might cool his office down. He had been Sheriff of Brunswick County for more than ten years, and he couldn't remember it ever getting so hot in here. He wiped the sweat from his brow and curled his lips as he exhaled. A knock sounded at the door.

"Hi, Glenn." Officer J.J. Haller waved from the doorway. "Do you have a few minutes?"

Jimmy James Haller, or J.J., had been Sheriff Hill's friend for over twenty years. They met while training at the police academy after J.J. had left the navy. J.J. was an exceptional police officer, and after several detectives retired over the past eighteen months, Sheriff Hill had leaned on him heavily. In fact, maybe too much.

"Sure, J.J. Come in and have a seat."

Usually, J.J. was impeccably dressed, but today his uniform was wrinkled. He also was unshaven, and his hair was unkempt. He was uncharacteristically disheveled. Officer Haller closed the door behind him, which immediately raised red flags for Sheriff Hill.

"What's wrong, J.J.?"

J.J. fidgeted in the chair. He wrung his hands and took a deep breath.

"I know you don't need to hear this now, Glenn, but I have reached the end of my rope. I'm feeling very run down and mentally drained too."

The Sheriff ran his hand through his graying hair. "I know I've put a lot on your shoulders, J.J."

"I don't want to let you down, Glenn, but as we've discussed, I need to go in a different direction with my life."

Sheriff Hill leaned forward and put his hands up. "Let's not do anything hasty, J.J. Maybe some help from the department psychiatrist—"

"It's not just the work," J.J. interrupted. "It's more than that."

Glenn Hill tilted his head slightly and scratched the back of his head. "It's our other responsibilities, isn't it?"

J.J. nodded. "You've been kind enough to listen to my concerns about that, which I appreciate. I feel like nothing we do is making a difference, though. I'm having a crisis of faith. I can't shake it."

"I know, J.J. I wish I had the right words to say to bring you some comfort."

"I'm totally exhausted."

J.J. sneezed and searched for a handkerchief. Sheriff Hill handed him a tissue box.

"I've had this cold for weeks, too. I just can't seem to shake it."

The Sheriff sighed. "Sounds like burnout to me."

"You are a good friend, Glenn. The best I've ever had, but…."

"As your friend, J.J., I want you to do something for me."

"Name it, Glenn."

"Don't put your papers in yet. I'll arrange a leave of absence. Take a sabbatical for a few months, and then we'll talk. Maybe it will help you clear your mind. You can do some soul searching and see how you feel then." Sheriff Hill put out his hand. "Agreed?"

J.J. gripped Sheriff Hill's hand tightly. "Okay, Glenn. Out of respect for you."

As J.J. opened the door, Sheriff Hill called out, "You stay in touch, J.J."

Turning back to Sheriff Hill, J.J. gave a quick thumbs up. "Sure thing, Glenn."

***

July 21st
Research Vessel Cape Fear, Waters off Ocean Isle Beach, NC
Noon

"Shark on!" J.J. Haller yelled as he began reeling in the piano wire that doubled as a fishing line.

Six scientists quickly exited the ship's cabin and peered over the vessel's side.

"Looks like an eight to ten-footer, J.J."

One of the Australian researchers added, "Just the size we are looking for, mate."

After a thirty-minute battle, the tired fish floated alongside the boat, and J.J. secured it with a harness.

"Okay, Doc." J.J. held the fish still. "Do your stuff."

Dr. Neil Frazier held up the spear and checked the tag on the tip. Reaching down, he prepared to push the spear's end into the shark's dorsal fin.

"This has an extra powerful sensor embedded in the tag. Hold the shark steady, J.J."

J.J. Haller gripped the harness strap tightly and pulled it upward to immobilize the animal.

Dr. Frazier stuck the spear's tip into the shark and quickly removed it. The barbs on the tag of the sensor were embedded into the skin, securing it to the fish.

"Let her loose, J.J."

He dropped the strap attached to the harness, and it drifted down below the shark. Now free, the shark hesitated and slowly began moving its tail and swimming away from the ship.

"Perfect!" Dr. Frazier declared. "That's how we do this!"

Later that afternoon, J.J Haller sat in the front of the boat, enjoying the refreshing sea breeze blowing on his face. He held his hands above his head, stretching his muscles and admiring his deep bronze tan. All the time spent in the sun had lightened his brown hair until it was almost blond. It was another long day of backbreaking work, but J.J. enjoyed the physical labor, and his chiseled physique was another nice fringe benefit. It wasn't easy to explain, but dripping with sweat in the hot sun felt almost cleansing.

It had been a month since J.J. had taken a leave of absence from the Brunswick County police. While he was feeling better about things, there were deep-seated doubts that he continued to be unable to shake. One thing J.J. was sure of was working on the ocean felt better than being a cop.

Dr. Frazier approached J.J. "Hey, J.J., did you hear the joke about…."

J.J. frowned as the professor went on with his bawdy joke. While J.J. enjoyed this job, he found the *schoolboy* antics of the professors, particularly Dr. Frazier, to be tiresome. Cape Fear was like a floating frat house at times. The innuendos about their female students and the filthy, off-color jokes were inappropriate in any setting and did nothing to restore J.J.'s faith in people.

The overgrown adolescent masquerading as a prim and proper professor was a dichotomy that had become all too familiar to J.J. It was what he referred to as *leading a double life,* and it was eroding his faith. His faith in his job, his faith in his people, and his faith in God. Sheriff Hill had done his best to try and help J.J. see the greater plan, God's plan. But J.J. could not see past humankind's suffering. What made it all worse was that J.J. believed his double life might make him an even larger hypocrite.

***

July 21st
J.J. Haller's residence, Calabash, NC
9:30 p.m.

Alone in the dark apartment, J.J. Haller downed the last drops of beer. He tossed the empty bottle, which shattered when it hit the hardwood floor.

"Protect the weak, the defenseless, and the helpless," J.J. slurred. "That was the oath I took as a cop."

He pulled another beer bottle from the ice chest and twisted the cap off. "Then there was my other oath." J.J. took a deep gulp of beer.

Looking up at the ceiling, J.J. declared, "Well, God. I haven't saved anyone. Nothing changes. We keep losing people while we wait for a message from you—all these secrets and contradictions. The higher-ups say that honesty is not always the best policy. Well, I'm being honest with you, God. I'm not sure I even believe in you anymore."

J.J. slammed the empty beer bottle on the table and saw the flashing red light. Slowly, he reached for the telephone and fumbled to hit the button to retrieve the message.

"J.J., this is Glenn. I've been trying to give you space to work things out. Unfortunately, I have some bad news. We lost Mac Jennings. When we speak, I will tell you more about it."

"That's perfect." J.J. shook his head and slammed his fist on the arm of the chair. He leaned back and instantly dozed off in a drunken stupor. As a result, he didn't hear the rest of the message.

"I know my timing is terrible, but J.J., I really need you to come back. No more drills. The computer broke one of the ciphers. They're coming, J.J. And soon."

***

J.J. was jolted awake by an audible crunch—like someone stepping on shards of broken glass. He shot up straight in his chair and rubbed his eyes to adjust to the bright light that now engulfed the room.

"What? What was that?" he asked coolly, still seated in his chair.

Shielding his eyes from the light, J.J. saw the outline of a large shadow on the wall.

"Is someone there?" he shouted.

No answer. J.J. reached for the military service pistol on the table next to him and got up from the chair. His heartbeat quickened as he pointed the weapon in the shadow's direction.

J.J. silently coached himself to take deep breaths, instinctively remembering his police training. The words of one of his academy instructors raced through his head. *Always remain calm.*

J.J. announced, "Unless you want to get shot, I suggest you show yourself."

The light quickly faded, and a figure stepped forward. It was a tall male with jet-black hair, dressed in a plaid shirt. J.J. could not immediately place the face, but he seemed familiar.

"Hello, Jimmy James."

Only one person had ever called J.J. by his real name.

J.J. slowly lowered his pistol. "Who are you?"

"Don't you recognize me, son?"

"My father was a racist, misogynistic drunk. He's dead."

"People can change, Jimmy."

J.J.'s jaw fell open slightly. "Dad? That's not possible."

The figure moved toward J.J. with its arms open. "Son, you have passed over."

"I'm dead?" J.J. asked in disbelief.

"Embrace your father, J.J."

J.J. hugged his father, who immediately disappeared, leaving J.J. alone in total darkness.

"What's going on?" J.J. asked aloud as he frantically searched the darkness. "This can't be heaven."

A loud, sinister-sounding phrase echoed around him. "No, J.J. This is not heaven."

"Wh-who's that?"

The menacing laugh that followed sent shivers down J.J.'s spine.

"You are not dead, although you will wish for death before this is all over. Mr. Haller, you now know what it is like to be possessed."

"NO!" J.J. Haller screamed.

A wicked grin came over the face of the figure standing in J.J. Haller's living room. Having assumed J.J. Haller's identity, the figure gloated triumphantly, "That was far too easy."

SINS OF THE FATHERS

***

August 15th, eighteen months after Amanda Aitken's death
Bristow Manor Golf Club, Bristow, VA

In August, Northern Virginia's weather usually brought what locals called the three Hs: hazy, hot, and humid. Today was no exception. It was only 10:00 a.m. as Jack, David, and Louis teed off on the tenth hole to start the back nine at Bristow Manor Golf Club. The thermometer in the golf cart already read eighty-seven degrees. Jack preferred early tee-off times for various reasons, not the least of which was the prevalence of afternoon thunderstorms. These storms caused David great anxiety when he was indoors, let alone out on a golf course.

Jack was surprised when, back in April, the boys suggested they go to the Broad Run Golf Facility to hit balls. He was delighted to fulfill their wish. Playing golf had brought the three men closer since Amanda's death. It enabled Jack to connect with his sons in a way he never imagined would be possible. It also began the process of healing Jack's heart.

The family's love of golf seemed to mirror their recovery from the loss of Amanda. Louis and David slowly improved as Jack began to teach them the game. Louis enjoyed the routine of developing a swing tempo, and the rote nature of hitting ball after ball on the driving range was soothing to him. David always enjoyed a challenge. The physical disability of being born without his left arm meant his life consisted of overcoming one obstacle after another.

Fortunately, David was naturally adaptive. Just like scooting on his butt in place of crawling, reading a book on the floor by holding a page down with his foot, or learning to zip his jacket with one hand, step by step, David taught himself how to grip and swing a golf club. Jack marveled at his determination and the steady improvement in his scores resulting from his fierce pursuit of the game.

The boys asked to go to the range regularly, and consequently, their game quickly improved. Jack had given each of them a copy of the rules of golf, which he knew they would soon learn and retain with their photographic memories. It wasn't long before they were reminding him what the rules were!

Once he started taking them out on a golf course, there was no stopping the trio. They played three to four times a week, often in the evening after Louis got home from work and if David felt up to it after any Leukemia treatments. Sometimes Jack could talk them into walking rather than taking a golf cart, which got the three of them much-needed exercise.

Jack was elated to have found something the three could enjoy together. He knew Amanda would have shared their enthusiasm, and for the first time, he felt as if he were genuinely honoring her memory. The more they played, the better the three men felt in mind and body. Both boys began to recover their social skills, and Louis decided to move from part-time to full-time employment. This increase in his hours was something Amanda and Jack had encouraged him to do for nearly two years. Louis began to socialize with his friends again, and David was preparing to go back to high school and complete his diploma, which had been interrupted by his Leukemia diagnosis.

As David boomed a drive down the left side of the fairway, Jack could not help but recall a philosophy class he took in college and the study of German philosopher Friedrich Nietzsche, who wrote, *"What doesn't kill you only makes you stronger."* His life was still a work in progress, but at least today, he felt strong enough.

Chapter 3

August 15th
IHOP Restaurant, Gainesville, VA
5:00 p.m.

"There they are!" David shouted.

"Over here, Mom." Jack waved, beckoning Amanda's parents to join them in a booth.

When Jack had called to invite them, he sensed a different tone in his mother-in-law's response. Perhaps it was wishful thinking, but he hoped he was not fooling himself.

"I'm going to have a waffle," Louis uttered gleefully as his grandparents sat down.

"Me too," Amanda's mother added, smiling at her grandsons.

The group quickly ordered dinner. Handing the menu to the waitress, Jack's mother-in-law happily asked, "So what did we shoot today, boys?"

"I shot eighty-eight," David declared. "I should have parred that last hole, though."

"Eighty-seven for me," Louis added. "I got you by a stroke, David."

"How about you, Jack?" asked his father-in-law.

"Eighty-five for me, Dad." Jack chuckled.

The boys giggled and teased each other as they played games on their phones while waiting for the food to arrive. As Louis and David played, Jack and his in-laws enjoyed a cup of coffee.

"Mom and Dad, thank you for the golf membership. We enjoy it immensely; believe me; we're getting our money's worth."

Jack's mother-in-law gazed lovingly at Louis and David. "Amanda would be proud of them, Jack. And of you too. You have turned your life around these last few months, and these boys are evidence of that. I know this has been hard on everybody. You are a good father, Jack, and you were a good husband. Amanda loved you, and so do we."

Jack wiped a tear from his eye and placed his hands on top of his mother-in-law's hand. "Thank you, Mom. You do not know how important it was for me to hear you say that."

A still emotional Jack took his glasses off to clean them.

"By the way, I never had a chance to thank you and Dad for hiring my attorney. It was beyond generous of the two of you."

Jack's father-in-law turned to his wife with a look of surprise. "Jack, there must be some misunderstanding. We didn't hire the lawyer."

Jack's phone rang. He saw Anne Bishop's name appear. "Mom and Dad, please excuse me for a minute."

Jack and Anne had kept in touch since they had dinner a little over a year ago. Shortly after leaving JESU, Anne accepted a position with the police department in Brunswick County, North Carolina.

"Hi, Anne, it's good to hear from you. How's life at The Brick?"

When Anne left, she moved into a golf community called Brick Landing Plantation in Ocean Isle Beach. When she told Jack, he laughed, telling her that it was the same community his parents had lived in years earlier.

While Anne was talking, a thought popped into Jack's head. Since working full time, Louis had accrued enough vacation time to take a two-week break. David could use additional rest before starting school in a few weeks.

Before Jack could mention it, Anne asked, "Jack, I could use your help with a case. Is it possible you could get away and come help me with it?"

Jack did not hesitate. After all, he owed Anne his freedom and his life.

"Absolutely. The boys have become avid golfers, and my brother is a golf instructor in Myrtle Beach. I haven't seen George in a while. We could leave tomorrow morning and be there around dinner time. I'll make hotel arrangements tonight."

"Why don't the three of you stay with me? I have room, and as you know, Brick Landing has a terrific golf course. I bet the boys would like to play the course that their grandparents once played."

"Anne, are you sure? Three men can become quite boisterous. We wouldn't want to intrude."

"Please, Jack. It would be no trouble at all. I would enjoy the company, and my cocker spaniel Daphne loves kids. I bet the boys would enjoy her."

"Louis loves dogs. He probably can tell you all you want to know about cocker spaniels—and any other breed, for that matter."

"It's settled, and I insist. I will leave a guest pass with the security office allowing you to come and go as you please. I can also leave a message with the golf pro to set the three of you up for nine holes of golf or a full eighteen if you're there early enough. I usually get home around six thirty. If that's not too late, we can have dinner together."

"The boys and I gratefully accept your offer! See you tomorrow."

Jack hung up and went back to the table.

"Is everything okay, Jack?" his mother-in-law asked.

"David and Louis, I have a surprise for you. We are going on a trip tomorrow."

***

August 15th
Anne Bishop's residence, Ocean Isle Beach, NC
5:45 p.m.

"Looking forward to it, Jack. See you tomorrow." Anne hung up the phone.

Anne let out a breath and looked down at Daphne. Her coat was the color of a gingersnap cookie, and she obediently sat at Anne's feet, waiting for her dinner. Anne lovingly patted Daphne on the head and made her way to the kitchen cabinet, with Daphne excitedly circling her legs.

"So, what shall it be, Daphne? Chicken, beef?"

Daphne barked once and put her front paws on Anne's leg.

"Beef it is."

Anne knelt to put the bowl of dog food on the floor. Her tail wagging a mile a minute, Daphne licked Anne on the face, then began to attack the food in her bowl. Anne stroked Daphne's back as she ate dinner. No matter how bad a day Anne might have, Daphne's unconditional love always made her feel better.

Anne placed last night's chicken on a plate and put it in the microwave. She set the table in the dining room, opened a bottle of red wine to let it breathe, and headed to the guest room to make up the boys' beds. The guest room was down the hall from her bedroom and contained two twin beds and a bookshelf filled with books about gardening.

This room will be perfect for David and Louis, she thought as she put sheets and a light blanket on each bed.

Once the beds were ready, she went to the den adjacent to the guest room and removed the couch cushions, which revealed a handle. She pulled on the handle, and a bed emerged from the piece of furniture.

Having finished her dinner, Daphne jumped on the bed and rolled over for a belly scratch. Anne happily obliged. After completing the challenge of making a bed with an energized dog vying for her attention, she sat on the edge of the mattress.

"Well, Daphne, I think this is comfortable enough for Jack. What do you think?"

Daphne barked her approval. Anne shut the lights off and headed back to the kitchen. Now it was her turn to eat dinner.

Anne poured the wine, tore lettuce leaves, and put them in a bowl. She opened the refrigerator, took out her favorite Italian salad dressing, and then grabbed a freshly picked cucumber and tomato from the countertop. Her mouth watered at the thought of how good homegrown vegetables always tasted.

The microwave chimed, and Anne carefully removed the hot plate of chicken and roasted potatoes. She placed it on the table in front of the wine glass and salad bowl. She took a sip of wine, poured the salad dressing on the greens, and reached for her fork with her right hand—but the spot on the table where she had put the utensil was empty.

Frowning, she murmured, "I know I grabbed a fork. Where is it?"

She searched the floor but saw nothing. Looking up again, she saw the fork on the opposite side of the plate next to the knife. She picked up the utensil and examined it.

"I could swear I put this to the right of the plate."

Anne began eating. *That was odd, but this is so good*, she thought to herself. She picked up the crossword puzzle that she had started at breakfast and proceeded to look once more at the clues.

Anne was always searching for clues, even at home when trying to unwind. Perhaps it made her a successful detective, but Anne was determined to find the answers, whether it was a crossword puzzle or a baffling case like the one she was working on now. Anne's one vulnerability was her tendency to look for evil intent beyond what might dwell within the typical perpetrator. Although she had left JESU more than a year ago, she reasoned certain aspects of the organization's training would never leave her.

Anne refilled her wine glass. She ran her hand through her strawberry blond hair and stared out the dining room window at the sun, which was only beginning to dip below the horizon. Anne watched Daphne, who was peacefully resting on the cool floor tiles. It had been another hot one, and even at the end of the day, the temperature still hovered in the upper eighties. The heat and humidity of coastal North Carolina were more intense than Anne and Daphne experienced in Northern Virginia.

Anne pressed her lower lip between her fingers and thought about the significant changes she had made over the past year. Mark Desmond was never far from her thoughts. Not a day passed that she did not think of him, and Anne struggled to accept that she had shot and killed him. Deep down, she knew Mark had given her no real choice, but he was her friend, mentor, and the unrequited love of her life.

After wrestling with her conscience for months afterward, she realized JESU was no longer the organization she thought it once was. During her pursuit of Mark and Jack, JESU had pressured her to find the two men before the burial mound incident. This demand for action was standard for a mission of that nature. But the bitterness toward Mark and the intensity of the accusations against him took her aback. The Council had kinder words to say about demons than they had for Mark. Mark had dedicated himself to JESU, and Anne believed he had earned the benefit of the doubt and their respect. The JESU Council thought differently.

Ultimately, JESU's treatment of Jack Aitken and his family pushed Anne to act on her convictions. She had never seen JESU treat a civilian like they treated Jack. After the burial mound mission debriefing, she was shocked that the Council considered Jack and his family a threat and expendable. Anne couldn't recall a situation where JESU had expressed such strident bitterness and contempt.

What pushed Anne over the edge was when the Council demanded she retrieve the key and sword from Jack; as they put it, *"Regardless of the cost and by any means necessary."* When she pressed the Council to clarify what they meant, the answer was simple: *"Kill him and his family if you must."*

Anne had to admit that Mark had been right about one thing; JESU was not the organization she thought it was. Anne refused to participate in the mission and resigned.

She tried to make a clean break from JESU, but her departure was rocky. It was almost unthinkable that someone would just walk away from the society. There were no written ethics that prohibited it. No part of the vow of loyalty that one swore when initiated into JESU required a person to serve the organization indefinitely. It was just an assumption that a warrior's commitment to JESU was for life.

At first, the Council pleaded with her to reconsider her decision. Then they threatened what might happen if she divulged anything about its activities. Finally, Anne requested a meeting with the Council, where she assured them she had no intention of disclosing anything about JESU or any of its covert operations. After another attempt to persuade her to stay, the Council members realized Anne's decision would not change. They acknowledged her choice and adjourned the meeting. No expression of appreciation for her service. No gratitude for the souls she had saved. Not even a word to wish her well in the future. Just goodbye and get out.

Suddenly, Daphne jumped into Anne's lap with her leash in her mouth.

"Real subtle, Daphne." Anne laughed as she attached the leash to Daphne's collar. She thought about putting the plates in the sink but decided she would clean them up when they returned. Daphne barked twice to ensure that Anne knew she was ready.

"Okay, Daphne. You win. We will go for your walk now." Daphne raced to the front door, practically dragging Anne with her. Anne locked the door behind her, and they stepped out into the night. Unfortunately, the darkness brought little relief from the heat as Anne immediately felt the sweat begin to run down her back.

***

After being cooped up in the house all day, Daphne usually enjoyed a long walk after dinner. Tonight was no exception. By the time they got home, and Anne had cleared the table, it was after 9:00 p.m. Anne was tired, but she still had work to do. She opted to shower, hoping that it would give her a jolt of energy. After her shower, her hair wrapped in a towel, she checked her email messages.

Anne, we will leave early in the morning tomorrow. I look forward to seeing you, and I admit to being intrigued about your case.

Anne responded.

Sounds good, Jack. I will make pasta for dinner. Just let me know if that is not good.

Shutting her laptop, Anne reflected on how good a friend Jack had been over the past year. When Anne told him about her potential move to coastal North Carolina, Jack connected her with a local real estate agent he knew. When she needed a job reference, he provided a glowing recommendation to Sheriff Hill, who just happened to be a friend of Jack's father—which Anne was sure helped "a city girl" get a job in a rural community.

Anne went to the kitchen and double-checked the pantry to ensure she had the ingredients she needed for tomorrow's dinner. Placing a box of pasta on the island, she recalled her first impression of Jack during the initial investigation of his family's disappearance. When she appeared unannounced on his doorstep, Jack had allowed Anne full access to his home. Anne was naturally suspicious, but her instincts told her that while Jack was not forthcoming, he was not necessarily hiding anything from her. He played his cards close to the vest.

It was only because of Amanda Aitken's unfortunate death and the aftermath that Anne came to know the real Jack Aitken. The paramedic on call that night quickly picked up on what likely had occurred in Jack's house and recommended that Jack speak with a lawyer. Instead, Jack insisted he would only talk to her. Anne was the one person Jack trusted. The one person he knew would understand the entirety of what happened that night. The one person who, it turned out, would be able to help him.

***

The morning after Amanda Aitken's death
Interrogation room, Manassas, VA
10:00 a.m.

Pressing down the record button, Anne resumed the interview.

"Okay, let's pick up where we left off, Jack. Amanda pleaded with you to release her from her predicament, and you shut off the machines. What happened next?"

Jack took a deep breath and continued his statement. "Once I had turned off the machines keeping Amanda alive, the room grew quiet. I stood at the edge of the bed looking at Amanda and saw what I perceived to be a peaceful look on her face ...."

"Go on, Jack," Anne encouraged him in a slightly garbled tone as she chewed on her pencil eraser.

Jack rubbed his forehead. "I heard a voice from the darkness behind me. It was unmistakable."

Raising his head, Jack locked eyes with Anne and forcefully stated, "It was Lucius Rofocale, the Prime Minister of Hell."

The interrogation room instantly grew quiet. Anne tried to remain emotionless but could not help being impacted by Jack's assertion. As a career detective, she could recognize when a defendant was lying or telling the truth. Jack spoke about Amanda in a way that told Anne he was completely and utterly devoted to her. She could hear the raw emotion in his confession, and his facial expression revealed the guilt he was wrestling with. But notably, he never asked for mercy or her help. Jack knew she was videotaping his statement but made no effort to hide any details of what had occurred the night before.

Jack stared into the corner of the interrogation room. "Lucius offered me a deal. He told me he would bring Amanda back if I would help him destroy JESU."

Looking up at Anne once more, he emphasized, "I told him I would sooner see him in Hell!"

As a member of JESU herself, Anne believed in and vigorously defended the right to life. She could never condone what Jack had done. However, hearing Jack tell her about Lucius Rofocale's offer, Anne knew it spoke volumes about Jack's character because he did not accept it. She knew men much more formidable, physically and mentally than Jack, who would have sold their souls to Satan to resurrect their wife or loved one. Anne realized he was honoring his wife's sacrifice and, in doing so, selling his soul to something that could be every bit as powerful as any form of evil: his guilty conscience. He and he alone would have to live with the consequences of his actions.

J.D. TOEPFER

***

August 15th
Anne Bishop's residence in Ocean Isle Beach, NC
10:20 p.m.

Anne downed a glass of water and put the cup in the sink. As part of her report in the aftermath of the Culpeper incident, she had disclosed Jack's revelation to the JESU Council. Anne came to see what the JESU Council members found morally repugnant; she viewed as a selfless act and, in her opinion, not capital murder. She could not help but respect Jack's sacrifice, but it was not up to Anne alone to decide Jack's fate.

She believed in the criminal justice system and always did things within its framework. However, she did go out of her way to find out who would perform the autopsy in the Medical Examiner's office. Katrina Myers was the best pathologist that the Medical Examiner's office had. Anne merely asked her to try to ascertain Amanda's actual time of death while casually reminding her that Amanda's condition, at the time, was very fragile.

Anne then did what she would typically do with any case assigned to her: she probed for the facts and investigated every possible angle. The more she delved into Jack's background, the more she realized he was a good man. She could not find a person who had a negative opinion about him. His finances were sound despite the substantial costs of his children's autism treatments, which medical insurance did not cover. Yes, Amanda had a life insurance policy, but there were no indications that it mattered to him. There were no other women in his life but Amanda. He did not gamble. He did not drink to excess, at least that she could tell. Jack had nothing to gain by confessing to her the way he did.

But then there was the issue of Lucius Rofocale.

As part of the framework of the agreement for Jack's statement, Anne alone had access to the videotape. If the District Attorney and the Grand Jury heard Jack talk about Lucius Rofocale, they would consider him insane. She spent days debating what to do, but in the end, Anne did not want anyone to lock Jack in an asylum any more than a prison cell for what she determined was an act of mercy. Jack and his family had suffered an immense amount of trauma. What Mark, JESU, and Lucius had done to Jack was punishment enough.

So, late one night, Anne went to the precinct's audio-visual studio and removed the portion of Jack's confession about Lucius Rofocale from the tape, using skills taught to her by JESU. What she was doing could cost her everything, but the thought of Jack's children losing their mother and then their father to any form of incarceration was more than she could accept. When Anne presented her findings to the District Attorney's office, the prosecuting attorney asked for her opinion on what they should be doing with Jack's case. Anne told them she understood bringing felony actions to the Grand Jury was required in Virginia, but if she were sitting on that jury, she would vote not to indict him.

Anne was relieved when the Grand Jury declined to prosecute Jack, and she thought the whole matter was now closed. Therefore, she was surprised when Jack contacted her, requesting they go to dinner. He indicated he had something else he wanted to discuss with her. Though she didn't blame Jack, Anne could not help but connect him with killing Mark. But with the case now closed, she saw no harm in accepting the invitation.

When Jack finally told her he felt she had influenced the case on his behalf, she was caught off guard and initially unsure what to say. Anne's instincts told her to be honest. Jack was very appreciative and considered her to be his friend. Anne was flattered. Now more than ever, she was grateful to have a friend. There was no replacing Mark, but Jack had shared experiences with Anne that allowed him to understand her perspective in a way that few people could.

For this reason, after an internal debate, Anne decided to take Jack up on his offer of assistance. A cold case that had recently come across her desk seemed straightforward at first glance. Still, additional information that had come to light was setting off her *'supernatural evil'* radar. She sensed something ominous, and she knew the only person she could turn to about it was Jack Aitken. Yet, there was one nagging doubt that was troubling Anne. If she were correct, would she be placing Jack and his sons in mortal danger?

Chapter 4

May 21st, three months after Amanda Aitken's death
Brunswick County Sheriff's Office, Bolivia, NC
10:00 a.m.

Sheriff Hill wiped the sweat from his forehead with the sleeve of his shirt as he reached for the next applicant's resume. He had already interviewed candidates for several hours and wanted to take a break, but three officers had recently retired, and there was still one last opening to fill.

After reviewing the resume, he reread the glowing letter of recommendation from Jack Aiken. He was George Aitken's son, and that meant something to him. George Aitken had always been a dependable supporter during Glenn's re-election campaigns.

Still, he had concerns about bringing a big-shot detective from Washington, D.C., into his department. He rubbed his chin and skeptically reviewed the application. She had impeccable credentials, and there was no disputing that. She was highly decorated and had a close ratio on her cases that far exceeded any of his current or former detectives. Why she would want to come here puzzled him, and he was determined to find out.

***

"So, Ms. Bishop, why would a big city detective such as yourself want to come work in our quiet, little community?" Sheriff Hill asked condescendingly.

Anne tried not to roll her eyes at the sheriff's tone and managed a small smile. She had been dealing with crap like this her entire career.

"Sheriff, Washington, D.C. has its challenges, but it's not Fort Apache in the South Bronx either. While Prince William County is far from a sleepy bedroom community, it is not Washington, D.C."

"Okay, detective." The Sheriff spoke with a hint of frustration. "You still didn't answer my question. Why move here for a job that will pay you half of what you're making now?"

"I have been in the same job for twenty years, and I want to avoid getting complacent. It is easy to become too comfortable, and sometimes shaking things up can be beneficial."

An impressive answer. Hill continued, "Give me one word that describes you as a detective?"

Anne immediately responded. "Resilient."

Sheriff Hill's eyebrows shot up. "Why resilient, Detective?"

"I believe every detective has their own style and way of doing the job. Each letter in the word resilient means something to me. It is a code word for how I have conducted myself on the job for twenty years, and I am proud of what I have accomplished.

"A resilient detective can recover quickly from the difficulties and challenges that inherently come with the job. The letters in the word resilient specifically stand for:

- **R**espect the people you work for and with. That includes the public whose taxes pay your salary, the victims of crime you advocate for, and your fellow police officers. It also means respecting the system of justice and the practices and processes that are components of it.
- **E**agerness can overcome the inertia of the system. Do the job with energy and passion, and dedicate yourself to your craft.
- **S**elf-discipline is a must. Be organized in your approach to the job. Self-discipline means good time management and detailed documentation. The details matter! It also means never lose your cool. Always keep your composure and maintain your professionalism.
- **I**nquisitive by nature—that is the foundation of a good detective. Use sound deductive and inductive reasoning. Do

not be afraid to embrace change, learn new skills, or acknowledge that the strange may be true.
- **L**anguage matters. Good oral and written communication skills are essential. So is learning to read people and what their body posture says that their mouths do not.
- **I**ntuition can and will save your life. Trust your gut instincts. Believe in that sixth sense that every good detective has. Rely on your experience.
- **E**thics are non-negotiable. Be honest and hold yourself to a higher standard than anyone else would. Never compromise your integrity.
- **N**ever give up. There is no such thing as a perfect crime. A solution is there if you only look hard enough. Be creative in your thought process.
- **T**rustworthiness is essential to everyone around you. You need to be dependable. Your partner, the victim, and the citizens you see each day need to know that you will be there and give them your best."

Sheriff Hill leaned back in his chair. He liked Anne's answer. He liked it a lot.

"Okay, Bishop. If you want it, the job is yours. You can start on June fifteenth. Is that enough time to settle your affairs and get down here?"

Anne rose from her chair and shook hands with Sheriff Hill. "Thank you, Sheriff. I accept. June fifteenth will be fine. I was moving here regardless of what happened today. My real estate agent already has a house lined up for me to look at this evening."

"That's great news, Bishop. Personnel will start processing your paperwork, doing a background check, etcetera. If you don't mind me asking, where has your agent been taking you?"

"Ocean Isle Beach. There is a planned community there called Brick Landing Plantation. Are you familiar with it?"

"Yup. You'll love it, Bishop. See you in June."

***

Early August
Brunswick County Sheriff's Department, Bolivia, NC

Anne waved her hand, trying to cool herself down. The ceiling fan turned furiously but could provide no relief from the heat. She had settled into her new job but felt like Sheriff Hill was still evaluating her. It was as if he was always convincing himself that she was the right person for the job, or he couldn't understand why she wanted to be here instead of where the action was.

Anne was documenting one of her files when Sheriff Hill knocked on the door and entered her office. He had a blue file folder in his hands—a cold case.

"Here, hotshot." He tossed the file on her desk. "Take a look at this. Animal Protective Services falls under our purview. Unlike the big city police departments, we don't have the funds to separate animal cruelty and abuse cases. This one has an interesting twist to it, though. Maybe a fresh perspective can find something we missed. It's not a glamorous case, as I am sure you are used to working on some high-profile crimes. However, each detective that works for me must work their share of 11-13 cases."

Sheriff Hill chuckled. "This comes with living in the Garden of Eden that is coastal North Carolina. Welcome to paradise, Bishop!"

As Sheriff Hill exited, Anne shouted, "10-4, boss. Copy that."

Anne reached for the file. Before she could pick it up, the folder flew open and the contents scattered all over the floor. It was as if the fan had blown the folder open, yet none of the other papers on her desk were moving.

That's funny, Anne thought to herself as she knelt to collect the pictures strewn all over the floor.

***

"It's me, Anne! Can't you hear me?" the voice screamed, but Anne gave no indication that she had heard anything.

"How am I going to get through to you? I thought for sure moving the papers would get your attention."

As Anne returned to her seat, the dark mist that had previously encircled her head materialized into a figure. It sat in a chair next to her desk and placed its hand over Anne's.

"You can't feel me either, can you?"

Anne raised her head and sat back in her chair. The figure got up and sat on the desk before her, so they were nose to nose. Anne should have felt the hot breath on her face, but she just continued to stare ahead, taking no notice of the presence that violated her personal space.

The entity gamely tried to become a solid mass but could not take on a form Anne could see.

Frustrated, it flung itself back into the chair. *"I've just got to get a message to you. I'm running out of time."*

Suddenly, the room began to shake as if an earthquake were taking place, but there was no reaction from Anne.

The figure trembled and declared, "Time for me to go."

Looking back at Anne before fleeing the room, it uttered, *"I don't know how much longer I can hide from them."*

***

Anne took the file home to review it. As Sheriff Hill indicated, it was not your average 11-13 case. Six animals had been killed around the small town of Bolivia, starting in December 2007 and continuing into the first several months of 2008. Initially, the department was investigating them as separate incidents. The first was a dog found along a country road; the second was a goat on a rural farm. Days later, a pig. At that point, it became clear that all three crimes were related.

Each incident report confirmed the cause of death as exsanguination. The animals had been completely devoid of blood. However, no body parts were missing, and the remains were otherwise intact. Except for punctures in the throat area, there were no other marks. Nothing suggested the perpetrator saw these animals as a food source. A panel of veterinarians spent time reviewing the findings. They could not identify any animal species that would kill in this manner or subsist solely by consuming blood.

Anne was certainly fascinated by what she read. A fourth animal death in the area came to light, and the file noted this victim's circumstances were even more peculiar.

Mark Robins lives in a trailer park on the outskirts of Bolivia. He owned a 150-pound male Pit Bull named Brutus. Mr. Robins was unaware of the other three animal attacks in the area at the time, so when Brutus was found dead in the yard, Mark buried him in the woods. Mr. Robins stated he was an experienced hunter and indicated that he found it unusual that there were no signs of any struggle around Brutus's body.

At dawn the next day, Mr. Robins awoke to find that Brutus's body had been exhumed and placed back in the same spot in the yard from the day before. Unnerved by this, Mr. Robins contacted the police. The authorities collected Brutus's body, and a veterinarian found puncture wounds in the dog's throat and no trace of blood left in the body. While searching the area around the Robins' home, officers found a paw print in the mud nearly five inches in diameter and made a plaster cast of the track.

Anne put the report down. She reached for the box and pulled out the plaster cast to examine it. Comparing the paw print to her fist, it dwarfed her hand. She put the plaster cast down on the table and found Post-It notes from the prior detective.

The vet indicates print does not match any known species.

What animal could take down a nearly 150-pound Pit Bull without a fight?

The detective working the case investigated the possibility that these deaths were acts of a satanic cult, but no such groups had ties to the area. A fifth death, a calf from a dairy farm, was found in a grazing field located at the edge of a wooded area. It, too, was drained of all its blood, so the locals decided to take matters into their own hands. They organized hunting parties, which searched every swamp, marsh, and backwood. They baited and set traps and erected trail cameras hoping they might catch an image of the killer, if not the killer itself.

As the locals began to refer to it, *The Vampire Beast* even made the local television news. Trappers caught a bobcat, and the image of a black bear showed up on one of the trail cameras, but no evidence of an animal species that killed only to consume its victim's blood came to light. There were no attacks for ten days until a sixth animal fatality turned up, this time a sheep devoid of blood.

Then the attacks ceased. Soon after, the story faded from the headlines, and after a few months, it became nothing but an urban legend to the residents of Bolivia.

***

August 15th
Anne Bishop's residence in Ocean Isle Beach, NC
11:30 p.m.

Anne yawned as she continued studying the map of coastal North Carolina on the table. One of her new home's attractive features was a large, finished room over the garage. Anne referred to it as her war room. In addition to the large table, she had equipped the room with an oversized bulletin board, a large screen, high-definition television, and a bed. She sometimes napped if she were sequestering herself in the room during a particularly challenging case. The room also had a pool table; shooting pool was an activity that usually helped Anne relax and clear her mind, but it was not working tonight.

She wondered if Jack's children might enjoy the game as she paced around the pool table, thinking about what had occurred earlier that day. It had taken her a little more than a week to review the entirety of the existing file on the Bolivia animal killings. Arriving at work early this morning, she had performed an Internet search to see if any additional information could have emerged about the case but may not have found its way into the file. She was hoping for a fresh lead to follow. What she found blew her away.

"How did this information never find its way into the file?" Anne had muttered to herself while blowing on the hot coffee in her cup. "I guess the prior detective was not that computer savvy."

Anne studied the Internet search results. The entire page was full of stories about an entity called *"The Beast of Bladenboro."* Several articles revealed a series of events like the 2007–2008 attacks. However, they had occurred over fifty years ago, in Bladenboro, which was sixty miles Northwest of Bolivia!

Anne immediately went to her car and pulled a roadmap of North Carolina from the glove compartment. While she believed in GPS and embraced modern technology, a physical diagram was sometimes an excellent visual aid in an investigation. Anne returned the map to her office and opened it on the desk. She located and marked Bolivia on the map and, after finding Bladenboro, drew a line connecting the two locations.

She had gotten sidetracked by matters associated with other cases. She was about to start thoroughly reviewing her Internet search results late in the afternoon when the phone rang.

"Hello, Detective Bishop speaking."

"Detective Bishop, this is Chief Charlie Bassett of the Lake Waccamaw police department."

According to the map in front of Anne, Lake Waccamaw was in Columbus County, a few counties to the northwest of Brunswick County.

Anne put her finger on the map to mark the location.

"The largest natural freshwater lake in North Carolina, I believe," Anne affirmed. "Chief, how may I help you?"

"I was speaking with Sheriff Hill earlier today. Unfortunately, there was a homicide here last night. We have been trying to keep things quiet. Some wealthier residents, particularly the Antonescu family, do not want an avalanche of outside people coming around and disrupting their peace and quiet."

While Chief Bassett was speaking, Anne tried to remember where she had heard about the Antonescus. Then she recalled that

Constantin Antonescu was the owner of a regional media empire in the Southern United States.

Chief Bassett continued. "Anyway, this is the second homicide involving young women in and around Lake Waccamaw in the past few weeks. I enforce a curfew to keep people home after dark, but I run a lean and mean department, Detective, and we could use some help. I asked Sheriff Hill for a detective experienced with homicide cases. When I shared the one detail that connects the two victims, he told me you were the perfect person for the job."

Bassett paused and then spoke hesitantly, more in the form of a question. "He told me you might be familiar with crimes involving victims who had all the blood drained from their bodies?"

Anne tensed up immediately, and the hair on her arms stood up. She remained calm but was stunned by what Chief Bassett had just shared. She was still processing it when she heard the Chief ask, "Detective? Detective Bishop, are you still there?"

Snapping to attention, she replied, "Yes, Chief. I will be there first thing in the morning."

"Good. We can meet at the department headquarters if you like, and I can take you out to the crime scenes afterward."

"That will be fine, Chief. See you tomorrow."

Leaving the map on the table in the war room had allowed the case to simmer for a few hours. Anne reviewed the map and sensed this was no ordinary serial homicide case. Something sinister seemed to be behind it all, and, in the past, she would have contacted Mark Desmond or a fellow member of JESU. With those connections severed, Anne knew the person who could help and dialed Jack Aitken's number.

Drifting off to sleep, she hoped she might be wrong. But there was no hiding from the reality that whatever was killing and drinking the blood of animals in Bolivia and Bladenboro might now have acquired a taste for human blood.

Chapter 5

August 16th
Route 95 South, VA
10:00 a.m.

The traffic always thinned out after passing Emporia. At least, that was Jack's recollection as they sailed past the last exit for the city. Not that it mattered, as they had left so early this morning, they avoided traffic all along the way. David and Louis were usually early risers anyway, but the excitement about their vacation had them up even earlier than usual. It was still dark when they pulled out of the driveway a little after 5:00 a.m. The sunrise traveling southeast on Route 17 was breathtaking, and then around Fredericksburg, they picked up I-95 South toward Richmond.

"Remember, Chick-fil-A at Exit 173!" declared David.

Jack laughed. "I would never forget that, buddy. You can count on it!"

His thoughts drifted back to another trip, nearly fifteen years earlier, when David was a little over three years old and barely speaking. The family was making this same trip to North Carolina to see Jack's parents. As they crossed the state line into North Carolina, David announced there was a Chick-fil-A at Exit 173, and they should stop there. Jack recalled looking at Amanda and their surprise when the highway sign confirmed David was correct. David had only traveled to North Carolina once before. At that time, he was not even two years old and non-verbal.

Smiling, he remembered waiting for Chick-fil-A to change over to their lunch menu for nearly thirty minutes. Amanda and Jack were ecstatic and happy to pause the trip, a reaction that perhaps only the parents of an autistic child might understand. It was a time of great apprehension as they waited to find out if David would be verbal or not, and if so, to what extent.

"There's the exit!" David shouted as he pointed to the sign, startling Jack and jolting him back to the present.

Jack's mind drifted back to the earlier trip as he exited the highway to fulfill his promise that they would eat at Chick-fil-A. David continued to be full of surprises. After enjoying their lunch, they returned to Route 95 South. Jack and Amanda had switched places, with Jack now behind the wheel. Jack had asked Amanda what the exit number was for I-40 East, which would take them toward the city of Wilmington and coastal North Carolina.

Before Amanda could answer, David, replied, "Exit 81."

"David, are you sure?" Amanda had asked.

"Yes, I am."

They did not see a highway sign until ninety minutes later. David was indeed correct. Jack and Amanda were discussing David's predictions when he made another one.

"Take Exit 414," he announced.

Jack recalled chuckling and telling Amanda, "I will take his word for it." Yet he remembered still being surprised when it turned out David was right.

However, when David gave them directions to his grandparents' front door, Jack became a true believer. Not only had they found out that David was verbal, but they now knew he had an eidetic or, as it is more commonly known photographic memory.

***

The Aitkens enjoyed their early lunch, but Jack had to bring something for Louis, as his self-limiting diet meant he would not eat anything off the lunch menu. However, Louis did enjoy a lemonade, and Jack welcomed the chance to stretch his legs. Neither David nor Louis were licensed, so he did all the driving. Jack was certainly not feeling as young as when they had last come this way.

The boys had to be convinced to allow him to turn on the radio, but they finally relented, and Jack was in heaven. Sirius Radio was custom-made for someone like Jack, as he could rapidly flip between multiple channels searching for a favorite song.

Jack pressed one of the buttons and heard a familiar piano melody on the radio. He recognized the song instantly. 'Truly' by Lionel Richie, Amanda, and Jack's wedding song. Jack concentrated on his driving but could not help but think of his wife. A tear came to his eye, and Jack wiped it to avoid a flurry of questions from his sons about why he was crying. Just like everything else, the trip they were taking reminded him of her, but her loss was not the only one he was feeling now.

It had been more than five years since Jack had last been to Ocean Isle Beach. Years earlier, Jack's parents had moved closer to him. Jack and his siblings hadn't known the extent of their parents' deterioration until they had been near him for a month or two. The most noticeable changes were physical, including difficulties with mobility and arthritis. But there were mental and emotional changes too.

Mom's memory was failing, and Dad had become increasingly frustrated with her decline and his own. Mom confided in Jack's brother that she missed their home in North Carolina and that the apartment they had moved into was unfamiliar. While the move to Virginia had been necessary, it bothered her that she felt she had no choice. Dad appeared overwhelmed by assuming so many responsibilities Mom once performed, from their finances to laundry.

In unison, Louis and David told Jack that Exit 81 was coming up, and he took the exit ramp toward I-40 East. Louis then added, "I miss Pop."

"I do too, Louis," Jack spoke solemnly. "I do too."

Roughly a year after moving to their apartment in Virginia, Mom fell and broke her leg. She never was the same after that, and neither was Dad. Mom could not return to the apartment and eventually moved to the facility's memory care unit. Now alone, Dad slowly deteriorated until suffering a heart attack about six months before the burial mound incident. He suffered a stroke months later and died that August. Mom was now in hospice care.

For Jack, their presence had become both a blessing and a challenge. He was grateful to spend more time with the two of them. He saw them far more frequently than he would have if they had remained in North Carolina. However, their medical difficulties required Jack to take significant time off work, creating additional stress. He often felt as if he were on call twenty-four hours a day, seven days a week. Trying to honor his father and mother while fulfilling his responsibilities as a father and husband felt like walking a tightrope. Jack always worried he would fail and take his loved ones down too.

Not too long ago, these remembrances would have sent Jack looking for a bottle of alcohol. Instead, he looked forward to reconnecting with pleasant memories associated with Ocean Isle Beach and possibly making some new ones. Anne's friendship had helped him tremendously, and they had become quite close. In fact, Jack was conflicted about his feelings for her. Jack took this to signify that his heart, soul, and mind were healing. At that moment, a Jim Croce song began playing on the radio.

"Movin' me down the highway, rollin' me down the highway. Movin' ahead so life won't pass me by."

The lyrics were not lost on Jack and brought a broad smile to his face.

***

August 16th
Route 17 South, NC
2:00 p.m.

Jack looked in his rearview mirror at Louis and then at David. The boys were laughing as they traded lines from *Toy Story* and *SpongeBob*. Louis would start the dialogue, and David would complete it. It reminded him of his relationship with his identical twin brother George. One extra benefit of this trip was the chance to see George. George was a teaching golf pro in Myrtle Beach, South Carolina. He had traded one type of teaching for another when he left a high school social studies position to get certified as a golf pro.

The miles between them could never diminish their bond. They joked with one another that they would always be *"wombmates."* Although Jack had been teaching David and Louis to golf, he was sure George would be a far more effective instructor, and he had already arranged for the boys to spend time with him.

Jack and George were as close as brothers could be, and they talked about everything.

Almost everything.

Jack had kept many of the details surrounding the last eighteen months from George. George had always been protective of Jack, and for some reason, this time, Jack felt that he was protecting his brother by keeping it from him. At some point, Jack would likely confide in George and tell him everything about his aborted attempt to be an author and what happened in Culpeper and the aftermath of it. But he was not ready to discuss it quite yet.

Louis slurped up the last of his milkshake and spoke overdramatically. "Ah! That was good, Father."

David laughed, and Jack shook his head. "Louis, why are you so silly?"

Louis grinned, put his earbuds in, and moved his upper body to the music. He would call Jack Father instead of Dad when he tried to be funny. It always made David laugh, which was a good sign since being in the car for so many hours usually had the boys ready to kill each other. Jack was thrilled to see David so happy after all he had been through with his cancer treatments. Jack could hardly believe he would be going back to school, but he still worried about the possibility of a relapse.

Jack was beyond thankful for David's recovery, but he had a selfish concern in addition to his fears of David's cancer returning. David's treatment had essentially defined Jack's life since the burial mound incident and Amanda's death. With David returning to school and Louis working full time now … *What comes next?*

He knew he had his gardening to keep him busy, but as summer faded into fall, there would be less for him to do outside. When winter arrived, he would have months with nothing but time on his hands. He had once hoped that writing would fill that void, but there was no way he was going down that path again. This trip was their first vacation in years, and he hoped that this time away might help him figure things out. Perhaps assisting Anne with her case might uncover something that interested Jack. He was more than intrigued by her invitation and a little nervous too.

Jack took Route 17 toward the town of Shallotte and drove through the business district. They came to a small bridge spanning the salt marsh that dominated the landscape, and to their immediate right was the small green of the 11th hole. As Jack went around the next curve in the road, a brick fence and a billboard that read Brick Landing Plantation appeared. They had arrived!

***

Jack drove to the guardhouse, and a security gate quickly dropped in front of his car. A formidable-looking uniformed guard with a flat-top haircut and a large tattoo on his forearm that read *Semper Fi* emerged with a clipboard under his arm.

"Good afternoon, gentlemen," the guard said firmly. "What can I do for you?"

"Good afternoon, sir. We are guests of Anne Bishop."

The guard scanned the notes on his clipboard and nodded confirmation.

"Do you know George and Louise Aitken?" the guard asked in a noticeably friendlier tone.

"Why, yes. George and Louise are my parents."

"It is nice to meet you, Mr. Aitken. I've worked here at The Brick for years. I remember your mother and father quite well. They were just lovely people." The guard continued to reminisce. "When they pulled up at the gate, we would always chat for a little while. I miss them."

Jack lowered his head. "I'm sorry to tell you this, but Dad passed away, and Mom is in hospice."

A look of genuine sadness came to the burly guard's face. "I am truly sorry to hear that, Mr. Aitken."

Jack managed a feeble smile in response to the condolence, while Louis and David had ceased their verbal banter and sat quietly

"Here is your guest pass. I assume you know the way?"

Jack nodded.

Leaning into Jack's open window, the guard added, "I hope you and your sons have a pleasant stay."

The guard waved as they passed, and Jack drove down the main road toward the clubhouse.

"Before we head to the golf course, let's go see Nana and Pop's house."

The mood in the car seemed to lighten at the suggestion, and Jack turned right onto Oakbrook Drive.

A minute later, Jack pulled up in front of a house encircled by live oak trees draped in Spanish moss. The red bricks and blue shutters were just as Jack remembered.

Looking through the windows of the garage door, Louis pointed excitedly. "Look, Dad, they still have a LiftMaster garage door opener!"

Jack laughed; only Louis would focus on something like that. He had always had an interest, almost an obsession, with garage doors and openers.

Then Jack noticed something different.

"Hey, guys. Look. The house number is no longer 1734. It's now 1815."

***

Brick Landing Golf Club, Eighteenth Tee, Ocean Isle Beach, NC
6:30 p.m.

"You need to have balls to play the Brick!" was the quote on the clubhouse wall, and Brick Landing had lived up to its reputation.

Almost every hole had a water hazard, and the trio lost their fair share of golf balls.

It had been three hours since they teed off, and it was still beastly hot. Jack's shirt stuck to him, soaked with sweat. The temperature had to be in the low nineties, and with the humidity, it was like sitting in a sauna. It didn't matter to the three of them; however, they were having a blast! The pace of play had been ideal, no one pushing them from behind and no one holding them up. Louis and David had played incredibly well and were going to break 100. Their scores were quite a feat considering the demanding test that Brick Landing presented to a new golfer.

Jack's prior experience playing the course had been helpful, and with a par on the final hole, he would shoot ninety. The boys were getting better each round, but they weren't ready to beat Jack yet! Jack knew that day would be coming soon, so he reveled in his victory. The eighteenth hole was a 370-yard par four, flanked on the right side by salt marsh. Behind the tee box was the Intracoastal Waterway. It was a beautiful vista.

Both boys had already struck their drives. Louis had found the salt marsh on the right, and David was in a sand trap on the left side of the fairway. The eighteenth hole was the signature hole on the course, and it was Jack's favorite. He pushed the tee into the ground and placed his ball on top of it. Before addressing the ball, he took a practice swing. *Okay, boys, let me show you how to do this!*

The sun, well on its journey toward its sunset in the western sky, sat over Jack's shoulder, causing his shadow to fall across the tee box. Exhaling, he took one last look down the fairway. He concentrated on the ball beneath his feet and steadied himself. He took the head of the driver back on an arc that paused in the space above his head and then brought it back down on the same plane, hitting the ball squarely in the sweet spot of the club. Jack followed through on the swing and watched his drive fade slightly from left to right, splitting the fairway down the center.

The three golfers headed back to their golf cart and proceeded down the path to their balls. Jack's second shot was as accurate as his first, landing twelve feet from the cup. Louis and David both missed the green with their next shots and missed their par putts, each settling for a bogey five. Jack stood over his ball, attempting to read what direction his putt would need to go to find the hole. He moved into position and struck the ball. He watched it fall into the cup—a birdie! The way every golfer would like to end their round!

They were tallying up their scores when Jack's phone rang.

"Hello, Anne. We just finished up our round of golf."

"Wonderful, Jack. It sounds to me like you had a good day."

"It was, Anne." Jack grinned broadly.

"You left a message. What's up?"

"Yeah. I have misplaced the paper where I wrote down your house number. I drove up and down Oak Brook Drive, and the numbers have all changed."

"It's 1815."

Jack roared, "I cannot believe it. Anne, you bought my parents' house!"

Anne, now laughing herself, chirped, "I guess I won't have to give you directions. At least you know their home is in good hands! I stopped by the house earlier in the afternoon and left the side door into the garage unlocked. I am on my way, but please let yourselves in and make yourself comfortable."

"Is there anything I can do to get dinner started?" Jack asked, still smiling from the irony of what he had just found out.

"If you could put some water on the stove for the pasta, that would be great. I do have a favor I would like to ask."

"Sure, Anne, name it."

"Can you and the boys take Daphne out for a walk?"

"Done. I'm looking forward to meeting Daphne. My sister Susan had a Cocker Spaniel. My parents did too." *Just another thing we have in common*, Jack thought to himself.

"Great. See you in a little while."

"Boys put the clubs in the trunk," Jack directed. "I have a little surprise for the two of you."

"I like surprises, Dad," David declared.

Louis chimed in, "Let's go!"

***

When Jack pulled into the driveway at 1815 Oak Brook Drive SW, the boys exclaimed, "This is Nana and Pop's house! Ms. Bishop lives here?"

"Yes. That is the surprise!"

They bolted from the car and headed around the garage to open the door. Jack followed them quickly as he heard Daphne barking. David was a little apprehensive around dogs. Jack stepped in front of the boys and opened the door from the garage into the kitchen. The paint colors were different, and the kitchen had gone through an upgrade, but the layout was the same. Jack could have walked the house blindfolded.

Daphne ran over to the three men, wagging her tail and barking. She pulled herself up on Jack's leg, ensuring he was paying attention to her.

Jack greeted Daphne. "You look a little like my sister's dog, Gizmo!"

"Hey, look, Dad. A dog!" Louis joked, stating the obvious. It was another one of Louis's attempts at being funny. Louis petted Daphne, who sat on his shoes and rolled onto her back to get a belly rub. Louis was smiling and laughing as he rubbed Daphne's belly. As Jack suspected, David stood behind Louis, unsure that he wanted to get too close.

Daphne refused to allow David to be a spectator and rubbed herself against his legs. She sat down and beamed at him with her big brown eyes and red tongue dangling from her mouth. She let out a softer bark, seemingly sensing David's apprehension. David petted the dog, who continued to snuggle up next to him. Slowly, David bent down closer to Daphne while stroking her gently. She saw her opening and licked David on the cheek. David giggled and wiped his face.

"Boys, I need to put a pot on the stove to boil water for dinner. How about you take Daphne for a walk, and I will empty the car."

The boys found Daphne's leash and attached it to her collar. Louis grabbed the handle on the leash and chuckled. "Dad, I sure hope that Daphne does not get dognapped." A reference to a *Scooby-Doo* episode he had watched so many times.

"Okay, Shaggy," Jack played along. "Now hold on to that leash tightly and take Daphne for her walk."

David and Louis took off with Daphne. Jack found a pot, filled it with water, and turned on the stove. He brought in the suitcases and items the boys would never leave home without, such as their pillows and electronic gadgets, including a digital clock that David wanted to take because it belonged to his grandfather. Jack told David his grandfather would be happy that he liked the timepiece so much and assured him it was okay to take it with them.

Jack cradled the clock tenderly and thought about his Dad and how he missed him. He had thought it might be strange to once again be in the home his parents had not only lived in but had designed and built themselves. He found that it felt just like it did whenever they had visited. It was welcoming, and the familiarity with the house was comforting. In a way, it felt like he was back home.

***

August 16th
Anne Bishop's residence, Ocean Isle Beach, NC
7:30 p.m.

Daphne's ears perked up at the sound of the garage door opening, and she dashed through the kitchen to greet Anne.

"Hello, Daphne." Reaching down to pet her, Anne asked, "Have you made our guests feel at home?"

Daphne barked and wagged her tail in response. Anne immediately smelled spaghetti sauce. "That smells delicious. I thought I was going to cook dinner?"

Jack warmly smiled while giving her a gentle hug. "I hope it was okay for me to go ahead and cook. I thought it was the least I could do to thank you for your gracious hospitality."

"I'll get dinner tomorrow, then."

"I almost have everything together here," Jack stated. "David! Louis! Ms. Bishop is here. Please come and say hello."

David and Louis had been watching television and playing games on their phones. They immediately came to the kitchen.

"Hi, Ms. Bishop," Louis waved. "Thank you for having us. Your dog is fun. Did you know that a Cocker Spaniel needs twenty to forty minutes of exercise daily? They live, on average, fourteen to sixteen years."

Jack interjected before Anne could respond. "Louis and David had fun with Daphne. They walked her when we got here." Then he whispered to Anne, "Be careful. He will tell you everything about Cocker Spaniels and then some."

Louis just grinned and nodded in agreement. Anne bent down to be at eye level with David. "Hi, David. I am so glad you are feeling better. It is nice of you to come to visit. Are you happy to be back in your grandparents' house?"

David shook his head up and down and softly replied, "Yes. I miss Pop. I wish Nana would get better like me."

Jack placed his hand tenderly on David's shoulder. "I know, David. Me too."

Anne gently tousled David's hair. Daphne inserted herself between David and Anne and put her paws on David's legs.

David reached down to pet her. He looked up at Anne. "I like your dog. Thank you for letting me stay here."

Anne tilted her head and smiled, clearly touched by David's gratitude. Before she could speak, he continued. "And thank you for protecting us in Culpeper."

Jack's face could not hide his surprise. David had absolutely refused to speak about what happened in Culpeper. He was never sure how much David or Louis remembered about what happened there.

Anne gently stroked David's cheek. "You are welcome, David."

David and Louis turned and went back to their games. After a moment of silence, Jack whispered, "Dinner is ready, Anne. The boys have already eaten. They have a narrow list of things they will eat."

The duo went back to the kitchen.

"Jack, I have had some police training on autism, but please do not be reluctant to share your 'real-world' experience with me. I want to learn more about how you care for David and Louis. It will help me be more effective in my job. Inevitably, I will meet more people with autism in the future."

"Sure, Anne. Be careful what you ask for, though. You are liable to get more information than you bargained for from the Aitkens."

Anne laughed. "I'm going to have a glass of wine with dinner. Would you like one too?"

Jack put his hand up and gently shook his head no. "Thank you, Anne, but I will have water. I have given up alcohol, at least for the time being."

Sliding a glance at him, the corner of her mouth turned up. "Water it is."

***

They sat in the dining room for several hours, enjoying a good meal and catching up on what had been happening since Anne left Northern Virginia. Anne was thrilled to hear about David's recovery and laughed as Jack told her about their steadily improving golf games. They also enjoyed a hearty laugh and marveled at the odds of Anne buying the house that Jack's parents had once owned.

While Anne got up to brew coffee, Jack checked in on the boys. It was nearly 9:00 p.m., and it had been a long day. The boys were in bed already, and Daphne had hopped up on the end of David's bed and made herself comfortable. David beamed, clearly enjoying her company. Jack wished them a good night and closed the door behind him.

Jack sat in a chair next to the fireplace and sipped his coffee. The sunken living room that his mother had designed was in the shape of a square, which allowed it to be accessible from all four sides. Jack rose, surveyed the crowded bookshelves, and thought about his mother. Due to David's cancer treatments, he had not seen her for months. He felt terrible about this but knew she would understand and that she would have insisted that David was his priority.

Anne joined Jack in the living room.

Jack waved his hand, "I love what you have done with the place."

"Does it look different than you remember?"

"Yes and no," Jack replied. "The colors are different, and you removed the wallpaper, but I still see Mom and Dad's touches throughout the home." Nodding, he added, "They would like what you did."

"Jack, how are you doing?" Anne asked warmly.

Jack sighed. "It has been a long road to get here, Anne. I will not lie to you; I was in horrible shape. I will never get over losing Amanda and must live with my decision. I can see now why guilt and grief are such a lethal combination. It may sound crazy, but I think the game of golf may have saved my life. It brought me closer to my boys in a way I thought impossible. I have stopped drinking, and each day is getting better."

"It's so uplifting to hear this," Anne chirped. "If anyone I know deserves a break, it is you and your family."

"Thanks, Anne. If not for you, I would be in a far different place than I am now. Both literally and figuratively. I so appreciate what you have done for my family and me."

Anne blushed slightly. "That is very kind of you to say, Jack."

A moment of silence passed between them until Jack asked, "So, how are things going for you? Does the new job agree with you?"

"I am settling in. It's a different pace of life down here than in Northern Virginia. For example, when someone says they will come on Tuesday, that can mean four weeks from Tuesday. I'm also working on cases that I have never handled before. It is one of these cases that prompted my call to you."

"Okay, tell me all about it."

"Let's go to the room over the garage. I have something I want to show you."

As Anne ushered Jack up the stairs, the boys were fast asleep on the other side of the house. Suddenly, Daphne picked up her head. She began to growl, prepared to protect her new friends.

The boys, tired from the day's activities, did not hear her warning. Daphne was getting ready to bark out an alert when the pair of red eyes staring in the moonlit window disappeared. Daphne growled again, and while she laid her head back down on David's legs, she remained vigilant.

Chapter 6

August 16th
Anne Bishop's residence, Ocean Isle Beach, NC
10:00 p.m.

Anne and Jack had played pool for nearly an hour. It was clear to Jack that she frequently played, as he had not yet come close to beating her in eight ball. Her last striped ball had just disappeared into a side pocket, and the cue ball perfectly aligned with the eight ball. Anne moved in for the kill.

"Eight ball in the corner pocket." Anne pointed the pool cue to the far-right corner of the table. She leaned over the table with one eye closed, lining up the shot. She pulled the cue stick back, moved it forward in a steady rhythm, and then struck the white cue ball, sending it forcefully into the eight ball. The eight ball was instantly set in motion toward the corner of the table while the cue ball abruptly stopped. Jack and Anne watched the eight ball disappear into the table's corner pocket, as Anne had predicted. Anne stood straight up, allowing the bottom of her cue stick to rest on the floor.

"It's a good thing we're not playing for money." Jack pretended to whistle as he exhaled. "I would be broke right now! You must practice quite a bit, but just how long have you been playing pool? You might have given Minnesota Fats a run for his money."

Anne laughed at Jack's suggestion that she could have beaten a hustler like Minnesota Fats. "Playing pool helps me think. My Dad loved the game. We had a pool table in the basement of our house." She tapped the table. "You just played on it."

Jack moved his finger along the felt portion of the side rail in front of him. "Wow. It is in beautiful condition, Anne. I can tell how much it means to you by how well you have maintained it."

"I have had to have it re-clothed several times over the years. It is a family heirloom, for sure."

Anne circled the table, thinking of her father. "Dad and I would spend hours playing. My Mom wasn't too happy about him teaching me to play. I think Dad may have hustled pool to keep food on the table. Mom was a devout Methodist who frowned on gambling."

Anne lovingly tapped the table with her fingers. "They've both been gone for more than ten years now. I guess you would say that this table helps keep me connected."

"I am sorry, Anne. I'm not sure if I told you, but I lost my Dad about two years ago. Mom is in an assisted living facility. I haven't been able to see her in quite some time due to David's illness and the concern about him catching something I might bring home with me from the facility."

"You have all been through so much these last two years," Anne emphasized as she pushed a ball into the corner pocket with her cue.

Jack blew the blue chalk off the pool cue tip and placed it on the wall rack. "Well, if not for your compassion, it likely would have been even worse."

Anne joked, "Just doing my job."

"Well, I think it was much more than that."

Jack paused. The smile on his lips disappeared, and his facial expression took on a more serious look. "So, I know you did not bring me up here just to embarrass me at pool. What is going on, Anne? I'm no detective, but I can tell something has you concerned."

Anne put her pool cue down on the billiards table and waved Jack over to the map on the desk. Jack walked to the side of the desk opposite Anne. "Okay. What should I be seeing?"

"Jack, I am honestly not sure yet. You are familiar with Spider-Man?"

Jack shook his head affirmatively, and Anne continued. "Spider-Man had what he called *spider-sense*. I often feel like I have developed something similar. I know that it is the influence of my JESU training. Let me ask you a question. When your parents were still living here, did they ever mention anything about a series of animal fatalities in the Bolivia area?"

Jack pulled at the gray stubble on his chin. "No. I never recall them telling me anything about a situation involving animal deaths. When did this happen?"

"Back in late 2007 and during the first few months of 2008. There were six attacks on animals in the area around Bolivia. My boss handed me a cold case file about two weeks ago. I've never investigated animal control-related cases, or as we refer to them in the police vernacular, 11-13s. Prince William County had its own separate animal-related crimes unit. Down here, they do not have the financial resources for a separate squad, so all the detectives manage these types of cases along with their normal caseload."

Jack listened intently while still studying the map. "Go on, Anne. I am following you so far."

"After reviewing the case file on these particular animal fatalities, there are aspects to the crimes causing my *spider-sense* to tingle. I would have contacted friends at JESU in the past, but that is no longer an option."

"So, you called me. Because I could be the only person who might also sense something out of the ordinary?" Jack half-joked.

"I was reluctant to call you, but I felt I had nowhere else to turn. I need your help to either prove that this is the work of a typical criminal or confirm if it is something more sinister."

Jack raised his finger and rubbed his lip. "I understand. I promised you that I would be there if you called. What can I do to be of assistance?"

"I'm trying not to get too far ahead of myself. What I could use is someone to do some research for me."

"I can do that. Tell me what you know already so we can determine where I should start."

"First, there is a signature, a common link between all six of the killed animals," Anne went on. "Each animal had bite marks in the throat, and their bodies were found to be without a drop of blood."

Jack closed his eyes and shook his head. When he reopened them, a look of astonishment was most surely on his face. He tried to speak, but no words were coming out. Finally, he asked, "W-what, what did you say?"

"You heard me right, Jack. It was total exsanguination."

Still trying to process what he had just heard, Jack asked, puzzled, "And no one made this connection before you?"

"Well, that is not entirely accurate. Due to the signature, a detective was assigned to the case to follow up on all six incidents. He treated them as the work of a single perpetrator. What probably happened is that after the incidents stopped, and with no new leads to follow, the case got pushed aside for more pressing matters. I'm afraid this is just a reality of police work."

"What else is in the file? There must be more."

"A panel of veterinarians performed autopsies on all six animals. They found no other bite marks and nothing to indicate that whatever killed these animals was doing so to eat them. The panel also stated they were unaware of any species that kill in this fashion, only drinking the victim's blood."

"Got it. Is there any physical evidence that might help determine what could have done this?"

Anne reached into the box and presented Jack with the paw print plaster cast. Jack held the plaster cast up in a way that allowed him to examine it from all angles. He placed his fist in the paw print impression, and the model engulfed his hand with room to spare.

"Just a guess, but I would say that you are looking at an animal … or something well over seven feet tall."

"I came to the same conclusion. And can take down a large male pit bull without a fight."

Jack flinched and bit his lip nervously. "Well, this just keeps getting better and better."

"One piece of good news—at least, I think it is good news. Just before I came home, I learned an officer found hair fibers and animal droppings at one of the crime scenes."

Jack's mood lifted slightly. "Did they test the items? Was there anything in the file regarding the results?"

Anne let out a breath. "There are results, but there is something strange about the findings. As well as how I had to go about locating them."

The tension grew, and Jack felt a bead of sweat roll down his temple. "What happened?"

"Each sample was viable enough to have drawn DNA successfully. What was weird is that the file confirmed the request for the tests made it to the lab, but there were no results in the file. It was as if someone requested the tests but never bothered to follow up regarding the findings. As unusual as this case appears, I find it hard to believe there was no curiosity on the part of the detective to get answers."

Jack folded his arms in front of his chest and frowned. "I would agree with you on that. Hell, I learned about all of this in the past ten to fifteen minutes, and I want to know the results. What did you do?"

"I had to call the lab that conducted the tests to get the results. They have a certified mail stamp that they emailed to show me they mailed them out to Detective Robert Wallace at the address for the police department in Bolivia."

"Is Detective Wallace still working there? I think he might have some explaining to do."

"He retired about eighteen months ago. I hear that he still lives in the area. I'm planning on following up with him."

Jack asked hesitantly, "So what were the results?"

"Positive results came back on the hair fibers and the droppings, indicating they were from an unidentified species."

Jack shook his head back and forth. "Why am I not surprised?"

"Take a look at this map, Jack. You can see I plotted Bolivia."

"I was looking at it before. What's with this line from Bolivia? It looks like it's connecting somewhere."

Anne pointed to another location on the map. "Bladenboro."

"Let me guess. That town had similar crimes there as well?"

Anne nodded. "Yes, they did. But here is the kicker: the cases occurred fifty-four years ago!"

Jack covered his mouth, and he shot Anne a look of concern before he spoke. "That explains your *spider sense*. The similarities prove, at least to me, that this is more than a coincidence. I am surprised no one in the sheriff's office made a connection between the two or attempted to question the results."

Anne replied in a steely tone. "That is another question I have for Detective Wallace. Jack, maybe it's the new job and the adjustment period that goes with it, but lately, I feel like I'm looking for something insidious in every case I work. Admittedly, for all the faults that JESU has, there was reassurance from knowing you had resources and people supporting you. I was reluctant to call you because I did not want to drag you into something that either turned out to be a wild goose chase or, much worse—something supernatural."

"Now I know how Michael Corleone felt," Jack joked, trying to relieve the tension.

Anne didn't laugh. She eyed Jack quizzically.

Jack motioned with his hands and quoted *The Godfather Part III*. "You know? Just when I thought I was out, they pull me back in."

Anne's lips curved upward, amused by Jack's cliche. "I get it now."

"Anne, I meant it when I told you I would be there if you needed me. Regardless of the outcome, I am glad you called me."

"I am too. Just recounting what I have learned so far is a relief. Being in a new job and living alone has its disadvantages. You are not sure who you can trust."

Jack removed his glasses and began to clean them.

"I know what you mean. Having a conversation with someone is easy, but learning to trust someone requires courage and a willingness to take some risk."

"I couldn't agree more, Jack." Anne sat on the edge of the pool table. "There is one more thing I want to share with you about the case. And unrelated to all of this, since I brought up JESU, there is something I need to share with you about them as well."

"Okay." Jack put his glasses back on. "The case first."

"There was a significant reason I was late getting home today. Yesterday afternoon I got a call from the sheriff's office in Lake Waccamaw."

Pointing at the map, Anne continued. "Here, Columbus County. Slightly northwest of Bolivia. Lake Waccamaw is a small town, and they did not have the personnel or expertise to investigate two recent crimes in their jurisdiction. The Sheriff, Chief Bassett, reached out to my boss and asked for our assistance. He let Sheriff Hill know one detail about both cases, and Sheriff Hill told him to contact me."

Intrigued, Jack encouraged Anne. "Go on. I'm listening."

"Chief Bassett explained that they had two murders of young women in the last few weeks. In and of itself, murders in Lake Waccamaw are unheard of, but the chief found something that connected the two cases."

Anne hesitated. "Jack, both of these young women had bite marks on their necks and had no blood left in their bodies."

Jack was glad to be holding on to the table; he might have found himself on the floor. Jack asked incredulously, "Are you telling me that there is a ... vampire involved in these two deaths?"

"Vampire. Cryptid. That is what I need your help to find out, Jack. I visited both crime scenes today. Were it not for the draining of blood from the two victims; I wouldn't be investigating a possible connection between the murders of these two women to what happened in Bolivia ... and what I think probably happened in Bladenboro."

"Did you find anything at the crime scenes?"

"Lake Waccamaw is an outdoor enthusiast's dream. It is two thousand acres of recreational paradise. The Green Swamp Preserve is very close to the lake, with more than fifteen thousand acres of untouched wilderness. There are foxes, bobcats, and black bears living in the area. It is where an animal, even a previously undocumented species, could easily live and hunt without being discovered."

Jack interjected with what he thought was a more rational conclusion. "Well, that certainly gives credence to the theory that this might be an animal attack rather than a cryptid of some kind."

"Both women were on hiking trails not far from the lake. There were no signs that either woman struggled. There were no footprints near the bodies. I found no physical marks on the women, except for the bite marks on their throats. The coroner will have to determine whether a sexual assault occurred, but they were fully dressed and not posed provocatively, so I doubt it. I found no traces of hair or any items that could yield DNA. Basically, I came up empty."

Jack rubbed his temple. "Any relationship between the victims other than how and where they died?"

"Impressive, Jack; you would make a good detective. The short answer to your question is no. They were both in town for recreational purposes, but not simultaneously. They do not appear to have known one another. We are working to inform the families of what happened."

Jack repeated, "Okay. So how can I be of help, Anne?"

Anne wavered, staring intently at the map, then went on. "There are other questions I need to answer. These two deaths occurred outside the fifty-four-year period between the incidents in Bladenboro and Bolivia. Is this relevant or not? It also occurs in the summer, not the winter, as the Bolivia attacks did. Finally, does this mean that whatever murdered these women evolved from killing animals to people, or is there no connection to Bolivia?"

"I am on it, Anne. My brother will take the boys tomorrow for golf lessons and a round afterward. While they're gone, I'll research what happened in Bladenboro and how it might compare to Bolivia's attacks. I can focus on that fifty-four-year gap for any significance. How will that be for a start?"

Anne let out a sigh of relief. "That sounds great. You have no idea how much I appreciate your help and understanding of my point of view on this."

Jack reassured her, "Anything for a friend."

There was a moment of silence between them, and the room was eerily quiet. Jack broke the silence by saying, "Now, tell me about JESU."

Anne's expression grew grave. She squinted and bit her lip. "I had already developed serious concerns about JESU and their tactics during the lead-up to the Culpeper incident. When you invited me to dinner after the Grand Jury had acquitted you, those concerns had mushroomed into a crisis of conscience. You, Reverend Miner, and even Mark had seen JESU for what it had become, but somehow I could not."

"And then they asked you to kill me."

Anne was amazed. "Yes. JESU is particularly sensitive to euthanasia, so they viewed Amanda's death with significant disdain. They demanded that I obtain the key and sword from you, by any means necessary, including killing you. How did you know?"

"After what happened in Culpeper, JESU offered to make me part of their organization. I guess they were unaware of the circumstances surrounding Amanda's death at that time. Otherwise, they would never have offered me a position."

"I am sorry that I told them about Amanda." Anne shook her head regretfully.

"You were honoring the oath you took. I understand. When I refused, JESU threatened my family and me. Until recently, they have pressured me to give them what they want. So much for religious brotherhood. As to how I knew, I did not know for certain until you just told me."

Jack gripped the edges of the table tightly. "After you told me you resigned, I suspected that they had asked you to do something that went over the line."

Looking back up at Anne, Jack continued. "Actions always speak louder than words to me. The sacrifices you have made for my family, for all of us, tell me all I ever need to know about you. Trust and respect are something that you must earn. You have earned it with interest."

"I once knew a man who had principles like you, Jack. He was an honorable man who valued friendship and had a strong moral compass. You may find this difficult to believe, but that man was Mark Desmond. I am sure that your perspective on Mark is different. I wish you had known him before all this Culpeper business."

"I did know that man, Anne. It might surprise you, but I have positive feelings toward Mark. He did meaningful things that I will never forget despite what happened. Mark heard my confession, and because of the Michaelmas, I found the strength to somehow get through what happened. He lost his way somewhere along the line, but I do not believe he was manipulating me the entire time. Perhaps I am naïve, but I am certain he was once a good man, and while he must be accountable for his actions, JESU has not accepted responsibility for theirs. The twisted views he held at the end were partly shaped by JESU's treatment of him over the ten years after the massacre."

Her voice cracked as she wiped a tear from her cheek. "Mark was my mentor and friend, and I suppose you have figured out by now that he meant much more than that to me."

"I sensed that based on how you reacted in the parking lot at the restaurant."

"Mark was an honorable man too, Jack. Nothing romantic ever happened between us. Not that I did not sometimes wish that could be possible. Mark had too much love for our God to compromise those vows. He would also have never put me in that position."

"I also know that as much as you believe he would not put you in a compromising position, you would not have done that to him either. Honor is not limited to only men."

"Thanks for saying that, Jack."

Anne quickly recovered her composure, and her face grew serious once more. "One last thing. When it comes to JESU, they underestimated you before. They will not make the same mistake twice. Be careful."

"I will, I promise."

Jack began to feel emotions he had not had for anyone other than Amanda, but he quickly drove them from his mind.

"Let's try to get some sleep." Jack glanced at his watch. "We will get to work on your case tomorrow."

Jack heard the door to Anne's bedroom shut. He turned out the lights and climbed into bed. After a long day in the car and being out in the heat on the golf course, he should have been tired, but he found it difficult to fall asleep. Jack heard thunder in the distance and saw a flash of lightning illuminate the room. It began to rain, and the sound of the rain became a steady pounding on the roof. Jack tried to force himself to think about something else. It was no use. He laced his fingers behind his head and leaned back, listening to the rhythm of the falling rain.

Jack knew coming here was the right thing to do. He had no regrets despite the feeling that he was again venturing into something that he could not comprehend. He owed Anne everything, and once more, with a strong sense of guilt, he wrestled with the power of the emotions he felt for her.

Then he thought about the recent dream he seemed to have most every night. These dreams of Amanda had become quite vivid. She was as beautiful as she had always been, and her shoulder-length curly brown hair showed none of the gray that had started to creep into it. There was no evidence of the injuries she sustained during the incident in Culpeper. She would ask him about David and Louis, and they would walk and talk as if they were catching up at the end of a long day. When Jack awoke, it always felt so real. Staring into the darkness, he thought, *How I wish it were real.*

Chapter 7

August 17th
Brick Landing Plantation Golf Club, Ocean Isle Beach, NC
6:00 a.m.

Jack heard a splash as he turned onto the 10th hole cart path. A mist hung in the air, limiting visibility. Jack guessed it was an alligator entering the pond to his left. He probably had startled the reptile. At least, that was what Jack hoped had happened. The last thing he needed was a confrontation with a hungry alligator!

The bright sunshine fought through the early morning fog as Jack continued his walk. Where it did, steam rose from the asphalt cart path. The air felt heavy with moisture, and Jack had already begun to sweat. Last night's thunderstorms had not cooled things down one bit. It was no surprise. August weather in coastal North Carolina always returned to one word: heat.

Jack crossed Route 179 and picked the trail up once more. The fairway of the eleventh hole sloped down from right to left, with a grove of tall pine trees from tee to green on both sides of the hole. Jack always found the scenery in this part of the course stunning. He heard a loud rapping noise and stopped to listen. Further down the path, a Pileated Woodpecker hung on the side of a pine tree, pecking at the bark, searching for insects. It was huge and had a bright red head. Jack was glad he had decided to get up and take a walk. He enjoyed the songs of the birds echoing through the otherwise quiet landscape.

Jack yawned. He always had trouble sleeping the first night in a new bed. Last night had been no exception. Of course, it could have also been what he had discussed with Anne that caused his restlessness, but Jack opted to tell himself that it was the bed and not the late-night conversation. Jack checked his watch and picked up the pace. The boys would be up soon, and he wanted to be there so Anne would not have to worry about making them breakfast.

One thing that Amanda had taught him was how to be a thoughtful guest. She always made sure that activities were planned for the boys so that Jack's parents would not be responsible for entertaining them. As a result, Jack arranged for his brother, George, to give the boys golf lessons in the morning and then play a round of golf after lunch. The boys were excited to see their uncle and play a golf course they had never seen before. Jack planned to use his free time to do research for Anne.

Nearing Anne's house, the sun had burned off the mist, and he could see the light shining through the drops of dew on the pine needles. While nothing rivaled the beauty of Virginia, in his opinion, North Carolina was a close second. As Jack reached down to pick up the morning paper from the driveway, a beat-up Jeep with the word SECURITY in large letters on the driver's side door pulled up next to him.

The driver, a security guard wearing black Wayfarer sunglasses and a ballcap pulled tightly down upon his brow, rolled down the window. "Good morning, sir."

"Good morning," Jack replied with a smile. "How are you today?"

The man ignored his pleasantries. "Are you staying with Ms. Bishop?" he asked suspiciously.

Jack fumbled with the newspaper in his hands, taken somewhat aback by the guard's tone.

"My family and I are staying with Ms. Bishop."

"You must be Mr. Aitken, then, I presume," the guard probed. "I was briefed about your arrival."

Jack thought the guard's demeanor seemed quite formal and rather direct in comparison to the Southern hospitality he was accustomed to in the past while visiting his parents.

"That's right. I am Jack Aitken."

The guard turned away, rolled the window back up, and murmured, "Enjoy your stay, Mr. Aitken."

Then he drove off up the road.

Jack watched the jeep disappear.

***

Once he was sure he was out of view, the guard pulled onto the shoulder and began to speak out loud.

"So, it seems for once my incompetent minions are correct. Jack Aitken did leave for a trip yesterday."

The guard leaned back in the seat and scratched his chin.

"Ms. Bishop is far more clever than I thought."

He continued with a smirk on his face and a tone of disdain. "Bishop even might rival Mark Desmond after all. We must not underestimate her, which means keeping a tighter leash on my 'friend'. Clearly, she has suspicions, and with her JESU connections severed, it is natural that she would turn to Aitken for assistance."

His facial expression quickly became grave, and the guard nervously rubbed his tingling throat with his fingernails. "I wonder if he brought that damn sword with him."

The car became silent, and time seemed to stand still for a moment. Thinking about what Jack Aitken had done to him before, the guard placed his hands on the steering wheel and gripped it so tightly he crushed it. His face grew red with fury, and his jaw locked. Through gritted teeth, he vowed, "Well, no matter. I will have my revenge on Mr. Aitken. On him and his whole accursed family!"

***

Daphne greeted Jack at the front door. Everyone was up, and the aroma of fresh coffee hung in the air.

"Sorry. No time for breakfast, Jack. I will call you later."

Anne dashed to her car, a coffee cup in her hand, and while the boys were eating breakfast, Jack took a shower. After getting dressed, he grabbed a cup of hot coffee and headed to the screen porch, accessible through a door in the dining room.

Jack flipped a switch, and the ceiling fan that his father had installed years ago, slowly started to rotate and move the air. The ninth hole was a par three, and the porch was less than fifty feet from the edge of the green. As Jack sipped his coffee, he waved at the golfers on the green. The porch was always a fun place to be in the morning, as you could often see some pretty good golf shots. Equally entertaining were the tee shots that were sometimes off-target and landed in the backyard or on the deck. An errant shot would sometimes hit the roof and wind up in the front yard.

After the foursome finished on the green, their golf carts meandered along the cart path toward the next hole. With no new group of golfers immediately behind them, it grew quiet. Jack could almost see his Mom and Dad in the chairs across the table from him. When they made their annual pilgrimage to see them, this porch was where he would find his parents every morning. Dad would read the morning headlines and provide Mom with a running commentary of the day's events. Mom would listen, but she did not let it distract her from the daily crossword puzzle.

Jack smiled at the remembrance but was thankful that Dad had not lived to see David battle cancer. David's illness, occurring so soon after Dad had to accept that Mom could not come back to live with him, would have been more than he could bear. It would have devastated him to see the impact of David's disease, including the hair loss, the lethargy, and David's pale, sickly appearance.

Jack felt the tears coming and picked up the morning paper to redirect his thoughts from the painful subject. Jack took another sip of coffee and leaned back in his chair. He read the front page: '*Antonescu Purchases Ocean Isle Beach Times.*' Jack could not place the name but read the article under the headline. It turned out to be quite interesting.

Constantin Antonescu VI owned Antonescu Communications, a multi-media company that dominated local and state media communications in the Southeastern United States. The purchase now gave Antonescu Communications ownership of local papers from Asheville, in the western part of North Carolina, to the coast. Newspapers were not the only part of their media empire. They owned television and radio stations throughout the South and participated in cable television, cellular communications, and social media platforms. In short, they had their fingers in every slice of the proverbial media pie.

The story revealed that the Antonescu family started in the newspaper business in South Carolina back in the 19th century. They owned the *Charleston Free Press,* which began publishing in 1809. While their roots were in South Carolina, they lived in a large family compound in Lake Waccamaw. Jack put the paper down.

"Lake Waccamaw." Jack put the paper down on the table. "Anne had mentioned Lake Waccamaw last night. Both murders had taken place in that area."

A sad coincidence, Jack thought as he returned to reading the article.

It turned out that the Antonescus were a huge family. They had seven children, all daughters! Large families were not the norm these days, so this was something that Jack found noteworthy. The article also stated that Constantin was seriously considering running for Governor. Jack finished reading the story and moved to the sports section and the local news. It struck him as odd that there was no mention of the murders that Anne was investigating. He pulled out his phone and texted Anne to let her know his thoughts on this. While it probably was not significant to the case, Jack thought it best to share it with her anyway.

Just then, the doorbell rang. Jack heard Louis yell, "Hi, Uncle George!"

***

"Hey, Louis! How are you, buddy?"

"I'm good, Uncle George. Do you know this used to be Nana and Pop's house?"

Uncle George stepped through the door. He had short, salt and pepper hair and a neatly trimmed beard, predominantly gray but with flecks of black, brown, and red. His lips curled up in a broad smile. Overlooking his nephew telling him something he already knew, he asked, "Isn't it great to stay here again?"

"Yeah, it is." Louis pointed toward the dining room, saying, "Dad is out on the porch. He is drinking coffee again."

"You need to make sure he does not drink too much coffee. Before I go see your Dad, where is your brother?"

"He is in the den watching TV."

Uncle George followed Louis down the hall. He had not seen David since right before he started his leukemia treatments. He peered into the room and saw his nephew. "Hey, big guy! Remember me?"

David looked up. "Hi, Uncle George. Are we golfing today?"

"We sure are, David."

Playfully rubbing his nephew's thick brown hair, his uncle chuckled. "Look at your curly hair! You look great!"

Daphne barked and got up, wagging her tail. She dashed over to greet George, who took a knee and, petting the dog, asked, "Who is this?"

Louis entered the room. "This is Daphne. She is Ms. Bishop's dog. She is a cocker spaniel."

Repeating what he had shared with Anne yesterday, he said, "Did you know that Cocker Spaniels need twenty to forty minutes of exercise a day? They live, on average, fourteen to sixteen years."

While Louis was speaking, Daphne had rolled over on her back, waiting for a belly scratch from George.

"I did not know that, Louis."

"Okay, Daphne, I will give you a belly rub. How does that feel, girl?"

Daphne rocked back and forth and arched her back, stretching out as far as possible, clearly enjoying herself.

"She is cute. Aunt Susan had a dog that was just like Daphne. He was named Gizmo."

George stood up. "Is a hug okay today, guys?"

Both boys came over and gripped their uncle tightly. "Okay, you two. I will talk to Dad for a while, and then you will come with me to play golf. How does that sound?"

Both boys grinned enthusiastically.

***

Before getting to the porch, Jack warmly greeted his brother in the hallway. "How are you, bro? It is so good to see you!"

Were it not for George's beard, it would have been like seeing a reflection. There could be no questioning that they were identical twins. The brothers hugged each other tightly.

"Better now that you are here," George shouted. "I've missed your ugly face!"

Releasing one another, Jack retaliated, "I haven't missed you at all. I see you every day when I look in a mirror!"

Jack chuckled. "I see you met Daphne."

"She is a sweetie, Jack; reminds me of Gizmo."

"I thought that as well. Daphne has Gizmo's disposition for sure. So, how does it feel to be here? I mean, what are the odds my friend would have bought Mom and Dad's house?"

George surveyed the room. "The paint on the walls is different, and the furniture is not Mom's style, but this house will always be Mom and Dad's to me."

"I know what you mean. Can I get you something? Have you eaten?"

"You know me, Jack." George grinned broadly, holding up a plastic cup. "I have my Dunkin Donuts iced tea right here."

"Some things never change," Jack chuckled and shook his head.

The brothers sat down in the screened-in porch. "This brings back memories, doesn't it?"

"It does, Jack." George shifted in his chair to get comfortable." Tell me, how are David and Louis doing? They look great!"

Jack gently touched his chin with his hand, paused, then replied, "My answer would have been much different six months ago. As I told you over the phone, David is in remission, and so far, he is doing well. He is closely monitored and still receiving treatments to boost his immune system. I am hopeful but try not to get too far ahead."

"That curly hair is a trip!"

Jack commented quietly, "Amanda would have loved it."

George leaned over and placed his hand on Jack's shoulder. "I just want to tell you how proud I am of you, how you have put the needs of David and Louis ahead of everything else. I know Amanda would be proud."

As George spoke, that little voice in Jack's psyche, the one that was an eternal thorn in his side, reminded him, *'If only he knew the truth. Would he feel the same way if he knew the real story behind Amanda's death?'*

Jack tried to drive the thought out of his head. "Thanks. That means a lot coming from you."

"How are Josephine and the kids doing? Are they fully acclimated to life in Myrtle Beach?"

George spread his arms out wide and emoted, "Jack, what's not to love? Mild winters, golf all year round! It beats working in school administration for sure! Jo's computer skills allow her to work anywhere. The kids are off at college. I never felt better in my life."

Leaning back in the chair, he asked, "But how are you feeling, Jack? You look and sound better than I can recall in a long time. I was very concerned about you after Amanda's funeral. What changed?"

Jack took a deep breath, released it, and simply replied, "Golf."

"Golf?" George sounded surprised. "What do you mean, Jack?"

"I guess a psychiatrist might say that golf became an outlet for my demons." Jack wiped a tear from his eye and went on. "It enabled me to connect with my boys. My children stopped the freefall I was in, and golf was the conduit that made that happen. The day that David and Louis asked me to take them to the driving range, totally out of the blue, is one that I will never forget."

Jack cleared his throat. "I am sure I have told you countless times about how their autism felt like a permanent state of grieving for me. Everything seemed to return to all the lost things and experiences I never got to have. Golf helped erase all that pain and regret. Watching David and Louis get excited about something.

Seeing their connection with one another over it and how it enabled the three of us to bond together, perhaps, for the first time. George, do you remember what we told one another about golfing with Dad?"

"Definitely. We told each other that we could finally understand Dad and see things from his perspective. Those discussions over breakfast in the diner at 4:30 in the morning and listening to him talk with Uncle Oskar in the car about work and politics before we got to tee off helped make him, well, it humanized him in a way. The golf course was where Dad seemed to be allowed to be himself."

"That's what has happened to the three of us. Golf allowed the three of us to be ourselves and, in doing so, helped us connect. Louis and David as brother to brother and me as a father to my two sons."

George reflected on what Jack had told him. He thought about golf's impact on the bond between his nephews and Jack. Then his thoughts drifted to his relationship with his son, James. James had been away at school, and it had been quite some time since they had golfed together. George made a mental note that they needed to play the next time James was home.

"You know Jack; Bobby Jones wrote that *golf is the closest game to the game we call life*. Think about it. Regardless of what score you shoot in a round of golf, good or bad, you still want to get up the next day and do it all over again. The beauty of golf is you want to return for more even when the best round of your life is over. When the worst round of your life is behind you, there is a resolve to come back tomorrow. Life gives us second chances, just like golf does."

George paused and went on. "Golf, like life, is full of good and bad breaks. How often have you stood in the fairway, watching your approach shot to the green, thinking it will end up right next to the pin, only to realize you did not hit it quite solid enough and ended up in the water? Conversely, how often do you slice or hook a tee shot into the woods, then search for the ball in frustration only to find it in the middle of the fairway? Even the best golfer hits a bad shot occasionally. The test is what they do to recover from it. Golf is a test, and so is life. Life can throw things at a person that drives them to their knees, but you only discover what is inside of you when you overcome adversity." George took the last sip of iced tea from his cup. "Jack, can I get this refilled with water and ice?"

"Sure thing." Jack went to the kitchen and returned with a refilled container.

George took a deep gulp from the cup and put it on the table. "Thanks. One final thing, golf and life both reward a strong work ethic. Ben Hogan became *'The Hawk'* by hitting golf ball after golf ball, day after day. Nobody was ever going to outwork him. Look at how your boys have improved their game by practicing. Dad and Mom drilled the importance of hard work into each of us. That is how we all became successful."

George locked eyes with his brother. "Jack, when I told you before I was proud of you, I meant every word. I look at what you and Amanda went through, and I marvel at your ability to take a punch and keep coming back for more. I am not bullshitting you when I tell you that the two of you are my heroes. If ever there were an example of how to respond to hardship, it is the one that the two of you set. So, I think I understand where you are coming from, Jack."

Jack chokingly replied, "I-I know you do, George. I know you do."

As well as Jack knew his brother, George, was, at times, an enigma. When they fought as children, George always went for the jugular. He knew just the things to say that would get to Jack, and he would show no mercy. At the same time, if anyone did anything to Jack, George would aggressively defend him, verbally and physically.

George took pride in telling others that he didn't take things seriously and had an irreverent sense of humor. But then he would say profound things like what he just shared, which flipped the script on who George wanted others to think he was. George may have been a joker and an armchair philosopher, but the one thing that Jack knew about his brother was that he would always be in his corner.

George grinned broadly and quickly changed the subject. "What is the story with the woman who bought Mom and Dad's house? How did you meet?"

Jack shook his head back and forth. "It is not what you may be thinking, George. Believe it or not, Anne is the detective who investigated Amanda's death. She has been a good friend since the Grand Jury acquitted me. Months ago, she told me she needed a change and interviewed for a Brunswick County Police Department position. I put in a good word for her with Sheriff Hill, and I gave her the name of the realtor we were using to sell Mom and Dad's house. I never knew that the realtor sold this house to her."

"Okay, but how did you end up staying here?"

"Anne called the other day, asking for help with some research on a cold case that she was reviewing. It seemed like a good opportunity to get away for a while. Louis is working full time, and David is going back to school. It allowed us to see you, and I need to figure out what I will do with my time once the boys get into their routine and I am home by myself. Anne insisted that we stay here. I accepted."

George eyed Jack with a wry smile, not quite sure he was 100% believing him. "If that is your story, I will leave it at that. You know you have a standing offer to move here, near us. As we get older, we need to care for one another."

George rose from his chair. "We should get going. I am taking David and Louis to the driving range and the Davis Love III course at Barefoot Resort. It is challenging, but not in a punitive way. The fourth hole is a 265-yard drivable par four. I thought they might like to take a whack at that one."

"I am sorry that I am going to miss it. If Louis and David like the course, maybe the four of us can play it together before we leave."

Jack handed George a plastic pass shaped like a credit card. "I packed their bathing suits. The pass gets them into the pool. You can take a swim to cool off if I am not here when you guys get back."

"Sounds good to me." George yelled, "Hey guys, are you ready to hit some balls?"

David and Louis turned off the television and raced past Jack in the hallway.

"See you, Dad." Louis quickly headed toward the door

"Bye, Dad," David added.

"Okay, guys. I will see you later. Have a good time and take it easy on Uncle George."

"We will!" the boys shouted in unison.

Jack watched the three of them drive off. He walked up the front stairs, and Daphne greeted him at the door. Her leash was in her mouth. Jack took the hint and allowed Daphne a long walk, although it might have been the reverse, and she might have been walking him instead. After the duo returned home, Jack located the knapsack containing his laptop. He set himself up on the dining room table and got down to business.

Based on last night's discussion, Jack typed *'Beast of Bladenboro'* into the search engine. He wondered just what information he was going to find. A sensation of excitement mixed with apprehension took hold as he began to read the list of results that came back. Jack pulled a notebook from his knapsack, and an entirely different feeling overcame him.

He had not seen it for a while and had forgotten that he still had it. The worn cover hung loosely from the spiral, and the ends of the pages were curling. It was his author's journal. Jack's hands trembled while holding the notebook, recalling some of the entries now seared into his memory forever. A chill ran down his spine.

Was the discovery of his notebook some sort of sign? A warning? Jack wasn't sure. The one thing he did know was that he had no intention of re-reading the journal. He rapidly leafed through the notebook until he found a few blank pages and started to take notes.

Chapter 8

August 17th
TPC Davis Love III Golf Course, Myrtle Beach, SC
11:30 a.m.

George Aitken held his glasses close to his lips, fogging the lenses, then wiped them clean with a cloth. "So, what are you guys going to eat?"

The trio had finished their golf lessons and elected to have an early lunch. Their tee-off time was set for 12:50 p.m.

"A hot dog for me," Louis told the waitress while fidgeting in his chair

David did not look up but just played with his silverware. "Chicken and fries for me."

George handed the menus to the waitress. "I'll have a Caesar salad, thank you."

Placing both hands on the table and leaning forward, George told his nephews.

"You two were very impressive this morning. It is hard to believe you only started the game six months ago."

"I like the driving range." David pretended to swing a golf club. "I like swinging hard!"

George's jaw fell open. "How you developed that swing with just your right arm is unbelievable!"

Turning toward Louis, George shook his head in amazement. "Your chipping and putting are incredible! I would not change one thing about your short game."

The trio talked about golf until the server arrived with a plate in front of him. "Who gets the hot dog?"

David quickly raised his hand, anticipating a delicious meal, but then saw the name on the server's badge, LUCIUS."

"666. The bad man." The happiness instantly drained from David's face. He repeated the words over and over.

Concerned, George placed his hand on his nephew's shoulder. "David, what is it?"

Suddenly, Louis dashed behind his uncle's chair.

The server placed the food on the table and looked on in complete confusion.

As he cowered behind the chair, Louis's eyes were wide open, darting from side to side. He was terrified.

George knelt next to his nephew, patting him on the back, trying to comfort him. "It is okay, Louis."

David was rocking back and forth in his chair. "The Bad Man. 666. The Bad Man. 666."

"Don't be afraid, boys." George tried to be reassuring, but he was unsure what to do. He turned to the server. "I am sorry. I'm going to get them outside. Put the bill on my tab, okay?"

The server stood with his mouth agape in stunned silence. George put a twenty-dollar bill in his hand.

"Louis. David. C'mon. Let's go outside."

**

August 17th
TPC Davis Love III 4th Hole, Myrtle Beach, SC
1:30 p.m.

George stopped the golf cart next to the sign for the 4th hole. As they waited for the group in front of them to tee off, he studied his nephews in the cart behind him. They appeared calmer. He took a deep breath and tried to process what had happened in the restaurant.

George took off his hat and ran his fingers through his hair. He could not understand it; nothing seemed to soothe his nephew's palpable fear. The more George spoke, the worse things seemed to get. He was particularly concerned about Louis, who started hyperventilating. Fortunately, starting their round diminished what upset Louis and David, but their first three holes had been disastrous. They both had gone double bogey, triple bogey, double bogey with a few lost balls. George did not care about their scores. He was concerned about their well-being and knew he needed to speak with Jack later.

The threesome made their way up the steps to the elevated tee box. "Okay, boys. Put those three holes behind you and play the golf that I know you can play. Louis, you are up first."

***

Louis pulled a driver from his bag and jammed a tee into the ground. He took practice swings and worked to slow his breathing. This hole was a shorter Par Four at only 265 yards, and there was a possibility of driving the green.

"Nice and easy," Louis whispered.

He pulled the club back slowly, paused his swing slightly as his hands got level with his ears, and then moved the club back down at the same speed he had pulled it upward. The clubhead struck the ball flawlessly, and his drive whistled down the middle of the fairway. It stopped short, twenty yards in front of the green.

George clapped his hands. "Great drive Louis! Now you do the same thing, David."

David's routine was like his brother's, but his golf swing's pace was considerably faster. His downswing crushed the ball, and the additional power he generated enabled him to find the edge of the green. David flashed a satisfied grin and leaned down to pick up his tee.

"That was a tremendous drive, buddy!" George spoke with a mix of awe and relief. "I cannot wait to tell your Dad about that one!"

George hit his tee shot in the rough, and the boys bounded down the stairs to their cart with a noticeable boost in their energy levels.

George kept the banter light, but for the remainder of the round, he wondered, *How am I going to approach Jack about what happened?*

***

August 17th
Anne Bishop's Dining Room, Ocean Isle Beach, NC
3:30 p.m.

Jack got up from the table in the dining room to stretch his muscles. He had been staring at the computer screen for hours, and it was time for a break. Jack paced around the main level of the house and thought about all he had read. Bladenboro, in the 1950s, was a typical rural small town surrounded by pine forests and swamps. What happened there was eerily like what Anne had shared with him about the 2007-2008 Bolivia attacks, but it was difficult to discern fact from fiction in the case of the *'Beast of Bladenboro.'*

Right from the start, Jack had trouble determining what day the attacks started. One account placed it on December 29th, 1953, while others indicated it was December 31st, 1953. Still, another story claimed attacks as early as December 15th. While such a slight variation seemed insignificant, it impacted the number of potential kills that had occurred, which in this case would have put the figure at nearly a dozen. A number far more than the six documented kills in Bolivia.

Jack laid down on the couch. An episode of the television show *CSI* came to mind as he marveled about modern forensics compared to the technology of the early 1950s. Back then, no accurate scientific testing was available to assist investigators in determining The Beast's identity. This fact allowed speculation to run wild, with eyewitness accounts suggesting a big cat, such as a panther or cougar. However, the description of what these witnesses saw indicated it was roughly four feet tall.

Jack thought about the plaster cast he held last night. Four feet tall would make the Bladenboro offender much smaller than the size suggested by the paw print found in Bolivia. Veterinarians brought into the case guessed it could be a rabid dog, and a few others indicated it might be a Wolverine, Coyote, Bear, or even a Wolf. Of course, Jack knew the information available today would confirm that none of these species are considered bloodsuckers.

The attacks' vampire-like modus operandi led to headlines in newspapers circulating as far north as New York and west to Arizona: *'Mysterious Beast Still at Large!' 'Vampire Tendencies Found in Bladenboro Monster!'* While this matched the cause of death in Bolivia, reports in the Bladenboro incidents spoke of mauled victims and missing body parts. The savaging and dismemberment of the victims differed from Anne's information about what happened in 2007-2008.

Jack opened the refrigerator door and searched for something to drink. After grabbing a bottle of water, he sat back down at his computer and re-read his notes.

He thought to himself, *It's interesting how Bladenboro generated a media frenzy, but Bolivia did not.*

Unlike Bolivia's investigation, which seemed to generate minimal interest on a local level, Bladenboro's attacks turned into a circus. The mayor told newspaper reporters about The Beast and admitted that he thought the publicity would benefit the town. A local painter sold bumper plates that read, *'Home of the Beast of Bladenboro,'* and the movie house showed a horror film titled, *The Big Cat* to capitalize on the mania surrounding the attacks. Even today, an annual festival in October celebrates *'The Beast of Bladenboro.'*

Eventually, this turned into a public relations nightmare for the town. They found themselves hosting hunters from all over the state, and several came from as far as Arkansas. They searched every swamp, backwater, forest, and marsh for *The Beast*. The police struggled to maintain civic order and more than once had to call off searches that ran the risk of groups accidentally shooting one another. By January 7th, 1954, nearly 1,000 people searched for the culprit.

Jack picked up his pen and resumed his notetaking.

SINS OF THE FATHERS

While the newspapers were growing suspicious of the validity of the animal attacks, there was real fear running through the local population. People living on the outskirts of town, far from the police's protection, were terrified. Men did not travel anywhere without a shotgun or sidearm, and children were kept inside after dark. One woman claimed that *The Beast* had charged her, only to be scared off by her screams and her husband's rushing to her aid with a shotgun blast.

In the middle of January, a local farmer trapped a Bobcat, and the mayor declared this to be *'The Beast.'* The newspapers reported other hunters killed the animal, but just like in Bolivia, the killings ceased as quickly as they had started. By the end of January, the town had returned to normal. No one gave Bladenboro a second thought, and The Beast of Bladenboro disappeared back into the darkness from which it had emerged.

Jack closed his notebook. George and the boys would be back shortly, so he sent Anne an email to summarize his findings.

Anne:

Hi. I hope your day is going well. I wanted to summarize what I found out about the 1953-54 Bladenboro attacks:

<u>Similarities to Bolivia</u>
- *Types of victims are similar. All animals.*
- *Bladenboro's victims are primarily dogs, but there is reason to believe that a goat and rabbit were victims.*

<u>Differences to Bolivia</u>
- *The number of killings varies in Bladenboro vs. Bolivia. Accounts are unclear, but upward of a dozen possible victims in Bladenboro vs. six in Bolivia.*
- *The Bladenboro attacks alluded to victims suffering a severe mauling, which the bodies in Bolivia did not.*
- *Accounts indicate that victims may have struggled, but they noticeably did not in Bolivia.*

- The attacker approached a person in Bladenboro, but there are no indications that humans were ever really intended targets of whomever or whatever the Bladenboro perpetrator was.
- Eyewitness accounts suggest that the attacker in Bladenboro was half the size we estimate for Bolivia's attacker. I base this assumption on the cast of the paw print we examined. We projected the height of the entity associated with it to be seven feet tall.
- The circus atmosphere surrounding these attacks makes it difficult to discern fact from fiction. My understanding is that relying on eyewitness testimony has its limitations. It is easy not to get the facts straight when you are in a situation occurring in the dark and a person is under duress. All of this aside, I believe there is enough here to consider the possibility that it could still be related even if this is not the same attacker as the one in Bolivia.

Unless you have another direction to recommend, I will research any similar attacks that may have occurred further in the past.

When should we expect you for dinner? If it is okay, I would like to extend an invitation to my brother. He should be back with the boys shortly. You mentioned that you wanted to cook, but I can put on burgers. I will walk Daphne and go to the store for what we need. Just let me know.

Jack

Jack checked his phone to make sure it synced up with his laptop. This way, he would not miss a reply from Anne while he was out walking the dog. He put the phone in his carrying case and went looking for Daphne.

***

"Daphne," Jack called out. "Where are you, girl?"

He checked the rooms where he and the boys were staying, and there was no sign of her. He stood in the doorway of Anne's room. "Daphne, are you in here?"

There was no response. After checking the screened-in porch and not finding the dog there, Jack became a little nervous. He found the door from the kitchen to the garage was locked. There was no way that Daphne could have gotten in there. Jack knelt to re-tie his shoes, then headed to the only place he had not checked yet, the room over the garage.

Jack got to the top of the stairs and saw Daphne staring into a corner of the room. "Daphne, didn't you hear me calling you?"

The dog did not respond and started to growl. Jack got goosebumps, and the hair on the back of his neck stood up. He had seen their cat react similarly to paranormal activity in their home. Jack warily scanned the room but saw only Daphne, who continued to growl at whatever she saw.

Jack's heart beat faster, and he carefully walked across the room, searching for anything different or out of place. It all appeared the same as he recalled it from the night before. Daphne stood her ground and started to bark. Jack took it as a defensive posture on the dog's part and guessed that whatever it was sensing made her uncomfortable.

As Jack passed the table with North Carolina's map still on it, something caught his eye. The pen Anne left on the map last night was now on the floor. The cap had been removed and was still on the table. As he inspected things more closely, he saw another line drawn on the map. This time, it went from Bladenboro heading east toward the coast. It stopped at a town circled on the map.

Jack picked up the pen, removed his glasses, and leaned closer to read the small print. "Saint Helena," Jack muttered to himself. "Never heard of it."

As he tried to make sense of the map, Daphne continued to growl, and her barking intensified. Jack went over to the dog, now looking at him with her tongue wagging.

"Come on, Daphne. Time for your walk."

Daphne stared one last time in the corner before turning and heading toward the stairs. Jack followed behind her but peered back at the corner and then toward the map. As he went down the stairs, he had an uneasy feeling.

As Jack walked Daphne, he talked to himself. "I know I did not mark the map, and I saw Anne leave this morning, and she did not go upstairs. David and Louis could not have done it either. So that begs the question, who did?"

***

August 17th
Anne Bishop's Dining Room, Ocean Isle Beach, NC
4:30 p.m.

Jack returned from walking Daphne and noticed George's car in front of the house. He found the three golfers sitting on the front stoop.

"So, how did we do today?"

"You have two very, very good players in the making. David even drove the green on the fourth hole I was telling you about."

Jack stood with his hands on his hips. "That's great, David! It is not very often that golfers like us get to hit a drive on a par four that makes the green! How about you, Louis?"

Louis continued to pet Daphne. "I shot a ninety, Dad. David shot a ninety-two."

Impressed, Jack puckered his lips. "What did your uncle shoot?"

Louis grinned. "Uncle George shot a seventy-two from the back tees!"

"Wow, George!" Jack exclaimed. "I can see this golf pro thing is paying dividends for you! How many strokes will you need to give me the next time we play?"

"We will have to negotiate terms." George teased, "Of course, if you want to be a real man, you'll play me even up."

Jack shook his head and laughed as he opened the door. "Not on your life, brother of mine!"

Stepping into the hall, Jack noticed the clock on the table. "There's time to swim before dinner if anyone is interested."

David ran off to get his bathing suit. "Yes!"

Jack's phone vibrated, indicating he had received a text. "Let me just check this quick. It is probably a message from Anne."

First, swiping the screen, he then entered his password. The message was indeed from Anne.

Jack.

I got your message, and thank you for your work today. I agree that we should dig into this a little deeper. We can talk more about it later. I won't be home until after 6:30 p.m. I would be delighted to have George stay for dinner. Hamburgers would be great. Thanks for walking, Daphne. See you shortly.

"Would you like to stay for dinner, George?"

"That sounds good to me. I was going to be alone tonight anyway."

Jack sensed something was up with George. He seemed distracted like he had something on his mind.

"Great. Let me just see if we need anything from the store."

Jack checked the freezer and found burgers. Anne must have anticipated having a cookout as a bag of hamburger buns was already on the countertop.

"I think we are all set. How about a swim, George?"

"Lead the way, brother."

The pool was only up the block, so they decided to walk.

"Woof! Woof!" Daphne barked, then began to whimper.

"Don't want to stay home alone, girl?" Jack asked Daphne.

Remembering what he had witnessed in the room over the garage earlier in the day, Jack grabbed her leash.

"All right, Daphne. You can come too."

Louis and David walked well ahead of their father and uncle, and the distance between them provided George the opening he needed to ask Jack about how the boys had behaved earlier in the day.

George kicked a pebble down the street, forcing them to slow down. "I have something to tell you, Jack." He shifted his towel from one shoulder to the other. "Something happened today at lunch, and I want to be sure you are aware of it."

"Something involving Louis and David?" Jack stopped walking.

"Well, we were having lunch, and the server brought our food. When the boys saw him, they both got highly agitated."

"Really? Did the server say or do something? How did they react exactly?"

"Uh, it was the name on the waiter's badge. His name was Lucius."

As soon as George uttered the name, Jack paled.

"What is it?" his brother asked. "Are you all right?"

Fearing his brother might faint, George grabbed Jack's arm.

Jack waved George away. "I am all right, George. Go on. What happened?"

George let go, but his hands lingered around Jack. Jack steadied himself, hoping to assuage George's concern.

"Louis ran behind my chair. It was almost as if he were looking for me to shield him from something. David, on the other hand, was muttering something to himself. He was saying something about a bad man."

Jack looked down the road as the boys entered the pool area.

"Did either of them say anything else?"

"David kept saying 666 over and over."

George grabbed Jack by the shoulders. "What is going on? Did something happen to the boys?"

Daphne barked and pulled Jack in the direction of the pool. "We need to catch up with David and Louis."

Louis and David were already in the pool splashing around when Jack and George grabbed lounge chairs. Daphne was anxious to join the boys, but Jack tied her leash to the chair to keep her out of the water. The boys were showing no aftereffects of the incident that George described. Jack was relieved to see this, but he still needed to figure out what he would tell his brother. He knew George was not going to drop the subject.

George finally broke the silence between them. "Jack. Come on. You know you can talk to me."

Jack looked down, still unsure of what to say. "They look okay now."

"Yes. We left the restaurant immediately. By the 4th hole, they had started to calm down, and by the back nine, they were themselves again."

Jack sat back in the chair, watching his sons enjoy their dip in the pool.

"George, I know I can trust you, and I can talk to you about anything."

George quickly responded, "But ..."

"I am not ready to talk about the incident behind what you saw and heard today. I know I owe you an explanation, and I realize you are looking out for the well-being of Louis, David, and me. I need more time to process it. Do you understand?"

George placed his hand on Jack's shoulder. "When you are ready to talk, I am ready to listen. If I can help in any way between now and then, all you need to do is ask."

Jack exhaled. "Thanks, George."

The two men sat back in their chairs and watched the boys toss a tennis ball to each other. But in Jack's mind, he was still trying to reconcile how he would tell George what happened to his family while still having his brother believe he was a rational man.

Daphne jumped into Jack's lap, and as he gently scratched under her chin, his thoughts wandered back to what he had researched today and Daphne's unusual behavior in the upstairs room. Daphne's reaction was another reason he did not want to tell George anything. He was not entirely sure what he was getting himself into, and he just might need his brother's help to protect his children if it was something evil.

***

August 17th
Anne Bishop's Dining Room, Ocean Isle Beach, NC
8:30 p.m.

"Would you like some coffee, George?"

"No, thank you, Anne. I would, however, accept some tea if you have it."

"Certainly, I will put some water on the stove now."

"Anne is great, Jack. Smart too. I love her stories."

Jack laughed. "Yes, she is the perfect person to know for many reasons. Were it not for her; I would be in jail, or worse."

Anne re-entered the room.

"Anne, I believe I owe you a heartfelt expression of gratitude. Thank you for all you have done for Jack and, by extension, our entire family."

Anne placed a pitcher of milk on the table.

"Jack has heard me say this several times before, but I was doing my job."

Anne shot a glance at Jack. "But I was happy that the result was what it turned out to be."

Anne sat down again. "George, how long have you lived in Myrtle Beach?"

"Roughly five years. I used to live in Maryland, and when I retired from my job with the Harford County School System, I came here to live out a dream I always had, playing more golf!"

The three of them laughed.

"Tell me, Anne, how are you adjusting to life on the coast? It is different from up north."

"I am sure you know what I am adjusting to most," Anne replied. "It is a much different pace of life around here. The heat and humidity are also more intense than Northern Virginia."

Then Anne heard the tea kettle whistle. Before she got up from the table, Jack rose. "Stay there, Anne; I'll get it."

Jack returned with the kettle and handed George a cup with a teabag.

Waving his hand above the cup, George inhaled the aroma of the tea.

"Mmm. Earl Grey. My favorite."

George poured milk into his cup. "You will enjoy the weather more once fall arrives. It stays nice and warm here until December; the winter has been mild. There certainly is a much lower likelihood of snow. I recall Mom and Dad saying it snowed once in the twenty-plus years they were here."

George finished his tea and checked his watch. It was 9:00 p.m.

"Anne, thank you for having me. It has been a pleasure to meet you. I have a forty-five-minute drive home, so I will go."

George left, and the boys turned in for the night. Anne took Daphne for a quick walk, and Jack cleaned the dinner dishes. The house suddenly became quiet. Jack sat down in the living room and closed his eyes.

***

"Jack." Someone was shaking him. "Are you awake?" It was Anne.

"Sorry, I must have dozed off for a minute. Anne, I have something I want to show you upstairs."

At the top of the stairs, he pointed toward the desk. "You need to check out the map."

Leaning over the map, an expression of shock immediately came across her face.

"I did not draw that line to Saint Helena, Jack, and based on the look on your face, I am betting that you did not do it either."

"Louis, George, and David were gone all day and never out of my sight, and I think we can eliminate Daphne as a suspect."

Anne pinched her lip and shook her head. "This is very strange."

"It gets even stranger, Anne. I went to take Daphne for her walk this afternoon, and I could not find her anywhere on the main level of the house. I finally found her up here."

Jack pointed at the right corner of the room. "She was staring at that corner, growling. She did not even notice that I had entered the room until I was beside her. I could coax her downstairs, but when George and the boys got back from golf and we decided to go to the pool, Daphne did not want to stay behind. She was whimpering. You know Daphne better than I do, but I only have seen animal behavior like this one other time. Our family cat acted this way when Lucius's demons haunted my house."

"Before we leave, I will smolder a mixture of herbs in the room's corners."

Anne opened the desk drawer and pulled out a box.

"It will either push something out of the room or provoke it to show itself. I will also bless each room downstairs to protect against any evil trying to set up a home here."

"Sounds good. I will focus my research on Saint Helena tomorrow and see if I uncover anything. Something or someone seems to be pointing us to that location, so I will play along."

While Anne collected the herbs in a bowl and ignited them to begin the smoldering process, Jack continued to study the map. As a result, neither noticed the black mass that had been carefully watching from another corner of the room. It slithered down the stairs behind them to escape the purification ritual.

***

August 17th
Lakeshore Drive, Lake Waccamaw, NC
11:30 p.m.

A bead of sweat ran down her back as Celine Romero struggled to shut the heavy oak door of the mansion. She finally heard the lock click and stepped out into the steamy night.

"I am so tired. I can't wait to get some sleep." Celine vented, then winced. "My feet are killing me!"

She removed the bandana from her head and used it to wipe the sweat from her neck. As she headed for the front gate, her jet-black hair felt damp in the night air.

Thankfully, her employer, the Antonescu family, had plans to leave for a Charlotte business meeting in the morning, which meant a few days off for her. They were a large family, which required them to employ her as a full-time chef. Celine had started working for them nearly ten years ago, and while Constantin Antonescu was cold and demanding, his wife and daughters treated her like family. She had watched the daughters grow into beautiful young women and the youngest daughter, Maricela, was like her niece.

She sighed, thinking about the journey that was in front of her. The seclusion and privacy that the Antonescu family achieved behind the walls of their estate meant a long walk to Route 214, where Celine's friend Abby would be waiting to pick her up. She planned to stay with her while the Antonescus were away.

Celine studied the night sky. It would have been pitch-black and hard to see the unpaved driveway leading from the family compound if not for the moonlight. Yet even the intense light of the moon could not pierce the veil of the impenetrable woods just beyond the walls. The surrounding forest remained dark and foreboding, and the deafening noises of the frogs and insects masked the breathing of a figure just beyond her view, which fixated on Celine.

As she walked through the front gate, the Spanish moss adorning the trees and the swampy lowlands around the lake reminded Celine of her hometown of St. Francisville, Louisiana. Built on a bluff overlooking the Mississippi River, St. Francisville was the home of antebellum homesteads such as The Myrtles Plantation, considered one of the world's most haunted places. Superstition was a way of life back home, and in Celine's belief system, the recent murders of two young women in the area showed that something terrible had taken up residence around Lake Waccamaw.

Celine felt uneasy. Shifting her tote bag to the other shoulder, she searched the pitch-black night for the eyes she was sure were watching. Glancing toward the lake, Celine recalled looking out her apartment window a month earlier and seeing a luminous ball of fire in the marsh at the edge of the swamp. Celine remembered the stories her grandmother had told her about the legend of Le Feu Follet. Also known as Cajun fairies, they inhabited the wetlands of the bayou. Sometimes they took the form of family members, but other times they presented as fireballs. Regardless of what state they assumed, their intent was malicious, luring victims deep into the swamp to their deaths. Celine feared that this was the fate that befell the two unfortunate women.

Upon reaching the paved road, Lakeshore Drive snaked its way through the swamps and forests surrounding Lake Waccamaw. Homes built along the water's edge occasionally came into view within the dense pine forest, but darkness dominated the woods that lined the road. Celine's fatigue dampened her senses, and this, along with the blackness of the woods, provided perfect cover for the figure that had tracked Celine's movements since she walked out of the compound's gate.

Celine stopped. She was sure she had heard a noise to her left, but she saw nothing. Celine searched around her for signs of an animal and listened for another noise. She heard only the racket of the insects. It was not just the night's humidity that caused the sweat to drip from her brow; something was wrong. She turned and started walking down the road once more but picked up the pace as she saw lights in the distance. She knew this meant she was not far from the service road connected to Route 214. What she could not know was that she would perish just in sight of it.

Without warning, the figure from the woods struck Celine with such force it left her unconscious. There was no chance to scream, and in her insensible state, no struggle was possible. The figure, walking upright, gathered Celine in its arms and stepped back into the dark woods. The forest shielded its movements again; it placed Celine down and stood over her.

A second figure, dressed entirely in black, emerged from the shadows.

"Your strike was flawless. Your aggression is sufficiently restrained. You have done well, my friend."

The assailant glared at the figure and salivated as it stood over the motionless body.

"I can tell that you remain resentful of my influence over you, but you have no choice but to accept it. Do we understand each other?"

A deep, guttural growl resonated from the protegee, who towered over its Master. Deep in its mind, it wanted nothing more than to tear the master's head off, but some power it could not understand restrained it.

"I can sense your fury," the Master stated sternly. "But you will obey me!"

The Master stood his ground to demonstrate his dominance, and the taller, more powerful figure backed away in deference. The Master motioned toward the unconscious Celine, and her assailant turned its attention back to its defenseless prey. Withdrawing to the shadows, the Master pulled a flask from his pocket and downed the contents. After the clash with his underling, whose hunger and extraordinary strength grew with each kill, the elixir reinvigorated him. As he understood the savage brute's true nature, the Master realized that controlling his minion would be an increasingly significant concern.

Celine's head had fallen sideways, with her cheek lying flat in the dirt, exposing her throat. The figure knelt in anticipation of satisfying its primitive, unquenchable hunger. It slowly lowered its head toward Celine's neck. An owl bore a silent witness to the nightmarish act unfolding on the ground below. With the nails of its bear-like paws dug into the hardened earth and massive arms holding its muscular bodyweight, the figure bared its slightly curved, needle-sharp fangs. Celine's eyes opened wide as the tips of the white canine teeth pierced her skin. She tried to scream, but only silence emanated from her mouth. Before everything went dark, the last thing Celine heard was the sound of her offender sucking her blood and life out of her.

Chapter 9

August 18th
Lakeshore Drive, Lake Waccamaw, NC
9:00 a.m.

Anne turned left from the service road onto Lakeshore Drive, and about fifty yards up the street were police cars and a Columbus County Medical Examiner's office van. Anne pulled her car over and parked it on the road's shoulder. A little after sunrise, Anne had received a call from Chief Bassett that a jogger had found a young woman's body. Anne flashed her badge to one of the police officers securing the area.

"The crime scene is over there, detective." The officer pointed toward the tree line.

Expectations were that the thermometer would top 100 degrees today, and even at this early hour, it was already sweltering hot. Anne tied her strawberry blond hair in a ponytail to keep it off her neck. Her shirt stuck to her back, and Anne squinted through her sunglasses at the blazing hot sun in the sky.

Ducking under the yellow crime scene tape and heading down an embankment toward the victim, she walked carefully, searching for inconsistencies, and constantly scanning the ground leading to the body. In one spot on the mound, the grass was flat. Anne stopped and surveyed the area.

Whoever or whatever killed the woman made its way through the grass to bring the body to its final resting place. She also noticed broken twigs and branches that the attacker might have stepped on. She took out a notepad and jotted down a reminder to have the broken branches and the grass collected and investigated for fibers of hair, clothing, or anything else that might connect to the attacker.

Anne reached the victim and found the body lying on the ground approximately fifty yards from the road. The Medical Examiner covered the body with a sheet to protect it from the heat and keep it away from curious onlookers. Anne found it odd that there were no reporters around. A story that involved the murder of three female victims in a small geographic area would typically bring out a horde of news people. She added this observation in her notepad. The media could help an investigation like this, and she might need to find out who she could talk to about it.

Anne put on rubber gloves to examine the body. "Hey Doc, can you pull the sheet back so I can see the victim?"

"Sure thing, Detective." The Medical Examiner pulled the sheet away from the body, revealing a fully clothed young woman lying on her back. Her head was turned to the left with her cheek in the pine straw. Anne knelt to inspect the body closely. There were two puncture marks in the throat area. A small streak of now congealed blood oozed out of each wound. The victim's mouth was agape, and her eyes wide open. The frozen look on her face indicated she was terrified by what happened in the last moments of her life.

Snap. Snap. Snap.

The Medical Examiner's camera shot pictures one after the other.

"That's it, Detective." The Medical Examiner stated.

Anne reached down and respectfully placed her fingertips on the victim's eyelids to shut them. Anne inspected the rest of the body and saw no blood or evidence of a struggle. The victim's fingernails were clean; her hands unclenched with nothing in them. The body lay on a bed of fallen pine needles, but the ground under them was as hard as concrete. Unfortunately, this meant the assailant's feet had left no imprints.

She pulled the sheet back over the victim. "What are your preliminary findings, Doc?"

"The victim is a young woman by the name of Celine Romero. A jogger found the purse earlier this morning and stopped to pick it up. When she saw the body lying there, she called the police. Ms.

Romero's identification was in the purse, along with money and her credit cards."

"I guess we can rule out robbery as a motive. What about the cause of death?"

Removing his rubber gloves and wiping the sweat from his forehead, the doctor exhaled deeply. "While I need to do an autopsy, I believe the cause of death is exsanguination. The wound on the throat looks very similar to the one I found on the other two bodies. There is a bump on the back of her head, so I believe the force that struck her had strength enough to render her unconscious. However, there are no other signs of physical injury. There are no cuts or abrasions on her arms or torso, which suggests that the attacker picked up Ms. Romero after subduing her and carefully placed her here before it killed her."

"Is that consistent with the other two victims? Were they placed in a similar position?"

"Yes, and none of the victims show any sign that the perpetrator was dragging them around."

"I am betting the autopsy will also show no signs of sexual assault, either?"

"I think that is a good guess, Detective. I found no such evidence during the autopsies of the first two victims, and like Ms. Romero, they were all fully clothed."

The Medical Examiner bit his lip for a moment and then spoke calmly. "Detective Bishop. I think we have a serial killer on our hands."

"I'm afraid you might be right, Doc." Anne watched an assistant place the victim in a body bag. "Please let me know as soon as you finish the autopsy."

Just then, a police officer interrupted. "Detective Bishop. I think there is someone here you might want to interview. She appears to be a friend of the victim."

***

Anne walked back up the embankment to the shoulder of the road and saw a slender woman standing by a squad car. Years of experience told Anne she was a little over five feet tall, probably in her early thirties. A white headband kept her long, curly brown hair out of her eyes, and the woman wore a tan shirt and red shorts. She held her head between her hands and was clearly distraught.

"Detective Bishop. Meet Abigail Redfern. She says she is a friend of Celine Romero."

"I regret to tell you this, Ms. Redfern, but Ms. Romero is dead. Her body is under the pine trees at the bottom of this mound."

With her face buried in her hands, Abigail Redfern started to tremble and muttered, "Oh God. No, not Celine. How could this have happened?"

"Ms. Redfern, come sit down?" Anne led Abigail Redfern to the front seat of her car.

Anne took out her memo pad. "Ms. Redfern, how did you know Ms. Romero?"

"Please, call me Abby. I-I was supposed to pick up Celine last night," Abby fought to speak through her sobs. "She, Celine, had a few days off and planned to spend them with me at my place. She is, was, my best friend."

"I know this is hard, Abby, but can you tell me why you were picking up Ms. Romero out here? This area is a remote location, particularly at night."

Abigail was trying to compose herself. Finally, she said, "Celine worked for the Antonescu family; their estate is further up the road. Celine was their cook. She lived there and did not own a car. They did not like the staff to have friends inside the house, so I waited here. When she came to visit, this is where I always picked her up, but she never showed. Her phone kept going to voice mail."

"I see. Do you know how long Celine has worked for the Antonescu family?"

"About ten years, I think. That was where we met. I worked for the family as a tutor for their children. They have seven kids."

"Seven children. You do not hear about families of that size much these days."

"I left to take a teaching job with the local public school system. The children are lovely, but Mr. Antonescu can be difficult. He is very brusque and demanding. Celine never really liked him much either, but she loved the children, and Mrs. Antonescu was always good to her."

"Did you see anything suspicious last night, Abby?"

She shook her head. "No, Detective. These streets have no lights, and even with a full moon, it is pitch-black after dark. I did not see anything at all."

Anne reached into her pocket and handed Abby a card with her contact information. "I am so very sorry for your loss. If you can think of anything else that might help, please contact me at the phone number or email address on the card."

"Thank-thank you, Detective," Abby's voice trembled. "Please find the person who did this. Celine was such a sweet person. She did not deserve to have this happen to her."

"I will do my best, Abby. I agree that no one deserves to die this way."

Anne got in her car, removed her sunglasses, and turned the ignition. She ran a hand through her hair, now soaked with sweat, and put the air conditioner on high. Then she dialed a number on her phone, put the speaker on, and dropped it in her lap.

Pulling onto the road, Anne drove down Lakeshore Drive toward the Antonescu family compound. She thought it best to tell them about Celine's murder herself. Her phone connected as she neared the front gate.

"Chief Bassett, this is Anne Bishop. Tell me, how well do you know the Antonescu family?"

***

August 18th
Ocean Waters off Ocean Isle Beach, NC
9:30 a.m.

The dark shadow swam effortlessly through the warm ocean waters. The blue tag and electronic tracking device attached to its dorsal fin identified her as Mary Lee. None of this was of any consequence to the ten-foot Blacktip shark. Instinctively, it made its way toward an underwater object it visited daily. Often hunting in a pack, whether through instinct or intelligence, she knew that the feeding was good in this location, especially when the water was illuminated, just like today.

A thin membrane protected her jet-black eyes from the shells and sand churning up due to the ocean waves' action. She usually saw everything that surrounded her, but the water was murky. It mattered little, as her superior sense of smell and ability to hear and feel the struggles of her prey more than compensated for her vision impairment. Mary Lee circled the underwater structure, and when she felt a vibration that echoed through the water or heard the low-pitched sound of an injured target, she headed for it. The smell of blood was all around, and the pieces of fish she regularly feasted upon were plentiful this day.

Mary Lee was oblivious to her heightened sensitivity and capacity to detect electrical impulses from her prey's beating hearts. Suddenly, she felt a sensation unlike any that she had felt before. A powerful impulse caused her to turn away from her easy meal, and the shark instinctively began to follow the echo. She ignored the noises that came from above and behind her. She was driven intuitively by the echoes, which got louder and louder as she approached the object in the water.

The object came into view. A large mass compared to the smaller prey the shark had been eating. Its appendages waved in the water, and periodically, the figure would float on the surface waves. The shark heard the beating of the figure's heart, and Mary Lee's brain suggested this was something worth investigating. Whether she nudged the object or took a bite to taste it, she had the urge to find out if it would satiate her hunger. She picked up speed and drew closer to the target.

***

August 18th
Public Beach, Ocean Isle Beach, NC
10:00 a.m.

Jack leaned back in his chair with a smile as he watched David and Louis toss a football back and forth in the surf. Jack could feel the particles of sand between his toes, and under the surface of the beach, the brown sand felt comfortably cool. As far as Jack was concerned, the sands of Ocean Isle Beach were one of the best-kept vacation secrets in the area. The beach was immaculate and rarely crowded.

The sun relentlessly beat down, and the heat index was over 100 degrees. According to the Weather Channel, the water temperature was warm, eighty-five degrees, and Jack recalled it staying that way into the fall. He imagined that swimming in the ocean would still be refreshing despite probably feeling like being in a bathtub due to the extreme heat.

Louis, in particular, loved the beach, and growing up, whenever he found out that they were going to visit Nana and Pop, the first thing Louis wanted to do was to go to the beach. Jack remembered one visit that they had made years ago. It was in April, around Easter time. David was still a baby, and Louis was five or six years old. Louis wanted to see the beach, so they had driven over for what they had anticipated would be a quick visit. Louis had other ideas.

Louis had broken free from Jack's grip and dashed toward the water as soon as they arrived. The weather was cool, and Louis was still learning to swim. He stopped and started to disrobe before he got to the water's edge. Fortunately, Jack caught up with him before Louis got too far.

Jack chuckled to himself, thinking about Louis's attempt to go for a swim and the whale of a tantrum he threw because he did not get his way. Grabbing a water bottle from the cooler, he opened it and took a large gulp. The water was cold and a perfect antidote for his parched throat. The tide was coming in, and the waves were getting higher. Louis and David were body surfing and trying to see who could ride a wave in and get closest to the beach. It gave Jack a feeling of déjà vu. It was as if he were watching George and himself at the same age. David and Louis were having a great time, and Jack decided he wanted to join them.

Nearing the water's edge, Jack noted the intensity of the wave action had caused the green water to turn murky from the sand and shells churning upward from the ocean floor. Off in the distance loomed the iconic Ocean Isle Beach fishing pier. Built in 1957, every inch of its 968 feet was full of fishermen. Jack had never seen it so crowded, and the sea birds were gathered in large numbers, having a feast. *The fishing must be good,* thought Jack.

Suddenly, the gulls and pelicans exited the water in unison. While seeing so many birds in flight at once was a beautiful sight, it appeared to Jack as if something had spooked them. A fisherman on the pier was pointing at something in the water and shouting, but Jack could not quite make out what they were saying.

Jack cupped his hands around his mouth. "Louis! David! Come back in now!"

Louis and David turned toward their father. Jack used hand gestures to have them swim back to shore. They started to head back in when Jack heard someone on the pier yell, "SHARK!"

Jack saw a large dorsal fin cutting its way through the water. Louis and David's efforts to swim quickly toward the shore had caught the shark's attention, and it was heading straight toward them. The anglers on the pier were making noises to distract the fish, but the shark did not change course. With his heart beating out of his chest, Jack charged into the surf and frantically swam toward his children.

As the shark got closer, it began to speed up and was now on a collision course with Louis. Jack had tried to swim out to protect the boys, but the shark was closing the gap faster than he could. Jack stopped swimming and stood in the chest-high water. Frozen with fear, Louis stopped swimming and saw the shark bearing down on him. Jack watched helplessly as the shark's body broke the water's surface. Its jaws were wide open, revealing row upon row of razor-sharp teeth. It was nearly within striking distance of Louis when Jack saw something from the corner of his eye.

Jack had not noticed it before, but a motorboat headed into the area at full speed. People on the pier pointed to the shark's position and appeared to be giving the boat operator directions on the path to take to intercept it. The shark's focus on Louis was so great that it did not notice the boat bearing down on it at a significant speed. The vessel slammed into the shark, stunning the fish. It floated briefly, then headed out to the open ocean, leaving Louis behind.

Jack swam to shore and ran to the pier while the pilot pulled up next to the boys and helped them into the boat. He moored next to the dock, and Jack hugged the boys tightly as they got off the vessel.

Nearly out of breath, Jack said, "That was a close call! Are you both okay?"

David and Louis spoke in unison. "Yes. We are both okay."

The boat operator stepped onto the pier. He was tall with the bronzed skin of someone who enjoyed the outdoors. Jack quickly approached the man and greeted him with his hand outstretched.

"Thank you for saving my boys!"

In a southern drawl, the man replied, "No thanks are necessary. My name is Jimmy James Haller. Folks around here call me J.J."

"Jack Aitken." He pointed at the boat. "Mr. Haller, I see the front of your boat is damaged."

Both men inspected the front of the boat, which had a significant dent in the bow. J.J. leaned over to inspect the damage further.

"Oh, don't worry about that. I can fix that myself without a problem."

"Are you sure? I would be happy to pay for the repairs."

J.J. shook his head. "Really, it is no big deal. The important thing is that your boys are safe."

A large crowd had now formed around the men. Big groups always made David nervous, and Jack could see he was getting agitated.

"I must get the boys back home. How about a drink later this evening? We could meet at the bar in the Brick Landing Plantation clubhouse. Is seven thirty okay?"

Embarrassed by all the fuss, J.J. replied, "There is no need to do that, sir."

Jack put his hands up in front of him. "I insist. It is the least I can do for your bravery and quick thinking. You saved Louis and David. They are what means the most to me in this world. Please, join me."

J.J. vigorously shook Jack's hand again. "Sure. Seven thirty is fine, and I know the location of the clubhouse. I live in Calabash. Are you familiar with it? The town refers to itself as the *Seafood Capital of the World*."

"Yes. We have eaten there many times. The Boundary House was my parents' favorite restaurant."

"An excellent restaurant, Jack. See you at seven-thirty."

Louis, David, and Jack thanked J.J. once more and left for Anne's house. J.J. got back into his boat and, as he was pulling away from the dock, whispered to himself, "I will look forward to seeing you again, Mr. Aitken."

***

August 18th
Ocean waters off Ocean Isle Beach, NC
10:15 a.m.

Mary Lee struggled to swim through the strong ocean current. After shaking off the stupor from the impact of whatever struck her, she fled the area around the shore and headed to open water. She nursed a large gash on the left side of her torso. A lesser animal would not have survived such a blow, but her remarkable restorative capabilities would eventually heal her wound. Until then, she would need to be vigilant and carefully watch out for predators that might seek to take advantage of her injury.

What had struck her? Mary Lee had no way to know. All she could remember was the increasingly loud echoes and a feeling that came out of nowhere and had driven her toward the mass floating in the waves. It was irresistible, and she could not have stopped her approach toward the figure even if she had the desire to do so.

Mary Lee swam farther out to sea in search of colder water and schools of fish.

***

August 18th
Antonescu Family Compound, Lake Waccamaw, NC
11:00 a.m.

"Is this going to take long, Detective?" Constantin Antonescu asked impatiently. "I have a plane to Charlotte that I need to catch. I have important business."

According to Chief Bassett, Constantin Antonescu was fifty-one years old, but Anne did not think he looked a day over thirty. The media mogul's perfectly coiffed jet-black hair had not even a hint of gray. His impeccably tailored suit flattered his lean and athletic build. He could have easily passed as a movie star. His piercing brown eyes glinted at Anne Bishop.

"I just need a little of your time," Anne stated firmly.

Before he could respond, Constantin's wife, Maria, entered the room. She was a slight woman, not even five feet tall. Her looks were plain, and she had the worry lines and gray hair that come with being the mother of seven daughters. "What is going on, Constantin?"

"Ms. …, what is your name again?" Constantin asked with increasing irritation.

"I am Detective Anne Bishop from the Brunswick County Police Department."

Maria turned toward her husband. "Is something wrong, Constantin?"

Constantin stood stiffly with his hands at his side. Seemingly unaffected by the terrible news, he made no effort to comfort his wife as he dispassionately told her, "Maria, Detective Bishop has informed me that Celine is dead."

Maria gasped and put her hand over her mouth. "Oh, God! What happened to her, Detective?"

"I am not at liberty to disclose that information, Mrs. Antonescu. As the assailant left Celine's body near your residence, I am here asking questions. I also am aware of her employment status with your family."

Constantin interjected. "May we get on with this, Detective?"

"How long was Celine employed by you, Mr. Antonescu?"

"Roughly ten years," Constantin responded curtly. He turned toward his wife. "Correct, Maria?"

Maria nodded in agreement. "Yes."

"What type of employee has she been for you? Were there ever any problems between you and Ms. Romero?"

Constantin frowned and replied coldly, "She was our cook. She did her job satisfactorily."

Maria glanced at Constantin and spoke in a soft and hesitant tone. "Celine was a good worker, Detective Bishop. Our daughters, particularly our youngest Maricela, are very close to her. She was like an aunt or big sister to them."

Constantin's brow furrowed, visibly annoyed with Maria's answer. "She was our employee, Maria. Not a member of our family. I have told you countless times that getting emotionally involved with our servants is unwise. When will you listen to me?"

Maria looked toward the floor. "You are right, Constantin."

Constantin grew more agitated with each second. "Are we done here, Detective?"

Ignoring Constantin's demeanor, she asked, "Are you aware of the murders of two young women in the Lake Waccamaw area?"

"Yes, yes." He waved his hand dismissively. "Chief Bassett told me something about it the other day. Something about excessive blood loss and bite marks." Constantin paused, then asked defensively, "What does that have to do with Celine's death? Do you think our family had anything to do with this?"

Anne schooled her features to remain neutral. *Why would Chief Bassett tell anyone about how the two victims died?*

"Mr. Antonescu, I must gather all the facts to solve a case. Ms. Romero worked for you, and her murder occurred not far from your home. I am merely trying to ascertain if you know anything to assist the investigation. I am not making accusations of any kind."

Constantin asked curiously, "Do you think there is any connection between these three murders?"

"It is too early in the investigation of Ms. Romero's death to determine a connection with the other two murders."

Anne continued. "I have one last question, Mr. Antonescu. I saw that you purchased another local newspaper recently. I have not seen anything in your newspaper or other media platforms about the murder of the other two women. Will the murder of Ms. Romero change that?"

Constantin stared at Anne as if trying to burn a hole through her. "Detective Bishop. I run a real newspaper, not a tabloid. The potentially salacious details of these murders are not news, as far as I am concerned. The local police should oversee the matter, and the wrong kind of publicity might impair their ability to perform their duties. Surely you can appreciate this."

Before Anne could respond, Constantin insisted in a steely tone, "I need to leave now to catch my flight. Good day to you, Detective. I hope you catch whoever did this to Ms. Romero."

Anne knew she had pushed the conversation as far as she could. "Thank you for your time, Mr. Antonescu."

Anne walked down the driveway and out the front gate of the estate. The Antonescus limousine sped by her on its way to the airport. Once inside her car, she wrote on her memo pad: *Need to dig deeper into the Antonescu family. Constantin is hiding something.*

Anne made a U-turn and headed back to headquarters.

***

August 18th
Anne Bishop's home, Ocean Isle Beach, NC
6:30 p.m.

After dinner, while Louis and David played video games, Jack and Anne sat down to discuss the day's events.

"Unfortunately, none of the broken branches or matted-down grass yielded any hair fibers or other evidence." Anne mindlessly tugged her ear and continued reading her notes from Celine Romero's crime scene.

Jack broke in. "So, what do you really think about all this, Anne?"

"While the results of the third victim's autopsy haven't come back yet, there are too many similarities between the first two deaths and the third victim. There is no doubt in my mind that the same offender committed the three murders."

They locked eyes and let her conclusion sink in for a few moments before Anne continued.

"The interview with the Antonescus was interesting. The victim's friend described the couple to me, and it was dead on the mark. The husband is demanding, abrupt, and cold. The wife is clearly subservient to him."

"You mentioned the need to investigate the family, particularly Mr. Antonescu, more thoroughly. Do you have any thoughts on where you might want me to start?"

"I would start with the family structure, including relatives. I'd also like to know more about Constantin's media empire and the family's overall history. My instincts tell me Constantin Antonescu is hiding something."

"Consider it done, Anne. I will get on that right after researching whether a cluster of murders in St. Helena might be like those in Bolivia or Bladenboro."

Jack tapped the table. "We had an eventful day too. The beach was great until...."

Anne noticed Jack stopped tapping the table. His hands shook. "Until what, Jack?"

"Until a shark almost attacked Louis."

"A shark?" Anne's eyes opened wide in disbelief, and she glanced down the hall to where Louis and David were playing. "Is Louis okay? What happened?"

"It was a close call for sure." Jack stared at the ceiling as if speaking to God. "The boys were body surfing when people on the fishing pier began yelling and pointing at something in the water. I saw the dorsal fin and finally figured out what the people were yelling about—a shark."

Jack shifted in his chair as he told Anne about the close call and the boat that saved them.

Anne placed her hands over Jack's. "That's unbelievable, Jack. Thank God nothing happened to any of you."

"Amen to that." Jack swallowed, choking back his tears. "The boat's bow had a huge dent from where it struck the shark. The operator wouldn't take any money to fix it but did agree to allow me to buy him a drink at the clubhouse tonight. I figured I owed him that much. Are you okay staying with the boys for an hour or so?"

"Sure, Jack. Take your time."

"My watch says it's nearly seven-thirty. I am going to head up there now."

The clubhouse was less than a ten-minute walk, so Jack opted not to take the car. As he walked, the entire incident at the beach replayed in his head. What could have been a catastrophe turned into one hell of a story that Jack would share with family and friends when he got home.

The sun was beginning its descent and would set within the hour. It was a hot and steamy night, and Jack felt a bead of sweat roll down his back. A seat in the air-conditioned bar with a cold drink sounded perfect, and Jack was looking forward to thanking the man who had saved his family.

***

August 18th
Brick Landing Plantation Clubhouse, Ocean Isle Beach, NC
7:30 p.m.

Jack took a table next to a window that overlooked the green for the eighteenth hole. The restaurant was appropriately named The View. The beginning of a spectacular sunset over the Intracoastal Waterway was underway. In keeping with his promise not to drink, he ordered a club soda with a twist of lime and continued to enjoy the crimson sky while waiting for J.J. Haller to arrive. Minutes passed, and Jack saw J.J. enter the restaurant. He got up from the table and waved to get his attention. J.J. waved back and made his way to the table.

"It is good to see you again, J.J. Please, take a seat." The two men sat down. "Some view, huh? I can't recall a more breathtaking sunset."

"Yes. It is lovely, Jack. Thank you for your invitation."

"It is the least I can do for your quick thinking. I am eternally grateful for what you did."

J.J. peered at the sunset out the window. "You are quite welcome, but no thanks are necessary. I just happened to be there at the right time and place."

A waitress came over. "May I get you something to drink, sir?"

"Do you have any locally brewed beers on tap?" J.J. never turned around.

"We have Carolina Tropical IPA from the Makai Company. They're located right here in Ocean Isle Beach."

"I will try it."

The waitress asked. "Can I get you a refill?"

Jack handed her his glass. "Please. Just club soda with a twist of lime."

The waitress left to place their drink orders.

"Just club soda, Jack? Did you not drive over? Well, I suppose it would be a short walk from where you are staying here in Brick Landing Plantation."

Jack bit his lip and began to blink rapidly.

"I did walk here. Funny, I don't recall telling you where I was staying…."

The corner of J.J.'s mouth curled up into an unpleasant smirk. "I know all about you, Jack. Don't you recognize me?"

Suddenly, J.J.'s eyes were ablaze with a piercing, fiery red glow. Jack recoiled as if a laser beam was burning a hole through his chest. The blood drained from his face, and he gripped his chair tightly to avoid falling to the floor.

"Luc ... Lucius?" he stuttered.

"In the flesh, Jack. It has been far too long since our last meeting when you turned down my offer to resurrect your beautiful wife. I suspect things must be going well since you are staying with that female detective—Anne Bishop is her name, I believe.? I hope you are not *'shacking up'* with her. That would be a poor example for your sons, don't you think? And so soon after Amanda's demise."

Jack was stunned, but the mention of Amanda's name instantly enraged him. He slammed his fist down on the table, startling the other patrons. "I knew you weren't dead!"

"Let's not make a scene, Jack." Lucius wore a Cheshire Cat grin, clearly enjoying pressing Jack's buttons. "Yes, reports of my passing were, shall we say, inaccurate."

Jack was still fuming, causing thousands of blood vessels in his skin to dilate, leaving his face flushed. "What the hell are you doing here?"

"Saving your sons' lives, it appears," Lucius chirped while sharpening his fingernails with an emery board. "You are welcome, by the way."

"I will ask you this one last time." Jack gritted his teeth. "Why are you here, damn it?"

Stone-faced, Lucius's posture stiffened further. "Do we have to go through this again, Jack? I truly thought you were smarter than that. You know I have no tolerance for ultimatums." He stared Jack down. "Your pathetic self-righteous indignation tries my patience. Do not make me do something that you will regret."

"I am not afraid of you, Lucius." Jack defiantly locked eyes with his tormentor.

"You should be, Jack. Unless you have that sword tucked under your shirt, you should be." Slipping the emery board back into his pocket, Lucius sat back in his chair. "But let's not put a damper on our reunion. If you must know, I am here for personal reasons. Let us leave it at that for now."

Jack laughed hollowly. "You're here on vacation?"

Not the least bit appreciative of Jack's attempt at humor, Lucius glared at him. "No, I am not, and I know you are not here for just a vacation either. Detective Bishop called and asked for your assistance, did she not?"

The bitter enemies sat staring at one another for what seemed like an eternity.

Finally, Lucius broke the silence. "Come, come, Jack. I know all about Detective Bishop. My sources have confirmed that she resigned from JESU—a rare occurrence, by the way—and moved here a few months ago. You would not be disclosing anything I do not already know."

"Why did you do it? Why did you save Louis and David?"

"Changing the subject, I see. Are you protecting Ms. Bishop's reputation? Bravo! Chivalry is not quite dead after all."

Under the table, Jack clenched his fists tightly, and the veins in his neck bulged as his blood pressure increased every second he sat in Lucius's presence.

Lucius tapped his sharpened fingernail on the table. "Cat got your tongue, Jack? Very well. Tell me, if I had not intervened, do you believe that you or your God would have been able to save them?"

Jack frowned. "You expect me to believe you were doing some noble deed?"

Lucius leaned in and whispered, "Such as keeping you out of jail?"

"*You?*" Jack recoiled.

"That's right, Jack." Lucius folded his arms and sat smugly in his seat. "I paid for your lawyer."

A muscle spasm in the nape of Jack's neck caused him to flinch in pain. Seeking relief, he instinctively rubbed the area with his fingers.

"If my understanding of human relationships is correct, this is a time you would normally say thank you." Lucius sneered.

Jack found it difficult to speak. Finally, he was able to ask, "But....Why would you do that?"

While always ominous, Lucius's stare felt incredibly evil. "I have plans for you, Jack."

"What plan?" Jack bit his lip nervously.

Lucius smirked. "Good things come to those who wait, Jack."

Growing frustrated by Lucius's cryptic statements, Jack asked impatiently, "So what is all of this really about?"

"Consider it a kind of warning. I spared your sons' lives—this time—but if you interfere in my affairs, there will be no saving them. Neither you nor any power from heaven above will be able to protect them from my wrath."

His stomach dropped. "Are you threatening my children?"

"I do not make threats, Jack. A threat implies an intent to inflict harm when the real goal is just intimidation and a desire to avoid physical violence. I do not avoid violence; I indulge myself in it. Get in my way, and I will skin your children alive and force you to watch."

Getting up from the table, Lucius leaned forward and advised Jack emphatically, "Consider our meeting here courtesy to an old friend. If you don't go home to Bristow, if you choose to stay, I will bring you nothing but heartache and death."

Jack sat passively in his chair as he let Lucius's words sink in, silenced by the knowledge that Lucius was not only physically capable of the monstrous act that he described but that he would revel in its performance.

Taunting Jack one final time, Lucius winked derisively. "Remember, Jack, since I saved the Aitken family, you owe me. Thanks for the drink."

Jack watched Lucius exit the building. He sat at the table and looked out the window into the darkness. The waitress grabbed the empty glasses on the table.

"Can I get you anything else?"

Jack hesitated. "Uh, yes. Jack Daniels on the rocks."

***

After downing another whiskey, Jack paid the bill and began to walk back to Anne's house. It was still muggy and hot. As he passed the main recharge pond for the golf course, he saw the moonlight reflection on the surface of the water. The red eyes of an alligator slowly meandered through the water, and the splashes of frogs and the echoes of their croaking seemed to surround him.

The alcohol should have dulled Jack's senses, but the opposite was true. Jack saw a demon behind every tree he passed. The bats voraciously eating mosquitos attracted to the streetlights and the thought of the drained bodies of the Lake Waccamaw murder victims reminded Jack of vampire legends. He constantly peered over his shoulder, expecting to see a hideous beast or Count Dracula himself following him. Jack picked up the pace and practically started running.

Every nightmare about Lucius Rofocale came flooding back. Jack felt like he was drowning in a sea of doubt. Sweat dripped from Jack's forehead and fell to the street like raindrops. At the end of Clubhouse Road, he turned left onto Oak Brook Drive, and Anne's house came into view. A small measure of relief came over Jack, but one thought echoed through his head: *What the hell have I gotten myself involved in now?*

Chapter 10

August 18th
Anne Bishop's house, Ocean Isle Beach, NC
9:30 p.m.

After Louis and David went to bed, Anne returned to the basics. Her police training and her missions for JESU had taught her details mattered. However, she could not uncover any new leads after reviewing her notes from the crime scene and her interview with the Antonescus.

Tapping her lips, she thought, *what would Mark do in this circumstance?*

"He always emphasized that solutions to present-day cases often could be found by studying the past," Anne mused. "Study the past…"

She dashed to the bookshelves in her living room and began scanning the titles.

"Aha!"

Pulling a heavy, leather-bound book, she read the title.

Mythes et légendes des animaux anciens

"Ancient Animal Myths and Legends." Anne turned the yellowed pages of the old text and walked upstairs to the war room.

Hours passed. Putting the book down, Anne stretched. Written in Old French, a dialect spoken until around the fourteenth century, it was challenging to read. JESU reference materials were often written in dead languages with ancient terminology to shield the book's contents from demons.

She had been reading about the Beast of Gevaudan, hoping to uncover something that might be useful in the Bolivia case. She had just found an interesting similarity.

"*Reports note that the Beast seemed to target the victim's neck.*"

The province of Gevaudan, located in the Margeride Mountains of South-Central France, had suffered upward of 600 attacks from an unknown assailant between 1764 and 1767. The attacker, thought to be a giant wolf, was supposedly killed by hunters using large-caliber bullets forged from melted down gold medals of the Virgin Mary.

What she read next quickly eclipsed her ray of hope, *"Many victims were actually eaten, and there is no hint of blood-sucking or vampirism."*

"Damn." Anne shut the book dejectedly.

C-R-E-A-K.

Anne heard the front door open and shut. The deadbolt turned.

"Is that you, Jack?"

There was no answer.

Anne met Jack in the hall and instantly knew something was wrong. When he had left to meet J.J. Haller, he was upbeat with a smile on his face. Now, the frown lines on Jack's forehead were deep, and his face was ashen. Anne had seen this look before on people who had come face-to-face with true evil.

"How was your meeting?"

He was unresponsive as he headed for the couch.

Anne sat down next to Jack and immediately smelled alcohol on his breath.

That odor cannot be good, Anne thought as she asked, "Can I get you something, Jack?"

"What? Oh, I am sorry, Anne. A glass of water would be nice. Thank you."

Returning with the glass, Anne placed it on the table next to Jack. The friends sat in silence for a few moments.

Suddenly, Daphne entered the room and hopped on the couch next to Jack. She laid down and put her head in Jack's lap. Jack stroked her ears and the fur on her head. A smile came over his face.

"Dogs are wise animals, Jack. Daphne knows something is bothering you. Her reaction is her way of trying to make you feel better."

"She is quite a dog, Anne." Jack continued to pet Daphne gently. "The boys love her. They haven't always been comfortable with dogs, but she is definitely the exception."

Placing her hand on Jack's, Anne leaned closer. "What's troubling you?"

"Amanda always told me I was like an open book. I could never hide anything from her." He took another gulp of water. "I guess you don't have to be a detective to figure me out."

"A look of worry, bordering on fear, is written all over your face." Softly, Anne whispered, "I know you needed a drink before you came back. You know you can talk to me. Please, let me help you."

"Remember when you told me about your supposed overactive supernatural spider-sense?"

Anne nodded her head affirmatively. "I remember."

"Well, you were not wrong, Anne. I wish you were, but you could not have been more on the mark."

A chill ran down Anne's spine. It was as if the room temperature had dropped ten degrees instantly. Years of training had taught her that maintaining her composure at times like this was necessary. She knew the best way to help Jack was to control her emotions.

"Okay. What happened between the time you left here and when you returned?"

"I got to the bar first. J.J. Haller," Jack stammered, "or at least who I thought was J.J. Haller, showed up a few minutes later."

A warning bell went off in Anne's head. She could think of only one thing, one person who could have upset Jack in this way. A thought entered her head as she heard Jack continue.

"We both had our drinks. There was small talk, and then J.J. shared that he knew where I was staying."

Jack stared at Anne. "I did not tell anyone other than George that I was staying in your house. The next thing I know…" He shook his head. "The next thing I know, J.J.'s eyes began to glow, and—"

"Lucius." Daphne picked up her head and began to growl upon hearing Anne mention Lucius's name. "I thought it might be something like that."

Jack scratched the back of his head. "How did you know?"

"An educated guess, Jack. As a detective, you learn to read people's faces. I reasoned that the only thing that could change your mood and demeanor so dramatically had to be something that scared you but, simultaneously, got under your skin. Something that would cause you to want a drink, to need a drink. After everything you've been through, the only answer I could come up with was Lucius Rofocale."

"When Amanda did things that made it seem like she could read my mind, I would tell her she needed to get out of my head. We joked about sharing the same brain. I guess I am entirely too predictable."

"What else did Lucius say?"

Jack blinked and shook his head several times, still trying to make sense of what Lucius had done.

"He told me he paid for my attorney."

Anne frowned. "Say again?"

"That's right, Anne. He hired Barrett and knew I was here because you had contacted me. Lucius mentioned your name specifically. He knew that you no longer had an affiliation with JESU. He told me never to interfere in his affairs again. He used that exact phrase."

"Clearly, something much bigger than I even thought is happening here." Anne got up from the couch and immediately started pacing around the room. "Lucius would not show up for anything other than a major event."

"I guess he has someone shadowing me. Hell, JESU and everyone else seem to be too. But I don't understand how he knew you called and asked me to come here."

"It may be a simpler explanation than you think. You told me Lucius knew I had moved here. That information would not be too difficult for him to obtain. His spies are everywhere, and judging from the number of contacts I received from my friends in JESU, my leaving is not a well-kept secret. It is not too much of a leap for him to conclude that I was somehow responsible for bringing you here."

Anne paused. "He likely came to the same realization I did. The only person I could turn to for help was you."

"Lucius told me I should take our meeting as a warning." Jack thought for a moment. "I could tell that something was making him angry. Under all his pompous bluster, he was seething."

Then Jack's head lowered, and he shifted in his chair anxiously. "He threatened my children, Anne. He told me that saving Louis and David from the shark meant I owed him one."

"Something just occurred to me." Anne's eyes narrowed, and she rubbed her chin. "Lucius makes threats constantly, but I am betting it is highly out of his character to save anyone. Why did he intervene to save their lives and keep you out of jail? He does not do anything without an ulterior motive."

Jack recalled what Lucius had told him: *"I have plans for you, Jack."* For the moment, he decided to keep that message to himself.

She sat down next to Jack again. "We will need to proceed cautiously. Demons do not do anything without expecting something in return. That means giving them something back, willingly or unwillingly. We should not let the boys out of our sight."

Daphne rolled over on her back. He rubbed her belly and chuckled. "We will put Daphne in charge of the boys. She'll look out for them. You saw how she reacted when we spoke Lucius's name."

Daphne's ears perked up, and she growled once more.

"Dogs have a sixth sense, Jack. You mentioned how she reacted upstairs to whatever she saw in the corner of the room. Even if she cannot physically protect Louis and David, she is a great early warning system."

Anne checked her watch. It was nearly 11:00 p.m. "I have a call tomorrow morning with the Medical Examiner."

"And I have some research to do tomorrow on Saint Helena," Jack added. "We will see if there are any connections to Bolivia."

"Good night." Anne went down the hall but stopped before reaching her bedroom door.

"I just want you to know, Jack...." Anne paused. "I won't let anything happen to Louis or David."

Jack nodded, then closed the door to the guest room behind him.

***

Jack hooked his jeans on the doorknob, and his wallet fell from the back pocket onto the floor. A picture had jarred loose; Jack and Amanda on their wedding day. Jack picked it up and reminisced.

How young we were. Jack imagined his fingers running through Amanda's wavy brown hair.

Lost in his reverie, he failed to notice a familiar face reflected in the window behind him. Jack turned off the lights, and the face disappeared.

Tears rolled down Jack's cheeks as he clutched the picture, sank to the floor in the corner of the room, and wept.

Staring through the window at the stars, Jack wrestled with the emotional pain that was tearing him up inside. He berated himself for his weakness and his inability to refrain from drinking. He could not stop worrying about Lucius and what he was doing here.

Tears running down his cheeks, Jack pleaded, "Why is it that no matter how hard I try to make things work out, it never goes as planned? I give it everything, but I can't figure out what I keep doing wrong!"

***

August 19th
J.J. Haller's apartment, Calabash, NC
3:00 a.m.

"I expel this agent of evil from my body! I demand that you depart from my vessel in the name of the Father, the Son, and the Holy Ghost!"

"You will have to do far better than that, Mr. Haller, if you want to expel me from your meat suit." Lucius laughed mockingly. "You need faith to make that work, and I can feel the doubts that have infected your soul."

Lucius was enjoying himself after his drink with Jack Aitken. Toying with J.J. Haller was all too easy, but it was entertaining, nonetheless. Lucius needed amusement after what had happened at the beach. He had been so close to avenging the pain Jack's children had inflicted on him in Culpeper! He had been doused with fennel powder before but had never experienced the unbearable pain this dose brought. It had almost been lethal, and Lucius was fortunate to have evacuated the vessel he was in before Jack beheaded him. Just recalling the incident made him seethe, and it took all his demon strength to reel in the fury inside him.

The frustration he was feeling was intense. The beach was the perfect setup, and vengeance had been within his reach. He was still trying to understand how the shark had broken free from his mind control. Something had short-circuited the electrical connection he had formed with the animal, allowing him to control it. This failure was now the second incident involving Jack Aitken's children where what should have been impossible turned out to be anything but, and Lucius did not believe in coincidence.

Ramming the boat into the shark had therefore served two purposes. Lucius had done it to punish the animal for failing to follow instructions, but he also needed to ensure Louis and David Aitken remained unharmed. Something was going on with those brats, and he needed to get to the bottom of it. Once their secret was out in the open, Lucius would dispatch them immediately and, of course, quite painfully. He owed it to them for what they had done to him.

Lucius's consolation was that everyone, including Jack Aitken, thought what he had done to the shark was heroic. He smirked as he considered how to leverage the fact that Jack thought he had saved his two sons. Jack had such high ideals. Lucius wondered if Jack would feel obligated to him somehow and need to repay Lucius for his benevolence. After everything that had transpired between them, he laughed out loud at the notion of Jack Aitken feeling indebted to him.

Lucius's fantasizing was interrupted by another attempt by J.J. Haller to exorcise him from his body. While Lucius prepared to teach J.J. a lesson he would not forget, he vowed to himself that he would impart to the Aitkens lessons about the concept of pain that would leave a permanent scar not only on their bodies, but their souls as well.

***

August 19th
Anne Bishop's house, Ocean Isle Beach, NC
6:00 a.m.

Night gave way to morning, and Jack again found himself up early. Daphne met him at the door to his room, and Jack placed his finger in front of his lips to keep his new best friend quiet. He grabbed her leash, jotted down a quick note to Anne and the boys in case they awoke before he returned, and headed outside through the garage. The sun was just beginning to rise, and the air was heavy. Daphne trotted down the road, her nose close to the ground, sniffing and processing the environment around her. Jack basked in the quietness of the dawn, which stood in stark contrast to the restless night's sleep he'd had.

It started with an inability to fall asleep. Perhaps Jack should have expected this after Lucius's surprising and unwelcome encounter at the bar. He tossed and turned for what seemed like hours. Unfortunately, once sleep came, it brought nothing but unpleasantness. While he appeared still able to block Lucius from his current sleep pattern, that did not stop his mind from replaying past nightmares. Lucius, in his demon form. The ritual sacrifice of his former soccer teammates and the looks of terror on the faces of his family. All these nightmares repeated themselves over and over again.

Jack waved to a couple of speed walkers, and when they broke their exercise routine to wish Daphne a good morning, he reciprocated their warm smiles. Looking into their faces, he saw happiness and contentment. Jack admired the apparent tranquility and peace they projected and contrasted it with his unsettled psyche. The mask of serenity he wore hid a now simmering cauldron of fear and concern. It was not just his nightmares. There was the dream—a troubling message delivered to Jack by his soulmate.

As they got to the front gate, Jack saw that Daphne was ready to go home. They turned left onto a path that cut through the golf course. Jack replayed last night's dream in his thoughts. It had started pleasantly enough with Amanda's visit, and Jack smiled at the thought of her. His previous dreams had been memorable, but this encounter was different. It was not light and uplifting. Amanda's demeanor was solemn, and her facial expression was intense. Jack recalled that this was a look he had never seen on Amanda before.

It was what Amanda told Jack that was even more disturbing. It was something that Jack could not forget…

"Jack, please, you must listen to me. What I have to tell you is very important. It is about David and Louis. We have always believed our boys were exceptional and that their disabilities were not liabilities but great gifts. I am here to tell you that we were right, but in a far more significant way than we could ever have imagined. Their destinies will lead them down a path where they will reveal a great truth."

Jack and Daphne turned onto Oak Brook Drive and headed back to the house. *What great truth? What did Amanda mean?* While trying to figure out what Amanda had been referencing, he remembered the rest of her message.

"But with the truth comes danger. Our boys are vulnerable, Jack. They will not only need your guidance as they discover their

true calling. They will require you to protect them from those who seek to silence the truth they will deliver."

The dream was surreal. Jack was not sure what it meant. Hell, he did not even know that it meant anything at all. After all, it was a dream. But it came to him from Amanda, which gave it relevance. Jack did not know what to make of it all, but as he entered the house, he knew he would ponder this potential revelation for some time.

***

August 19th
Brunswick County Sheriff's Department, Bolivia, NC
9:00 a.m.

Anne sat, staring at the computer screen. The Medical Examiner's report on Celine Romero's death had just come in, and she was reading it carefully. The report indicated that the victim had no pre-existing conditions. The autopsy confirmed that the victim had died of massive blood loss. Like the two earlier victims, her body was bloodless.

The rest of the report was all too familiar. No indications of assault beyond two puncture marks in the throat. No evidence of any sexual crime. No fluids, hairs, or anything else that would potentially be a source of DNA. In other words, no information that would help Anne get any closer to identifying the killer. Anne knew losing patience could cause her to fail to recognize the one clue that could break the case open. However, she could not help feeling like she was starting to run out of time.

There would be three more victims if the pattern held, and the killer would disappear. Equally concerning was that if the routine changed, she could deal with an even greater unknown than she was already facing. Add Lucius Rofocale being in town, and a recipe for an even greater potential calamity was at hand.

Anne leaned back in her chair, took a deep breath, and exhaled loudly. She got up from the chair and headed to the break room with her coffee cup. She needed a refill, but Sheriff Hill was standing in the doorway.

"Good morning, Bishop," Sheriff Hill thundered. "I just made a fresh pot. After you get a refill, come to my office. I want you to update me on what's happening with the Lake Waccamaw murders."

Anne freshened her cup and headed to Sheriff Hill's office.

"I heard there was a third murder. Anything back from the M.E. yet?"

"I was just reviewing the report, boss. There is a definitive link between the recent murder and the other two victims. They have a serial killer on their hands."

Sheriff Hill's demeanor changed. He frowned, and his ordinarily booming voice was quieter, more solemn. "Any suspects?"

"No one specific yet. I did speak with the Antonescu family as the third victim was their employee and lived on their estate. Constantin Antonescu was less than helpful. I will do some more digging into his relationship with the victim."

Anne paused for a moment. "I am also planning to speak with former Detective Wallace about the Bolivia case you gave me."

Sheriff Hill bit his lip. "What do you want to speak with Bob about?"

"There are some inconsistencies in the file that I need to clear up."

Sheriff Hill asked pointedly, "Care to tell me what this is about?"

Anne thought carefully about how she would respond to her boss. She was unsure of the relationship between Sheriff Hill and retired Detective Wallace. For all she knew, they could have been best friends outside the squad room, so it was important to tread lightly.

"Notwithstanding that the victims are human in Lake Waccamaw and were animals in Bolivia, there are undeniable similarities between these crimes. Specifically, the victims' exsanguination and the absence of physical injuries other than two small puncture wounds in the throat. Additionally, I have found similar crimes occurring with the same modus operandi in Bladenboro. I want to understand why he could not connect Bolivia and Bladenboro. Finally, there appears to be a failure to follow up on possibly critical evidence in the Bolivia crimes. I consider it enough of a concern to speak with the Detective about it in person."

Anne waited for a response with trepidation. She was somewhat surprised when the sheriff told her, "Good work, Detective. Keep it up, and if you find that things get uncomfortable, call me right away. I am heading out to do some surveillance on another case."

Knowing she had the sheriff's approval, Anne responded confidently, "Copy that, boss."

Anne returned to her office, picked up the phone, and started dialing former Detective Wallace's phone number.

Chapter 11

August 19th
Pender County Museum, Burgaw, NC
1:00 p.m.

The day had started sunny, but storm clouds gathered by mid-morning, developing into a steady rain. Jack heard rumbles of thunder as he pulled into the unpaved lot that served as the Pender County Museum's parking area. Usually, he would feel concerned about the weather, as David was always anxious about the potential for wind, hail, or worse yet, a tornado. However, when Jack was leaving, Daphne parked herself right next to David. It was as if she sensed his anxiety. The dog had even put her head in his lap to calm him down. Jack felt a sense of relief knowing that David was in good hands—or paws, as the case might be.

Numerous searches on the Internet had revealed very little about Saint Helena, NC. The village's formal founding occurred in 1905, and there had never been more than 450 residents at any one time. There was nothing unique about the town. It was a very rural area that consisted exclusively of farmland. The Saint Helena website stated there were five churches in the village and that number virtually matched the total size of the town itself, which was 5.65 square miles.

An online photo of the Saint Helena Village Hall showed only a former single-family house. When he called, the contact person there told Jack that few historical records were on the premises. They had the deed establishing the town and little else, let alone documents, for years before the village's formation. She had suggested he try the Pender County Museum and Historical Society in Burgaw. Fortunately for Jack, George had been able to come over on short notice and take the boys to the bowling alley.

Jack had been driving for more than an hour when he finally got to the museum. The Pender County Historical Society was the museum curator and had an office in the two-story red brick building. The structure was well-maintained from the exterior, but its slate roof betrayed its age. Playing a game of hopscotch across the now muddy parking lot, Jack tried to avoid the puddles filling the potholes, but just as he almost reached the front porch of the building, he heard a splash and felt his shoe immersed in a pool of water. He sighed. *I sure hope that is not a sign of things to come.*

Jack turned the knob and pushed in the front door, which stuck slightly to the jam due to the humidity. As he stepped in, a short, gray-haired woman greeted him. Jack estimated that she was nearly eighty years of age as he watched her shuffling slowly across the floor to greet him, using a cane to steady herself.

"Good afternoon," she addressed him in a Southern drawl. "How may I help you?"

"Good afternoon, ma'am. Earlier this morning, I spoke with someone in the Saint Helena Village Hall about my research. She suggested I might try coming here, as the information I am looking into pre-dates the actual formation of the village."

The older woman grinned. "Well, that is wonderful! There are not a lot of visitors to our museum, dear. As you can see, we are rather modest in size. We are only open three days a week until 4:00 p.m., so you showed up on the right day and at the right time. My name is Amy Scowle, but my friends call me Miss Amy."

Jack shook Miss Amy's hand. "It is very nice to meet you; my name is Jack Aitken. Is it possible you might have a room with a table where I can spread out a little to take some notes?"

"Certainly, dear, but first, you must allow me to give you a tour of our museum."

Jack was glad he took the time to allow Miss Amy to show him around. Considering its size, the museum was quite interesting. Downstairs, it displayed military memorabilia from the American Revolution through World War II. The second floor had exhibits, including antique medical instruments and utensils. Another room was full of wedding dresses that women in Pender County had donated. Jack thought to himself, Amanda *would have liked to have seen this.*

Finally, Miss Amy showed Jack a space that displayed some beautiful turn-of-the-century furniture.

Upon finishing the tour, Miss Amy stated proudly, "The Noel family donated this home to us. It was the first brick home in Burgaw and is more than a hundred years old."

Jack peered down at his watch and saw it was now 2:00 p.m. Miss Amy noticed this. "Look at the time. I am sorry for going on so, Jack."

He chuckled. "That is quite all right, Miss Amy. Your museum is fascinating. You have a right to be proud of it."

"Oh, Jack. You are very kind. Thank you for indulging me. Now, let us get down to business. How may I help you?"

"I am seeking information on the history of Saint Helena and, more specifically, any information about that area in the late 1890s into the early twentieth century."

"Are you looking for birth records, land deeds, or something else?"

Rubbing his chin, Jack inquired, "Were there any local newspapers in publication around that time?"

Miss Amy put her finger to her lips and thought for a moment. "Well, *The Pender Chronicle* ceased publishing in 2012. They were located here in Burgaw and covered all of Pender County. If my memory serves me right, I believe they began publishing around the period you mentioned."

"That's great, Miss Amy!"

Before Jack could utter another word, she put her hand up. "Unfortunately, Jack, North Carolina has put all defunct newspaper back issues on microfilm. The nearest location you could access this information would be in Raleigh. The local library has some issues, but they are all from the 1950s."

"That is too bad." Jack sighed dejectedly. "Raleigh is a haul from here."

"Wait!" Miss Amy declared eagerly. "If you do not mind getting dirty, there is a chance we might have some back issues in the storage room. It is very dusty, dear. We do not go in there often."

"I am game if you are," Jack replied hopefully. "Show me the way."

Miss Amy led Jack down to the basement. She pointed to a door behind one of the old exhibits. Jack walked around the glass display case and took the door's handle in his hand. He turned the knob, but the door would not budge. Eventually, he pushed harder, the door gave way, and he peeked into the room. Jack took out his cellphone to better illuminate the chamber. It had a musty smell as if no one had been in it for years. There were cobwebs on the shelves, and dust was everywhere.

"I think it would be best if you did not come in here. Can you give me an idea of where I might look for the newspapers?"

Miss Amy bowed her head slightly and bit the nail of her index finger as she thought about where the newspapers might be. After a few moments, she replied, "Jack, try the last shelf on the right. The oldest documents would be on the furthest shelves from the door. We can start there."

Jack slowly made his way to the back of the room. Debris littered the floor, and Jack was careful not to trip over it. When he arrived at the shelves, there were several cardboard boxes. Jack managed to drag two of them upstairs and returned for the other two. Miss Amy had already opened the office door and waved Jack into the room. There was a circular table in the middle with four chairs around it.

"We can work here. If you do not mind, I want to help you look, Jack. It is not every day that I get a chance to do something this exciting."

Jack smiled. "Of course. What I am looking for are stories about animal attacks in St. Helena. Specifically, there were multiple attacks over a short period, such as four to six weeks, around the turn of the century."

"Ooh, a mystery!" Miss Amy exclaimed. "Where would you like me to start?"

Opening one of the boxes, Jack attempted not to breathe in the decade's worth of dust that now permeated the air. He carefully removed documents and placed them on the table.

"Good news, Jack! These are old issues of *The Pender Chronicle*!"

They frantically searched the contents of the box.

"I'm sorry that these are not the years you are looking for, Jack."

They put the papers back in the box and went on to the next.

The second and third boxes proved unsuccessful as well. Jack checked the clock on the wall and saw it was after 4:00 p.m.

"Miss Amy, I do not want to keep you here past closing time."

Miss Amy waved her hand in front of her face. "Don't you worry about that, Jack! We will stay until we get through all of these boxes!"

"Okay. I just need to make a phone call to my family. Please excuse me for a moment."

Jack stepped away from the table and phoned George while Miss Amy continued to look through the newspapers earnestly.

"Hey, Jack. How are things going?"

"All right, George, but I have one more box I need to look through. How late are you able to stay?"

"As late as you need me, bro. We had a ball bowling. Can I take Louis and David for something to eat and maybe a movie? Do you think they would like that?"

Louis and David overheard the conversation and shouted in unison. "All right! A movie sounds great! What will we go to see?"

Jack laughed. "I guess you have your answer."

"I guess so! I am happy to spend time with these two guys. They remind me of the two of us. Do what you must do and keep me posted."

"Thanks, George. I owe you one."

"No problemo." George ended the call.

Jack's phone vibrated. It was a text from Anne.

I will be late. Going to see Detective Wallace in Leland.

Jack typed a quick reply. *Okay. I am in Burgaw. I will explain later.*

Miss Amy looked up as Jack returned to the room. "I think I may have found something."

Jack rubbed his hands together. "Is it me, or did it get cold in here suddenly?"

Miss Amy shivered. Grabbing a sweater, she wrapped it around her shoulders. "I thought the same thing."

Pushing a paper across the table toward Jack, she pointed. "Here, look at this."

Jack remained standing, carefully examining the document. The tattered edges hung loosely, but the fading print was still legible. The entire newspaper had yellowed, and a pungent, moldy odor filled the air. It was the front page of *The Pender Chronicle,* dated January 26th, 1901. The date seemed appropriate, as the room seemed even colder. Jack blew into his hands to keep them warm.

"Miss Amy, where did you find this?"

"To tell you the truth, I thought we were out of luck, dear. I was about to close the box when I saw this on the other side of the table. Maybe it slipped out of one of the piles we were going through."

Jack scanned the front page, which was full of only advertisements. He flipped to page two and found news stories, most of which were about Queen Victoria of England's recent death. Then a headline toward the bottom of the page caught his eye: *'First Anniversary of Saint Helena Crimes.'*

Despite everything that had happened in the past few days, he still found himself surprised by what he read. The story confirmed that while the paper had not yet begun publishing when the attacks started, they were so unusual that a follow-up story about them seemed warranted. The first documented incident was right before Christmas in 1899. Harv McRae, a local goat farmer in Saint Helena, reported to authorities that he found several dead animals. Jack slowly read aloud, *'The animals had not been mutilated and appeared only to have been drained of their blood.'*

Miss Amy viewed Jack anxiously. "Is this the information you were looking for?"

Jack nodded his head up and down and continued to read. Early in 1900, a third attack involving a farm on Saint Helena's outskirts left residents uneasy. The farmer found unusual tracks in proximity to the corpses of farm animals. There was a great deal of speculation about the footprints as they were enormous. Hunters had killed off Wolves and Mountain Lions decades earlier, and there were no known predator species capable of such attacks in the area. The residents formed a posse to hunt the attacker, but they had no success tracking it through the swamps and woods surrounding Saint Helena.

The following paragraph confirmed that a fourth and fifth animal attack followed the three earlier events. The last attack happened on the Mizerak farm. This time it involved the family dog, not farm animals. The Mizeraks were sheep farmers and found their sheepdog on the edge of the property, not far from the house. The night before, the family had heard growls from the woods, and when they checked the area in the morning, they found their dog dead. They did not find any signs of a struggle and only found blood on the white fur around the dog's throat.

The Mizeraks buried the dog, but on the morning of the 26th, they found the unearthed remains on the house's front steps. Jack was shocked. *Like in Bolivia,* he thought to himself, but 100 years earlier! A genuine chill crawled up Jack's spine, and he slowly sat down in his chair. There was no doubt now that all three sets of attacks were related.

"Jack, are you all right? You look like you have seen a ghost."

"I am not sure. I have just read a story about animal killings in 1899-1900 that are eerily like attacks in Bladenboro in the 1950s, and Bolivia in 2007-2008."

"Miss Amy," Jack asked hesitantly, "have you ever heard of any similar attacks occurring in Saint Helena or Pender County?"

Miss Amy, her mouth slightly agape, just shook her head. Then she announced, "Strigoi."

"Strig-oi?" Jack asked, sounding it out. "Miss Amy, what is Strigoi?"

Miss Amy squirmed in her chair. "Jack, I have lived here in Pender County all my life. It is very rural, so animal attacks are not unusual. Immigrants from Eastern Europe, mostly from Romania, settled in this area over the past fifty years. Psychiatrists here even advertise that they can provide counseling emphasizing knowledge of Romanian culture. They are friendly, but they keep to themselves and are very superstitious. Myths and legends and all of that. Do you know what I mean?"

Jack nodded as Miss Amy continued. "I have heard them whisper about the legend of the Strigoi. I do not know much about it. I do not put much stock in such things, but I often hear it brought up in conjunction with bad luck or unfortunate events."

"Something like an animal attack?"

"Yes, Jack. I only mention it because I know the myth's premise is that this is a creature, sort of like a wolf. I do not know if that helps you at all."

Jack placed his hand on Miss Amy's. "It does, Miss Amy."

The pair sat in silence, the only noise being the rain hitting the roof and windows.

"It sounds like it is still raining. Can I at least give you a ride or follow you to ensure you get home all right?"

"A true gentleman. A dying breed these days." Miss Amy smiled. "Thank you, but that won't be necessary. I do not live that far away."

"At least let me help you to your car."

Miss Amy locked the door to the museum, and Jack held her umbrella so that she would not get wet on the way to her car. Jack waved as Miss Amy drove away and called out, "Thank you again."

Returning to Ocean Isle Beach, Jack thought about Miss Amy's statement about the Strigoi. At a stop sign, he wrote a note to at least familiarize himself with what it was, assuming there was any information available about it. Jack could not stop thinking about the article. He had difficulty convincing himself that what he was reading could have happened and wondered if a search of records in the span from 1845-1846 would find another series of attacks. As

Jack considered it, the question was not if there would be another series of attacks. The problem was, where should he look next?

***

Amy Scowle still felt excited as she turned the corner toward home. She could not remember the last time she felt so helpful. Assisting Jack Aitken was exhilarating, and at her age, she wondered if such an opportunity would ever come again. Miss Amy planned to savor this for a long time. As she pulled into her driveway, however, she did have one nagging thought. Should she have told Jack about the Strigoi?

Miss Amy exited her vehicle and headed toward the front door. A figure stepped onto the front porch as she put her key in the lock.

"Ma'am, I want to ask you some questions about Jack Aitken."

Chapter 12

August 18th
Retired Detective Robert Wallace's home, Leland, NC
4:45 p.m.

Anne Bishop pulled up to a gray brick ranch-style residence on Wyland Court. The pouring rain made it difficult to read the house numbers, so she had to exit her car to see if she was at the right home. The black iron numbers above the front door read *1093* and confirmed she was at the right place. Retired Detective Robert Wallace lived in the Magnolia Greens development, just outside Wilmington, about a thirty-minute drive from the police station.

Magnolia Greens was an amenity-rich, gated community, with the centerpiece being its championship golf course. Anne recalled that her realtor had provided information about the neighborhood during the move associated with her new job, but it was far out of her price range. As she reached the opulently designed front door, she thought, *Pretty high-end on a cop's salary.* Anne rang the doorbell. Moments later, a middle-aged woman with red hair and a pale white complexion opened the door.

"Good afternoon, ma'am." Anne showed the woman her identification and handed her a card with her contact information. "My name is Detective Anne Bishop, and I am here to see Mr. Wallace."

The woman invited Anne inside. "Yes, I am Mrs. Wallace. Robert told me you would be stopping by. My name is Theresa, but you can call me Terri. Please come in. May I take your coat?"

Anne handed her wet overcoat to Mrs. Wallace. "Thank you, Terri. It's coming down hard out there right now."

"I know," Terri Wallace agreed. "I hope it lets up soon. I have a card game to go to this evening." Terri pointed down the hallway. "Robert is waiting for you in his study."

As she walked, Anne surveyed the home. It was spacious, open, and lavishly decorated with top-of-the-line furniture, murals, and hardwood floors. It was not what you would expect to find in the house of a retired cop.

A very tall man without the belly that men tended to get in their middle age got up from behind the desk and reached out his hand. "Good afternoon, Detective. It is nice to meet you. Please, have a seat. Can I get you something to drink?"

"No, thank you, Mr. Wallace. I'm fine."

Robert Wallace closed the doors behind him and sat again behind his desk.

"How is Glenn doing these days? I know it came as a surprise to him when I put in my retirement papers."

"He is doing fine," Anne replied. "If you do not mind me asking, why did your retirement come as such a surprise?"

"Please, call me Robert. I may not look like it, but I am only in my mid-fifties. Glenn was sure I had another ten years on the job before retiring."

"I see. You got out while you were still young enough to enjoy life?"

"You have that right, Detective," Wallace gloated. "I feel great. I play golf three to four times weekly and work out daily. I never thought life could be this good."

Anne tried to hide her envy when she spoke. "Congratulations, Robert. It is good to see one of our own making the most of his hard work. You have quite a place here."

"Thanks, Detective. I did work hard for all of this."

"You must have saved almost every penny," Anne stated, attempting to probe more deeply into the former detective's ability to afford the lifestyle he was living.

Robert Wallace sensed what Anne was trying to do and replied coyly, "I collaborate with good financial people."

Wallace leaned back in his chair and laced his fingers together. "So, when you called, it sounded like you have something important that we need to discuss. What can I do for you?"

"I do not want to take up too much of your time, but I am here about a case assigned to you in late 2007."

Robert Wallace quickly sat up straight in his chair and coolly countered, "I worked a lot of cases back then, Detective."

"I am sure." Anne kept her calm, feeling that she had struck a nerve. "This case involved a series of attacks on animals in Bolivia. Does it sound familiar?"

Sounding annoyed, Wallace answered, "Not really. Why don't you try to jog my memory?"

Anne sensed he knew more than he was letting on. "Six attacks that have the same cause of death would be difficult to forget, would it not?" she pressed.

Wallace paused for a few moments. "Maybe that is why I do not remember it. I think there were one or two, but I do not remember six."

Anne replied pointedly, "I do not need to remind a former law enforcement officer about the penalties for evidence tampering, do I?"

Robert Wallace's eyes narrowed into tight slits, and his jaw clenched. He was pissed. "What are you insinuating, Detective? I do not know what you are talking about."

"But I think you do, Robert." Anne stared defiantly at Wallace, giving no indication that she would back down. "Exsanguination in animals is unusual. So is not defiling the remains. Don't you agree? Yet, your file suggests you saw no connection between these crimes. I also found the results of the DNA tests that you buried. Your work was more than sloppy, Detective. I believe you deliberately hid those results. In 2007 and 2008, a twelve-year-old could have searched the Internet to look for animal exsanguination information. They would have found more than a passing reference to the Bladenboro killings from 1953 and 1954. You made no mention of it at all. It is time for you to come clean about all of this, or the District Attorney will hear from me."

Robert Wallace leaned forward in an apparent attempt to intimidate Anne, but she didn't move a muscle. Realizing he could not bully her, Wallace uttered only one word: "Antonescu."

Anne asked emphatically, "What about the Antonescu family? How are they involved in this?"

"That is all I am going to tell you." Wallace's tone got rough. "You do the detective work from here."

"What about Sheriff Hill? Is he involved in any way?"

Wallace shot up from his chair. The veins on his hands were bulging as he tightly grasped the sides of the desk. "How dare you!" The former detective declared indignantly. "Glenn is my friend. Do you think I would betray him?

"Time for you to go, Detective." He angrily pointed toward the door. "I believe you can find your way out."

Anne got up. "Have a good evening, Detective," she replied brusquely.

After fetching her jacket, she opened the front door to go and could not help but notice the dark, ominous clouds. While the weather all day had been miserable, the sky confirmed something very intense was on its way now. A booming thunderclap shook her car as she got behind the wheel. Lightning bolts illuminated the darkness, and the rain picked up in intensity once more. She turned right onto Route 17 South and thought *I was right about Constantin Antonescu. Now I must find out what dirt he has under his fingernails.*

She knew she would have to proceed carefully, especially if Sheriff Hill was somehow a part of this.

***

In his study, Robert Wallace sat with his elbows on the desk, his chin supported by his folded hands, absorbed in his thoughts. Detective Bishop's visit caught him off guard, and he pondered his next move. This case was, both literally and figuratively, dead and buried. How did it get on Anne Bishop's radar?

Wallace picked up the receiver on the phone and quickly put it back in the cradle. He waited, then dialed a number, but stopped before hitting the last number. Wallace picked up the phone a third time and finally placed a call that he hoped would ease the dread that was only beginning to build in his soul.

Ring, ring, ring ...

***

August 18th
Detective Anne Bishop's home, Ocean Isle Beach, NC
7:00 p.m.

Jack finished drying the dinner dishes and handed them to Anne. They laughed at David and Louis giggling with their best buddy Daphne barking along. Anne poured coffee for them both, and they sat in the living room to update each other on what they had learned that day. They both had an exciting story to tell.

"What you learned about the animal deaths in St. Helena leaves no doubt that what happened in Bolivia and Bladenboro are not isolated incidents. I continue to be impressed with your investigative instincts, Jack."

"Thanks!" Jack replied enthusiastically. "I take that as a compliment but cannot take all the credit. Miss Amy was a tremendous help." Pointing at the ceiling, toward the room above the garage, he added, "And without direction by whomever or whatever drew the line on the map upstairs, I would not have known where to begin to search."

Anne frowned and scratched her chin. "I am still trying to understand that myself. I am grateful for the assistance, even if it is weirdly unexplainable. It is also fascinating what Miss Amy told you about the—what did she call it, Strigoi?"

"Another in a long line of legendary creatures from Romania," Jack joked. "What do you make of Robert Wallace's insinuation of the Antonescus potential involvement in all this? Do you think they are covering up details about what happened in Bolivia?

"It seems far from a coincidence. I am wrestling with whether the Antonescus Romanian origins have a connection to any of this." Sipping her coffee, she added, "I think we should investigate the

Antonescus background. Then we can delve into the legend of the Strigoi."

"I agree, Anne. Let me check on the boys and get my laptop."

Jack poked his head into the den. David was playing games on his iPad, and Louis was texting his friends about their vacation. They looked up at Jack. "We are good, Dad."

"Okay, guys. If you need something, I'm in the dining room."

Daphne wagged her tail and panted with her tongue hanging out of her mouth. "That goes for you too, Daphne."

The dog barked, and the boys laughed as Jack grabbed his laptop from the guest room. He found Anne at the dining room table, already pounding away at her keyboard. While the two of them researched, the hours passed by quickly. Louis and David went to bed; before Jack or Anne realized it, it was after 11:00 p.m. The only sound besides their typing was the air-conditioning unit's humming.

Jack sat straight in the chair, hunched his shoulders, and rolled his neck, trying to stretch his tight muscles.

"Anne, I am not sure if this is helpful or not. I found significant Romanian-American populations around the United States. One of them is in Georgia. Before moving to Lake Waccamaw, the Antonescus lived around Atlanta, a mecca for multi-media companies. Antonescu Communications headquarters is still there."

"Listen to this, Jack. According to the Foundation for Eastern European Family History Studies, Father Samuel Damian, an Orthodox Priest from Transylvania, was the first Romanian recorded in America. He traveled extensively in Maryland, North Carolina, and Virginia in 1748 and corresponded with Benjamin Franklin regarding electricity before settling in Charleston, South Carolina. His name appears in the *South Carolina Gazette* as far back as 1748."

"That is very interesting." Jack got excited. "South Carolina could easily be the portal through which an influx of Romanian immigrants entered the country and eventually settled in Georgia."

Anne continued, "Census data indicates that a major wave of immigrants from Romania entered the United States from 1895 through 1920."

She paused for a moment and then read slowly, "The overwhelming majority of these immigrants were from Transylvania and its neighboring region of Banat. Both of which share a border with Wallachia."

"Count Dracula's stomping grounds." Jack smiled playfully. "I guess you would not get a more superstitious group than immigrants from there. It supports what Miss Amy told me about the Romanian residents in her area and their fear of the Strigoi."

"So, what have we got on the Antonescus?"

"This is from Antonescu Communications Annual Report," Jack answered. "Constantin Antonescu VI was born in Atlanta in 1960. The family got into the newspaper business in the early eighteenth century. When Constantin VI was born, they owned regional newspapers, including the *Augusta Morning News*, *Savannah Chronicle*, and *The Brunswick Times*. He worked in the family business while attending the University of Georgia and graduated in 1982 with degrees in communications and journalism. His father, Constantin Antonescu V, died in 1989. His son became the owner and Chief Executive Officer. Constantin VI continued to buy up regional newspapers, television, and radio stations throughout the South. Still, the company really took off in the 1990s when it invested its assets in Internet-related businesses. By 2000, its revenues exceeded one billion dollars. They were twenty billion in 2020."

"That is an impressive resume. Any information on Constantin's personal life?"

"Constantin married Maria Iancu in 1984, and they have seven children, all daughters. Daria is the oldest, born in 1985. Then Ana Maria, Gabriela, Alexandra, Daniela, Sofia, and finally Maricela in 1998. They lived in Buckhead, the most affluent suburb of Atlanta, until 2005, when they moved to the large family compound in Lake Waccamaw."

"Anything else, Jack?"

"Nothing that appears to be of any importance. I read in the paper the other day that Constantin has formed an exploratory committee to consider running for Governor."

Just then, a loud noise startled them.

"What was that?" Jack asked.

Anne grimaced. "I think the air-conditioning unit just died. I have been putting off getting it repaired or replaced. I just have not had time to get to it. I have some fans we can set up to get us through the night, and I will call a repairman in the morning."

In the garage, Anne checked the unit and determined it was not repairable. Jack helped set up fans in each of the bedrooms. It was nearly midnight, and they decided to pick up their research in the morning. The effects of the loss of air-conditioning were instantaneous. Despite the movement of the air by the fans, both Jack and Anne tossed and turned, struggling to fall asleep.

***

August 18th
Robert Wallace's study, Leland, NC
10:30 p.m.

Robert Wallace sat nervously in his study. The desk lamp provided the only source of illumination in the room. Outside, a vicious thunderstorm that had gone on for hours had finally diminished, but the wind had not died. Still being lashed by the gusts, the trees caused shadows to fall upon the walls, adding to the eerie atmosphere consuming the room. Despite the nasty weather, Robert had encouraged Terri to go to her weekly card game, leaving him alone.

For hours, Wallace had sat waiting for the phone to ring. While not an easy man to rattle, Detective Bishop's visit had caught him off guard. He had thought the Bolivia case was closed, and the last thing he expected was a confrontation. The tense conversation between the two could not conceal that Detective Bishop was right;

he had buried the DNA evidence and fraudulently closed the case, citing a lack of evidence.

Now, he was seeking reassurance from the one man who could help him, the only person up until now who knew what he had done.

Wallace picked up the vodka bottle on the desk and poured it into the glass before him. The bottle had been nearly full when he took his first drink earlier that evening, but it was now almost empty. The former detective brought the glass to his lips and gulped half the contents down. He wiped his mouth with his sleeve.

RING! RING! RING!

The phone's sound nearly made the former detective jump out of his skin. He checked the caller ID and recognized the number immediately.

Wallace composed himself and picked up the phone. "What took you so long? I have been waiting here for hours."

"What do you want?" the person on the line asked curtly. "I told you never to call me."

Wallace responded bluntly, making no effort to hide either his fear or anger, "I did you a favor thirteen years ago. You owe me something in return."

"I owe you nothing," the caller responded coldly. "You got paid handsomely for your efforts. I do not want to hear from you again, ever. Are we clear, Wallace?"

"Listen." Wallace was furious. "I was visited today by a Brunswick County detective about the Bolivia case. She knows everything. We need to do something about this."

"NO! *You* need to do something about it! Make this go away, Wallace. I do not care what you must do, but this is your problem to solve."

Robert Wallace paused for a moment, then asked pleadingly, "What the hell do you want me to do? You want me to kill a police detective?"

"Do what you have to," the voice replied callously, "or I will have to get our mutual benefactor involved. I do not think either of us wants that."

The phone clicked, and then there was nothing but silence. Wallace put the phone back in its cradle and opened the bottom desk drawer. Reaching in, he pulled out a case and put it on the desk. He opened it, revealing his old service weapon, a .45 revolver. Wallace had always taken pride in the meticulous care of his pistol. It was like it had only recently come off the factory assembly line.

Opening the loading gate of the pistol, he filled each cylinder. While putting six bullets into the chamber, he began to consider his options. As despicable as the thought of killing Detective Bishop, a fellow officer, was to him, the idea of having to see the unnamed *benefactor* once more was even worse. It sent a chill up and down his spine, just having to consider it. He finished loading the pistol and put it on the desk.

CRASH!

With his back to the arched window behind his chair, Robert Wallace could not see the entity speeding toward him. It burst through the window, sending shards of glass in all directions. The force of its entry was powerful enough to split the massive oak desk in two. Despite his size, Wallace was hurled against the built-in bookcases as if he were a small leaf blown away by a hurricane. Amazingly, he was still conscious.

A second entity swaggered into the room as Wallace struggled to regain his senses. The figure surveyed the damage and, looking at the enormous creature in front of him, announced sarcastically, "How uncivilized. We really must teach you how to turn a knob and use the front door."

The creature, which had been on all fours, stood upright, its massive, red hairy chest heaving with every breath it took. A low growl emanated from its mouth, lined with razor-sharp teeth and two pronounced canines on its upper jaw. The beast's eyes locked in on Robert Wallace, who could finally stand but struggled to remain on his feet.

The second entity was tall, but the creature overshadowed him. This figure appeared to be a male human.

Examining his fingernails, he spoke pompously. "You will have to forgive my friend, Mr. Wallace. I am afraid he is all brawn and very little brain."

Still feeling the effects of the sneak attack, Robert Wallace's head spun as he looked at the creature and man in front of him. Breathing heavily, he asked, "Do I know you?"

The man's eyes flared a fiery red, and he replied icily, "Do you remember me now, detective?"

Robert Wallace staggered backward. "My God, it is you."

"Oh no, not God, detective," the man declared mockingly. "You remember my name, do you not?"

"L-L-LLLucius. Lucius R-R-RRRofocale," Wallace stammered.

Lucius smirked wickedly. "Yes, Detective. We have something to discuss."

"What do you want? What do you need me to do now?" Wallace asked more coherently.

"Funny, you should ask. Tell me, what was Anne Bishop doing here this afternoon?"

Robert Wallace replied without hesitation. "She knows everything about Bolivia. I told her about Antonescu. I know you will kill me, so there is no sense in trying to play dumb or pretend that I do not know what is going on."

Instantly seething with anger, Lucius sneered, "That is indeed a disappointment, Mr. Wallace, and particularly unfortunate for you."

Wallace scanned the room; his gun was within reach. He picked it up and pointed it at Lucius. The creature towering behind Lucius prepared to launch an assault on Wallace.

Lucius held up his hand. The beast stilled but continued to stare the former detective down.

Lucius tauntingly laughed. "I can assure you that will do you no good."

Wallace fired the gun anyway. The first bullet should have struck Lucius in the forehead, but it stopped before his face and fell at his feet. Wallace fired another shot at the creature. It hit the beast in the chest but did not back it up an inch nor inflict any noticeable sign of pain.

Wallace was stunned. Dropping the gun, he begged, "What if I kill Detective Bishop? If she dies, then the secret will die with her."

Lucius folded his arms and started shaking his head back and forth. He paused, then replied contemptuously, "You forget one small detail, Mr. Wallace: you would still be alive. No matter. You will indeed kill Anne Bishop, just not with a gun."

The creature leaped across the room and was on top of Wallace instantly. Wallace was no match for the strength of the hairy beast, whose size dwarfed his and whose power enabled him to toss Wallace around the room like a ragdoll. In short order, Wallace was sprawled on the ground, nearly beaten to death.

Lucius raised his hand again, and the creature immediately stopped its attack.

"Taste him, my friend, but do not drain him. Let him turn, and he will kill Anne Bishop for us. That will leave only one loose end to tie up, which will happen soon enough."

The creature approached a now defenseless Robert Wallace, who was barely conscious. The hairy beast, its fangs exposed, lifted Wallace from the floor. The former detective moaned in agony as the monster roughly pushed his head to the left, exposing the jugular vein.

The creature plunged its fangs into Wallace's flesh, and as it sucked his blood, Wallace, in agony, silently prayed for mercy.

None was forthcoming.

Chapter 13

August 19th
Anne Bishop's house, Ocean Isle Beach, NC
3:00 a.m.

Sweat rolled down Jack's face and back. The bed sheets stuck to his legs, and he finally kicked them off in frustration. He had watched the ceiling fan for what seemed like hours, but it just kept turning around, providing no relief from the heat and humidity that had invaded the house after the loss of air-conditioning. He heard Daphne's claws clicking on the tile floor as she wandered the home in search of a comfortable place to sleep but then heard another sound and got up to investigate it. A light was on in the kitchen, and Jack decided to see who was up; it was too hot to sleep.

He found Anne surveying the refrigerator. "I hope I did not wake you. I could not fall asleep and thought a cold drink might help. Are you interested?"

Jack exhaled. "What do you have in there?"

"Ordinarily, I would offer you a cold beer. How about a bottle of ginger ale instead?"

Jack yawned. "Sold."

She handed Jack a bottle and grabbed one for herself. Sitting at the dining room table across from each other, they opened the bottles and jokingly toasted one another. "Cheers."

They both took a large gulp. Staring at the bottle, Jack commented, "It is funny how much we take for granted. We do not realize how important something like air-conditioning can be until we do not have it."

Anne concurred. "I am surprised that Louis and David are still asleep."

"Me too, but I did poke my head in there, and they are both out like a light."

Jack wiped his brow with his wrist and took another mouthful of soda from his bottle.

"When I was a younger man, I slept as they do, but nowadays, I am the antithesis of what I used to be. I am a restless sleeper, and it is a rare morning that I wake to feel refreshed. I have tried melatonin, but it does not seem to work."

After finishing the bottle's contents, Jack declared, "I think if I exercised more frequently, that might help."

"I hear you. Work is what keeps me up at night. I cannot keep my mind off this case."

A black mass suddenly darted across the living room, and Jack jolted.

Anne glanced at Jack. "Did you see something?"

"Yes," Jack whispered. "It was a shadow or something like that."

Anne and Jack got up and stepped into the living room. They searched the room for a sign of what they had seen, but nothing was out of place. They began to move around the room, investigating as they went.

Jack saw something out of the corner of his eye. It was in the hallway, suspended in midair. Jack shot Anne a look, and her worried expression told him she saw the same thing. They both slowly moved in that direction.

As they stepped into the hallway, the mass darted up the stairs to the room over the garage. Jack muttered, "Have you ever seen anything like this before?"

"Seen, no. Read about it while I was part of JESU, yes. I don't recall much about entities like this. Let's follow it."

Anne started toward the stairs, with Jack right behind her. They got to the landing but saw nothing. Suddenly, the lights came on in the room. They looked at one another and slowly made their way up the steps. When they reached the top of the stairs, they could not believe what they saw. The black mass was visible yet at the same time transparent. They could see right through it as it hovered over the map on the table.

Jack and Anne hesitated, then unhurriedly walked toward the table. The black mass did not move. When they were only feet away, the pen on the tabletop slowly rose in the air. It hovered for a few moments and then descended toward the map. Jack and Anne watched incredulously, their mouths slightly agape, as the pen swept across the map's surface. Then the ballpoint pen dropped, and the black mass darted away from the table to the corner of the room where Daphne had been barking just two days earlier. It hovered there briefly before seemingly exiting the room through the wall.

Jack whispered, "I thought the smudging you did the other day would get rid of something like this."

"It has worked well in the past, but maybe it does not affect entities not driven by evil intentions. That mass made no aggressive movement toward us whatsoever. It was as if it wanted to lead us up here. We need to look at the map."

They encircled the table. The pen, which only minutes ago was hovering in the air, was in the middle of the table. It appeared innocuous enough, but Jack's superstitions about objects having the capacity for malicious attachments told him not to touch it. He noticed the map had a new line drawn on it. It went from St. Helena, the location Jack had just researched, to a tiny circle in the southwestern quadrant. Jack had to remove his glasses to read it.

"Bughill Township. I have never heard of it. It looks even smaller than St. Helena."

He stepped back and examined the map again. "It may be nothing, but that looks like an '*X*' on the map."

"I see that too, Jack. I would not discount or assume anything associated with this case. It is getting weirder and weirder all the time."

"Well, I know what I am doing tomorrow. Bughill Township, here I come."

Anne opted to attempt to sleep, but Jack knew it was pointless. He sat reading in the living room. Jack thought about what they had just seen. He peered over his shoulder to make sure he was still alone.

Jack recalled what Mark Desmond had told him: *"The most challenging part of the battle between good and evil is determining one from another."* Jack wondered if this entity was as benign as it appeared, or was it something malevolent just setting them up for the kill? He slowly fell asleep in the chair.

The black entity hovered nearby before exiting the house again.

***

August 19th
A Sawgrass Marsh Near Brick Landing Plantation,
Ocean Isle Beach, NC
3:00 a.m.

The beast examined the struggling animal in his hands. What would have been a bobcat to Robert Wallace only hours before was now his next meal. The cat desperately slashed at Wallace with its claws in a last-ditch effort to escape but to no avail. Wallace barely felt pain from the bobcat's counterattack as he pinned the creature to the ground with his left hand. Gripping the cat's head with his right hand, he effortlessly twisted it 360 degrees until it fell away from the bobcat's body.

The cat's torso continued to writhe and twitch while Wallace tossed the head behind him into the marsh. Kneeling on the damp earth, he tore an arm from the body and began biting into the flesh. The being that once was Detective Robert Wallace stared into the darkness. It had no memories or thoughts of its own any longer. It only gnawed on the bones of its prey to appease the insatiable appetite coursing through its body.

The beast pulled off another limb from the carcass, and while it consumed more flesh, it listened to the sounds of the insects surrounding him in the marsh. The other sound it heard was a thought emanating from its now primitive brain: *Kill Anne Bishop*. The beast could not remember that it once had the power of human speech, but the sound in its head was familiar. A voice leading it to a destination it did not recognize, but its animal instinct knew was now within reach. *Kill Anne Bishop,* the voice repeated. *Kill Anne Bishop.*

Then a different impulse began to reverberate through the beast's body. It told the creature it was time to rest. After finishing the last pieces of the bobcat's flesh, the entity began pushing on the sawgrass with its hands and feet. Ignoring the cuts from the sawgrass's sharp ridges, it continued matting the grass into a temporary bed. The crude mattress provided enough comfort for the beast to sleep.

Kill Anne Bishop. Kill Anne Bishop.

***

August 19th
Anne Bishop's house, Ocean Isle Beach, NC
7:00 a.m.

Still groggy from the night before, Jack slowly rose from his chair and headed to the breakfast table. Several months ago, a cold Corona with a twist of lime would have been his breakfast of choice, but today he settled for coffee and two Tylenol. Daphne tried her hardest to get his attention, and Jack could not resist petting her even in his current stupor. *At least someone got some sleep last night*; he thought as he tossed back the two Tylenol with a coffee chaser. Louis and David were still asleep, but Anne was already sitting at the table.

"If you do not mind me saying so, Jack, you look like hell," Anne teased. "I feel the same way. After our *visitor* left last night, I bet you did not get much sleep either."

Jack nodded in agreement as he gulped down his first cup of coffee and poured himself another. He offered to pour her some more coffee. Anne held her cup out, and Jack filled it to the brim. He sat down across the table from her.

"I dozed a little in the chair. I honestly am not sure if it was the ghost, apparition, or whatever else we might call it or the heat. I felt that I was not alone … that I was being watched. I will need more than two cups of coffee this morning."

Anne shook her head. "I am so sorry, Jack. I knew the air-conditioning unit was on its last legs. I feel like a real idiot."

They heard a gasp before Anne could continue and found Louis and David standing behind them. Louis told David. "She used the *'I'* word."

David agreed. "I heard it too."

Jack began to laugh. With a puzzled look, Anne asked, "What is so funny? What is the *'I'* word?"

"It's okay, boys, Anne and I were just talking about the air-conditioning not working. Go to the bedroom and watch television. I will get your breakfast ready."

The boys turned and headed toward the bedroom with Daphne right behind them. Jack continued to chuckle and turned back to Anne. "The 'I' word, as Louis and David refer to it, is the word idiot. Do you recall the comedian George Carlin's monologue about the seven dirty words you can never say on television? My boys have a slightly broader list than Mr. Carlin."

Anne began laughing. "I see. I will try to watch my language from now on."

Getting ready to leave for work, she asked," Is there anything you need before I go?"

"Nothing I can think of, Anne. I'll call George and see if he can hang out with the boys again so I can research Bughill Township. Would it be okay if I asked him to stay for dinner again?"

"I would enjoy that, Jack. I will call or text you to let you know how my day is going. Thanks for your help and for looking after Daphne once more."

"No problem. I am happy to do it."

Jack watched Anne drive away, then prepared Louis and David's breakfast. He sat at the table with another cup of coffee and the telephone. He dialed George's number and took a sip while waiting for someone to pick up.

After three ringtones, he heard someone on the other end. "Hello, George's Mortuary. You kill 'em, and we chill 'em."

Jack laughed. "Hi, George, it is your brother. Nice message. Still working on that comedy career?"

"You know it, Jack! What's up?"

"I know this is asking a lot, but are you able to hang out with Louis and David again today? I must do more research, which will probably involve another road trip."

George responded instantly. "Say no more, Jack. I have vacation days left to take, and today will be one of them. Let me get my act together. I can be there by nine. Do Louis and David like amusement parks? There is a great one down here."

"Perfect, George. I can always count on you!"

"You know it, dude. See you in a little while."

Jack hung up the phone and went to get dressed. After cleaning the breakfast dishes, he sat at the dining table with his laptop. Jack waited for the computer to boot up, and his thoughts turned toward Bughill Township. His intuition told him that he might discover something significant there, but after the ghostly encounter the night before, he was not quite sure he wanted to find it.

***

August 19th
Detective Robert Wallace's home, Leland, NC
10:00 a.m.

Anne turned onto Wyland Court and found the cul-de-sac cut off by a barricade. While on her way to the office, she had received an urgent call from Sheriff Hill to hightail it out to the Wallace house.

Dozens of people had assembled in front of a makeshift barricade, along with television news trucks with satellite uplinks. The location was crawling with Brunswick County Police. Anne parked the car. As she approached the Wallace residence, she flashed her credentials to the officers, who moved the barricade to allow her to go through.

A posse of police personnel ran back and forth from the Wallace home, and crime scene investigators were visible from the street. Anne knew something terrible had happened. Sheriff Hill exited the house as she went to the front door. The serious look of concern on his face confirmed that Anne's conclusion about the situation was valid.

"Good morning, Bishop. Thanks for getting out here so quickly."

"Certainly, boss. What happened?"

Shaking his head, Sheriff Hill answered, "You are not going to believe it. It looks like a tornado ripped through the place. I received a phone call from Terri Wallace, Robert's wife, early this morning. Terri was hysterical, but I could calm her down enough to find out that she had played cards late into the evening, and with the weather so bad, she decided to spend the night at her friend's house. She called Robert last night and left a message to that effect. He did not return her call, but she did not give it a second thought. Terri came home around 8:00 a.m. and found ..."

Sheriff Hill paused to compose himself. Anne could not help but notice how his eyes darted back and forth—as if the sheriff was continuously scanning the area around him, expecting to see something. It was a look Anne had seen countless times before, during her missions for JESU. It was a look of fear.

Sheriff Hill took a deep breath and slowly exhaled. "I cannot find the words. Come with me."

Sheriff Hill led Anne into the house and down the hallway to the study where Anne had confronted Robert Wallace the day before. What she saw shocked even her.

The room was unrecognizable. The window behind Robert Wallace's desk was gone. Glass and wood splinters were everywhere. The massive oak desk that Wallace had sat behind lay on the floor in pieces.

Before she could ask, Sheriff Hill shared, "There is no sign of him, Bishop. I am unsure how anyone could have survived this destruction, but he is not here. We have searched the entire house, and officers are canvassing the neighborhood. There is no sign of Wallace anywhere."

Anne scanned the room, attempting to make sense of it all.

"I know you must ask the question, Sheriff. I left here around 5:30 p.m. yesterday, and Robert Wallace was very much alive. I discussed the Bolivia case with him, as I told you I would. He refused to admit that he buried or doctored the evidence. He did, however, tell me one thing."

"What was that, Bishop?"

"Antonescu."

"Antonescu?" Sheriff Hill asked, rubbing his temple with a perplexed look on his face.

"Yes, boss," Anne reiterated. "Just that one word. Then he told me to do my own detective work and asked me to leave. So I left."

Sheriff Hill pressed his lips together, seemingly satisfied with Anne's explanation.

Anne continued. "I asked him if you knew anything about the case."

The sheriff seemed surprised by Anne's admission. "And what did he tell you?"

"That you knew nothing about it. While Wallace was evasive about everything else, the one thing he told me that I believe to be true is that you were unaware of what he was doing."

Looking at Anne, Sheriff Hill stated, "I think we can safely say that we have cleared one another of any involvement in what happened here. Look around and see if you can find anything in this mess that might help us trace Wallace. By the way, I did check with the weather service, and there is no record of any tornado action in this area last night."

"Copy that, boss," Anne replied respectfully, and the sheriff left.

The evidence technician in the room told Anne they had a lot of trace evidence to go through. It included broken glass, wood fragments, blood, and fingerprints belonging to Detective Wallace and his wife. The technician left the room. Anne was now alone. She surveyed the debris but saw nothing that would be of any value.

Anne made her way to the gaping hole that had once been the room's wall and window. Shards of glass were everywhere. Anne put a pair of latex gloves on and knelt to sift through the rubble. She picked up and carefully examined several bricks on the floor, but they yielded no clues. Anne saw the desk pieces and remembered how large a piece of furniture it was.

What could have possibly broken up that oak desk in this way? It's like a freight train came through this place.

The fragments of wood from the desk were everywhere. She moved a larger piece of rubble and saw something hanging on the corner of what was once a drawer. It was a piece of hair! It was red and relatively coarse. Anne knew it was not from Robert Wallace as his hair had been black with a hint of gray. She called for the evidence technician, who held open a plastic bag as Anne carefully used a pair of tweezers to gather the hair sample.

"How long will it take to get the test results back on this sample?"

"At least twenty-four hours, Detective."

Anne spoke with the lead crime scene investigator and gave him her card, asking that he call her immediately when the results were ready. Anne exited the crime scene and made her way to her car. She noticed that the television reporters were taping their news stories for the next broadcast and wondered if any of these crews were working for Antonescu Communications. Anne made a mental note to watch the news broadcasts tonight to find the answer to that question.

Chapter 14

August 19th
Family Kingdom Amusement Park, Myrtle Beach, SC
11:30 a.m.

George Aitken exited onto the log flume platform and felt the water ooze out of his shoes, but the smiles on his nephews' faces made it all worth it. The three men were soaking wet, but it was a relief on such a hot day. They were having a blast, and seeing them enjoying themselves was a wonderful feeling. George could see that the boys were thriving. Whether it was just the passage of time or, as Jack insisted, the introduction of the game of golf to their lives, there was no doubt that it all had a healing effect on Jack and his family.

"Hey, guys, how about riding the roller coaster?"

"YEAH!" yelled David.

Louis was far less enthusiastic. "Okay. I guess so."

They waited for their turn, and by the time they got to the front of the line, the blazing sun had almost dried out their clothes. David grinned broadly, but Louis was more subdued.

"Don't worry, Louis," George reassured him, patting his nephew on the back. "This is going to be fun!"

After the attendant strapped them in, the coaster slowly pulled away from the platform. The car made its way up to the top of the trellis, where it paused for a moment; then, it began its descent, picking up speed as it fell toward the first curve in the track. David waved his hand while Louis gripped the car's restraining bar. As far as Louis was concerned, the ride seemed to go on forever, but David could not get enough.

"Let's do it again!" David begged, exiting the ride.

Glancing over at a nervous-looking Louis, George suggested, "Why don't we have lunch instead."

They found the snack bar, and George breathed a sigh of relief that there was something available that both Louis and David would eat. David munched on chicken nuggets and fries, while Louis was more than satisfied with a hot dog.

"So, what should we do next?" Uncle George grabbed fries from David's plate.

David playfully put his hands over his plate to prevent further theft of his lunch.

"I vote for mini-golf."

"I am a better putter than you!" Louis declared.

David quickly retorted, "We will see about that!"

"Okay, miniature golf, it is. You two are going down!"

As they headed toward the miniature golf course, a giant billboard featuring Ripley's Haunted Adventure came into view. Both boys saw the sign and stopped in their tracks. The billboard was an advertisement for a haunted house attraction. A picture of a devil dressed in red holding a pitchfork and a werewolf figured prominently on the billboard.

The fun that the three men had been enjoying ceased immediately. Louis pointed at the sign yelling, "666!"

David sat down on the ground with his hands covering his face and started to rock himself back and forth.

Like the time at the golf outing, their uncle was caught off guard. "It's okay, boys. It is just a sign. It cannot hurt you."

George's attempts to comfort them were futile. A crowd began to assemble, making things worse for David, who struggled to catch his breath. Louis continued to point at the billboard, shouting, "BAD MAN! LUCIUS! BAD MAN!"

Louis made a fist and began striking himself in the head. Jack had tried to describe incidents like this, but words could not explain George's helplessness. The more attempts he made to reassure Louis and David verbally, the worse things seemed to get. After what seemed like an eternity, George found an opening to shepherd the boys away from the billboard, and they began to calm down.

Minutes later, they were back in the car, and George sat behind the wheel, trying to process what had just happened. Compared to the incident at the golf course, this was far, far worse.

Louis could still be heard mumbling to himself, "Culpeper. Culpeper. Culpeper."

George turned out of the amusement center parking lot, heading on Route 17 North. He was heading back to Brick Landing, and this time he was going to get answers from Jack about what Louis and David were afraid of and just who Lucius was.

David sat in the back seat, trying to calm himself down. He continued to rock back and forth and, under his breath, repeated, "Beware the S-t-r-i-g-o-i. Beware the S-t-r-i-g-o-i."

***

August 19th
Joe's Barbecue Kitchen, Whiteville, NC,
One Hour West of Wilmington
1:30 p.m.

Jack sat dejectedly at a table in Joe's Barbecue Kitchen, waiting for a server to take his drink order. The day had been a total bust. Jack had no other leads to follow. After George had arrived to take Louis and David to an amusement park, Jack had left for Bug Hill Township. Internet searches failed to yield any helpful information about the location. It was almost as if it did not even exist.

Picking up Route 904, Jack arrived roughly forty minutes later in Bug Hill. At least that was what the GPS told him, but Bug Hill was a town in name only. There were no signs of civilization to be found. After some difficulty, Jack finally found a place to pull the car over and look around. There was nothing to see except farmland. While Bug Hill was devoid of people, its name was appropriate, as swarms of flies and mosquitos engulfed Jack. The smell of manure from the cattle farms was as overwhelming as the insects, and both quickly sent Jack back to the car.

His next idea was to go on to Whiteville, the Columbus County seat and the likely location of historical records. The initial disappointment at Bug Hill merely meant that he would move on to the next research phase a little earlier than expected. Arriving in Whiteville, unfortunately, would prove to be an even greater disappointment.

"I'm sorry, Mr. Aitken," the County Clerk apologized, "but the records from 1845 to 1846 fell victim to a fire that occurred in the early 1900s. Unfortunately, this is not uncommon as North Carolina's rural towns often had no fire department back then."

Jack sighed and could not hide his disappointment.

The County Clerk added timidly, "You might try the local library."

But at the library, the librarian confirmed she had no historical records or resources to help him.

"There is no Miss Amy or historical society in Whiteville," Jack muttered with resignation as he pushed open the door and exited the library.

His mood sank, and he thought that lunch might improve his frame of mind. The librarian had suggested Joe's Barbecue Kitchen, telling him it was the best barbecue in the area. Jack sat with his elbows on the table and head in his hands, considering how this failure would impact Anne's case and what he should do next.

"Hello, hon." A waitress with long black hair, whose name badge read Viviana, greeted Jack. "What can I get you to drink?"

"A diet soda would be great. What do you recommend for lunch?"

The waitress grinned. Her deep red lips drew back and exposed pearly white teeth. "Try the barbecue buffet." She brushed her hand against Jack's as she took the menu. "I eat it every day."

"Sounds good." Jack was too deep in his thoughts to notice her flirtation. "I will have it."

Viviana returned with Jack's drink and handed him a plate. "Please feel free to help yourself, hon."

Jack headed to the buffet table in the center of the restaurant. Every barbecue delicacy Jack could think of was in front of him.

Fried chicken, pulled pork, ribs, and coleslaw were Jack's favorites, and he sat down at his table with a full plate. He started with the fried chicken, which was hot and juicy. The librarian was not kidding; the food was delicious.

As Jack eagerly ate his lunch, three older gentlemen sat at a table adjacent to him. Viviana took their drink orders, and one of the men observed Jack eagerly consuming his lunch.

"Son, you eat as if you have never been here before today. It is good, isn't it?"

Jack wiped his lips with a napkin. "This might be the best barbecue I have ever eaten."

The man chuckled. "You had that look about you. My name is Ray Perkins. These other two old goats are Carl Ford and Billy Johnson."

Ray and Billy dressed like any other farmer in the area. They wore jeans, a dirty t-shirt, and a baseball hat. Their skin was deeply tan from years of working in the hot sun and was like worn leather right down to the deep wrinkles in their necks. Carl, on the other hand, was unforgettable. He wore a black patch over his left eye and was missing his right arm.

"Jack Aitken. It is good to meet the three of you. You are right. I am just visiting for the day from Ocean Isle Beach."

Viviana shot another flirty look at Jack as she placed the men's drinks on the table. Carl asked, "What brings you to Whiteville, Jack?"

Still oblivious to Viviana, Jack replied, "I am doing some research for a friend. Unfortunately, I am striking out. I thought lunch might make me feel a little better."

"I don't want to pry into your business, son," Ray said with a heavy southern accent, "but we have been living around here all our lives. Maybe we could be of some help?"

Jack thought about the offer and figured he had nothing to lose.

"Well, it has to do with some animal deaths in Bug Hill back in the 1840s. The County Clerk told me all records from that period did not survive a fire in the early twentieth century. The library had no resources either. I went to Bug Hill this morning, but I am sure you already know what I found out; there is nothing there."

Ray and Billy immediately looked at Carl, who was trembling. He shifted in the booth and coughed as if he had choked on something.

"Are you okay, Carl?" The tone of Ray's question had more than a hint of concern.

The color had drained from Carl's face. "Yeah, but I think I lost my appetite."

Carl got up from the booth and headed out of the restaurant, leaving Billy and Ray staring at each other, their mouths agape.

"Did I say something wrong?" Jack watched the door to the restaurant swing in and out in the wake of Carl's departure.

Billy quickly got up from the table to go after Carl as Ray tossed a few dollars on the table to pay for their drinks. Ray slid out of the booth and stood by Jack's table. His face was solemn as if he were heading to a funeral.

"If you take my advice, Jack," he replied quietly. "You'll go back to Ocean Isle Beach and forget about Bug Hill."

Ray headed out the door, and Jack sat at his table, scratching his temple. He was stunned by what had occurred. Then he almost jumped out of his skin as Viviana pulled a chair across the floor and sat down across from him."

"It's not your fault," she whispered reassuringly.

"What?" Jack asked, wondering why she was sitting down with him.

Viviana's lips curled upward as she slid another bottle of soda across the table, "Here, have another drink, and I'll explain everything."

***

"I saw what happened." Viviana locked eyes with Jack. "You'll have to forgive Carl. He hasn't been the same since the accident."

"Accident?" Jack questioned.

"Yes. We're pretty sure Carl got drunk and fell off his tractor or something like that," she declared dismissively. "But Carl claims a beast attacked him, slashed his face causing him to lose an eye, and then ripped his arm off."

"When did this happen?' Jack asked with a mix of concern and curiosity.

"Back in 2007 or 2008."

Jack shot up straight in his chair and muttered, "Bolivia."

Viviana seemed surprised. "How did you know Carl claims the attack was in Bolivia?"

Finally able to break away from her seemingly magnetic charm, Jack responded carefully not to disclose too much information. "I'm doing some research on animal attacks. Do you know why Carl was in Bolivia?"

"I think he was doing some hunting or something," Viviana chuckled. "You should hear old Carl after he has had a few drinks. He'll talk on and on about the Bug Hill Fiend."

"Bug Hill Fiend? What's that?"

"A local legend about a vampire-like creature. I don't know too much about it. It does sound an awful lot like what my grandmother would call a Strigoi."

Jack's jaw opened slightly, and he instinctively placed his hand over his mouth to hide his amazement over what Viviana had just shared.

"Do you know anyone I might be able to speak with about all of this?" Looking at her name tag. "Viviana?"

"Sure." Viviana leaned in closer. Her expression was almost hypnotic. "Go see Madame Volha."

She grabbed Jack's hand and wrote the address down on his palm.

Jack slowly pulled away from her. "Th-thank you, Viviana."

"Sure thing, sugar." Viviana winked at Jack, who practically ran to his car.

***

"Turn right at the next intersection."

The navigation system indicated that Jack was almost at his destination. He raised his hand and flexed it several times, then re-read the address the waitress had written on it. He thought about her stare, from which he could not break away.

"Something about her was weird," Jack mumbled. "Those eyes."

"You have reached your destination on the right. Route guidance has ended."

Jack pulled into an empty gravel parking lot in front of a white mobile home with tan curtains. A neon sign in the window indicated the establishment was open. Above the door was a sign that read *Madame Volha's Psychic Readings.*

Removing the key from the ignition, Jack shook his head.

"What am I doing here?" His steps crunched on the parking lot stones. "Psychic readings, really?"

Despite his misgivings, Jack reasoned he had come this far, and without any suitable alternatives, he turned the knob and pushed in the door, which caused a bell to ring gently.

"Hello?"

Jack expected the sound of the bell to summon someone, but no one responded. Looking around the room, he saw a crystal ball on a table and mirrors on the walls. To his left was a glass display case with crystals, necklaces, and other jewelry.

PRRR ...

Looking down, a black cat with green eyes rubbed against his legs. Jack reached down to pet the animal, which quickly retreated.

Hiss.

The hair on the cat's back stood straight up, and its tail waved back and forth in an expression of displeasure over Jack's attempt to touch it. It slowly backed away and slipped behind a curtain in a doorway at the room's far end.

Almost immediately, an older woman dressed in a loose-fitting blouse with embroidered beads and a floral design came through the curtain. Her burgundy skirt hung down around her ankles, and upon her head, she wore a bandanna with tufts of gray hair sticking out from under it. She slowly made her way toward Jack.

"Welcome, I am Madame Volha." The woman spoke slowly with an accent that Jack could not quite place. She had a long pointy nose and deep wrinkles on her face.

"Good afternoon, I'm Jack—"

"I know who you are," she interrupted. "Come sit at the table, Jack Aitken."

Jack's eyes opened wide, surprised that Madame Volha knew his name. *The waitress must have called to tell her I was coming.*

Fidgeting in his chair, Jack tried to get comfortable. Never having been to a psychic, he was nervous.

"Give me your hand."

Placing his hand on the table, she pushed his fingers apart and then began to rub her fingers up and down the lines in his palm. Something about her touch was familiar.

"Mmm…interesting." She scrutinized his hand. "Now, give me your ring."

"Why do you need that?" Jack never took his wedding band off, even after Amanda's death.

Madame Volha scowled. "Do not ask questions. Do as I tell you."

The woman's eyes were bloodshot, and Jack tried to resist her demand at first, but the longer he stared into them, the more relaxed he felt. It was like floating in a tranquil lake. It felt good. He twisted the ring from his finger and placed it in front of Madame Volha.

"Good, Jack. That is good. Now, look into my crystal ball."

All Jack saw was darkness, but he could not stop gazing into it. It was like he was losing himself, and suddenly, he could not remember why he had even come there in the first place.

The psychic's face was shielded from Jack by the crystal ball, but then her head slowly began to rise. The green eyes were the first thing he saw, other than the darkness. Then the jet-black hair followed by the blood-red lips. The face he saw was no longer that of an older woman.

"Viviana?"

She strutted around the table. "Yes, Jack." She slowly stroked his hair.

"But how?"

"Shhh…" Viviana held up her finger, then sensually rang her tongue along her lips.

"Don't speak." She slid a shot glass across the table toward Jack. "Just drink."

Jack studied the liquid, which was red, like wine, but thicker in its consistency. He looked up, and Viviana's intense leer reached into Jack's subconscious and took hold like a vice. He had no choice. His free will was gone, and Jack raised the glass and drained its contents.

***

"Wake up, sleepy head."

A feminine voice managed to pierce the stupor that gripped Jack. He fought to regain consciousness. His upper body swayed back and forth, then side to side, but something held him up and would not allow him to bend over. Jack shook his head vigorously, trying to sweep the cobwebs from his brain.

"Time to get up, lover," she whispered, then Jack felt a tugging on the side of his face. The sensation helped jolt him back to the present, and he realized someone was gently biting his earlobe. Then they released it.

Still slightly groggy, Jack nevertheless recognized the face in front of him.

"Viviana." Jack blinked several times, still adjusting to the light of the room. "What's going on?"

"Good, you are coming around," Viviana cooed. "Just in time, too. I'm famished."

Now dressed in a short skirt and a red lacy top with her long hair tied back with a black bow, she circled from behind Jack. Teasingly biting her fingernail, she stopped, and Jack helplessly watched as Viviana lifted her long leg over him. Her stiletto heel clicked as it hit the floor, and she straddled him, slowly lowering herself onto his lap. She leaned forward, her ample cleavage nearly spilling out of her top, and wrapped her arms around Jack's neck as she pressed her ruby red lips against his.

Jack's eyes opened wide as her kiss overwhelmed him.

Pulling her lips away, Viviana whispered seductively, "I bet you're awake now."

Her lips curled into an evil grin as she fondled his wedding band. "Once you gave this up, I knew you were mine."

Locking eyes with Jack once more, she continued. "Of course, non-compliance is not an option once you are lost in my web. You managed to ignore me briefly in the restaurant, but I always get what I want in the end."

Viviana raised her arms toward the ceiling and laughed over and over.

Still riding Jack, she feigned a tone of concern. "I suppose you want to know what's going on. Are you scared, Jack?"

She leaned in and whispered wickedly, "I do hope so. You'll taste better that way."

***

Jack nervously scanned the room from left to right and back again, searching for some way out of his predicament. He realized he was literally stuck in the chair, and the only movement he could make was to wiggle his fingers slightly. Jack was not physically restrained in any way, but he was essentially paralyzed. He felt like prey caught in a Black Widow's web.

Facing Jack again, Viviana smirked, revealing row after row of jagged, triangular teeth.

"I admit you are a little old for me, but it has been so long since I have fed," she slowly licked Jack's cheek, "and we don't get many strangers around here these days."

Shrugging her shoulders, she declared, "What's a succubus to do? A meal is a meal."

Jack's heart was beating a mile a minute. Viviana leaned in and placed her ear on Jack's chest.

Pulling back, she was giddy. "You are scared! Yum!"

Jack was unsure why; perhaps Viviana was weak from not feeding, but her grip over his hands and arms loosened, and he was now in control of his body. He tried to stay still, not wanting to warn her that he could move.

A weapon. The words echoed in Jack's head. *What do I use as a weapon?*

Now moaning in anticipation of her meal, Viviana's mouth opened as if she had the jaws of an Anaconda.

"Dinner time, lover!"

Instinctively, Jack reached inside his shirt and ripped the chain from around his neck. The two halves of the Mizpah coin he and Amanda had once worn for one another hung from the necklace, and Jack grabbed them tightly in his right hand. Struggling to hold off Viviana, whose ravenous jaws snapped at him, he forcefully shoved the religious icon down the succubus's throat.

Viviana fell backward, clutching her throat. Smoke emanated from her mouth as the silver burned into her body. Suddenly, there was a flash of light and...

BOOM!

***

"Ohhh," Jack moaned.

He felt the hot sun on his neck and began to spit out the grit and dirt in his mouth.

"What the hell..."

Pushing himself up, he watched small pebbles falling to the ground. He reached up to his cheek and removed several more pieces of gravel embedded in his face. Looking around, he realized he had been lying face down in a gravel parking lot.

"What a headache." Jack rubbed his temples. "If I didn't know better, I would think I got drunk and passed out."

Jack managed to get to his feet and stumbled to the car. He put his hands in his pockets but could not find the keys. There was no sign of them as he searched the area around the vehicle.

"I didn't." Jack peered through the car window and saw the keys hanging in the ignition. "You idiot."

He prayed that he had left the door unlocked. Jack exhaled as he pulled on the latch. Thankfully, the door opened, and he slid into the seat. He grabbed the water bottle in the cup holder and took a sip.

"Ugh, that is warm." Jack stared out the windshield and saw an empty lot in front of him. "How did I get here? What is going on?"

A bead of sweat fell from his forehead onto the steering wheel.

"It is hot as hell in here." Jack turned the ignition and put the air conditioning on full blast. He fanned himself, waiting for the car to cool down. Still trying to figure out why he could not remember anything, Jack's left thumb reached for his ring finger. Spinning his wedding ring was a mindless, nervous habit.

"Shit!" Jack held his hand in front of his face and saw the indentation where his ring used to be.

Then he reached inside his shirt. "The necklace isn't there either!"

Jack sighed. "I guess someone robbed me." Rubbing a bump on his head, he muttered, "They must have hit me pretty damn hard."

Pulling out of the parking lot, Jack shook his head.

"Well, this day has been a disaster. I got robbed and lost two of my most treasured reminders of Amanda. I have a massive headache and no information to share with Anne. To top it all off, I can't remember a damn thing after leaving the library in Whiteville. It is definitely time to go home."

***

As Jack pulled onto North Carolina Route 904, he saw a sign that indicated that Bug Hill Township was two miles up the road. "What there is of it." Jack chuckled, recalling the stop he made earlier and how isolated the area turned out to be.

Jack saw a sign for the Wilcox ranch; the impressive stone and iron entrance gate was hard to miss. The ranch's fence line seemed to go on forever before the last rails were no longer visible in his rearview mirror.

BAM!

Jack's front right tire hit a pothole, and he screeched to a stop. From the corner of his eye, he saw his hubcap rolling off the shoulder of the road into a dense clump of trees. Jack crossed the yellow line and parked the car to check on the condition of the tire. Exiting the vehicle, the smell of manure no longer hung heavy in the air, but the bugs remained merciless.

"Well, the tire looks okay." Jack waved his hand to scatter the swarm of mosquitos around him and checked his watch. "It's a little after 4:00 p.m. If I am going to find that hubcap, I better do it quickly."

Approaching the stand of trees, Jack saw nothing out of the ordinary; just a thicket of wild raspberries greeted him, along with heavy amounts of vegetation around the tree trunks. It was not looking promising. There was nothing but leaves, and he knelt to get closer to ground level, where the hubcap should be. He noticed something that appeared made of metal entangled in the foliage.

"That might be it." Locating a loose branch, he poked the undergrowth around the object. Jack struck it with the limb and heard a clang. There was no doubt it was metal and made by people, as it was square-shaped.

"That's not a hubcap." Jack strained to get a better view. "What is that?"

Using the tree branch, Jack carefully pushed the vegetation from around the object, and after a few minutes, he knew what it was.

"It's a historical marker. What is it doing out here in the middle of nowhere?"

His curiosity getting the best of him, Jack risked the possibility of getting poison oak or poison ivy and pulled the vines from the top of the plaque. It read: *The Bug Hill Fiend.*

A pulse of excitement ran through his body as he hurriedly pulled more foliage off the marker.

SINS OF THE FATHERS

Seventy-five years ago, starting on December 1^{st,} 1845, and ending on January 10^{th,} 1846, six animal mutilation incidents took place around Bug Hill. Local farmers eventually came to call the assailant The Bug Hill Fiend, as the attacks all occurred after dark, with each victim drained of their blood. The Wilcox family cattle farm, the final killing location, stands three miles northwest of this spot. The crimes remain unsolved as of the placement of this plaque on December 1st, 1920.

Dedicated by the Bug Hill Farmers' Cooperative

Jack dropped to his knees. "My God, this confirms another series of similar attacks."

Forgetting about the hubcap, Jack ran back to the car to get his cell phone and then snapped a picture of the plaque to show Anne. He then googled 'The Bug Hill Farmers' Cooperative' but found no mention of the organization. Unfortunately, the explanation for why the memorial plaque was there was likely lost forever.

Turning off his phone, he headed back to the car. As he pulled back onto the road and made his way back to Brick Landing Plantation, Jack thought to himself; *there is no doubt that the animal mutilations are related. The unanswered question is, what does it all mean?*

***

A black SUV pulled into the parking lot where Madame Volha's trailer once stood. The gravel crunched under the heavy black shoes of the figure exiting the vehicle, who surveyed the field in front of him. Seed heads from the tall grass danced in the gentle breeze as the visitor slowly walked and scanned the ground before him.

Then the late afternoon sun's rays reflected off something, and the figure reached down to inspect it. The figure read the inscription as he held the gold ring up to the sky:

"*Jack, I love you always.*"

Chapter 15

August 19th
Anne Bishop's Den, Ocean Isle Beach, NC
6:00 p.m.

Anne sat on the couch, watching the six o'clock news on WSFX Channel 26 out of Wilmington, a television station that just happened to be owned by Antonescu Communications. The lead story was the disappearance of retired Detective Robert Wallace. After broadcasting the initial report and pictures of the destruction of Robert Wallace's study, the story cut to a live feed.

"This is Janet Finley, reporting on a still-developing story from the Magnolia Greens community in Leland. Earlier today, Mrs. Robert Wallace arrived home to find a portion of her home destroyed and her husband Robert, a former police detective, missing. The cause of the extensive damage we showed you earlier remains a mystery, and Robert Wallace's whereabouts currently remain unknown."

Sheriff Hill and Mrs. Wallace then joined the reporter on screen. Terri Wallace was visibly upset and made no eye contact with the camera.

"Sheriff Hill, what can you tell us about the status of the investigation? Do you have any leads on the whereabouts of Robert Wallace?"

"We are still in the early stages of our investigation. We are asking for the public's help, and if they have seen Robert Wallace, please contact us at 910-253-2777."

A picture of Robert Wallace appeared on the television screen with the phone number that Sheriff Hill had provided.

Terri Wallace, through her tears, pleaded, "Robert, if you can see or hear this, please call or come home …."

Sheriff Hill escorted her away as she began to sob. Anne turned off the television and headed toward the kitchen. She passed the door to the porch, where she saw Jack and George having what appeared to be a tense discussion. Jack had barely gotten home when George cornered him, and they had been outside ever since. Louis and David were upstairs playing pool, and Daphne was sleeping on the stairwell landing. Since they arrived, Daphne had not left the boys' side, but Anne could not help but notice that ever since Jack shared the story of finding Daphne staring in the corner of the room, Daphne would not go upstairs.

As Anne thought about this, the phone rang. She picked up the receiver on the second ring.

"Hello, Anne Bishop speaking."

"Detective Bishop, this is Brenda Johnson, the medical examiner's office technician."

"Hi, Brenda." Hopeful, Anne asked, "Do you have something for me?"

"I do. I have preliminary test results on the hair sample you found at the Wallace residence today. The M.E. still has some testing to do, but he thought what he found out so far was significant enough to call you."

Anne was immediately curious. "Okay, what did he find out?"

"It is from an animal, but there is something odd about it. It is like a wolf or coyote, but not an exact match for either. The M.E. stated he had never seen anything like it. It will take some time to get more definitive results."

"It is not dog hair?"

Brenda quickly responded, "He knew you would ask that. He told me to tell you that it is not canine or cat hair."

"Thank you, Brenda. Please let the M.E. know I appreciate him expediting this for me."

"Will do, Detective."

Anne hung up the receiver. *Why would wolf or coyote-like hair be in Wallace's study? Neither animal has the strength to do the damage that I saw there.*

Anne sat at the dining room table, waiting for an opportunity to let Jack know what she had found out. It was a clue, but she was unsure what it meant. The Strigoi legend came to mind, and Anne wondered if such a beast could exist and, if it did, would it be capable of doing the damage she saw in the study. While significant, this new information could not replace one nagging thought running through her head all day: *What happened to Detective Wallace?*

***

August 19th
Screened Porch Anne Bishop's Home,
Ocean Isle Beach, NC
6:30 p.m.

"Come on, Jack, I don't want to sound overly skeptical, but do you hear yourself? How can you expect me to believe this story? It all sounds like an episode from *Supernatural.* We both love the show and see ourselves in Sam and Dean Winchester, but this is a bridge too far, even for me."

Jack had spent the better part of an hour telling his brother about Route 666, what happened in Culpeper, the existence of JESU, and Lucius Rofocale. It sounded like some Hollywood script or a graphic comic book. Call it brotherly instinct or being identical twins, but George knew there was something he was still not telling him.

"I know how this all sounds, George. As they say, truth is often stranger than fiction, but it is the truth, every word of it. Think about it. Why would I lie to you? I have no reason to hide it from you … other than preventing you from questioning my sanity."

Jack threw up his hands in frustration. "You asked what happened to Louis and David, and I told you."

George eyed Jack with raised eyebrows. "Does Anne know about all this?"

"Yes, she does."

George wanted to read his brother's face, but Jack just looked out into the woods.

Jack continued. "If not for her, Louis, David, and I would not be here. She saved all our lives."

"What about Amanda's? You told me Amanda died from complications arising out of her kidnapping."

There was a moment of silence, and somehow, George sensed the other shoe was about to drop.

He saw Jack's chest expand as he took a deep breath, then exhaled loudly. "That is not entirely true."

Frustrated, George turned away from Jack. "What the hell does that mean? Jesus, Jack, what else have you been hiding from me? I don't want to hear more about Gates to Hell or Lucius Rofocale!"

George spun back and slammed his hand on the table. "God damn it, Jack, talk sense to me!"

Jack peered down at the brick floor. "George, you remember what Amanda's condition was like after we brought her home from the hospital?"

"Yes." George compassionately put his arm around his brother's shoulder. "I remember that she was unresponsive and on life support."

George could see a torrent of tears forming in Jack's eyes as he struggled to speak. "It was month after month of the same thing, George. I would come home each day, and the reports were always the same. Most nights, I would sleep by Amanda's bedside, hoping to see anything that would indicate that she would be able to come back to us. Then, one night…."

The creases in George's forehead deepened as a look of worry came over his face. "Go on, Jack. What happened?"

A tear rolled down Jack's cheek. "Amanda woke up George. I saw her fingers move, and she started talking to me."

George abruptly sat down, shocked by Jack's revelation. He whispered, "What did she say?"

Jack was rubbing the tears away. "I got so excited I reached for the phone to call a doctor. Amanda asked me to stop…."

Despite being on the edge of his seat, George remained quiet as Jack paused to compose himself and stammered, "She-she told me I needed to let her go. She had no feeling in her legs and could not explain how she even moved her fingers."

George felt a wave of guilt for being so hard on his brother. "My God, Jack. I am so sorry. I had no idea."

Jack stood, shaking his head from side to side. He waved his hand, and George took the hint and stopped speaking.

"There's more," Jack sighed. "Amanda made it clear that I needed to make the boys my priority. She told me she knew I would want to save her and that it would be detrimental to Louis and David if I tried. Amanda told me that I needed to let her go. She stopped speaking, drifted back into unresponsiveness, and the only sound I could hear was the machines keeping her alive. After what seemed like an eternity, I did it."

"You did what?" George's eyes opened widely, fearful of what he might hear next, but he asked again, "What did you do, Jack?"

Jack looked George directly in the face. "I turned off the machines. One by one, I shut them off." Then, gritting his teeth in anger, Jack stated, "I killed her, George! I killed Amanda!"

George instinctively pulled away from Jack in horror at what Jack had confessed.

"George. I know you do not want to hear this, but Lucius Rofocale appeared in my living room and told me that Amanda did not have to die. He offered me a deal that would bring her back to life. Unlike the pact that Dean Winchester accepted to bring Sam back from the dead, I would get more than a year, but the price was still the same. Unlike Dean, however, I did not take it. Can you believe that? I could have saved her. I should have rescued her even at the cost of my soul, but I know that is not what she would have wanted me to do."

The brothers sat together in silence. Even the insects and birds were quiet. It was as if they were bearing witness to what Jack had confessed.

George fumbled for something to say. "Jack, I do not know what to…."

Jack interrupted. "There is no absolution for what I have done. I know there will be no forgiveness for my sins. My punishment is living, knowing what I did, and knowing I could have chosen a different path. Amanda would still be here if I had given up writing that book or accepted Lucius's proposal. My punishment is just, and I will not shy away from it or attempt to avoid it."

Before George could utter a word, Jack went on. "It does not matter if you believe my story or not. I know what happened, and the two incidents you experienced with Louis and David attest to the truth."

Still dumbfounded, George scratched his head. He suddenly felt drained. Their conversation played with his emotions like the roller coaster he was riding with Louis and David earlier in the day. Removing his glasses, Jack took another deep breath. "George, a few nights ago, Amanda visited me in a dream. She told me that Louis and David are on Earth to fulfill some great purpose, but they are in danger because of it."

Clutching George's hands, he pleaded, "Whatever their destiny might be, I need your help to protect my sons."

George gripped Jack's hands tightly. "Jack, regardless of whether I believe your story, you know you can always count on me where it concerns Louis and David. Whatever you need."

"George, you have always been there for me."

Just then, Anne knocked on the door. George was thankful for the interruption as he was suffocating. Everything Jack had told him was proving difficult to process. Regardless of what he thought about Jack's story, he was sure of one thing. Jack believed every word of it.

***

August 19th
Family Room Anne Bishop's Home, Ocean Isle Beach, NC
6:30 p.m.

Louis Aitken came downstairs, looking toward the porch. He could see his father and uncle talking, and even though he could not hear them, he could tell they were talking loudly. Anytime Louis saw or listened to his father getting angry or frustrated, it made him nervous. He sat down on the landing and began to pet Daphne. Louis used to rub his cat, Ivy, the same way. It always made him feel better. He missed Ivy, and even though he was afraid of dogs and the loud barking noises they made, he felt comfortable around Daphne. He particularly liked when she slept with him.

Louis went to the family room and, making no eye contact with his brother, announced, "Dad and Uncle George are talking loudly, David."

Deeply engrossed in a video game, David appeared to ignore his brother, but after a moment of silence, he replied, "I don't like that, Louis. It is not good for brothers to fight. That is what Dad tells us all the time."

Just then, Anne Bishop appeared in the doorway. "Boys, I called for a pizza, and the delivery person will be here soon. I need to speak with your Dad for a few minutes before dinner."

"I like pizza, Ms. Bishop. Just cheese, though."

"That is what I ordered, Louis. Just cheese. David, your Dad told me you don't eat pizza, but he will make you macaroni. I am boiling water on the stove."

David never stopped playing his game. "Okey, dokey."

Anne noticed Daphne, who was looking up at her from the floor. "Daphne, I am relying on you to let me know when the pizza arrives. Just bark a few times."

As Anne left the room, Louis laughed at her suggestion to Daphne. He watched David play his game and anticipated the pizza. Suddenly, Daphne's ordinarily floppy ears perked up. She walked toward the windows and peered out into the front yard. Then she began to growl.

"What is it, Daphne?" Louis asked. "Is the pizza here?"

Louis bolted up from the floor and peered out the window. He thought he caught a glimpse of something moving around the corner of the house but saw nothing.

Louis sat back down on the floor. "David, I think something bad is going to happen."

David continued playing. "Me too, Louis. Me too."

***

August 19th
Anne Bishop's home, Ocean Isle Beach, NC
6:45 p.m.

Anne poked her head into the porch. "I am sorry to interrupt the two of you."

"Jack. I just received some new information about the case we are working on, and I need to discuss it with you."

George replied, "It is okay, Anne. I think Jack and I are through for now. I will keep Louis and David company. Is there anything you need me to do for dinner? I could set the table or something like that."

"Thanks, George, but everything is all set. The pizza should be here soon. If you could listen for a knock on the door, that would be great. My doorbell is not working right now."

George gave the thumbs-up sign. "You got it." He asked Jack, "Are we good?"

"You know we are, George. I appreciate that you are looking out for Louis and David."

"Always, Jack. I love those two like they are my kids."

George exited the porch and closed the door behind him.

***

Rubbing the bump on his head, Jack told Anne, "Before you tell me what you found out, let me update you on my research in Bughill Township."

Jack held up his phone and showed her the picture of the historical plaque.

"This is it. It is all I can remember."

"That is some lump on your head." Anne pulled the hair back from Jack's scalp to look closer. "You are fortunate that whoever robbed you didn't kill you. Maybe we should take you to a doctor, just in case."

"I am all right, and besides, we've got your case to solve!"

Anne placed her hand on Jack's hand. "I am sorry about your wedding ring and chain. Are you sure you don't want to file a police report?"

Jack sighed. "Thanks. If we had the time, I would go back to make a complaint. Maybe when the case is over."

Clapping his hands to change the subject, Jack summed up what they knew so far.

"Each town we investigate has the same number of incidents. They happen every fifty-four years, except for the series of attacks in Bolivia. The animals are all drained of blood and not mutilated in any way. There is no disputing the connection between them, but who or what is doing this?"

Anne folded her arms and paced around the porch. "I don't know yet, Jack, but for the first time, I might have found some physical evidence that begins to answer that question. About an hour ago, I got a call from the Medical Examiner's office. While at the Wallace house today, I found strands of hair that did not appear human. Wallace does not have a pet, but the preliminary test results suggest it is from an animal of some kind. The technician says they are like a coyote or wolf, but they are definitively not from either species. My gut tells me this is a clue that identifies the perpetrator if we can figure out where and from whom the hairs came from."

Anne hesitated. "What concerns me is the damage at the Wallace house was so extensive that no animal I know could have done it. You might hate me for saying this, but I wish Mark Desmond were here. If anyone could figure this out, it would be him."

Shaking his head, Jack replied, "I don't hate you for saying it. Frankly, I was thinking the same thing. I know his research skills were superior to mine. I am not saying my contributions to the case are not helpful, but he probably would find something I am missing."

Just then, Jack and Anne heard Daphne bark.

Louis yelled, "Pizza is here!"

Jack chuckled. "I better get David's macaroni ready."

"The water is probably boiling by now, Jack."

As Jack made his way to the door, Anne grabbed his arm. "I don't want to pry, Jack, but is everything okay with you and your brother?"

Jack stopped. "Over the past few days, George has had a few incidents with Louis and David that he was unsure how to manage. I was just giving him advice on what to do if something similar happens."

Jack headed to the kitchen as George started giving out pizza slices. Everyone and everything appeared fine. As they sat down to eat, the conversation was light, and on the surface, all seemed to be well. Anne joined in the fun, but her gut instincts told her something was off. Perhaps it was her years as a detective or her intuition, but Anne looked at Jack, wondering, *what aren't you telling me?*

***

August 19th
Anne Bishop's home, Ocean Isle Beach, NC
8:00 p.m.

The enjoyable meal allowed Anne and the Aitkens to forget their work and worries, if only for a moment. Even Louis and David remained at the dining room table laughing over a wild game of *Uno*. As a result, none of them saw the figure at the edge of the wooded lot next to Anne's house, staring at them through the darkness. As it moved toward the house's side door, the foamy saliva oozing from its mouth fell to the ground.

The fading light across the windows confirmed that the day had finally yielded to the night. Daphne barked. Anne chuckled at her beloved Cocker Spaniel, then turned to her guests.

"Will you, gentlemen, please excuse me? It is time for us ladies to go for our nightly stroll."

Louis and David yelled in unison, "Can we come too?"

Anne was pleasantly surprised that the boys would want to go along and took it as a positive sign that they were getting comfortable around her.

"It is alright with me if it is okay with your dad."

"Go ahead, guys, and listen to what Ms. Bishop says."

Jack told Daphne, feverishly wagging her tail, "Daphne, you are in charge."

Daphne barked as if she understood Jack's instruction and pawed at Anne's legs to get her to hurry up.

"Okay, girl." Anne grabbed the leash. "Let's go."

The crew headed through the kitchen to the garage while Jack and George moved to the living room. The brothers heard the garage door open, and before they could sit down, they heard Daphne barking incessantly and the boys screaming, "DADDD! Help!"

Jack and George quickly ran through the kitchen and threw open the door to the garage. They found the boys crouching behind a car and Anne, apparently unconscious, on the ground against a wall. A hulking figure, over six feet tall, approached Anne's motionless body, foaming at the mouth. Daphne inserted herself between Anne and the attacker and angrily growled when she was not loudly barking. Jack leaped down the stairs leading from the kitchen into the garage and charged at the massive aggressor while George positioned himself between the boys and the assailant.

The figure sensed Jack's approach and faced him. Jack flung his body at the attacker to tackle him, but the behemoth caught Jack in mid-air and wrapped its arms around him like a python might constrict its prey. Jack instantly saw that the figure was indeed a man, but in appearance only. The figure's bloodshot eyes and the white frothy foam around its lips made it appear anything but human.

Jack struggled to free himself from the figure's vice-like grip, but it was no use. The attacker squeezed harder, and Jack was finding it difficult to breathe. The assailant drew Jack's throat closer with its mouth open and teeth bared. George saw what was happening and searched for something he could use as a weapon. He saw a shovel, grabbed the handle, and swung it at the being with all his might. In an instant, Jack hit the floor, and a massive hand grabbed the shovel before it hit its target. George was stunned and released the handle of the shovel. The figure tossed the shovel aside and turned its attention back on Anne.

Kill Anne Bishop. Kill Anne Bishop. The phrase kept repeating in the mind of the figure that once was Robert Wallace. He stepped over Jack, lying on the floor, struggling to catch a breath. Anne was now kneeling and trying to get to her feet. Daphne charged the beast, snapping at its legs. The small dog was no match for the monster, who ignored the animal entirely. As the former Robert Wallace approached Anne, George jumped on his back, trying to restrain him. The beast spun around, trying to throw George off, and then backed up into the side of the car, crushing George between its torso and the vehicle. George cried out in pain and released his grip. He slid down the side of the vehicle toward the floor.

The beast detected Louis and David, both of whom were still crouching behind the car, frozen with fear. The same voice in his head telling him to kill Anne Bishop also told him not to touch them. His focus returned to George, sitting on the floor with his right side against the car. Leaning down, the former Robert Wallace pulled George closer and sunk his teeth deep into the nape of George's neck. George let out an agonizing cry of pain, but the beast immediately released him. Jack had struck him in the back with the shovel.

What once was Robert Wallace reached for Jack, but before he could move against him, a gunshot struck him in the chest, pushing him backward. The beast heard a word that he could not understand, a command to which he was no longer capable of responding.

Anne demanded, "Wallace, get down on your knees and put your hands behind your head."

The creature tilted his head as if trying to understand what Anne was ordering, then continued forward. Anne unloaded the rest of the bullets from her service revolver. The monster staggered but would not stop. It continued moving toward Jack and Anne.

Jack noticed Anne pulling the trigger, even after emptying her gun. A sign that she was stunned that this being remained standing. *What do I do now?* Jack thought to himself. Then six more shots rang out, and the former Robert Wallace dropped like a rock.

Jack and Anne turned toward the sound and saw Sheriff Hill standing in the garage entrance with his gun still pointed at his friend and smoke emanating from the pistol barrel. Sheriff Hill slowly moved forward and knelt to check the body for any signs of life. He held his fingertips on the carotid artery and felt no pulse. Wallace, or what had been Robert Wallace, was dead.

Sheriff Hill looked up at a still stunned Anne Bishop. "Silver bullets."

Jack ran to his brother's side and saw the jagged wound left by the animal's bite oozing blood down the front of George's shirt. He pulled the cell phone from his pocket and dialed 911. "I need an ambulance at 1815 Oak Brook Drive in Ocean Isle Beach. The Brick Landing Plantation subdivision. My brother has suffered a severe bite."

Glancing down at Wallace's body, Jack continued, "From an animal of some kind."

Anne handed him a towel, and Jack jammed it into George's wound to stop the bleeding. George grimaced. "Why am I always taking one for the team? Are Louis and David okay?"

Jack saw the boys standing next to Anne, who assured him they were unharmed.

"They are fine, George. Thanks to you." With a sarcastic smile, Jack went on. "You always do what Dad told you to…when taking care of your younger brother."

George shook his head. "Yeah, well, this is the last time, Jack. And whoever or whatever that thing is, it did not come for the boys."

Jack heard the sirens in the distance and assured George that he would be okay. Then Louis and David declared, in unison, "Strigoi, Dad. Strigoi."

Jack's jaw fell open, puzzled by the boys' assertion. Anne's facial expression mirrored his own. They had not mentioned the Strigoi legend in the boy's presence. How could they possibly know about the myth of the Strigoi?

Before Jack could say another word, he saw Sheriff Hill looking at the boys. The sheriff's eyebrows narrowed, and he muttered grimly, "Strigoi. Mr. Aitken, we must talk."

Chapter 16

August 19th
Brunswick Medical Center, Bolivia, NC
10:00 p.m.

Anne stepped off the elevator, went to her left, and saw Jack down the hallway, waving to get her attention. She had dropped Louis and David at George's house and immediately headed to the hospital. Jack was in the waiting area with Josephine, George's wife, anticipating an update from the doctors treating George's wound. Sheriff Hill was down the hall on the phone.

"Any word yet, Jack?" Anne asked. "Don't worry about Louis and David; they are fine. They are concerned about their uncle, but their cousins Kate and Erin are with them."

"No news yet. Thanks for dropping the boys off. After everything Louis went through with his Leukemia treatments, I think another trip to the hospital would have freaked him out."

Jack swallowed. "In all the confusion, I did not get a chance to ask if you are okay. Wallace tossed you against that wall hard. We should get a doctor to look at you. You might have a concussion."

"I am fine. I was just a little stunned, but I don't feel or see any after-effects other than some scrapes. I am sure there will be bruises tomorrow. Nothing I haven't felt after a few of my JESU missions. I'll let you know if anything changes."

"Okay. Do you have any ideas about what happened to Wallace? You emptied your pistol into him, and it didn't seem to have any effect whatsoever. I wonder if he was on drugs or something. Have you ever seen anything like that before?"

"I have seen plenty of weird things in my time, but nothing like this, Jack. Whatever happened to Wallace, he was no longer human. No human being could have taken those shots."

"You've got that right, Bishop," Sheriff Hill interjected. "That was not the man I knew as Robert Wallace. Robert Wallace is dead; that thing was just using his body."

Anne and Jack faced the sheriff.

"Chief, I am sorry about your friend."

Jack added, "Me too, Sheriff. I am grateful, however, that you showed up when you did with the right weapon. You saved all our lives. Thank you."

"Unfortunately for Robert," Sheriff Hill sighed, "he got himself involved with the wrong people, and it cost him his life."

"Jack, the doctor is here," Josephine called down the hallway.

"Will you both excuse me?"

***

The fluorescent lights in the ceiling reflecting off the powder blue painted walls of the space outside George's room enabled Jack, from a distance, to see the doctor's face. It was a look he had seen too many times before, and Jack braced himself for the bad news.

With a clipboard in his hand, a doctor in blue scrubs stepped toward them. "Mrs. Aitken, we have been able to stop the bleeding and pack the wound. It is quite deep, and there is a significant risk of infection. We are giving your husband intravenous antibiotics. He is also in great pain, so we have given him a shot of morphine. When you see him, he may be a little out of it, so don't be concerned."

Josephine ran her hand through her shoulder-length blond hair and frowned. "How long will he need to be here, doctor?"

"If he responds well to the antibiotics, he probably can go home tomorrow. But there is something else we need to be concerned about, Mrs. Aitken."

Jack and Josephine glanced at one another. They were now more worried than they were just a few seconds earlier.

"What is it, doctor?" Jack asked.

"Whenever someone suffers an animal bite, we are required to notify the Department of Health. It is a routine procedure for them to test the animal's blood, or in this case, a person, for diseases."

The doctor hesitated, then went on. "Mrs. Aitken, the attacker tested positive for rabies."

"Rabies?" Josephine flinched, and her hands began to tremble. Struggling for support, she grasped Jack's arm. "How is that possible?"

"We found bite marks in the attacker's throat area. There is no way to know what animal bit him."

Jack thought, *Bite marks in the throat. That sounds way too familiar.*

"There's more." The doctor exhaled. "Normally, rabies is 100% preventable with a vaccine that I would administer immediately after exposure."

The doctor's tone concerned Jack, who muttered anxiously, "But...."

"The strain of rabies is one the medical examiner has never seen before, and it does not appear in the national database. They are also checking international sources, but that will take time."

Jack's jaw stiffened. "What are you saying, doctor?"

"We will start the vaccine regimen immediately, but we do not know if it will be effective on this strain. If Mr. Aitken does not respond to the treatment...." The doctor trailed off.

Jack questioned, "He could die? Rabies is fatal if not promptly treated, isn't it?"

The doctor cradled George's medical chart in his arms. "Nearly 100% of people infected with rabies will die from it. Rabies is the most lethal virus known to man. Fewer than twenty people have survived the disease after they begin showing symptoms."

Josephine gasped, and her hand covered her mouth. Tears burst from her hazel blue eyes, and she sobbed into Jack's shoulder. Standing together in the hallway, Jack hugged his sister-in-law, trying to comfort her as the doctor stepped away to give them time to process his problematic diagnosis.

After a few minutes, a hospital employee approached them. "Mrs. Aitken, I am sorry, but there are some papers I need you to sign." Josephine stepped into an office across the hall from George's room and left Jack standing alone, lost in his thoughts about his brother. He wondered, *am I responsible for getting George involved in this situation?*

The declaration of Father Mark Desmond rang through his head: *Jack, you have got your weaknesses too. For instance, your tendency toward introspection and self-flagellation regarding how things impact your family.* Jack took a deep breath and steadied his nerves. He knew that George, Josephine, and their children would lean on him now. He had to make sure he provided the support they needed. Anne and Sheriff Hill approached him.

Anne immediately noticed the deep furrows on Jack's forehead. "Bad news, Jack?"

"Unfortunately, yes," Jack replied. "They ran some tests, and Robert Wallace had rabies."

"Rabies?" Anne asked incredulously, but Sheriff Hill stood like a man of stone, his arms folded across his chest.

"Don't they have a series of shots they can give him?" Anne queried. "It was always my understanding that the shots were painful, but with immediate treatment, it is possible to cure rabies."

"George's situation is more complicated, Anne. The test shows what appears to be a previously unknown strain of the disease. The doctor is not sure the current vaccine will be effective against it."

Jack brushed the tears from his eyes with the back of his hand. "Where could Wallace have gotten an unknown strain of rabies?"

"Strigoi," Sheriff Hill quickly responded.

"Strigoi?" Jack challenged. "What are you talking about?"

"I heard your boys utter the word back in the garage." Hill stared at Jack. "I know you heard about the legend of the Strigoi from Amy Scowle when you were in Pender County."

Jack stepped back and bristled. "How the hell do you know about that?"

Looking at Anne, the sheriff responded, "I think you have that figured out already, haven't you, Detective?"

"You hired me to fill more than a vacancy in the force," Anne grilled her boss. "I am not in Ocean Isle Beach by accident, am I?"

Sheriff Hill smiled. "It isn't every day that someone trained by JESU walks into my office."

Forgetting the sheriff was her boss, Anne's eyes glazed over. "Where did you get that information?"

"Sorry, tactfulness is not my strong suit." Hill put his hands up, attempting to reassure Anne. "But background checks are my specialty. Don't worry, Bishop. The secrets of your past are safe with me."

"It was no accident that you gave me this unsolved case either, is it?"

"Right again." The sheriff pointed his index finger toward Anne. "I knew your JESU skill set was just what was needed to investigate this case. Robert's sudden retirement caught me off guard. He never mentioned retirement, ever. He never discussed it in the twenty-plus years we had known each other. I would have done the investigation myself, but my friendship with him meant I was too close to the situation. I had my suspicions about Robert's actions or the lack thereof, but I have a soft spot where friends are concerned. It is my Achilles heel, I'm afraid."

"I know the feeling." Anne grimaced, thinking of Mark Desmond.

"What does this have to do with a Strigoi?" Jack brought the conversation back to Sheriff Hill's original assertion.

Just then, Josephine touched Jack on the arm. "I am sorry to interrupt. Jack, George is asking to see you."

Looking at Anne and Sheriff Hill with raised eyebrows, Jack asked, "We'll pick this up later?"

Anne and Sheriff Hill nodded.

Jack walked away, and Sheriff Hill waved. "Come on, Bishop, I'll buy you a cup of coffee."

***

August 19th
Brunswick Medical Center, Bolivia, NC
10:30 p.m.

Jack cracked the door to his brother's hospital room and peered in to see George, in a green hospital gown, lying in bed with his eyes closed.

"Hey, George. Are you awake?"

George opened his eyes. "Come on in, Jack."

Jack made his way to George's bedside and grabbed his brother's hand, squeezing it firmly. "How are you feeling? Are you in any pain?"

"They have me numbed up pretty good." George raised his arm to show Jack the IV. "After the shot they gave me, I can't feel a thing."

George hesitated momentarily, then shifted in the bed toward his brother. "Jack, I want to apologize."

"For what, George? I know what I told you was unbelievable."

George shook his head. "Please, Jack. I should have known you would never lie to me. After what happened earlier, I won't ever doubt you again. I am still trying to understand all of it."

Jack joked, "I've got more experience with the world of the surreal than you do. I don't think anything will surprise me anymore."

"Jack, what was that, that thing?"

"We're still trying to figure that out. We are kicking around a theory, but I don't know enough about it to share it with you. I'll keep you posted."

George grinned. "You do that. By the way, can I ask you to stand on the other side of the bed, away from the machines? I wouldn't want you to pull the plug on me."

Jack winced at his brother's poor and, under most circumstances, highly inappropriate attempt at humor. However, he took no offense from George's joke. George always had a unique perspective on what was funny and enjoyed shocking people. At this point in their lives, Jack knew he would never change. Jack just shook his head.

"I couldn't help myself," George teased. "Under the circumstances, I hope you can forgive me."

"George, nothing you say surprises me anymore. You're incorrigible."

Jack laughed. "You know, that's something Lucius would say."

George cringed. "Ouch! You know me. I go to see *Nightmare on Elm Street* to root for *Freddie Krueger*!"

Jack snickered. "Or drive the winding roads of Long Island's North Shore at night, with no lights on."

For a few moments, the atmosphere in the room was light, but then George grimaced in pain. "Seriously, Jack. You know how we all loved Amanda. I am truly heartbroken for you and the decision you had to make. No one should have to make that choice. Initially, I was upset by what you did, but the more I thought about what I would do if I were in your shoes and Josephine asked me to let her go, well, I can understand why you did it."

"George, I don't know if you realize how much I needed to hear that from you."

George's expression grew serious. "Speaking of Lucius. I'm also glad you didn't sell your soul to him."

Then, trying not to laugh, George joked, "You saved me the trouble of figuring out how I would save your ass again! All our lives, I have been protecting you. It's getting a little tiring."

Tears rose in Jack's eyes—from the laughter, not sadness. George always knew how to make him laugh.

Eventually, Jack stopped laughing. "You know how severe your condition is, don't you?"

George waved his hand dismissively. "It will be all right. I'm much too important to die. I'm sure the treatments will work, but those shots will hurt."

George smiled once more and, referring to a character from the 1970s show *Good Times,* joked, "You know, Jack, *Sweet Daddy is afraid of needles.*"

Jack and George roared, and while struggling to get the words out, Jack conceded, "You do not have a serious bone in your body, do you?"

George simply replied, "Nope."

Jack grabbed his brother's hands tighter. *"Don't worry about a thing, Frankie Five Angels."*

George beamed, understanding Jack's reference to one of their favorite movies, *The Godfather II*. It was Jack's way of assuring him that everything would be okay and that he would take care of George's family, no matter the outcome.

"Will you and Josephine be okay for a while?" Jack asked. "I've got some things to take care of with Anne and the sheriff."

Holding up his phone, Jack continued. "I am only a phone call away if either of you needs anything."

"Thanks, Jack. Sheriff Hill told Josephine that he called the Myrtle Beach police, and they would post a squad car at the house twenty-four hours a day. Louis and David will be safe."

Jack leaned over the bed rail to hug his brother. "I will see you soon."

As he left George's bedside and made his way to the door, Jack thought that Sheriff Hill was very kind *to* make that call. *However, after what we just experienced, I am not convinced it will do much good if something like the being that was Robert Wallace shows up.*

***

Sheriff Hill and Anne entered the nearly empty cafeteria. A janitor had placed most of the chairs on top of the tables and mopped the floor. A young cashier with purple hair sat behind a register chewing gum like a cow chews grass, blowing giant, pink bubbles.

"Hi." The cashier put down the magazine she was reading. "What can I get you two?"

Holding up a near-empty pot, Hill asked, "Any chance we can get some coffee?"

"Sure, Sheriff, I will brew you a fresh pot."

The duo sat in a booth with lime green upholstered seats, waiting for the coffee.

"It's been a long day." Anne placed her hand in front of her mouth as she yawned."

"I'm afraid it will be an even longer night." Sheriff Hill twisted his torso, stretching his back muscles.

While still technically boss and employee, Anne and Sheriff Hill now sat across the table from one another as two detectives working a case. The cashier placed the coffee pot and two cups on the table between them. As she watched the sheriff pour black coffee into the white porcelain mugs, Anne realized her view of him was evolving. It had started with her believing he was a male chauvinist, but she now knew that had been more of an act than reality. She guessed there was more to the sheriff's background that he was yet to reveal.

"Okay, Bishop." Hill blew to cool the hot coffee. "Let's talk about what pieces of information you have about this case and see if we can start putting this puzzle together."

Anne quickly glanced around to make sure no one would overhear their discussion.

"Okay, boss. So far, our research shows that starting with 2008, every fifty-four years, dating as far back as 1845, there are a series of similar attacks as those that occurred in Bolivia. All the crimes occur in six-week intervals, and there are always six attacks. Then the crimes abruptly stop."

"That's good research." Showing his approval by giving the thumbs-up sign, he added, "I would never have thought to look back in time to validate it."

Anne thought, *we had hints from other-worldly sources, but I will keep that to myself for now.*

"I must credit Jack for that," Anne conceded. "I have been focusing on what is going on in Lake Waccamaw."

The smell of disinfectant hung in the air as the janitor finished cleaning and left the cafeteria.

"What have you found out about those attacks?" Sheriff Hill questioned. "When Chief Bassett called me for help and mentioned the exsanguination being consistent with each victim, I figured your background in JESU made you the logical choice for that assignment too. Tell me, how significant a piece of evidence is the blood loss?"

Shifting in her seat, Anne confirmed, "The blood loss is a factor in all of these cases, including the historical ones."

"That is interesting." Hill scratched his ear. "Any mutilation to the bodies?"

The room was quiet, except for the clock ticking on the wall.

"No. The bodies are all intact, and Jack has found that the historical documents support the same condition of the corpses in the past attacks as well."

"So, let me sum this up, Bishop." The sheriff tapped the table with his fingertips." Until now, all the victims were animals. For some reason that I am guessing we haven't discovered yet, the killer, this entity, has switched to human prey."

Anne tilted her head slightly and, with a look of surprise, interrupted, "You did say entity. What makes you think it is not a human?"

"The hair sample you found at the Wallace house. I know the Medical Examiner has not determined what animal it is from, but it sure as shit isn't human."

Anne frowned. "Chief, you are a contradiction wrapped in an enigma. Candidly, I am not quite sure what to make of you."

Sheriff Hill refilled his coffee cup. "You will in good time. Has it occurred to you that the numbers six and fifty-four might have some relevance?"

The quiet room was suddenly louder as a few doctors ordered eggs, and the smell of bacon now permeated the room

"Jack and I have considered it but have not yet discovered its meaning," Anne whispered.

"Fifty-four is the number of times you will find a reference to demons in the *Bible*," the sheriff asserted. "Six, well, that seems like an easy clue for a former JESU member."

Anne looked at Sheriff Hill quizzically.

"You know what I mean? Six-Six-Six." He rolled his eyes." Didn't they teach you this stuff?"

"You believe all of this has supernatural origins?" Anne asked candidly, in a tone that made her statement seem more like a declaration than a question.

"Well, don't you?" he asked somewhat astonishedly. "Another concern is, why did the fifty-four-year pattern change, and why go after humans, now?"

***

Before Anne could respond, Jack slid into the booth. "I thought I might find you two here." Jack placed a coffee mug that he received from the cashier on the table. "How about filling me up?"

As Sheriff Hill poured, Anne asked, "How is George?"

"He is okay, for the moment anyway. I know he is scared, but he is cracking jokes and being himself. I'm not sure if I was comforting him or if he was comforting me. It's typical of George. Am I interrupting anything?"

Anne eyed Sheriff Hill. "Uh, no. I was just updating the sheriff on our findings. He has put forth an interesting theory."

Jack raised the mug to his lips.

"Let's lose the formality and get down to the facts," Hill announced impatiently. "I told Anne I believe we are dealing with something supernatural. I pointed out that the fifty-four-year historical gaps between the attacks correlate to the number of times the *Bible* mentions demons. I guess that might vary depending on which version of the Bible you read, but I'll stand by my interpretation of what you discovered. The six deaths associated with each series of attacks—I think that number has an obvious meaning. Finally, Anne finding the hair at the Wallace crime scene points in the direction of this perpetrator falling into the category of a what, not a whom."

Slowly putting his cup down, Jack stared at the sheriff, his mouth agape and eyes wide.

Sheriff Hill continued. "This leads me to what I heard your sons say back in the garage. I heard Strigoi, loud and clear. As I acknowledged previously, I know all about what Amy Scowle told you about the legend of the Strigoi. But what do your kids know about it?"

Jack was taken aback by how much Sheriff Hill knew about the case and how strongly he stated his theory. It was the same premise that Jack and Anne had been working toward but had not yet definitively articulated to each other. However, after the events of the last few hours, Sheriff Hill's theory was well beyond the line of plausible. It was now a fact.

"The truth is, Sheriff, I don't know. Anne and I discussed what Miss Amy told me about the Strigoi, but not in Louis and David's presence. I want to ask them the same question. My sons are autistic, and one trait of their disability is an inability to lie. It is quite literally not in their DNA. I don't know that any answer we get would be helpful. But I will grant you that it is odd they would even utter the word."

Jack hesitated. "Now, how do you know about Miss Amy?"

"It's quite simple, Jack." Hill straightened his tie and matter-of-factly responded, "I followed you."

"What?" Jack felt a rush of heat on his neck and instantly became agitated. "Why would you do that? How did you know?"

Sheriff Hill reached into his pocket and slid a gold ring across the table toward Jack.

"I think you'll want this back."

Examining the ring, Jack realized that it was his wedding band.

Astonished, Jack asked, "Where did you find this?"

"I told you I have been following you, didn't I?"

Jack clenched his fist and started to rise from his seat.

Still waiting for their food, the doctors heard the loud discussion and questions from the booth and peered around the potted plants that separated the kitchen from the seating area.

Anne grabbed Jack's wrist and convinced him to sit back down before he drew further attention.

Anne asked bluntly, "How is it that you seem to know so much about the supernatural? Are you from JESU? You must excuse me for being so direct, but I am tired, sore, and more than a little suspicious."

"No, I am not. And I am telling you the truth, Anna Grieve."

Anne's spine stiffened. "How the hell did you know that? Who sent you?"

Jack was confused. "Who is Anna Grieve?"

Anne shot Jack a look. "Me. That was my name before the first Culpeper massacre. I changed it when JESU requested that I keep watch over activities around the burial mound. Very few people knew about it. Even Mark thought I was dead."

"I told you, Anne," Sheriff Hill bragged, "I am good at background checks, and as I stated before, your secrets are safe with me. I used your former name, so you know you can trust me. I will say it once more. I have no past or present affiliation with JESU."

"That's not good enough!" Anne gritted her teeth. "Who are you really, Sheriff?"

Sheriff Hill sat up straight with his hands in front of his chest. "I know you both want answers. You deserve answers. Hear me out about the Strigoi, and I will tell you everything. Agreed?"

Jack and Anne exchanged glances and nodded their agreement. Hill took a long sip from his coffee cup, shifted in his seat, and removed a worn leather notepad from his pocket. He flipped through the pages and, when he found what he was looking for, began to read.

"Miss Amy told you that local immigrants associate the Strigoi with misfortune. The reality is that it is a superstition deeply rooted in Romanian culture with far more ominous overtones."

The sheriff flipped to the next page. "Romanian mythology says that a Strigoi is a troubled spirit that has returned from the grave. Reports say it can transform into any shape or form or remain invisible. Its powers increase by consuming the blood of others."

Anne interrupted, "Well, that accounts for the exsanguination and could explain the damage to the Wallace house. It also could explain Wallace's seemingly superhuman strength."

"Yes, and no," the sheriff continued. "I think a Strigoi is responsible for the destruction at the Wallace house, but the determination that Robert Wallace had rabies meant there was still blood in his body. Those bite marks tell me something fed on him, not the other way around. It may be that the Strigoi bit him, but it did not drain him. Robert Wallace was no Strigoi."

Jack added, "If a Strigoi bit Wallace, I bet that is why they can't identify the rabies strain from my brother's bite. I only hope that the vaccine will be effective."

"So do I, Jack." Hill's demeanor was calm, his following statement sobering. "Otherwise, we may have to put him down like we did Robert Wallace."

Jack scratched his forehead, not wanting to consider what the sheriff had just suggested. Not long ago, he would have found the suggestion shocking and appalling, but now he knew it was a possibility he could not ignore.

As he returned to his notes, a bead of sweat ran down Sheriff Hill's temple. "It probably comes as no surprise to either of you that Bram Stoker's Dracula has origins rooted in the Strigoi legend, but his characterization is a modern interpretation. What we are talking about is not a suave vampire in a cape. It is far more primitive. Its ability to pass on the rabies virus to Wallace and Wallace in turn to your brother is a characteristic of an animal, not a human."

"The hair sample we found was also not human," Anne interjected. "The Medical Examiner confirmed it was from an animal."

Jack added, "One of the eyewitnesses from the Bladenboro accounts mentioned catlike features. Sounds like an animal to me."

Sheriff Hill cautioned, "We need to remember that if it is a Strigoi, it may be able to shapeshift. It could look like just about anything if it is visible at all."

"Sheriff, are there any written accounts about it?" Anne asked. "Historical records or something that brings the legend into the real world."

Sheriff Hill flipped through the pages once more. Putting up his finger, he replied, "Listen to this. The Greeks and Romans wrote about the *Strix* or *Striga*, which they associated with witchcraft and consuming infants' flesh. The first modern written account of a Strigoi is associated with Jure Grando Alilovic. Local records from Istria, located in present-day Croatia, indicate Alilovic was responsible for terrorizing the area sixteen years after his death in 1656."

Sheriff Hill paused, then told Jack and Anne, "Until the local priest and villagers cut off his head."

Jack turned to Anne. "You know who would be fascinated by this?"

"Mark Desmond," Anne answered instantly.

Sheriff Hill shuddered as if a cold breeze ran through his body.

"Is something wrong, Sheriff?" Anne asked.

"Yeah," Jack added. "You look like you saw a ghost."

"It's nothing. As I was saying, this is the first but by no means the last story about the Strigoi. To the present day, there are still news reports in Romania about small, isolated villages where bodies have been exhumed and desecrated in an apparent effort to destroy some perceived evil entity."

"Desecrated? How?" Jack asked.

"The head has a nail driven into it, or the heart is removed and sliced in two."

Jack cringed. Anne was not surprised by what Sheriff Hill had indicated. While unfamiliar with a Strigoi, her JESU training included studies of vampires. Vampires were real adversaries at one time, even if they might not exist today.

Hill drank down the last drops of coffee from his mug. "One piece of information I found interesting was an assertion by Dimitrie Cantemir, a Moldavian statesman and author, and Romanian folklorist Teodor Burada. Both men indicated that, unlike a vampire, created only by the bite of another vampire, the Strigoi can be born from a human mother."

With skepticism, Jack asked, "You are saying they can breed?"

Anne exclaimed, "It could support their ability to shapeshift into a human form."

"If the past few days have taught us anything," the sheriff stated, "it is to believe that even the improbable is possible."

"Talk about *Rosemary's Baby*," Jack joked.

"You're not kidding," Anne agreed.

"It may be far worse," Sheriff Hill concluded, shoving his notepad in his pocket. "One story contains a quote from a vampire, who refers to the Strigoi as *the true monster of our nightmares.*"

Chapter 17

August 19th
Lake Waccamaw State Park, Lake Waccamaw, NC
11:00 p.m.

Moonbeams danced across Lake Waccamaw's calm water and illuminated the small, sandy beach adjacent to the boat ramp. The night was still warm from the heat of the day, and the smell of Star Jasmine hung in the air. The sounds of frogs echoed through the darkness, and the cattails and pampas grasses waved in a gentle breeze. Maricela Antonescu and her boyfriend, Reid Bowman, lay on a blanket, holding hands, staring upward at a spectacular full moon.

    The young couple met as juniors in high school, and despite the objections of Constantin Antonescu, Maricela's domineering father, they spent as much time together as possible. Reid was a straight-A student and headed to Duke University. He did his best to make a favorable impression, but nothing seemed enough for Constantin. As the youngest of Constantin and Maria's seven daughters, Maricela tried hard not to replicate her older siblings' rebellious behavior, but she refused to give Reid up no matter what her father demanded. As Maricela saw it, she and Reid were in love, and her father was just going to have to learn to accept it.

    A shooting star raced across the sky, and Maricela wished this night would never end. Reid would soon be off to college, and Maricela would be heading to Atlanta to begin her internship at the headquarters of Antonescu Communications. A tear fell from her cheek just thinking about it, and she quickly drove the thought from her mind. She squeezed Reid's hand tighter.

    "Did you see the shooting star?" Maricela asked, fluttering her eyelashes.

"I did," Reid responded. He turned toward Maricela and whispered in her ear, "I made a wish too."

"Care to tell me what that wish was?" Maricela inquired with a smile.

"If I tell you, it won't come true, will it?"

Maricela cooed softly, "I bet I know what it was."

Maricela's lips met Reid's. The romantic moment was quickly interrupted by a piercing howl reverberating across the lake.

"What was that?" Maricela nervously looked around.

"I don't know." Reid put his hand around Maricela's shoulder. "I have never heard anything like that before."

Reid stood up and marked the direction from where the menacing sound originated. He scanned the shores of the lake for a sign of what could have made it but saw nothing.

"Maybe it is a coyote," Reid tried to reassure Maricela. "The lake does share a border with the Waccamaw National Wildlife Refuge."

"Whatever it is," Maricela murmured anxiously, "I hope it stays on the other side of the lake."

Reid raised his arm, pretending to shield his face like Bela Lugosi. "In the darkness comes the evil of the night."

Then he smiled playfully. "Or it could be a Bigfoot."

Maricela punched Reid weakly in the leg. "Stop it! You know I don't like it when you tease me!"

Reid sat back down on the blanket. He ran his finger down Maricela's cheek and gazed longingly into her eyes. "I am going to miss you when I go to school. I know we can FaceTime, but it is not the same as being with you."

Reid stammered, "I mean seeing each other face-to-face. In person."

Maricela placed her hand over Reid's. "I know what you are saying. I am not looking forward to going to Atlanta. I wish I could make my father understand that I have no interest in the so-called *family business.*"

Reid shook his head. "Please don't be angry at me for what I am going to say. Your Dad gives new meaning to the word controlling.

But look at it this way, at least when you are in Atlanta, he will not be watching over you so closely. He can't since he is not there all the time."

Maricela sighed. "Yes, but unfortunately, you won't be in Atlanta either."

Reid embraced Maricela, who leaned her head on his shoulder. The breeze that had previously been gentle began to increase in intensity, causing small waves to break on the shoreline. The young couple just sat in silence. While the quiet often made young couples uncomfortable, it never troubled Reid and Maricela. They did not need to speak to convey their love for one another.

Reid ran his fingers through Maricela's long red hair. The wind continued to blow harder, but lost in the moment, neither Maricela nor Reid noticed. Their embrace grew more passionate until a flock of birds suddenly scattered out of the pampas grass and cattails adjacent to the boat landing.

The noise created by the dispersed birds startled the couple. Turning toward the boat landing, the last few birds flew away, and they saw the grass rustling and heard splashing along the water's edge.

Maricela's nails sunk into Reid's arm. "Do you see anything, Reid?"

"I see movement in the grass, but I am not sure what is causing it."

Reid strained to see through the darkness. He placed himself between Maricela and the boat landing and slowly moved forward.

"What the hell are you doing?" Maricela whispered pointedly. "Have you lost your mind?"

Reid placed his index finger in front of his lips to signal her to remain quiet. He faced the grass again and continued forward to get close enough to identify what was responsible for scattering the birds. As Reid got closer, the thick grass along the water's edge shook. Reid believed it might be an alligator for a moment, but then he heard loud breathing and a growl. A hostile and angry guttural sound. Reid was sure he saw a massive, hairy figure moving through the grass. He slowly backed away.

"Maricela, I don't know what it is, but we should get out of here. Help me pick up the stuff slowly, and we will make our way to the car. Don't run or turn your back. Running will only encourage it to follow us. Understand?"

Maricela nodded and picked up the picnic basket and the blanket. Whatever was stirring in the grass did not attempt to reveal itself. Maricela and Reid finally made it to Reid's car; they got in and locked the doors. Reid put the key in the ignition, then checked to see if the figure had moved in their direction. What he saw was unexpected.

Pointing toward the spot where they had just had their picnic interrupted, Reid asked, "Do you see a person down there?"

Maricela leaned in toward the windshield.

"Yes. I see someone too. Do you remember the creepy guy I was telling you about the other day? You know, the one that seemed to be following me around school and stuff."

"Yes, I remember. I didn't know whether to deck the guy or …."

Reid's answer was interrupted by a light in his eyes. Startled, he saw someone next to the vehicle with a flashlight in his hand.

The figure knocked on the glass. "Open the window, please."

Reid instantly recognized the police officer and hit the button to roll down the window. The light flashed toward Maricela and the back seat as the window disappeared.

Before Reid could speak, the figure asked, "Son, are you aware that there is a curfew in effect? You shouldn't be here."

"Well, uh. Yes, officer. I know."

The officer flashed his badge. "I'm Chief Bassett. What are you two doing here? Reid, is that you?"

"Yes, Chief," Reid replied sheepishly. "It's me."

"Reid, I am surprised at you. You know better than this."

Not wanting to alarm the young couple, the Chief did not mention the murders. "There have been some people injured in this area recently. I am going to have to insist that you leave immediately."

"Okay, Chief." Reid pointed toward the lake. "But you better tell that guy down there too."

Chief Bassett scanned the area and saw someone standing near the boat landing on the sand.

Glancing at Maricela, Reid continued. "Maricela thinks it is a guy that has been following her around."

"Ms. Antonescu, is that true?"

"Yes, Chief. It's creepy. He has been following me all over town."

Chief Bassett exhaled. "All right. I will investigate it, but you two need to leave now. Reid, I expect you to take Ms. Antonescu home right away. Are we clear?"

"Yes, Chief. Crystal."

"Good. Now, get out of here."

Chief Bassett watched as Reid backed the car out of the parking space and drove toward the park entrance. He saw the car's lights disappear and then turned back toward the lake. The figure was no longer there. Chief Bassett went to the shoreline and saw where the couple had spread their blanket on the sand. He shined his flashlight in all directions but saw nothing. He moved toward the cattails and pampas grass along the water's edge, but all he heard was the frogs croaking, the crickets, and the sound of the wind blowing through the grass.

Returning to the squad car, he surveyed the area for any sign of the stranger that Reid and Maricela had described. He saw no one. He opened the door and picked up the radio receiver to check in with the dispatch officer.

"Chief Bassett to dispatch. I kicked some kids out of the Lake Waccamaw Park."

The dispatch officer replied, "Roger that, Chief."

"Dispatch, have any reports in the past few days come in about a stranger in town?"

There was a moment of silence, and the answer came across the radio: "No, Chief. No reports."

"Roger that."

As the Chief got into the car, he saw something shiny on the ground. He reached down and picked up a bracelet. He held it up to the flashlight and, flipping it over, saw something etched on the back, *To Reid, with all my love. Maricela.*

Chief Bassett put the jewelry in his pocket, and as he slid into the front seat of the squad car, he heard the dispatch officer say, "Chief, we just got a call from the park ranger, Tom Davis. There may have been a break-in at the snack bar on the other side of the park."

"I copy, dispatch. I'm en route now."

***

August 19th
George Aitken's home, North Myrtle Beach, SC
11:00 p.m.

David Aitken lay awake in his bed, staring at the ceiling. Usually, he would be fast asleep by now, but with his Dad at the hospital with his uncle, this unfamiliar bed caused him to toss and turn. Uncle George and Aunt Josephine's house was new to him, but at least Louis was here too. Suddenly, Louis broke the silence in the room.

"There's no need to hide when it's dark outside," Louis whispered, quoting *Pajama Sam* from an old computer game they played as kids.

"Darkness lives in my closet, but I'm not scared," said David with a smile.

Louis jumped out of bed, put a blanket across his shoulders like a cape, and declared, "This looks like a job for Pajama Sam!"

David giggled and sat up in bed. "You'll need your mask, the Illuminator Mark V Jr. flashlight, and your lunchbox, I mean your portable bad guy containment unit."

Louis answered, "You know that the Illuminator Mark V Jr. takes two D batteries, right?"

David got out of bed and sat down on the floor. The brothers laughed, and it made them both feel a little better.

"I hope Uncle George is going to be okay," David told Louis as he rocked back and forth to calm himself.

Before Louis could respond, a bright ball of light appeared in the room and floated in the air between the boys. It hung in the air at the bottom of David's bed and began to expand from a ball into a person's outline. David and Louis sat mesmerized by the light and somehow understood that they had nothing to fear from it. They recognized who the figure was.

"Mom!" Both boys exclaimed.

"Where did you come from?" David asked.

"We miss you, Mom!" Louis added.

Their mother's spirit, Amanda, sat smiling in front of them. The boys got up off the floor and sat next to her on the bed. She put her arms around their shoulders, and the boys moved closer. Despite her not being a physical being, Louis and David could feel the warmth of her touch.

"I miss you both so much." Amanda's spirit told them. "More than you can know!"

"What are you doing here?" Louis asked.

"I'm here to see you both one more time before I go." The apparition patted their backs.

Disappointed, David frowned. "Why can't you stay, Mom?"

Amanda's spirit tried to reassure David. "My time here is short. After tonight, you may not be able to see me again for a long time, but I will be with you. You will be able to feel me all around you. Do you believe me?"

Louis scratched his head. "I guess so. I'm not sure."

"Louis darling, you will understand soon. Each of us is born with extraordinary abilities and talents. You have an exceptional memory. It will allow you to remember all the words that someone will begin teaching you, just like all the types of train cars and time schedules you can recite from as far back as you can remember."

Louis smiled, thinking about what his Mom had just told him. He loved everything about trains.

David interjected, "What about me, Mom? Do I have special abilities too?"

"Yes, David. Despite being autistic, you have discovered a way to have many friends. You are everyone's cheerleader. The gift of friendship and the optimism you provide to others will enable you to spread the words that Louis will memorize. You both will be messengers."

David responded, "That sounds like fun and a little scary at the same time."

"Don't be afraid, David. You too, Louis. Dad and others are going to be there to help you."

Amanda's spirit spoke lovingly to her children. "Boys, there is genuine goodness inside of both of you. People will come to see that neither of you can say anything other than the truth. Don't be afraid to shout it out loud when the time comes!"

The spirit placed a hand under each boy's chin. "You are both going to change the world."

David tilted his head and asked warily. "Mom. Why is the Strigoi here?"

Amanda's spirit looked at the boys with concern. "The Strigoi is evil. It is here to do a terrible thing. I don't know if anyone can stop it from happening, but Dad, Ms. Bishop, and others will try."

"What about Uncle George, Mom? Louis asked. "Is he going to be, okay?"

"Boys, I want you to remember something you need to tell Dad."

Louis and David nodded.

The spirit continued, "The vile waters of the river Styx, a Strigoi bite they say will fix. The blood of man, it will congeal. The river water is said to heal."

Instantly, the apparition disappeared, but Louis and David heard their mother's voice.

"I love both of you, my angels."

***

August 19th
Lake Waccamaw State Park, Lake Waccamaw, NC
11:45 p.m.

Tom Davis was a veteran of the Gulf War and a Park Ranger for nearly thirty years. He was six feet five inches tall, and despite his gray hair and being almost sixty years old, he was in better shape than men who were half his age. He enjoyed the solitude that came with working the night shift. Being a Park Ranger in a small town like Lake Waccamaw could be dull, but that was the way Tom liked it. Vandalism was an uncommon occurrence in the park, and due to the curfew, he was more than a little surprised to see someone breaking into the snack bar. Usually, Tom would have managed the incident independently, but when he witnessed the perpetrator rip the steel door off its hinges and toss it aside like a piece of scrap metal, he thought a call to the sheriff's department was in order.

After confirming on the radio that Chief Bassett was on his way, Ranger Davis slowly made his way to the building. He heard a noise inside the snack bar as he approached the back door. *Whoever is in there is not trying to hide their presence,* thought Ranger Davis. Strangely, along with the noise, he heard what sounded like growling. Davis grabbed the nightstick hanging from his waist and peered inside. He saw a massive shadow moving around the floor.

"This is Ranger Tom Davis of the Park Service. Turn around slowly and come out with your hands above your head."

Ranger Davis heard loud breathing, but the figure made no effort to comply with his demand.

"I have my nightstick drawn. We can do this the easy way or the hard way. It is up to you."

Still, the perpetrator did not move or follow any of Ranger Davis's instructions. After roughly thirty seconds, the Park Ranger stepped through the doorway, keeping his shoulder against the wall and his nightstick held high. He carefully moved forward, and crouching with its back to him was an enormous individual covered in red hair. At first glance, it could have been a bear, but in the thirty years Tom Davis had worked in Lake Waccamaw, he had never seen a bear with red hair or an animal of this size.

"Now, turn toward me, slowly," the park ranger demanded.

The figure rose, and Ranger Davis was shocked by its size; even he felt small in its presence. The giant turned around quickly, and the Park Ranger could not believe what he saw. Confronting him was a creature whose head nearly touched the eight-foot ceiling. It had an elongated snout and large jaws prominently displaying jagged canine teeth. It watched Ranger Davis with its piercing, red eyes and saliva dripping from its mouth to the floor.

Ranger Davis froze, and his jaw dropped open, but before he could react, a massive paw with razor-sharp claws slammed into his face, tearing his skin away, exposing ligaments and the mandible. The swat's force sent the Park Ranger flying into the brick wall behind him, causing a gaping hole in the cinder blocks used to construct the building. Before Davis could react, the ravenous creature was on top of him, tearing at his torso with its deadly claws. The Ranger screamed in agony, but only briefly. The beast picked up the Ranger's bloody body and pushed Davis's head to the side. Then it sunk its canines into Davis's throat. He drained the Park Ranger so quickly that Tom Davis lost consciousness and died almost instantaneously.

The beast dropped the dead body to the floor, and another human stood before him. Chief Bassett had arrived on the scene. Upon hearing Tom Davis's scream, he entered the building with his gun drawn. Chief Bassett and the creature were face-to-face for a moment, and then the Chief began firing his weapon into the hairy beast at point-blank range. As he shot round after round into the torso of the creature, it kept moving toward him. The Chief backed up as the creature approached him. Even after emptying his gun, the Chief continued pulling the trigger.

Chief Bassett tried to run, but it was no use. The creature grabbed his arm, pulling it from its socket. The Chief screamed from a combination of fear and pain. The screaming quickly ceased when the beast twisted the Chief's head off and tossed it on the ground.

Unexpectedly, a third figure stood in the doorway of the building and yelled at the creature, "No! What have you done now?"

The creature let go of the body and watched it fall to the floor, coming to rest next to its decapitated head. Chief Bassett's face remained contorted, preserving the final moments of his painful death. The beast angrily snarled and growled at the figure now standing in the building.

Lucius Rofocale stood before the creature and rebuked it. "You fool! Did I not order you not to kill humans without my consent? This incident will bring more unwanted attention to our plan."

The creature eyed Lucius warily. Its instinct was to tear Lucius's head off, just like the human's, but it could not do so for a reason that it could not understand.

"Quickly!" Lucius ordered. "Take these bodies to the deepest part of the lake and weigh them down with rocks. Perhaps the alligators will help us dispose of the remains. Then meet me back at the cave and make sure you bring the head with you."

The creature snarled at Lucius scornfully and did not comply with his command. Lucius instantly transformed himself into his demon form to intimidate the monster.

"Damn it!" Lucius thundered. "You heard me! Now get going!"

The creature shook its head and continued to growl but picked up both bodies like they were playthings and walked into the lake, eventually disappearing below the water's surface. Once the creature was out of sight, Lucius reeled and stumbled out of the building. Finally, he propped himself against a wall and reached into his vest for a flask. Opening the flask, Lucius quickly downed the liquid and held the flask loosely in his hand, waiting for its contents to take effect. He felt no impact for what seemed like an eternity, but eventually, his strength returned.

***

Dragging Chief Basset's head by its hair, the Strigoi followed Lucius back to a cave beneath a house bordering the lake. As the creature settled back in its nest and fell asleep, Lucius reached out in his thoughts to his Lord and Master Lucifer.

"Yes, Lucius," Lucifer responded curtly. "What is it?"

"It is about the Strigoi, my master. His brutality and constant hunger make him more difficult for me to compel. Unlike lower animal forms that I can easily control using the techniques you taught me, I am increasingly unable to influence his behavior. I am also running low on the elixir, which is taking longer to refresh me."

"I see. The Strigoi's primitive brain is more difficult to alter with your meager power of suggestion." Lucifer's response dripped with contempt. "Tell me, is the Strigoi powerful enough yet to achieve our plan?"

"He fed for a fifth time tonight, Master. After the next feeding, he will have reached full strength."

"Good. Excellent, Lucius. You will need to finish the remaining elixir immediately after his final feeding. The timing will be vital, as consuming all the liquid will give you the power to telepathically stimulate that portion of the Strigoi brain that allows him to transform into an acceptable vessel and perform his functions as required."

"I understand, Master. I will not fail you."

"See to it that you do not, Lucius," Lucifer seethed. "The consequences could be disastrous for you."

Lucifer abruptly cut off their communication. Lucius was silent, contemplating his fate if he failed the Master again. Then he recalled finding a bracelet on the ground while waiting for the Strigoi to return from disposing of the bodies. He pulled it from his pocket and, looking at it, read the inscription on the back, *To Maricela, with all my love. Reid.*

Glancing over at the sleeping Strigoi, Lucius thought, t*his trinket might be just what I require to successfully conclude this mission and save me from Lucifer's fury.*

Chapter 18

August 20th
Brunswick Medical Center, Bolivia, NC
1:00 a.m.

Jack sat on a chair and leaned forward with his hands clasped in prayer. He bowed his head toward the tan tile floor of the meditation room, hoping that God was listening. The news about his brother's condition was not good. George's bite wound continued to bleed, and he would soon require a blood transfusion if the situation did not change. Jack could not help but ask, *why do these things keep happening to my family?*

Josephine remained with George, speaking with the doctor, while Jack stared at the wall. The window shades were drawn, and the room was dark and quiet, except for his heartbeat. The silence was soon interrupted by the noise emanating from his phone, telling him he had a new text message. Jack swiped across the screen and touched the text message icon. It was from his niece Kate.

Uncle John. Louis and David are okay. They are sleeping. Don't worry about them. They are fine. How is my dad?

Jack studied the screen. *How do I answer that question?* It took a minute for Jack to respond, and he took great care not to send anything that might upset his niece.

Kate, thank you for the update and for looking out for your cousins. Mom is in with the doctor now. We will know more soon. Love U, Uncle Jack.

Jack put the phone back in the carrying case attached to his belt and heard a knock. Through the small window in the door, he saw Anne and Sheriff Hill. Jack waved his hand, letting them know they were okay to enter. Anne pushed the door inward and stepped into the room. Sheriff Hill made sure the door shut behind him.

Anne immediately noticed the troubled look on Jack's face. "What's wrong?"

"It's that obvious?" Jack replied as he sighed. "The doctor is saying that George's wound is not clotting. He will need a transfusion if they can't stop the bleeding."

"I wonder if that has anything to do with the rabies strain they identified in Robert's blood?" Sheriff Hill questioned out loud.

"They don't know." Jack pulled at the stubble on his chin. "I suspect what you shared probably is at least part of the problem. I have got to figure this out and do it fast."

Jack sighed. "I wish Mark Desmond were here right now."

As Jack finished his sentence, he felt a chill run down his spine. "Is it me, or did it just get cold in here?"

The sheriff searched the room and saw a vent for the air conditioning system. He placed his hand in front of the grate. "There is no air coming out."

"It's not you, Jack," Anne answered, and as she uttered the words, her breath condensed in front of her as if it were the middle of winter.

"W-h-a-t, what's going on?" Jack wrapped his arms around his torso, shivering.

No sooner had Jack asked his question than the window embedded in the door to the room frosted over. Sheriff Hill reached for the doorknob, and the deadbolt lock clicked before he could get to it. He turned the knob and shook the door.

"It won't open!"

The trio searched the room and then at one another with an equal amount of bewilderment and fear. A gray, smoky fog appeared from the vent that only seconds earlier had not had any air flowing out of it. The mist hung in mid-air for a moment and began to take form.

A transparent figure appeared before them. "Peace be with you."

Jack, Anne, and Sheriff Hill were mesmerized by the figure. With an astonished look, Anne asked, "Mark?"

"Wait a minute. I've seen you before." The sheriff pointed at the figure. "Mark Desmond!"

The apparition nodded its agreement to the sheriff's assertion. "Anne. Jack. I am the spirit of the person you knew as Mark Desmond."

Jack's jaw was open, and Anne mirrored the same look of disbelief on her face.

"Are you a g-ghost?" Jack asked the figure. "What are you doing here?"

"I realize this is difficult for you to believe, but I am not a hallucination. Jack, you asked me why I am here. The answer is simply this, atonement. My soul has been in limbo since our encounter in Culpeper. I have been evading the Seraphim, the most senior of angels, hoping to make some amends before I face my final judgment."

The apparition paused, its face winced in agony, and then spoke in a voice filled with anguish and regret. "I betrayed you, Jack. You came to me seeking help, and I used you for my sinful and selfish ends. Amanda is dead due to my actions. I presented myself to you as God's servant and violated the trust of such a position. There is no healing the pain I caused you and your family. Even the most heartfelt apology cannot erase, let alone ease, your awful suffering. I am truly sorry for the heartache I caused you and your children. I know I have no right to ask, but please, forgive me. I beg you."

Jack stood before the apparition, dumbfounded, unsure how to respond to its admission of guilt, the grief-stricken confession, and profound request for forgiveness.

The figure gazed at Anne. "My friend, if I may still address you in that manner, I am ashamed that you had to be the one to end my madness. I put you in the position of being my executioner. I tore the bonds of our relationship and shredded the respect you gave me. In one night, I managed to destroy a lifetime of trust and left your faith in tatters."

A visible tear streamed down the cheek of the apparition as it pleaded, "Anne, please find it within your heart to pardon my vile actions. Pity me and forgive my trespasses against you and the violation of the trust you put in me."

Anne wept and trembled; she whispered, "You have it, Mark. I do forgive you. I miss you terribly."

Jack, whose lips were quivering emotionally, added, "Mark, I know there was more to you than who you were in Culpeper. Our journey together was brief, but you strengthened my resolve and helped me be there for my sons. If it is forgiveness you seek from me, you already had it long ago."

The spirit managed a sad smile. "I love both of you. I am grateful for your compassion and wish I had the courage when I was alive to show mercy to each of you the way you are giving it to me now."

"You have been helping us all along, haven't you?" Anne held on to Jack's arm to steady herself. "That black mass in my home, it was you. You left the hints on the map for us to follow."

Still suspended in mid-air, Desmond's ghost nodded. "Yes. I tried many times to manifest myself to you in my present form but have been unable to do so until now. I have more that I need to share with you before facing our God's swift and just judgment."

The glowing light shining brightly around the spirit began to dim. Anne exclaimed, "Mark! What is happening to you? You are beginning to fade away."

"My time with you is almost up." The regretful apparition began to fade. "Please listen very carefully."

The apparition locked eyes with Anne and Jack. "Do you both recall our discussions about the balance between good and evil?"

Jack and Anne responded in unison. "Yes."

"The *Codex Gigas* is Satan's version of the *Bible, Quran*, and other similar religious texts. Lucifer also has his version of the Book of Revelation and intends to begin the final confrontation with God….on his terms. Lucius is here to light the fuse, and the Strigoi is the ignition source."

As the specter faded, Jack asked, "How do we kill the Strigoi?"

"I don't know that you can," the spirit answered solemnly. "It is a powerful being whose origins go back to the beginning. The time of the book of Genesis."

The spirit grew weaker, and the trio strained to hear every word.

"Ingold. Samuel Domien," the apparition whispered. "Domjen."

Just before the ghost faded away, Jack yelled, "Is there a cure for the bite of a Strigoi?"

"Ask your boys. Their destiny. Your destiny. There is no escaping it. From the day you are born, your destiny is planned." The fading figure muttered.

Looking toward Sheriff Hill, Mark Desmond's spirit vanished, but his final declaration echoed through the room: "The sheriff can tell you."

Then the room was silent, with no trace of Mark Desmond's ghost.

Jack asked Anne and Sheriff Hill. "What did he say? I could barely hear him at the end."

Sheriff Hill was pale. "I know what he is referring to, and I think you need to take a seat. If you are shocked by what you just saw and what Desmond had to say, you will be stunned by what I tell you next."

***

August 20th
Deep in a Cave near Lake Waccamaw, NC
3:15 a.m.

Located in front of a crude altar, a ceremonial baptismal carved from the same stone as the foundation of the building became an ideal receptacle for the hundreds of gallons of water from the River Styx Lucius had brought to the cave. While consuming the water provided the most immediate benefits, immersing himself in the potent bath was necessary to supplement his strength and allow him to maintain control over the Strigoi's actions. While the Strigoi

SINS OF THE FATHERS

needed to feed to build the energy required to perform its role in Lucifer's plan, the risks of supplementing its powers also increased.

While floating in the pool, Lucius used precognitive telepathy, a form of extrasensory perception, to embed in the Strigoi's primitive brain the information it would need for the next phase of their operation. Lucius routinely practiced the mental exercises allowing him to manipulate the electrical brain impulses of the Strigoi. Unfortunately, the telepathic effect on the Strigoi was fleeting. Feeding on human blood was necessary and enhanced the Strigoi's strength, but Lucius grew weaker with every attempt to control the primal beast.

Precognitive telepathy was not yet impactful on people, and Lucius found this amusing. The theory's basis was mental exercises first discovered and developed by human beings. One quite legendary human being, at that. Nearly ten years earlier, construction workers were renovating a London home owned by Dr. Benjamin Franklin before the Revolutionary War when they made a ghastly discovery. Digging up the basement floor revealed human skeletons. What type of ghoulish behavior the *Good Doctor* had been up to remained a mystery to the present day, but Lucius knew.

During his experiments with electricity, Dr. Franklin inadvertently discovered what would later become the basis for telepathic science. As he continued to float in the water, Lucius's lips curled into a wicked smile as he reveled in the next thought that entered his head. Lucius did not realize it then, but his interception of Dr. Franklin's correspondence on his electrical experiments with Father Samuila Domien was fortuitous. Father Domien had been the *Mark Desmond* of his day and was a dangerous and constant threat to Lucius and his demon legions. Domien followed Lucius and the Antonescu family to North America in secret, where he gave up his priestly robes and changed his name to Samuel Domjen.

But he was no match for me. Lucius discovered Domjen's deception, and in exchange for Lucius not pursuing a vendetta against Dr. Franklin, Domjen agreed to reveal the importance of

Franklin's research. Domjen attempted to resist Lucius's probes into his mind but was unsuccessful. *Pathetic Fool*-Lucius snickered. Domjen divulged everything and was driven insane by Lucius's mental torture. Lucius enjoyed himself so much that he opted not to kill Domjen but left him to live in perpetual torment. He cast a spell that ensured Domjen's spirit would remain captive even after his physical death.

With his reminiscing complete, Lucius got back to the job at hand. Gaining access to the Antonescu house would be required, and what better way to do so than by assuming the identity of Maricela Antonescu's boyfriend, Reid Bowman? Using the electricity in his brainwaves, Lucius embedded a vision in the Strigoi's memory, an image of it transforming into a clone of Reid Bowman. He emphasized that the bracelet's return to Maricela was the reason for Reid's visit. As he mapped out the plan in the Strigoi's ancient brain, he reiterated one thing above all else. Lucius told the Strigoi that under no circumstances was it to harm Maricela Antonescu.

***

August 20th
Brunswick Medical Center, Bolivia, NC
3:15 a.m.

It was very late, and Jack should have been exhausted, but the opposite was true. Unfortunately, his brother's condition worsened, and he was at that very moment receiving a blood transfusion. Jack had offered to donate his blood as an identical twin and, therefore, a perfect match, but the doctor assured him that it was not necessary at this time. Jack sent Josephine home to attempt to get some sleep and assured her he would stay and let her know if anything changed.

After visiting hours, Jack, joined by Anne and Sheriff Hill, sought refuge in the hospital chapel. It was a small, softly lit sanctuary with tan walls and brown wood paneling. An altar with candles lit for prayer was flanked by two stained-glass windows: one depicting a rainbow hovering over Noah's Ark and the other Christ's crucifixion. Several rows of white oak pews with green cushions faced the altar. They had the room to themselves.

For the past hour, Sheriff Hill had shared with Anne and Jack that although he was a small-town lawman, he had another identity too. He described an organization, a brotherhood calling itself *Logos Confraternity*. Jack had his fill of secret societies from his dealings with JESU, but Logos Confraternity seemed, at first glance, to be like any other non-profit organization. As the sheriff portrayed it, the religious organization's purpose was to perform charitable acts for the poor and needy, which it did. However, the true mission of the group, not disclosed to the public at large, was startling.

Hill explained that Lagos Confraternity stood for *protectors of the word of God*. The organization had existed for nearly three centuries in its present form, but its roots reached back to the early Christian church's formation. The mission of the brotherhood was to protect God's prophets. At the same time, it sought the destruction of the false prophet, as revealed in the Book of Revelation.

"I apologize for not revealing my group and its mission earlier. Before I felt I could do so, I needed to be sure of a few things."

"Father Desmond's appearance was as much of a surprise to me as it was to the two of you, but for different reasons. You knew the real Mark Desmond. I only came to know him in my dreams."

Jack glanced at Anne, then asked, "What did he tell you, Sheriff?"

"A great deal." Sheriff Hill looked Jack straight in the eyes. "Much of it has to do with your boys."

Jack glared back and asked firmly, "What about my boys?"

"I will get to that. There are some other things I need to tell both of you first."

Sheriff Hill leaned against one of the pews and folded his arms. "Anne, Desmond first came to me a few months before I hired you. He told me about the Bolivia case and that I should assign it to you to investigate. He told me all about you. That's how I knew your real name and about JESU."

Anne laced her fingers together and rested her chin on her hands. "That explains it. Go on."

"He warned me about the existence of the Strigoi. I should have acted on what Mark told me much earlier than I did. Even after you applied for the job, just like he told me you would, I wasn't sure if I imagined it all. I stood back while you investigated to see if you would prove or disprove my sanity."

Sheriff Hill shook his index finger at Anne. "Regardless of what Desmond did in guiding you on the investigation, you're still one hell of a detective, Anne."

"Thanks, Chief. Just doing my job."

"After I hired you, Mark told me about a demon legend. I considered if he might be a demon himself. He knew so much about it."

The sheriff's gaze shifted back to Jack. "When Mark sensed my doubts, he brought a woman, an angel, with him to prove he wasn't a demon. When I saw the beautiful aura surrounding her, that was proof enough for me."

Jack asked pleadingly, "Was it, Amanda? What did she say, Glenn?"

"At the time, she did not identify herself." Hill began to pace in front of the altar. "She spoke of her children and her husband, but not by name."

"What Mark told me made the hair on the back of my neck stand up." The sheriff stopped to study the stained-glass window of Christ's crucifixion. "He began with the same thing he told us tonight. Lucifer wants to write his version of the Book of Revelation."

Turning back to Jack and Anne, he declared, "Mark told me that the Strigoi was the sign that the arrival of the false prophet was looming."

The sanctuary was silent as Jack and Anne processed what the sheriff had just told them.

Anne gulped. "You mean Satan's false prophet."

Glenn Hill breathed deeply, then exhaled. "As a part of Logos Confraternity, I have heard stories about the false prophet. Still, I never thought I would be fighting to prevent its arrival in my lifetime."

"But that's not everything, is it, Glenn?" Anne asked. "I can see it in your face."

Sheriff Hill shook his head in amazement. "Very perceptive, detective. Mark told me something even more difficult to comprehend or believe. The Strigoi was consuming human blood for a very sinister purpose."

Glenn Hill's face suddenly lost all expression. "I find this hard to say, but the Strigoi needs human blood to be potent enough to mate. According to the legend, the Strigoi is the father of the false prophet."

"What?" Anne and Jack cried incredulously.

"You heard me right. According to Mark, the Strigoi will fulfill an ancient curse involving the seventh child of the same gender in the same family. A child with red hair."

Jack looked at Anne, but she spoke before he could. "Antonescu. The Antonescus have seven children, all daughters. I'm betting the youngest daughter is a redhead."

"Now we know why Lucius Rofocale is here," Jack stated. "He is here to fulfill the prophecy."

Jack's thoughts went to his visit from Amanda. He recalled what she told him about Louis and David. *What was it she mentioned? They would reveal a great truth. What great truth?* Jack remained silent, and then another statement Amanda made began to echo in his head. *They will require protection from those seeking to silence the truth they deliver.*

Once more, the chapel was quiet. So quiet that you could hear the dripping wax from the candles fall on the altar.

Anne noticed that Jack's face had grown pale. "Are you all right, Jack?"

Jack wiped the sweat from his brow. "I'm okay, Anne. Glenn, you stated that the purpose of your organization was not only to defeat the false prophet but protect God's prophets as well. Did I hear you correctly?"

Sheriff Hill placed his hands on the pews and leaned in toward Jack. "You know. Don't you?"

"Know what?" asked Jack, trying to hide what he in his heart already knew. "What are you saying?"

Anne glanced at both men with a puzzled look on her face. "Tell me what you both appear to know but which I don't."

"As I know you are aware, Anne, the Book of Revelation tells of two witnesses who will appear before the Messiah's second coming," Hill replied. "These witnesses are supposed to be the reincarnation of two biblical prophets. Their names remain a mystery. Some say they are Elijah and Moses, while others speculate they are Enoch and Abraham. Our Order has a hypothesis too."

Anne's eyes opened wide. "And that is?"

"The two witnesses will bring the word of God to a spiritually sick populace who need healing. Jesus is the balm that will soothe the wounds of a world in need of its *Great Physician*. One witness will be the Old Testament prophet Isiah who made numerous prophecies about the Messiah's coming and his ministry. The other will be the New Testament's most effective proselytizer, Paul of Tarsus, Saint Paul."

"One prophet to confirm the fulfillment of Jesus's promise to return," Jack added. "The other to convert the non-believers and strengthen the resolve of those who have wavered in their faith."

"Exactly!" exclaimed the sheriff.

Suddenly, Jack felt very alone. He softly whispered, "Amanda was trying to tell me about their destiny."

"Amanda?" Anne asked with surprise. "What do you mean, Jack?"

Jack looked at Anne and dropped a bombshell. "David is Isiah, and Louis is Paul."

Anne had a look of both wonder and concern. Jack let the magnitude of what he heard sink in for a moment.

"Several nights ago, I had a dream about Amanda. She was telling me things about David and Louis. She predicted their future would involve revealing a great truth, but she cautioned they would also need protection. I did not think it was more than my subconscious wishing to see Amanda again."

Anne asked in a tone filled with great concern, "What sort of danger, Glenn?"

"Lucius and his demons will want to silence God's prophets. They will not like anyone confronting the false prophet's deceptions and lies."

Sheriff Hill tapped the top of the oak pew with his finger. "There is one thing that occurs to me."

"What's that?" Jack asked.

"David and Louis's true identity. It must still be intact. Otherwise, the Strigoi most surely would have killed them by now."

The sheriff sat beside Jack and placed his hand on his shoulder. "I could not tell you this earlier, but Father Desmond informed me about who your sons are right before you arrived in town. The Order has been shadowing all of you to protect Louis and David. The man who rammed the boat into the shark before it could attack them, J.J. Haller, is part of the Brotherhood. We work together, and he is a good friend of mine. I am sorry, but trust you understand my reasons for not disclosing this to you until now."

Jack's thoughts became a torrent of questions. *J.J. Haller. All this talk of destiny. Was it his destiny to be possessed by Lucius Rofocale?* Jack wondered. *How many casualties would there need to be on this road to heaven?*

"Glenn, there is no easy way to tell you this, but your friend is gone."

"What do you mean, gone?"

"After the boat incident you were referencing, I met J.J. Haller to thank him for saving the boys. Unfortunately, the figure I met revealed himself to be Lucius Rofocale, the leader of Lucifer's demon legions here on Earth. J.J. Haller is possessed, Sheriff."

Sheriff Hill flinched as if punched in the gut. "J.J. had confided in me that he was struggling with his faith. But I never thought it would lead to this. The Order warns us that casualties are inevitable."

Looking at Anne, Sheriff Hill pleaded, "Isn't there something we can do?"

"I'm sorry, Sheriff. I wish I had something encouraging to tell you, but my experience with possession cases is always the same. It ends in death for the possessed. Always."

Jack interrupted, "I know this is a lot for all of us to process, but it is late. We could all use some rest. I think we are going to need it. I'll head to Ingold tomorrow morning and look for some more answers."

"I'm going to see Constantin Antonescu again," Anne announced. "His daughter's life is in danger, and in not so many words, Wallace implied Antonescu knows more about all of this than he has let on. It is time for him to come clean about it."

Sheriff Hill placed his hand firmly on Jack's shoulder. "The Order and I will protect your boys at all costs, even if it means our lives. I will also have guards here at the hospital. They will be undercover, but here if the need arises. I will make all these arrangements personally and let you know if anything changes with your brother's condition."

Jack thanked the sheriff and went to George's room. George was asleep, and Jack sat in a chair beside the bed. As he watched his brother resting, Jack contemplated what lay ahead for Louis and David. *God, I realize that your choice of my children to be your prophets should be considered an honor beyond words. After all, who am I to question your judgment? However, if I am being truthful, I must tell you that it is a destiny I don't want for them.*

Chapter 19

August 20th
Antonescu Family Compound, Lake Waccamaw, NC
12:15 p.m.

Just as Anne turned the corner and approached the Antonescu mansion, her phone began to ring. She considered answering it, but since she was almost at the front entrance, she allowed it to go to her voice mail. Anne pulled up to the compound's security gate, and armed guards surrounded her car. One of them gestured that she should lower her window. Anne complied with the request, and the leader questioned her curtly. "What is your business here? The Antonescus are not receiving any visitors."

Anne flashed her badge. "Inform Mr. Antonescu that Detective Anne Bishop is here to see him. Tell him this is not a request."

The other guards watched Anne as the leader spoke into his walkie-talkie. The security gate opened, and the leader waved Anne into the compound. As she pulled up the drive toward the mansion, she could not help but notice that the place was crawling with more armed security personnel. It was clear that the Antonescus were trying to keep someone or perhaps something out. The heightened security level confirmed Anne's suspicions about Constantin Antonescu. It made Anne more determined than ever to uncover what he was hiding.

Anne parked the car and reached for her phone. Before she could check the message, Constantin Antonescu was standing beside her car door. Anne could tell by his facial expression that he was not pleased to see her. She pulled the door handle, and as she pushed the door open, she heard, "It did not take long for you to get here, but I suppose I should not be surprised."

Constantin's blunt statement caught Anne off guard. *Why would he not be surprised by her visit?*

"I'm sorry, Mr. Antonescu, but I don't understand what you mean."

Constantin eyed Anne disbelievingly. "You're here about Chief Bassett's murder, are you not?"

Anne was stunned. Chief Bassett. Dead? Anne's police instincts quickly took over. She slammed the car door behind her and spoke calmly. "I was unaware of it, Mr. Antonescu."

Anne thought about the phone call and wondered if this bad news was the subject of the message she had received a few minutes ago.

"What happened?"

"I thought you were here to tell me, Detective," Constantin answered as they headed toward the front door. "I only heard early this morning that Chief Bassett is dead."

Anne's phone rang again, and a text message immediately followed. As Anne swiped the screen to answer the phone, she asked Constantin, "Is there somewhere in private I can take this call?"

Constantin Antonescu ushered Anne into his study and closed the doors behind him.

"This is Detective Bishop."

She instantly knew who was on the other end. "Anne, it's Glenn Hill. I have some unfortunate news, and there is no good way to tell you this, so I am just going to say it, Chief Bassett is dead."

"Constantin Antonescu just informed me." Anne said with concern. "What do we know, boss?"

"His mutilated body was found floating in Lake Waccamaw this morning."

"Mutilated?"

"Yes. The body was headless. It appears as if someone had tried to weigh the body down, unsuccessfully. Fortunately, the animals had not yet gotten to the body, and since the Chief was in law enforcement, the state police could identify his body by the fingerprints on file."

"There's one more thing, Anne. They found a second body at the scene."

The phone line went silent before Sheriff Hill continued. "The body had no blood left in it."

Anne winced. "That's five victims. We're running out of time."

"Do what you do best, Anne. Keep working the case, and let's hope that Jack finds something in Ingold that can help us."

"Speaking of Jack. Any update on his brother's condition?"

"I won't lie to you. Jack's brother is in and out of consciousness. His condition is deteriorating."

Anne sighed. "I'll be in touch."

She was slipping her phone back into her pocket when it began to vibrate. Anne had forgotten all about the text and the other message, and she pulled the phone back out and read the text.

Anne. Please call. Have news to share. Jack.

Anne listened to the voice mail, which had also been from Jack. He had information about George's situation to share with her. He sounded optimistic, which led Anne to think that he was likely unaware of George's worsening condition.

Anne peered out of the study's glass doors and saw Constantin Antonescu in the hallway with a drink in his hand. *A little early in the day for a drink, perhaps, but* Anne thought right now one sounded pretty good. She decided to return Jack's call first, then confront Constantin Antonescu. She hit the return call feature on her phone. It began to ring.

***

August 20th
U.S. 701 N, nearing Ingold, NC
12:45 p.m.

It was a beautiful day with bright sunshine. The driving conditions were perfect. The time had gone by quickly, and he was already on the outskirts of Ingold. Jack had not seen another car in quite some time, which told him he was out in the middle of nowhere. He was thankful for the solitude. It gave him time to think about what Louis and David had told him earlier that morning.

Jack scanned the road ahead for a sign telling him he was approaching Wright Bridge Road. He needed to make a right turn where U.S. Route 701 N, the road he was currently traveling on, intersected with it. According to the GPS, Ingold was only a quarter of a mile down the road once making the turn. The Internet search revealed very little information about Ingold. It was a tiny town, and despite the apparent importance it now assumed due to the spirit of Mark Desmond's guidance, its insignificant size left Jack wondering what he could find there that would be of any use.

Before heading to Ingold, he had left Josephine at the hospital with George and stopped to check in on Louis and David. As was usual, the boys were up early. Jack's nieces and nephew were still asleep, and he found Louis making breakfast for his brother.

Before his brain could generate another thought, Jack's cell phone rang. He had sent Anne a text earlier, then left her a voice mail and hoped that this was her returning his call.

Jack touched the hands-free button on the steering wheel. "Hello."

"Hi, Jack. I got your text and message. I'm at the Antonescu house. What's going on?"

"Am I interrupting anything important, Anne?"

"Not at all. At least not yet anyway."

"I'll try to make this quick. I stopped by George's house to see Louis and David, and they told me something quite remarkable."

Jack caught his breath and continued. "They told me Amanda was there last night and spoke to them."

Only hours ago, a statement like this would have seemed peculiar. But after seeing Mark Desmond's spirit, it was something she accepted without question.

"What did she tell them?" Anne whispered, looking around the room to ensure no one was listening in on their conversation.

"She told them a little more about their future, and in her own words, told them *they will change the world.*"

"All of this is just unbelievable, Jack. I am still trying to get my head around it all."

"You and me both, but she had something more to say. The boys asked her questions about the Strigoi and George."

Anne was already hanging on Jack's every word, but something about this statement piqued her interest even more.

"And? What is it, Jack?"

Jack was unable to temper his enthusiasm. "Amanda told them something that sounds like a possible cure for a Strigoi bite. I know it is cryptic, but it is more than we had to go on previously. She told them, *the vile waters of the river Styx, a Strigoi bite they say will fix. The blood of man, it will congeal. The river water is said to heal.*"

"The River Styx is the river of death in Greek mythology," Anne stated. "It sounds like she was saying that there are some healing properties associated with the water."

Anne paused. "Jack, the River Styx is a myth, isn't it?"

"I thought the same thing, but before I left for Ingold, I searched on my phone and found articles indicating that modern science believes the Mavroneri River in Greece is the mythical River Styx. Even if this turns out to be the real River Styx, there is another problem."

"Of course, there is," Anne fumed. "Besides the obvious, our being thousands of miles from this Mavroneri River. What is the problem?"

"The water is probably poisonous."

Anne thought for a moment. "Do you remember how Mark always talked about the balance between good and evil?"

"Yes. I remember."

"Well, perhaps, a toxic bite from an evil entity like a Strigoi is only curable by something equally toxic. In this situation, maybe that is how the virus is neutralized and puts things back in balance, so to speak."

"That has to be it, Anne!" Jack exclaimed. "It is the only way what Amanda shared makes any sense!"

Anne checked down the hall and saw Constantin Antonescu approaching.

"Jack, I must go. Antonescu is coming. We'll pick this discussion up again later, for sure."

"Sounds good, Anne, and good luck with Antonescu."

***

During the phone conversation with Anne, Jack had made the required right turn onto Wright Bridge Road. He pulled the car onto the shoulder in front of the only structure he could see for miles around; a dilapidated plantation-style house with an abandoned cemetery next to it. Jack removed the key from the ignition. He opened the door and felt a blast of hot air hit him in the face. It was now mid-day and already well above ninety degrees. The humidity was high, and Jack began to sweat instantly.

He surveyed the decaying structure before him. It was apparent from its look that no one had lived there for a long time. Where windows had once been, gaping holes left the structure's interior exposed to the elements. Wisteria vines encircled the porch columns, making it seem like they were choking the building. The few shingles left on the roof were flapping up and down with the breeze.

To his right, Jack noticed a cemetery, overgrown with brown grass and dense brush that hid the tombstones from view. Rust covered the wrought iron fence surrounding the graveyard. The only sound heard was the shaking leaves on a large oak tree adjacent to the cemetery. In front of him, he saw something in the grass. Jack picked up the road sign and read it; *Town of Ingold. Population 424. Population 424? I haven't even seen a sign of one person, let alone 424.*

A feeling of uneasiness swept over Jack as he quickly did the math in his head. *2 + 4=6. 4+2=6 4+4-2=6.* A shudder went down Jack's back as he thought…666. The scene reminded him too much of the Bradford home and family cemetery in Culpeper. But time was of the essence, so he took a deep breath and started toward the graveyard. He hoped to find evidence there to tell him who once owned this house. More importantly, he hoped to find some reference to Samuel Domjen.

***

August 20th
Squad Car outside Aitken Home, N. Myrtle Beach, SC
12:45 p.m.

"That's right, Brother Dickerson. I want to double the security detail at the Aitken residence. We need to protect those boys at all costs. Equip the rest of the team with silver bullets, and if you or any of the other Brothers see anything—I mean *anything*—suspicious, you shoot to kill. If you need anything else, call me. Over and out."

Sheriff Hill put the radio handset back in its holder and grasped the steering wheel tightly with both hands. While he was at the hospital earlier that day, it was apparent from observing Josephine Aitken's demeanor that George Aitken's condition was getting worse. Having seen what happened to Robert Wallace after being bitten by the Strigoi, he was very nervous that something similar might happen to George. Sheriff Hill was unsure of how quickly such a transformation might occur, and having failed to reach Jack, the sheriff took no chances and brought in all the reinforcements from Logos Confraternity that he could muster.

Hill wanted to warn Jack about George's apparent decline and the necessary measures he might have to take to protect Louis and David. Safeguarding Louis and David Aitken was the primary objective of his organization, and they would do whatever they had to do to protect the boys. That included killing their uncle if he became a threat. Unfortunately, his calls to Jack had gone to voice mail.

I wish J.J. were here right now. In addition to being the sheriff's most trusted friend, J.J. was a valuable advisor regarding tactics. J.J. had been a Navy SEAL, and the extensive training J.J. received while in the military would be of great assistance to the sheriff right now. The news that a demon now possessed J.J. was hard for Sheriff Hill to swallow. Until now, the sheriff had not had time to consider this tragic piece of information, and thinking about it made him furious.

J.J.'s faith may have been shaky recently, but Sheriff Hill believed he deserved a fate better than the one he must be experiencing. *If I were the one possessed, what would J.J. do right now?* Glenn Hill asked that question in his mind repeatedly. He finished the last gulp of coffee and hesitated before putting down the cup. While his head told him that they both knew the risks of being part of Lagos Confraternity, in his heart, Glenn knew somebody must do something for J.J. He could not just leave his best friend to a fate that would end in damnation. At least not without a fight.

Grabbing his cell phone, the sheriff quickly typed out a message and hit the send button. He started the car and pushed the accelerator to the floor, causing the rear wheels to spin rapidly. The friction of the rubber tires on the asphalt road generated a cloud of smoke, and the car fishtailed as he pulled away. The message he sent reached Jack and Anne's inboxes.

I doubled security measures for Louis and David. I think I know where to look. On my way to find this Lucius Rofocale and try to save J.J. GBWU. Glenn

***

August 20th
Antonescu Family Compound, Lake Waccamaw, NC
1:00 p.m.

Anne's frustration level with Constantin Antonescu was growing by the minute. For the past half-hour, he had deflected every question she had asked him. He repeatedly refused to admit he knew Detective Robert Wallace or why the Detective would even mention his name. However, when Anne told him Wallace was dead, Constantin grew agitated.

"People seem to die frequently after associating with you, Detective," Constantin sarcastically asserted while trying to change the subject. "I do hope you aren't carrying anything catching."

"Mr. Antonescu," Anne snapped. "I can say the same thing about you! Need I remind you that you knew Chief Bassett far longer than I did, and Ms. Romero was your employee? Do you think I am blind? I see all the armed security guards around the compound, and I know fear when I see and feel it, Mr. Antonescu. I have seen it in the faces of many people. I see it in yours."

Constantin's hands trembled, and the ice in his glass echoed like someone shaking dice before rolling them in a game of craps. Constantin made his way over to the liquor cabinet in the living room and poured himself another glass of Tuica.

Constantin saw Anne Bishop watching him and held up the empty bottle. "Tuica is unique to Romania. It once was considered only a drink for peasants. They distill it from plums. I have it imported directly from Bucharest. It is an acquired taste, but you should try it sometime, Detective."

Anne felt a vibration from her phone and pulled it from her pocket. She saw the text message and softly repeated it: *"On my way to find this Lucius Rofocale and try to save J.J."*

"Oh, God! He's going after Lucius."

Constantin froze. "What about Lucius?"

Anne looked directly into the face of Constantin, whose eyes were wide open. His complexion was pale, as if all at once, the blood had rushed out of his head. There was no longer the look of fear on Constantin Antonescu's face. It was a look of sheer terror.

"What do you know about Lucius Rofocale?" Anne demanded. "Antonescu, I can't help you if you don't talk to me."

Constantin regained his composure and turned away from Anne, muttering, "Help me? You can't help me. No one can."

Constantin stopped and stood in the middle of the room like a statue. He just kept mumbling, "Lucius. Why? What did I do? I did it...."

Anne grabbed Constantin Antonescu's arm. "What is it? What did you do?"

Constantin was jolted back to reality, shaking off Anne's hand. "You need to go now, Detective. No more questions."

Anne persisted. "What do you know about Lucius? How do you know Lucius Rofocale?"

Constantin Antonescu turned and faced Anne. Then he waved his hand dismissively. "I don't know what you're talking about, Detective."

Before Anne Bishop could speak another word, Constantin screamed, "GET OUT! DIDN'T YOU HEAR ME? GET OUT!"

Anne automatically retreated. Constantin Antonescu's face took on the look of a caged animal. Both fear and rage emanated from his being. Anne realized that he was beyond help. Whatever his dealings with Lucius Rofocale were, he was bound to them. Anne could see there was no chance of redemption for Constantin Antonescu.

Two Antonescu security team members had heard his scream and escorted Anne from the study.

***

From a second entrance to the study, Maria Antonescu had been a silent witness to Anne and Constantin's conversation. She heard Anne's car door slamming and the crunch of her tires on the pea gravel driveway. She quietly entered the room and approached her husband, who stood in the middle of the room, pensively staring into space.

"Constantin."

Constantin was startled by her voice. He turned and asked in an exhausted tone, "Yes, Maria. What is it?"

"Why didn't you tell her? Perhaps she could help you? Help us?"

Constantin shook his head. "Maria, you don't know what Lucius Rofocale is capable of doing? There is no way out of this."

Constantin sighed. "I should have seen the devil I was dealing with when I first met him."

He sighed ruefully, feeling sorry for himself. "I guess Albert Speer was right." Referring to Albert Speer, Adolf Hitler's architect and Minister of Armaments. *"One seldom recognizes the devil when he is putting his hand on your shoulder."*

Constantin turned away from Maria and continued contemplating his fate. Maria knew better than to continue speaking with Constantin when he was like this and left the room. She headed to the kitchen for a cup of tea, thinking *there must be a way I could save our family from all of this. But how?*

***

August 20th
Woods outside Antonescu Compound, Lake Waccamaw, NC
6:00 p.m.

Sheriff Hill walked for hours through the pine forest surrounding Lake Waccamaw. He took a long gulp of water from his canteen and checked the monitor for the signal he had been following. The indicator on his GPS had finally stopped moving, and he knew he was close to its location. He weakly laughed, thinking that *even J.J. would have been impressed with this plan.*

While driving to Lake Waccamaw, his thoughts had been about what he would do if he came face-to-face with the Strigoi. He hoped his silver bullets would be as successful in killing the Strigoi as they had been on Robert Wallace, but he knew there was no way to be sure they would be effective. He also had to consider what he would do if he confronted Lucius Rofocale. Sheriff Hill had missed demonology class but sensed that Lucius would be no ordinary adversary. Regardless, he was determined to rescue J.J. at all costs. But he knew he needed to find him first, and this idea was his best one yet.

Hill reasoned that the Strigoi would need a remote lair, one not easy to find. Along with privacy, the sheriff thought of a cave or a structure that would protect it from the weather. That was when he noticed the bats. While bats were usually active from dusk until dawn, they sometimes came out during the day if their roosting area was too warm. These bats, however, were juveniles that had somehow become separated from their mother. It gave him the idea for what he called *Operation Nightwing*.

The sheriff captured one of the young bats and attached a device to its leg to track with his watch's GPS app. If the plan worked as he thought it might, the bat would continue to search for its mother and, hopefully, make it back to its roost. Initially, the bat was very disoriented, but eventually, it started to fly in one direction. Since the signal had stopped, Sheriff Hill took out his binoculars and searched the area for a likely location for the bat to stay. So far, he saw nothing but a large house surrounded by dense trees and a tall fence.

The house was opulent but not out of place with the neighborhood and other homes Sheriff Hill had seen when he arrived in Lake Waccamaw. One dominant feature of the landscape was Lake Waccamaw itself. There was a dock extending into the lake from the property's shoreline. A tall grouping of cattails, close to the shore, obscured his view of the home's foundation, which was relatively close to the water.

Birds were flying around that area, and the sheriff scanned it closely. What appeared at first sight to be birds were bats!

"There must be an entrance of some kind under the house," Sheriff Hill muttered.

He slid the binoculars back into their container and began to search for a way to get to the opening. Glenn Hill knew this was something he had to investigate.

***

August 20th
Somewhere on NC Route 701 S
9:00 p.m.

Jack sat impatiently at a deserted intersection, waiting for a green light. He found it difficult to resist the temptation to run the red light, but at this point, he didn't want to risk getting caught by a traffic stop. To say that the last few hours had been bizarre was an understatement. Suddenly, his phone, which was not working for the past hour, began to ring.

"Hello," Jack answered in a tone filled with surprise and frustration. "This is Jack."

"Jack. Where have you been?" Anne Bishop asked with a sound of relief. "I've been calling for hours. It would ring, and then the line would go dead."

"I don't know what is going on, Anne. This phone had a dead battery. At least that was what I thought, and then it began to ring. I am still about thirty minutes away from the hospital. How are the boys?"

"Louis and David are fine. They are still at your brother's house. Daphne is keeping an eye on them."

Jack nodded. "Thank you for looking in on them, Anne. I appreciate it. I am sure that Daphne is keeping everyone entertained. Where are you now?"

"I am at the hospital. I've been sitting with Josephine."

Anne took a deep breath. "Jack, George isn't doing well. He is in and out of consciousness. His limbs are rigid. The doctors are unsure but think paralysis might be setting in."

Jack mumbled, "We're running out of time, aren't we?"

"Jack, I got nowhere with Constantin Antonescu. He knows Lucius. I pressed him for answers, but he threw me out of the house. The compound is like an armed camp. He is afraid and, with good reason, based on what you and I know."

"Great," Jack uttered sarcastically. "This just keeps getting better and better."

"I'm afraid it gets worse, Jack," Anne added ruefully. "Sheriff Hill isn't here either."

"What?" Jack was open-mouthed.

"His text indicated he went to Lake Waccamaw to find his friend, J.J. Haller. We didn't have time to tell him much about Lucius. No matter how careful he is, I'm afraid he is unprepared for what he may face."

A hush came over the car as Jack focused on the road. Anne broke the silence. "Jack, are you still there?"

"I'm still here. I tell you, Anne, my day was as bizarre as yours was disappointing. I'm still trying to figure out what the hell happened."

As Jack prepared to tell Anne what occurred in Ingold, his mind drifted back to a few hours earlier.

***

Ingold, North Carolina, Earlier That Day

Jack had spent the past hour searching through the cemetery with no success. The overgrown brush in and around the graveyard made it nearly inaccessible, and the wind had weathered the words on the crumbling grave markers beyond recognition. Since the burial ground had yielded no answers, Jack turned his attention to the adjacent dilapidated house. As he made his way toward the opening, which used to be the front door, he couldn't help but be surprised that the building was still standing.

The noise of each step Jack made on the floorboards sounded more like groans than creaks. It was like the house was suffering tremendous pain from every move he made. Jack peered up the stairs in the main hallway, but the gaping holes in the staircase were confirmation that it was far too dangerous to attempt to investigate the second floor. Glancing around the main floor, Jack found it hard to imagine that the home was once an elegant mansion rather than the crumbling structure it had become.

The smell of rotting wood and mildew was pervasive, as was the dust and the cobwebs that hung everywhere. The broken pieces of furniture and shards of glass littering the floor made moving around the house hazardous. Jack explored the rooms on the ground floor but found nothing. Just more trash and animal droppings. There was no sign of anything related to Samuel Domjen, Samuel Adams, or Samuel L. Jackson, for that matter. Jack sat down, carefully, on the front steps, dejected. His shoulders slumped, and he stared at the ground, thinking of his brother.

It was hard for Jack to explain, but George was more than his brother. Being identical twins cemented a unique bond between them. Yes, sometimes they had been the fiercest of competitors. They beat the crap out of one another more than a few times, but ultimately, they were always there for each other. Despite only being ten minutes older, George had taken it upon himself to be Jack's protector. George never looked for trouble but wouldn't back down from anyone or anything. Anyone messing with Jack was messing with him.

But now, their roles were reversed, and George needed Jack to be his protector. He needed Jack to figure out how to heal his wound. Jack was in Ingold to find a cure but had nothing. He was growing desperate. He tried to think about what to do but was too disappointed to think straight. Jack didn't notice the odor right away, but an aroma of smoke began to permeate the air. Jack got on his feet. There was a fire burning somewhere close. For some reason, he couldn't explain; he needed to know from where it was emanating.

***

Jack passed a road sign indicating that the next two miles were subject to frequent deer crossings, which along with the pitch blackness of the night, made Jack increasingly vigilant as he continued to fill Anne in on the strange events of the day.

"After I smelled smoke, I followed the odor, and it led me to the rear of the house. Turning the corner, I saw two weathered doors to the cellar and wisps of gray smoke escaping through the cracks."

"That's weird, Jack."

"It got much, much weirder. I could see a glow, like something you might see radiating from a fire in a hearth. I couldn't see anything else, so I carefully opened the doors. It revealed wooden stairs that went down into the cellar."

"Go on, Jack. What happened next?"

"When I started downstairs, I could still smell smoke, but also an overwhelming aroma of mildew and mold. It is hard to describe, other than to say it smelled of decay. Opening the cellar doors was like unsealing a container someone buried long ago. I suppose it smelled like opening a tomb."

Jack was silent for a moment. "Anne, I still can't believe what happened next, but when I got to the bottom of the stairs, a fire was burning on the dirt floor in the middle of the room."

"A fire?" Anne questioned in a shocked tone. "Why was there a fire there?"

"The question turned out not to be why the fire was there, but who was sitting next to it."

"Jack, did you say there was someone in the basement? Did I hear you, right?"

"You did. An elderly, no, an ancient man, was sitting by the fire. He was dressed in rags and had a long ratty white beard. One of his eyes drooped to the point of almost being closed. The thing is, he never really acknowledged that I was there. He was speaking gibberish. Nothing he was saying seemed to make any sense."

"That is unbelievable," Anne gasped. "Do you remember anything else?"

"It was hard to understand him. He would chuckle and laugh to himself between words. Fortunately, I had a pen on me and found a scrap of paper. I wrote down what I thought I heard. The first thing I recall him saying was *1737 Misbegotten.*"

Anne interjected, "That means nothing to me at all."

"Me either." Jack struggled to read the words on the paper in his hand.

"Then he spoke the following in quick succession. One right after the other."

Jack read the letters. "*O-l-t. V-a-s-c-e-a. O-l-t-e-n-i-a. R-a-m-n-i-u.* I'm hoping I spelled them right."

"Let me do a quick check on my phone. Give me a minute."

"Okay." Jack reached the outskirts of Shallotte and turned onto Route 17 South toward his brother's house and the hospital.

Anne returned, filled with enthusiasm. "Jack, there is a Valcea County in Romania."

"I knew I probably spelled something wrong." Jack shook his head. "Anything else?"

"These all seem to be places in Romania."

"How about *Ashram NonaKris*? Does that ring any bells?"

"I've heard the word, Ashram. It is usually associated with Hinduism. It is another phrase for a religious retreat. I don't know about NonaKris."

Anne quickly added, "Wait. Listen to this. NonaKris is a region of Greece. It is reputed to be the source for the River Styx."

"What? So, whoever this person said this area is a religious retreat? Louis and David were talking about the River Styx. They insisted Amanda told them about it."

"That seems more than coincidental, Jack. Is there more?"

"Yes. The next thing I wrote down was *Eden. Dominion over animals. Ben was a thaumaturgist.*"

"I would say he was referring to Adam and Eve, but who's Ben?" Questioned Anne.

"I don't know. But the last thing the old man yelled out was w*all and mezuzah.*"

"Jack, a mezuzah is a talisman of sorts. Jewish families often hang it on a wall outside of a residence to ward off evil."

"That explains it!" Jack shouted. "I thought the symbols were familiar. They must be Hebrew."

"I'm not following you. What are you referring to, Jack?"

"Sorry. It is a metal object of some kind. It was on the wall. I picked it up after the man pointed at it. It was the only time we had anything that resembled a real interaction. I kept asking him questions like what his name was, but he never answered me."

"I'll look at it when you get here. If I can't figure it out, I might have some old contacts at JESU that I could covertly ask about it. Was that it, Jack? Did anything else happen?"

Jack pulled in front of his brother's house and shut off the car. He took a deep breath before he answered Anne.

"This is the strangest part of the whole thing, Anne. It was beyond bizarre. I have no explanation for it."

"What happened?" Anne asked with a concerned tone.

"As soon as I took the mezuzah off the wall, everything disappeared!"

"Disappeared?!"

"I don't know, Anne. One minute, I was in the basement, and the next minute I am standing next to the abandoned cemetery, and the entire house is gone."

"G-gone?" Anne stuttered.

"Yes, gone. There was only the foundation left. Not only was the house not there, but I know I couldn't have been in it for more than a few minutes, and I checked my watch, and it was more than five hours later!"

There was a long period of silence as the two friends struggled to comprehend Jack's experience in Ingold and what it meant.

"Anne, I made it to George's house, and I'm going in to check on Louis and David. Then I'll head over to the hospital. I'll bring this object with me. Tell me, how is my brother?"

"When you get here, I'll fill you in on my meeting with Constantin Antonescu."

"And my brother?" a concerned Jack asked.

Anne paused and answered, "Hurry."

Chapter 20

August 20th
Antonescu Family Compound, Lake Waccamaw, NC
10:00 p.m.

Constantin Antonescu knelt and placed another log in the fireplace. It was the middle of summer, but the shivers running up and down Constantin's spine were chilling him to the bone. He stepped back and observed the flames in the hearth. He gulped down the brandy in his glass, a glass that had rarely been empty the entire day. After the amount of alcohol he consumed, Constantin should not have been able to stand up, but his senses were on high alert. He could not have relaxed, even if he were able to do so.

"Mr. Antonescu," the security guard interrupted the silence. "There is a Reid Bowman at the front gate to see Maricela. Do you want me to send him away?"

Constantin stopped and considered the guard's question. He never cared much for Reid but did not dislike the boy either. Frankly, no one would ever be good enough for his little girl. *Sweet Maricela.* Constantin thought to himself. Suddenly, Constantin felt a wave of remorse wash over him.

"Escort him up to the house."

"Yes, sir."

The guard turned and left the room, and Constantin returned to the bar to fill his glass. As he poured the brandy into his tumbler, his thoughts drifted back to eighteen years earlier, when his destiny changed forever.

***

"Please come in, Mr. Rofocale." Constantin stepped aside, allowing his guest to enter. "It is good to see you again."

"Certainly," Lucius Rofocale uttered. "It is indeed my pleasure."

"May I offer you a drink? Scotch, bourbon, or perhaps a glass of wine?"

"A glass of red wine would be lovely," Lucius replied.

Constantin poured a Domaine Leroy Musigny Grand Cru Burgundy into a fishbowl-shaped glass and handed it to Lucius.

Lucius sipped the wine. "My compliments, Constantin. The wine is exceptional."

"Only the best, Lucius." Constantin nervously held up his glass. "Here is to a profitable relationship."

The two men drank to seal their deal.

***

At least, that was what Constantin believed at the time. Mesmerized by the flames of the fireplace, Constantin's ruminating continued.

***

"About that," Lucius stated. "There is one formality to address, Mr. Antonescu."

Constantin remarked, "Of course, Lucius. Anything. Your capital infusion is vital to my company, and I know all your sage advice will make us successful beyond our wildest dreams."

Constantin paused and continued, "With our financial future secure, we'll be ready to pursue the power that comes with higher office."

"Yes. Yes. Constantin. We'll get to that."

Lucius reached into his pocket and pulled out a piece of parchment paper. He unfolded it and placed it on the table in front of Constantin.

"Read it carefully, Constantin," Lucius cautioned. "Be sure it is what you want."

Constantin scanned the document and looked up at Lucius's eyes, glowing a fiery red. Lucius also had a most unpleasant smile *on his face. Deep down inside, Constantin knew what he was doing was wrong, but his company was on the brink of bankruptcy, and his wife, Maria, was pregnant with their seventh daughter. Constantin had managed to run the business his family had built into the ground and never would be able to live with the shame of failure. His father never believed in Constantin, and he would prove him wrong!*

Constantin had spent months searching for venture capitalists to invest in his company and his vision for the future. No one had been willing to take a chance on such a highly leveraged company. That is until Lucius Rofocale introduced himself to Constantin. He could not even remember exactly where or when he met Lucius, but it was immediately apparent that Lucius had the financial wherewithal and insight that Constantin needed.

After a brief negotiation, Lucius's only condition seemed odd, but Constantin managed to find a way to justify it. They would name their new baby Maricela, and when she turned eighteen, she would go to live with Lucius. Constantin attempted to ask Lucius about his contract terms, but that was the first time he saw Lucius's dark side.

"That is my business, Constantin," Lucius coldly declared. "It is only on a need-to-know basis, and you do not need to know. Understand?"

***

"Maybe she still can run away and escape him," Constantin mumbled.

Unfortunately, what happened next should have made Constantin reconsider. It should have made him run for the hills, but the temptation of what Lucius was offering was too much for Constantin to reject. Constantin began to tremble, thinking about the end of the meeting. He guzzled down the brandy in his glass.

***

"I'm onboard, Lucius." Constantin's voice quivered. "I'm ready."

Suddenly, Lucius grabbed Constantin's hand, except Lucius's hand wasn't a hand at all. It was a CLAW! He roughly pulled Constantin's finger over the parchment and pricked it with a talon on his finger. As the drops of blood spilled onto the document, Lucius demanded that Constantin sign his name on it. Too scared to refuse, Constantin sealed the document with his bloody signature.

"Excellent, Constantin," Lucius gloated triumphantly. "Excellent."

Lucius swallowed the rest of his wine and folded the document, placing it back in his pocket.

"You will find that I have already deposited the agreed-upon funds into your banking institution."

Lucius reached into his jacket and handed a folder to Constantin.

"This is a list of the companies you will purchase, Constantin, to create your media empire. Follow my instructions to the letter, and you will quickly acquire the wealth I promised you."

Lucius got up from his chair and headed for the door.

He turned to face Constantin and smiled menacingly. "We will not see one another again until I come to collect Maricela."

After Lucius's departure, Constantin, his hands trembling, finished his drink and hit the intercom, telling his secretary, "I'm leaving for the day."

***

Constantin arrived home and found Maria lying on the den couch. Nearly nine months pregnant with their seventh child, Maria had sought some much-needed rest before their new arrival. She immediately could tell that something was not quite right.

"Constantin, what is wrong? Did the meeting not go well?" Maria asked.

Constantin thought carefully before replying, "It was a challenging negotiation, Maria."

"How much did he demand from you?" Maria questioned.

***

Just then, a sound broke Constantin's train of thought. Reid Bowman stuck his head into the room. "Good evening Mr. Antonescu."

"Yes, Reid," Constantin replied. "Maricela is upstairs."

Reid waved and headed to the stairs. Constantin's thoughts immediately returned to how he had responded to Maria's question.

***

"A great deal," Constantin whispered to Maria. *"He demanded a great deal."*

***

August 20th
Brunswick Medical Center, Bolivia, NC
10:30 p.m.

Jack slowly made his way to the waiting area down the hall from his brother's room, and once there, a combination of fatigue and extreme worry caused him almost to fall rather than sit in a chair. Jack leaned backward and rubbed his fingers across the sandpaper-like stubble on his chin. An overwhelming feeling of helplessness began to set in, and Jack tried not to panic. George had fallen into a coma, and the outlook was bleak. The doctors were saying it was just a matter of time.

Jack's sister-in-law, Josephine, approached. "May I sit with you?"

"Certainly, Jo."

Josephine sat next to Jack. The black bags under her eyes betrayed her exhaustion. They sat together, not uttering a word, for what seemed like an eternity. Eventually, Jack broke the silence between them.

"Jo, I am so sorry for all of this. I know this is no consolation to you or the kids, but George is a hero. He saved David and Louis's lives."

A tear fell from Josephine's eye. "There is nothing to be sorry about, Jack. You know, George and I have talked about you so many times over the years."

Jack sat up with a slightly surprised look on his face. "About what?"

"C'mon, Jack. You take the weight of the world on your shoulders. I admire your sense of responsibility. In a world filled with people who want to blame someone else for their problems, you never do. But, at times, you hold yourself accountable for things that are not your fault. This current situation is one of those times."

Jack took a deep breath and struggled to hold back the tears.

"I know you and Anne are doing everything you can to save George."

Jack placed his hand on hers. "You are stronger than you realize. George would be proud of you."

Josephine smiled sadly. "George would tell you that he and I learned a lot about strength by witnessing the struggles you and Amanda went through, particularly what you've had to do since Amanda has been gone. You have no idea, Jack, how much we admire you."

"Amanda was always the strong one, Jo." Jack shifted in his chair. "She was the Rock of Gibraltar in our relationship. I think my survival instinct is mistaken for strength."

"You know," Jack chuckled, "George would say I'm more like a 'wham-it' toy or a Rocky Balboa doll. I don't have the good sense to stay down after being beaten."

"Whatever it is inside of you, Jack, I hope George has some of it too."

"I know my brother, Jo, and he has it. Trust me; he has it."

Jack reached down to tie his shoe. "Besides, he is an Aitken. Surrender is not in our creed!"

***

Across the hall, Jack saw Anne speaking with a man wearing gold wire-rimmed glasses containing thick circular lenses and dressed in black from his shoes to the satin yamaka on top of his head. He appeared to be around fifty years of age with a neatly maintained beard containing splashes of gray mixed among his black hair. The white shawl around the man's shoulders had a stripped blue pattern on each end, and Jack surmised he was a Jewish cleric or Rabbi.

Anne finished speaking to the man, and the two of them approached Jack and Josephine

"Are we interrupting?" Anne asked.

Josephine got up from her chair. "No, Anne. I need to get back to George. They are allowing me to stay in his room tonight."

Hugging her brother-in-law, Josephine whispered, "Jack, remember what we talked about. Don't ever forget it, okay?"

Still moved by Josephine's commending words, Jack cleared his throat. "I promise, Josephine. Thank you. I'll stick around for a while longer in case anything changes or you need something."

Reaching out to Anne's acquaintance, he shook his hand. "I'm Jack. Jack Aitken. It is nice to meet you. And you are?"

"I am Rabbi Shimon Levi. It is a pleasure to meet you as well. I must say I was very intrigued by Anne's message about the mezuzah."

Jack spoke to Anne. "So we found out something about the mezuzah?"

"I arranged for us to use a meeting room." Rabbi Levi pointed toward a door down the corridor. "I thought we might examine it in private."

The room was small, with sanatorium-white paint on the walls. It felt almost claustrophobic. A round, wooden table and several chairs took up most of the space. If not for a painting of a bouquet of daisies hanging on the wall, the room could have been a padded cell in a mental institution.

"I sent a picture of it to a friend at JESU," Anne explained. "And he read the Hebrew inscription on the outside. It read *Shomer Delatot Yisrael*. He texted me. It's in Hebrew and means *Guardian of the Doors of Israel*."

Rabbi Levi added, "That makes sense as the purpose of a mezuzah is to protect a structure and its inhabitants against evil."

Anne continued, "He told me that a mezuzah often has a scroll inserted inside it."

"Is there a scroll on the inside?" Jack asked excitedly.

Anne nodded. "I also sent a picture of that to my friend, but he could not decipher it. He thinks it is an ancient variation of Hebrew. He's never seen it before."

"That is disappointing," Jack sighed. "But, somehow, not surprising."

"I didn't know where to turn," Anne went on, "so I reached out to Rabbi Levi, an associate with the hospital. His online profile indicates he graduated from Hebrew College. It is the premier university for rabbinical studies in the United States. Trust me, if anyone can read it, he can."

***

Anne reached into her pocket and handed the mezuzah to the Rabbi, who meticulously examined it.

"It is quite beautiful." Rabbi Levi carefully studied the symbols on the outside of the religious object.

Holding the mezuzah in the palm of his hand, he commented, "It is fairly heavy. A mezuzah is typically not this substantial."

The creases in the Rabbi's forehead narrowed as he squinted to read the inscription.

"Sorry." The Rabbi removed his glasses. "I'm afraid my vision is not what it used to be. Small words are the bane of my existence these days."

Rabbi Levi turned the mezuzah over.

"I will open it to read the scroll, with your permission, of course."

Jack glanced at Anne. "Please go ahead, Rabbi."

Flipping the tiny clasp on the side of the mezuzah, the Rabbi gently opened the religious artifact. He pulled out a small, yellowed scroll and carefully unrolled it.

"Are you able to read it, Rabbi?" Anne asked.

"This scroll is not paper as you and I know it. The author of a mezuzah scroll writes it on the skin of a kosher animal. This one has inscribed verses from the Torah written in an ancient Hebrew text. These verses come from the book of Deuteronomy, Chapter 6 Verses 4-9 and Chapter 11 Verses 13-21. It is God's charge to write his laws on the doorframes of your home so that you will prosper under the protection of the almighty God of Israel."

"The fact that I found this on the wall of a house in the middle of nowhere isn't unusual?" Jack asked.

"While the location may be odd," Rabbi Levi replied smiling, "This mezuzah is not."

Jack held the mezuzah open as the Rabbi placed the scroll back in the cylinder. "Thank you, Rabbi, for helping us understand what the scroll says."

***

There was a knock at the door. Anne opened it and found a woman standing in the hall with a bundle of papers in her arms. She peeked into the room.

"Mrs. Antonescu?" Anne stood in the doorway, surprised. "What are you doing here?"

"Ms. Bishop, please forgive my intrusion. I called the number on the card you left with Constantin, and the person who answered told me I might find you here at the hospital. An orderly told me you were in here. I must speak with you."

Rabbi Levi got up. "I should get back to looking in on some of the patients. It was nice meeting you both, and thank you for letting me look at the mezuzah."

Rabbi Levi smiled at Mrs. Antonescu as he turned and went down the hallway.

"Mrs. Antonescu, please have a seat."

"I'll leave the two of you alone. I am going to check on George."

Jack offered his seat to Mrs. Antonescu and headed to his brother's room.

"Ms. Bishop. I need your help. My family needs your help."

"Has something happened?" Anne asked with concern. "I saw Constantin today. Your home has become an armed camp."

"He is only trying to protect us."

"Protect you from what?" Anne countered. "He was less than forthcoming. He made it quite clear that he wanted me to leave."

"Constantin is a proud man, Ms. Bishop. What he did, he did for his family."

"And that is?" Anne asked. "Constantin seemed ready to tell me, but then he demanded I get out of the house."

Maria Antonescu's eyes lowered, and she was quiet for several moments.

"Ms. Bishop. I have been married to Constantin for nearly thirty years, but I won't pretend to know everything that goes through his mind."

Maria paused and continued, "Around twenty years ago, Constantin's business was not doing well. In truth, it was on the verge of bankruptcy. Constantin had great ideas for building a media empire but lacked the capital investment to pursue them. Every bank and venture capitalist turned him down. That is except for one."

Anne listened intently. "Go on, Mrs. Antonescu."

"Constantin told me that the man's name was Lucius. He never told me Lucius's last name, but he did say that Lucius made him very nervous. But true to his word, this Lucius immediately transferred all the funding that Constantin needed."

Deep inside, Anne had suspected something like this all along, but hearing it only made her wish she was wrong.

Maria went on. "Constantin's success far exceeded anything we could have imagined. Beautiful homes. Expensive jewelry. Luxury cars. I guess it blinded me to what was happening to Constantin. His ambitions had no limits, and he grew increasingly obsessed with the pursuit of power and influence. Constantin even spoke of seeking political office. Then, about a year ago, something happened."

"What?" Anne asked.

"I overheard a phone conversation between Constantin and Lucius. After that call, Constantin became fixated on protecting Maricela. He tried to stop her from seeing her boyfriend, Reid and insisted that Maricela take a position with Antonescu Communications in Atlanta this fall. This job would keep her far away from Reid, who will attend Duke University."

"Mrs. Antonescu, it isn't unusual for a father to be overly protective of his daughter. I think that might be particularly true of the youngest child."

Mrs. Antonescu shook her head. "There's more, Ms. Bishop. After the phone call, Constantin became intensely interested in importing wine from Romania. He saw the catacombs beneath the house as an ideal wine cellar. Soon after receiving the first few shipments, a strange odor emanated from behind the kitchen door leading to the catacombs. I mentioned it to Constantin, and he became furious. He demanded that I stay away from the door and that I was never to open it."

"Did you go down into the catacombs?"

"I did not have the nerve. I'm unsure if I was more afraid of what I might find or how Constantin would react if he found out. But I am ashamed to say that I searched Constantin's office and found a packing slip from one of the wine shipments. There was something strange on it."

"What did it say, Mrs. Antonescu?" Anne asked with great interest.

"Constantin has not been importing wine from Romania. It is water from Greece. But it is not ordinary water. It is from the River Styx."

"What did you say? Did you say from the River Styx?"

Maria Antonescu shook her head. "That's right. Coming from Eastern Europe, I am well aware of the myth surrounding the River Styx."

Anne was stunned but at the same time excited. She peered down the hallway at the room where George Aitken lay in a coma. She finally had potentially good news to share with Jack. Water from the River Styx could be an antidote to the virulent virus killing Jack's brother, and now there was a possible source within reach.

During their entire conversation, Maria had been cradling a book tightly to her chest. The leather-bound cover was cracking, and the book's distinctive musty smell confirmed its age. The yellowing pages' edges were curling, and the book was bound with leather straps to prevent it from falling apart. Maria presented the book to Anne.

"This book has been in the Antonescu family for generations. It is in a language that I do not recognize. It is not Romanian. I would be able to read it if it were. Perhaps, in this book, you can find the answers to the secret that Constantin is hiding. He is highly protective of it and doesn't know I have taken it."

As Anne examined the book's cover, Maria got up from the chair and stepped toward the door.

"I need to get back before Constantin realizes I'm gone." Maria pleaded. "Ms. Bishop—Anne. Please help us."

"I will do everything I can, Mrs. Antonescu," Anne replied, touching Maria on the arm.

A tear fell down Maria Antonescu's right cheek as she turned and quickly made her way to the elevator. Anne undid the leather straps to the book, opened it to the first page, and began to read.

***

August 20th
Brunswick Medical Center, Bolivia, NC
11:00 p.m.

SINS OF THE FATHERS

Jack Aitken stood at George's bedside in the dark, holding his brother's hand. The only visible light was the green glow of the medical instruments monitoring George's vital signs. Nurses strapped George's arms to the bed for his protection. Violent muscle spasms were just one of the symptoms caused by the rabies virus coursing through his body. George remained in a coma, and his condition continued to deteriorate. The medical staff did everything possible to make him comfortable, but the doctors indicated that George would be gone in a day or two.

"I wish I knew if you could hear me, George. There are things I want to tell you. Something that I need to say to you."

Emotionally, Jack declared, "I am so proud that you are my brother. You have always been there for me...."

***

George was wondering where the tent in the Onteora woods had gone. Had it been a dream? Perhaps he had gone to heaven? At first, he sat with Jack around a campfire, swapping stories about their childhood. The smell of fresh air, pine trees, and smoke from the campfire was unmistakable. Then he was on the Powerline trail; the terrain felt the same. George could walk it blindfolded and quickly found his way to the trading post with the Scout Troop 200 totem pole beside it. George searched for his name etched into it, but the totem pole suddenly disappeared. He was sure he could hear Josephine and his children and even saw their faces, but these images and sounds were becoming more infrequent. George went into the trading post; it was empty. Jack was gone, and the only thing that remained was the darkness.

At first, it surrounded him, but now George sensed the darkness seeping through his skin's pores and invading his soul. The visions of his children were fading, and he struggled to remember their names. George felt locked in his own body. While initially afraid of the silence and the thought that it meant he was dead, he now begged for its return and a respite from the near-constant humming in his ears. The noise reminded him of electricity pulsing through a live wire. George screamed, "STOP!"

***

Jack saw George flinch but dismissed it as another involuntary reflex. He reasoned that there would have been a change in the heart monitor or the blood pressure gauge if it were something else, but neither of these devices fluctuated. They just kept up their steady, monotonous beeping. The beeping rhythm and fatigue caused Jack to zone out for a while. The opening of the door and the sliver of light associated with it brought him back to the present.

"Jack." Anne's voice penetrated the darkness. "May I speak with you?"

Jack patted George's shoulder. "Sure, Anne."

Jack touched George's hand and pulled up the blanket on a sleeping Josephine before following Anne to the waiting room. Anne showed Jack the book that Maria Antonescu had left with her. She opened it to a page that she had marked.

"Jack, Maria Antonescu left this book with me, and you are not going to believe what it is."

Anne's statement immediately stirred Jack's interest. He leaned in to look at the worn leather journal on the table. There were cracks in the cover and strings hanging from the binding. Jack was sure if he tugged on them, the book would go to pieces like a sweater unraveling when the loose yarn is snagged and pulled.

"Jesus, Anne, this book stinks! There must be centuries' worth of mold and mildew on the pages. It looks ready to fall apart. I'm afraid to touch the pages."

Despite the book's condition, Jack was drawn to the text.

"What language is that?" Jack asked. "It's unfamiliar to me."

"It is an old Greek dialect. It is what the Catholic Church used before the split of the Roman Empire into the Western and Eastern kingdoms and the development of Ecclesiastical Latin."

"Odd." Jack slowly ran his fingertips over the print. "The book looks old, but not something you would see from ancient Rome."

Anne seemed surprised. Jack declared, "I've learned something from you and Mark."

"Turns out, you're right, Jack. It is a journal from the 1700s. It begins in 1737, to be exact, and it has entries up until the 1750s."

"I'm not sure I understand." Jack's eyes narrowed. "Who would write a journal in a nearly forgotten language, and why would they do it?"

"Only someone schooled in ancient Greek. Say, someone associated with the church. I've seen this done to limit who would be able to read it. I guess you could say it's a form of secret code."

Anne paused and then dropped a bombshell. "Jack, It's the journal of Father Samuel Domjen."

Jack's jaw dropped open, and he slowly muttered, "Samuel Domjen."

"That's right. Mrs. Antonescu told me it was a family history of the Antonescu family. She was half right. It's Samuel Domjen's journal, but much of it is about the Antonescus. I haven't had time to read all of it, but I can give you a summary of what I know so far."

Jack lowered himself into a chair while Anne pointed to a journal entry.

"In June 1737, the Antonescus left a small village called Ramnicu. I checked it on my phone, and it is in present-day Romania. According to the journal, they arrived in Venice, Italy, in July and left on a ship whose destination was Charleston, South Carolina. By then, Charleston was starting to be an important trading port."

Anne's finger traced the writing in the journal. "Wait, here is another reference to Constantin Antonescu."

Anne continued hesitantly, "Had seven daughters. *The youngest of which was named Maricela and was with child.*"

She looked at Jack. "Seven daughters, just like Constantin and Maria have now. Their youngest daughter is named Maricela, isn't she?"

Jack gulped. "Do you remember what Sheriff Hill told us? Mark had warned him about an ancient curse involving the seventh child of the same gender. The Antonescus have seven girls."

The room seemed to take on an ominous feeling. Like Jack and Anne were heading deeper and deeper into the heart of something dark and profoundly evil.

Anne flipped through the pages of the journal urgently, trying to read as fast as she could.

"The voyage took thirty-two days. Father Domjen indicates nothing unusual occurred during the trip, but one passenger on the ship did make him very uneasy."

Jack asked, "Did he say what his concerns were about the passenger?"

"The passenger was Doctor Lucian Resu. Initially, Father Domjen thought it fortunate to have a doctor on the ship, and naturally, the doctor was happy to look after Maricela. However, the doctor soon became overly interested in her. His exact phrase reads *unnaturally attentive*."

"Are you thinking what I'm thinking?"

Anne shook her head up and down, and the duo spoke in unison. "LUCIUS!"

"Does it say what happened to Maricela?"

I'm looking," Anne answered as she feverishly scanned through page after page. "So far, nothing. There are a series of entries about experiments with electricity. I wish I could understand their meaning, but science was never my best subject in school."

"Wait!" Anne excitedly tapped the book several times with her finger. "I think I found something. This journal entry has letters much larger than the others."

<u>*August 21st, 1737. The Outskirts of Charleston*</u>
MY WORST FEARS HAVE BECOME REALITY! THE HORROR OF HORRORS HAS OCCURRED TODAY! THE CURSE IS REAL! Maricela Antonescu bore not a son or daughter but an abomination. One of Maricela's sons came to town in search of Doctor Resu. I overheard him in Romanian tell the doctor that his

mother was in labor and suffering incredible pain. It turns out my suspicion of Dr. Resu was well-founded.

The doctor is no physician. He is my arch-nemesis, the enemy of humanity; he is the demon lord Lucius Rofocale! When I arrived at the Antonescu farm, what I saw was hideous. The very thought of it sickens me still. As hard as I try, I will never be able to forget it for as long as I live.

Maricela lay sprawled on the table. Her head turned sideways, her mouth agape and eyes wide open, just staring into space. This expression was not the face of a mother experiencing the joy of childbirth but of someone who was terrified. Blood was everywhere. Maricela's womb had burst. It was as if something clawed its way through her abdomen to freedom. The massacre was beyond description, with every child, man, and woman at the farm lying dead. The lucky among them only had their neck broken. A crueler fate befell the less fortunate.

I found what I thought was an animal, covered in gray hair with a red hue throughout its hide. It was feeding on one of the bodies. When I got closer, it stood up like a man. It stared at me, blood dripping from its prominent fangs. I do not doubt that this is the Strigoi that the legend foretold. It fled at the sight of me but soon returned along with its master, Lucius Rofocale.

Lucius boasted of how he masqueraded first as an older woman living in the forests of Ramnicu. Sightings of the woman allowed Lucius to manipulate the villagers and stir their fear of witches. Lucius then assumed the form of Mihail, Maricela's devoted husband, to have relations with her. The resulting pregnancy provoked the superstitions of the already vulnerable villagers. They murdered Mihail and then drove the Antonescus from the town.

Before departing with his demon child, Lucius confirmed that coming to the New World was part of his sinister plot. North America was sparsely populated, and unlike Europe and Romania, most North American inhabitants knew nothing of so-called myths like the Strigoi. It would allow this beast to flourish free from concerns about legends and ancient curses until the Strigoi would be called upon to fulfill its ultimate purpose. An undoubtedly nefarious objective that Lucius did not disclose.

My failure is complete. I should have killed Maricela and destroyed her offspring, but I hesitated. Her six sons were already without a father, and if I were wrong, I would be taking away the love and stability provided by their mother. My compassion may destroy humankind. Perhaps not today or tomorrow…… I know I must carry on, but August 21st will now be notorious. Beware of this seemingly harmless day on the calendar.

Jack suddenly interrupted Anne. "Anne, look at the clock on the wall!"

Anne saw the clock hands were slightly after midnight.

"My God, Jack!" Alarmed, Anne shouted, "It's August twenty-first!"

They leaped from their chairs, and Anne exclaimed, "You drive. I'll read and see if there is anything in this journal that can help us."

"I hope you find something." Jack's hands shook nervously. "I'm not sure what we'll do if you don't!"

***

August 20th
Rabbi Levi's office, Brunswick Medical Center, Bolivia, NC
11:30 p.m.

Rabbi Levi nervously fumbled to put the key in the lock as he glanced in each direction down the hallway. Finally, he turned the key and pushed the door to his office. The Rabbi quickly made his way to his desk and frantically began searching through the drawers.

"Where is it?" the Rabbi cried out loud. "I know it is here somewhere."

As he continued searching, Rabbi Levi could not shake the feeling of déjà vu he got when he held and read the scroll from the mezuzah. He wasn't sure if it was the paper's texture or its troubling message, but it all felt like he had seen or read it before. This intense feeling led him to do something the Rabbi would have thought unthinkable. He stole the mezuzah!

One morning, roughly a year earlier, Rabbi Levi found an envelope on his desk. There was no return address or postmark on it. When he opened the envelope, the Rabbi could instantly tell the document inside was ancient. The torn and curling edges were like a piece of paper ripped from a book.

"Got it!" the Rabbi declared.

He picked up the envelope and shook the contents onto the desk. Then, pulling the mezuzah from his pocket, he removed the scroll, placed it next to the document from the envelope, and found that the writing paper was an exact match!

Rabbi Levi re-read the writing on the document from the envelope, recalling at the time that it made no sense.

Soak iron chains in the fat of a hog killed on the Feast of Saint Ignatius.

Decapitation

Removal of the heart

Facedown on sacred ground

At the time, he was intrigued enough to do an Internet search and found that Saint Ignatius's feast was an obscure Catholic observance on October 17th. Rabbi Levi could not understand what this mostly unknown celebration had to do with any words or phrases on the page. Even stranger was why the envelope and its contents found their way to his desk at all. Yet, something told him to hold on to the envelope and its contents, so he put it in his desk drawer and forgot about it.

"The chains." Rabbi Levi scratched his chin. "They are in the trunk."

Perhaps an even odder incident, which now was no longer looking like a coincidence, was his purchase of iron chains for his car tires. While visiting relatives in Chicago, he had found himself at a hardware store. On an impulse, he purchased the chains and could not explain why, as it never snowed enough in Wilmington, North Carolina, to have a use for them. They had taken up room in his trunk ever since.

Rabbi Levi read the mezuzah scroll once more. The first half was unmistakably apocalyptic, and like the Christian book of Revelation, Jews believed in the coming of a Messiah. However, Judaism parted company with the Christian *Bible* about battling evil; yet this scroll predicted just that forthrightly.

"What does it mean?" Rabbi Levi asked out loud.

While contemplating it, Rabbi Levi read the second half of the scroll. The Rabbi's hands were shaking from the suggestion to break the mezuzah. Desecrating a mezuzah in this manner to a Jew was a horrific act, but the author told Rabbi Levi, as the scroll recipient, to do it! Rabbi Judah Lowe ben Bezalel, a great historical figure in Judaist studies, had signed his name to the document, which was the only reason Rabbi Levi would even consider the idea.

"Sands of Waccamaw?" the Rabbi muttered. "Is this a place?"

Rabbi Levi pulled out his phone and typed the phrase into the search engine. Lake Waccamaw appeared at the top of the search results. Rabbi Levi clicked on the link and found, surprisingly, that Lake Waccamaw was a town and a body of water roughly one hour away. Suddenly, the papers in the Rabbi's office began to blow around. Rabbi Levi shot up out of his chair as the wind grew more intense.

"What is going on?" Rabbi Levi shouted.

Then, a heavy book hit the floor with a thud.

Chapter 21

August 20th
Catacombs under Antonescu Compound, Lake Waccamaw, NC
10:00 p.m.

Sheriff Glenn Hill hung from the tunnel system's stone ceiling. He had found the cave entrance under the Antonescu home only hours earlier but felt like he had been in this hell hole forever. Were it not for the shackles on his wrists that attached him to the chains bolted into the bedrock above him; he would be a heap of flesh on the floor. The pain he was experiencing was beyond anything he had ever imagined.

The sheriff recalled how carefully he had made his way through the cave. Eventually, he heard a conversation but accidentally triggered the trap that caught him. Somehow Lucius had managed to restrain the Strigoi, who was ready to suck the sheriff dry. Sheriff Hill wished that the beast had been allowed to finish him off. Lucius had spent hours torturing him and extracting every piece of information he fought so hard to hide.

"So, Sheriff," Lucius Rofocale scoffed. "God has decided that Jack Aitken's children will be his messengers?"

Lucius scratched his temple and paused, allowing this revelation to sink in.

"Louis and David Aitken will proclaim the second coming of the so-called almighty's, son?"

"Are you lying to me, Sheriff?" Lucius's eyes narrowed as he viciously grabbed Hill by the hair and forcibly raised his head. Lucius's prior abuse had resulted in Sheriff Hill's right eye swelling shut. The left one was rolling back into his skull.

Placing his hand on Sheriff Hill's chest, Lucius shoved his hand through his ribcage and grabbed his heart. The result was that the heart ceased beating, and Glenn Hill fell limp while letting out a painful cry.

Lucius removed his hand from the sheriff's heart and, using an electrical impulse from his finger, jumpstarted Glenn Hill's heart back to life. The jolt caused the sheriff's body to convulse, and he gasped, trying to breathe.

"We are having far too much fun for you to die, Sheriff." Lucius grinned wickedly, relishing the torture he was inflicting. "At least not yet."

Lucius pointed toward the Strigoi. "After all, my friend has not even had his chance to welcome you formally."

The enormous brute stepped forward, saliva dripping down its elongated fangs.

"Not yet!" Lucius declared forcefully, holding his hand in front of the Strigoi's massive, hairy chest.

The Strigoi glared at Lucius. While tired of taking orders from this *little* demon, Lucius held power over him that he could not ignore. As a result, against his primitive instinct, he stepped away from the meal he saw in front of him.

Folding his arms, Lucius mocked the sheriff, who hung helplessly in front of him. "You know, Officer Hill, I actually believe you."

"What say you, Mr. Haller?" Lucius loudly taunted the lost soul whose body he now claimed as his vessel. "Do you believe your friend, the sheriff?"

Lucius's lips turned downward in mock compassion. "Sorry, Sheriff. Mr. Haller is too tied up now to answer."

But then Lucius grabbed Glenn Hill's chin and held it in his claw-like fingers. "Your feeble attempt to save your friend has failed, and, in fact, he looks even worse than you do right now."

Lucius glanced at the ceiling, and his sinister laughter echoed through the catacombs.

***

Lucius took a long drink from the Teflon flask filled with water from the river Styx and then returned the acid-resistant container to the pocket of his suit jacket.

"Now, where were we, Sheriff?" Lucius tapped his lips with his index finger. "That is right!"

"I still cannot believe it." Lucius snickered. "Two defective boys as prophets."

Lucius gloated with no signs of pity at Glenn Hill. "Your God is losing it, Sheriff. Sending his son to Earth as one of you pathetic humans is one thing, but two autistic children as emissaries? I can hardly believe his stupidity."

Using what strength remained in his body, Sheriff Hill replied faintly, "God's glory is made manifest in weakness."

"Oh, please," Lucius retorted. "How many times have I heard that one from fools such as yourself? Your friend J.J. was weak. You are weak. Where is God's glory in your failure? Losing you and Mr. Haller will neuter your order; what was it called, Logos Confraternity? Just like JESU, you will both be irrelevant. Your defeat will be complete when I destroy those two so-called prophets."

Sheriff Hill gritted his broken teeth at Lucius's boasting. He no longer had the physical strength even to express his rage. The pain was so intense it once again brought the sheriff to tears.

"What? No more quoting of scripture?" Lucius questioned sarcastically. "How about a cryptic warning of what will happen to me if I persist in my pursuits? Perhaps a threat of retribution if I lay one hair on the head of God's prophets?"

While brushing the dirt from the cave off his impeccably tailored black suit, Lucius waved his hand, and the Strigoi, growling, and snarling, approached him.

"Sheriff, my friend, and I will go now to settle accounts with Mr. Antonescu. Please hang around a while longer?"

Lucius turned and smirked. "You do not have my consent to die just yet. Your failure to comply with my wishes will mean that my friend here, upon our return, will have to rip your head off. Do you understand?"

Lucius put his hand to his ear. "What is that? Nothing? I will accept your silence as a yes."

Looking to the Strigoi, Lucius ordered, "Come, it is time for you to fulfill your destiny."

***

August 20th
Maricela Antonescu's room, Lake Waccamaw, NC
10:30 p.m.

Maricela sat on the floor, her hands covering her face. While *The Walking Dead* was Reid's favorite show, it was far too gory for her taste. Reid pulled her closer, sensing that Maricela found what was on the television frightening. A corpse on the ground behind one of the characters began to reanimate. Fortunately for Maricela, the show cut away to a commercial.

"How do you watch this show? It is nauseating."

Reid grinned. "C'mon, Maricela. We all have our guilty pleasures, don't we?"

"I guess so. You know, you are lucky that I love you so much. How many girlfriends agree to watch television instead of going out?"

"You're right. I am lucky! But, with the curfew, I don't think anyone is going out at night around here. I wish they would catch this guy so we can feel safe again."

Maricela Antonescu chimed in, "So we can have some fun too!"

Reid fixated on Maricela's large, sparkling blue eyes. He ran his hand through her thick, vibrant red hair. He sighed; *her beauty is beyond compare.*

"Your Dad is taking no chances. I think it would be easier to get into the White House. What is with all the security, anyway? Isn't he overdoing it a little?"

"You know my father, Reid. He's always been overprotective, but something else is going on."

"There must be. Your Dad was civil to me when I poked my head into the study to say hello. He even told me you were upstairs. I mean, when has he ever let me come up here?"

Maricela laughed. "Yeah, we even have the door closed."

The young lovers embraced, and Reid touched her cheek.

"You look tired, Maricela. Are you still having those dreams?"

"Yes. I had another one last night."

She touched Reid's cheek with her right hand.

"I know you would never hurt me, Reid. If only I could understand what these dreams mean."

Her boyfriend attempted to reassure her. "I know you have no control over this."

Holding her close to comfort her, he whispered, "I love you. With every ounce of my being, I will protect you."

"The dreams are just so vivid. They feel so real. It's your face, I see, but it's as if you are not really you. I know this doesn't make any sense."

Reid spoke softly. "If you feel it, then it makes sense to me."

Then he got up, walked to the window, and studied the night sky.

"Come see this." Reid beckoned Maricela.

Reid pointed at the bright white moon, whose beams danced across Lake Waccamaw. The stars were as bright as diamonds in the moonlight.

"Native Americans called this a Sturgeon Moon," he indicated. "The moonlight lit up the darkness so vividly they could catch fish, even at night."

Maricela was about to suggest they take a walk and sit on the bench at the end of the pier when she saw something on the shoreline. Two figures emerged from behind the cattails. One towered over the other. Even from a distance, she could see the massive muscles and one other prominent feature, hair. The gigantic entity had hair covering its entire body.

"Reid, look toward the cattails. What is that?"

"I don't know," he replied slowly, shaking his head in disbelief.

POP! POP! POP!

Their guns blazing, guards rushed toward the brutish, hairy giant. The lesser figure only had to wave his hand, and the creature immediately engaged the security team. In shock, Maricela and Reid watched the confrontation, which was brief and one-sided. The beast was unaffected by the burst of bullets while being gang rushed by the guards. Bodies were flying everywhere.

The hairy giant picked up a guard, grabbed his arm, and tore it from his body. The guard screamed in agony, and other anguished screams echoed across the compound. More guards dropped limply at the feet of the monster, their necks snapping like small twigs. The skirmish was over before it even got started. Dead and dying guards littered the lawn and the hulking entity, along with its master, continued walking toward the house.

Reid quickly ran and locked the door to Maricela's room. He dialed 9-1-1 on his phone, but there was no reception. Although he knew it wasn't, it was as if the battery was dead.

"I told you something was wrong, Reid!"

Maricela trembled as she asked, "Now what do we do?"

Reid, sounding flustered, replied, "I'm working on it."

***

August 20th
U.S. Route 74 West, outskirts of Lake Waccamaw, NC
11:00 p.m.

Jack kept one hand on the steering wheel as he reached into his pants pocket. Everything Anne had found in the Domien/Domjen journal thus far had been fascinating but not altogether helpful. Were it not for the current situation; Jack would have seen the correspondence between Samuel Domjen and one of the Founding Fathers, Benjamin Franklin, as intriguing, even if discussing their experiments with electricity was something he could not understand. But at that moment, the journal proved that it belonged in a museum rather than being a source of beneficial information.

"Damn it!" Jack shouted. "It's not there!"

Anne flinched but then asked, "What's not there?"

"The mezuzah." Jack slammed his fist on the steering wheel in frustration. "I was sure I had put it in my pocket. I know it is a longshot, but I was hoping it might be a protective talisman."

Jack reached under the seat.

"It's not there either. I guess we'll never know if it has protective properties or not."

Putting both hands back on the wheel, he asked with concern, "Anne, do you have any idea what we're walking into here?"

Anne scratched the back of her head and studied the journal. Without looking up, she answered, "I keep a bag of blessed weapons in the trunk. I have two crossbows equipped with silver-tipped arrows that have a coating of anointing oil. Exodus 30, Verses 21 to 22, provides the recipe for it. It includes cinnamon, olive oil, and myrrh. It has protective properties, and if it was good enough to anoint the Ark of the Covenant, I believe it will provide us some protection. I confess that I am unsure if the silver-tipped arrows will affect the Strigoi."

Jack thought about Saint Michael's Sword, hidden in his home, and uttered ruefully, "I sure wish I had the sword of Saint Michael right now. It is the only weapon I know Lucius fears."

Anne interrupted. "Listen, here is something that Father Domjen wrote about the Strigoi."

November 8th, 1737, North Carolina Wilderness
I have been tracking Lucius Rofocale and the Strigoi for months now. They are easy to follow. They leave a trail of dead animals wherever they go. There is not much blood around the corpses, and the only markings on the victims are two distinctive fang marks from elongated canine teeth. Oddly, the victims have not been eaten, at least not by the Strigoi, but I have had unfortunate encounters with human victims of this abomination. They are the undead—walking flesh-eaters who consume the carcass that the Strigoi will only drink dry. After several near-fatal encounters, I have discovered that only a silver bullet through the head or the heart will end the madness.

"Well, Anne, that confirms what we already know." Jack hesitated. "Unfortunately, it also reinforces what will happen to George."

Jack nearly broke into tears when he finished the following sentence. "Unless we find some water from the River Styx somewhere."

Anne placed her hand on Jack's. "Don't lose faith."

Jack collected himself and drove on into the night. The car fell silent as Jack carefully scanned the road ahead of him, and Anne continued to read the journal.

Minutes later, Anne exclaimed, "Jack, I jumped ahead while reading about more science experiments. Listen to this."

March 5th, 1753, Domjen Home Ingold, North Carolina
While I consider myself a man of science, I am a man of faith first. I do not know how, but Dr. Franklin has obtained water samples from the river of death. The River Styx.

"What did you say?" Jack interrupted.

Anne replied, "The River Styx. Wait, there's more."

I cautioned my friend to carefully handle something so inherently evil—a liquid from the bowels of Hell itself. Dr. Franklin has theorized that something fundamentally evil can also be a medicinal cure for a wound inflicted by something equally vile. He believes we can cure people who suffer bites from the Strigoi.

After sharing my journal entries from 1737, Dr. Franklin became obsessed with the Strigoi and my accounts of the effects of its bite on humans. He believes he can either cure them as I suggested or control them through electrical impulses from the brain.

The experiments he suggests are pure madness. I can hardly believe the lengths to which Dr. Franklin would go to prove the efficacy of his theories. It is wise to communicate through ancient Greek, a language lost too many. If what we correspond about were read by church leadership, we would likely be declared heretics and excommunicated. I fear that we might even find a noose around our necks.

I warned my friend that his only faith could not be science. I fear that we are meddling with powers that we cannot comprehend. There are things not meant to be understood by men. Faith means trusting that God should remain the sole entity to know the process used in man's creation. I told Dr. Franklin that there is a line that we must not cross and that his theories and experiments were reaching that line. We might already be stepping over it. I hope he will listen to reason and abandon this pursuit before it is too late.

I remain here in Ingold as the sentry on guard against Lucius and his evil partner. The killings ended almost as quickly as they started. By January 1738, the trail had gone cold, and there had been no attacks for more than a decade. I pray that the Strigoi will not return, but I stand ready to confront it if it does. I don't pretend to know how to kill it, but I will do all that is within my power and, with God's providence, will destroy it. And so...I wait.

Samuel Domjen

"That's the end, Jack. It's the last entry in the journal."

"I can't believe it." Jack was stunned. "I thought I knew a lot about Benjamin Franklin."

Anne pointed. "Make a left turn here onto Lakeshore Drive. There's room on the shoulder. Park there for a minute."

Jack pulled the car onto the shoulder. The lights of the Antonescu house on the hill were visible in the distance.

"Jack, I know we are both trying to digest what I was reading from Domjen's journal, but we need to clear our minds before we head to the Antonescu house. If we are distracted by other thoughts, we could make a mistake. In this situation, one misstep could get us killed."

Jack thought back to the Michaelmas conducted before he left to confront Lucius in Culpeper. While listening to Anne, he scanned his arms, hoping to see the armor appear that he had worn that night.

"So, what is the plan, Anne? How do you suggest we approach this?"

"First, we're going to wait. I want to watch the compound for a while. When I was here last, it was crawling with security. I don't see any flashlights moving around the grounds or searchlights scanning the woods outside the fence line. Earlier, there were guards posted everywhere. Now there is no movement at all. I can already sense that something isn't right."

Jack and Anne sat in the car for nearly twenty minutes, watching the Antonescu house.

"Okay, Jack. Let's get going. The shoulder dips down below the road level and has more cover. We'll approach the front gate slowly. If we can't access the residence through the front entrance or see security personnel, we can quietly walk through the woods down to the lake. I remember seeing that the fence did not extend into the water. We might get wet feet, but we should be able to get in that way."

"Copy that, Chief," Jack acknowledged with a slight chuckle.

The duo exited the vehicle, retrieved Anne's crossbows and arrows, and headed toward the Antonescu home, neither knowing exactly who or what awaited them there.

Chapter 22

August 20th
Maricela Antonescu's room, Lake Waccamaw, NC
11:00 p.m.

Reid Bowman's trembling hands fumbled to lock the door, and it took him several attempts to flip a switch and turn off the lights. Maricela Antonescu's bedroom was dark, and Reid hoped this would hide their presence as the room was devoid of weapons. The moonlight revealed that after the brief battle on the lawn, the hideous twosome was heading toward the front door, and they were not alone. The giant hairy figure following closely behind his apparent superior carried what appeared like a body in its arms.

Reid watched from behind the window curtain and held his hand up to signal for Maricela to remain quiet. Maricela attempted to look over his shoulder to see what was happening. The taller being was impossible to miss, and Maricela saw it hauling something.

"Can you tell what it's carrying, Reid? I can't see it clearly from this angle."

Reid muttered, "I think it's a body."

"My God." Maricela placed her hand over her mouth. "What is going on here?"

"Somehow, I don't think God has anything to do with it," Reid responded curtly.

"That's not funny, Reid."

"I'm sorry. It's my nerves. Maricela, is there any way out of this room other than the door?"

"Just the second-story window."

Maricela sat down on the bed. "We're not going to get out of here alive, are we?"

Reid knelt, hugging Maricela, and whispered, "We will. We will. Don't be afraid. Don't lose hope."

The young lovers held hands tightly when suddenly, a loud thud emanated from the study on the first floor directly under Maricela's room.

A startled Maricela nervously asked, "What the hell was that?"

"I don't know." Reid gulped. "But I'm going to find out."

He headed to the door with Maricela right behind him. She grabbed his arm to pull him back.

"Don't leave me here alone! Reid, please don't go!"

Reid turned. "I am just going down the hall to peer down the staircase. Lock the door behind me. I will be back in a minute or two."

Maricela stared fearfully at Reid.

"I promise, Maricela." Reid gently ran his fingers across her cheek. "I'll be right back."

"You better." Maricela forced a smile.

Reid unlocked the door. He carefully stepped into the hallway and gestured for Maricela to quietly shut the door behind him. Reid slowly walked down the hallway to the staircase. He could hear a conversation in the study on the first floor.

***

August 20th
Constantin Antonescu's Study, Lake Waccamaw, NC
11:00 p.m.

Constantin Antonescu got up from behind his desk. Ordinarily, the sound of gunfire would have startled him and been a cause for panic, but not tonight. All day long, Constantin had sensed that his moment of reckoning was near. He attempted to protect his family, particularly Maricela, by deploying his security team. But Constantin knew it would be a futile act.

He powerlessly watched the destruction of his security detail through his study window and waited silently for his *business partner* to arrive. Constantin felt like his heart would beat out of his chest. His fight-or-flight instinct was on high alert, but he realized neither was an option. The tortured screams of injured and dying men emanating from the front lawn were confirmation that fighting was pointless. From the day in his office when Lucius Rofocale pricked his finger, Constantin was all too aware that there would never be anywhere to run or any place to hide that Lucius could not find him.

He wondered to himself, *How did I end up here?* But Constantin knew the answer to the question. Constantin hated to admit it, but he did not need a push to accept Lucius's deal. He was successful immediately, starting a chain reaction that made Antonescu Communications a regional media juggernaut and almost launched Constantin into the Governor's chair. Constantin found that he was never satisfied. Even when he rose to the top of the media industry, he couldn't get enough. Every deal was an adrenaline rush, but it eventually spun out of control. Now, he was moments away from complete destruction.

Constantin's life began to flash before him. The memory of the night he first met Maria brought a sad smile to his face. While the borders of Communist Romania were officially closed during the Cold War, Maria's family still made it to America. It was 1985, and Maria was an exchange student living in the Stage XII dormitory at the State University of New York Stony Brook on Long Island. English was still a second language, and Constantin was the first person she met outside her family who spoke Romanian.

It was a packed room, and the deejay had the music blaring, but Constantin didn't notice. Spellbound by Maria's beauty, Constantin knew he had to get to know her.

What was the song they danced to at the party? Constantin thought to himself. Then he remembered. *The Hooters!* He could hear the music in his head. Closing his eyes, he could see the two of them dancing.

And we danced, like a wave on the ocean romance. The song continued as Constantin saw Maria spinning like a top. *Swept away for a moment by chance…* Constantin whispered the lyrics: "And we danced and danced and danced."

Maria was always there for him. Constantin admonished himself for the years of unkind treatment and disregard he showed her. He often yelled at Maria or criticized her when he wasn't ignoring his wife entirely. Constantin shook his head. What a fool he was. Blinded by his greed and lust for power, Constantin had willingly walked the path that would now lead to his ruin. Only at this moment did he allow himself to realize that his family would share in his suffering. In fact, their nightmare might very well turn out to be worse than his.

While lost in his thoughts, Constantin absentmindedly wandered around the study. Throughout the room were objects that reminded him of his loved ones. Pausing for a moment, he stared at the family portrait hanging over the fireplace. *My beautiful daughters*, Constantin thought to himself. The picture of his grandchildren only hammered home the future he was about to lose. However, his most significant regret by far was for Maricela.

Thinking about Maricela, a wave of immense guilt swept over him.

"What have I done?" Constantin muttered to himself.

No longer blinded by his avarice, Constantin considered the available options.

"Reasoning with Lucius is out of the question," Constantin debated with himself out loud.

Constantin rubbed his chin, then bit his fingernail. "Perhaps Reid could help Maricela escape."

Constantin stared up toward Maricela's room. *Reid is here already.* Constantin thought to himself. *All I would have to do is go upstairs.*

"Going somewhere, Constantin?" The sound of the question boomed across the room. Constantin was startled and turned instantly toward the doorway.

"Or are you looking toward the heavens for a miracle?" Lucius smirked.

"Mr. Ro-Rofocale." Constantin stuttered.

"Oh, Constantin." Lucius's lips curled upward in a sinister grin, revealing his black teeth. "We are partners, remember? There is no need to be so formal. Please, it is Lucius to my friends."

Constantin observed Lucius with a combination of disbelief and fear.

"I know what it is." Lucius wagged his finger in the air. "I do not look the same, do I?"

Lucius pretended to frown. "Time has a way of marching all over a person's face, you know."

Pulling at the skin on this face, Lucius declared, "Of course, it could be that I am wearing a completely different meat suit, altogether, than I was the last time we saw one another."

Lucius laughed loudly. "At least my voice is the same, right partner?"

Constantin cringed at Lucius's obnoxious attempt at humor. He quickly glanced at his desk and the drawer where he kept his revolver.

"I see a look in your eye, Constantin, that concerns me." Lucius scowled. "I have kept my end of our deal. I delivered the success, wealth, and power you desired. I am sensing that you are having second thoughts about holding up your end of our bargain."

Lucius's eyes glowed a scorching red, and he demanded, "Look at me, Constantin! Do I look like someone who tolerates a partner who goes back on his word?"

Constantin began to tremble. Those terrifying eyes! Just like their meeting eighteen years earlier. It felt like they were burning a hole right through his body.

Constantin put his hands up in front of him. "No-No, Lucius. I would never double-cross you."

"That is better, Constantin," Lucius spoke in a slightly less ominous tone. "I knew you would come around."

Lucius clasped his hands behind his back and started to pace around the study.

"You know, Constantin, you may find this hard to believe, but I genuinely like you. As a matter of fact, we have a lot in common."

"We do?" Constantin asked, with a perplexed look on his face and a sickening feeling in his stomach intensifying.

"Yes," Lucius continued. "Take personnel matters, for instance. We both know how hard it is to find good help these days."

Lucius put his hand on Constantin's shoulder and uttered sarcastically, "It pains me to be the one to tell you this, Constantin, but your security team is …. no more. Come, I will show you."

Lucius grabbed Constantin's arm and roughly escorted Constantin to the window.

Pointing at the mangled dead bodies, Lucius declared, "Have you ever seen such incompetence?"

Lucius squeezed Constantin's arm, causing Constantin to flinch from the pain.

"If I did not know better," Lucius whispered to Constantin, "someone could persuade me to believe that their deployment was an attempt to kill me."

Lucius shoved Constantin back to the middle of the room and proclaimed scornfully, "Let me let you in on a little secret, partner. Their guns and whatever you have in that desk drawer do not work on me."

Constantin backed away from Lucius and asked fearfully, "Wh … Wha … What are … are … you?"

Lucius answered contemptuously, "I should think that would be obvious by now."

Lucius paused, then roared in Constantin's face, "I AM A DEMON! Your worst fucking nightmare come true!"

Constantin was driven to his knees by the force of Lucius's proclamation, but Lucius dragged Constantin to his feet.

"Get up." Lucius was disgusted. "Begging does not become you."

"What's going to happen to my family?" Constantin asked plaintively. "What do you want with Maricela?"

Lucius frowned. "What will happen to your family, you ask? Regardless of what you may think, I do not need your six other daughters. They are free, as they have always been, to live life as they choose."

Constantin, who had been holding his breath, let loose a small sigh of relief.

"Eighteen years ago, I warned you about asking me that second question." Lucius's lips turned upward in a menacing smile. "The time is coming very soon when you will have your answer."

Lucius raised his right hand and yelled, "COME!"

Loud, lumbering footsteps echoed down the hallway, and the floor began to shake. Constantin was afraid yet found himself curious at the same time. The noise grew louder as whoever was coming down the hallway neared the study door, but the footsteps stopped. The house was quiet for what seemed like an eternity when suddenly a body flew and landed at Constantin's feet. Constantin instinctively jumped back, but looking down, he recognized who it was.

"No. Please, no." Constantin tilted his head sideways with a look of horror and dismay.

Dropping to his knees, he begged, "Maria. Not my Maria."

Maria Antonescu lay twisted on the floor. Her back was arched, with the heels of her shoes touching her lower back. A position that was only possible due to the fracturing of her spine. Her head was unnaturally at rest on the carpet, the result of a visibly broken neck—the look of terror from the moment of her death frozen on her face.

While coming to grips with the shock of the moment, Constantin could not help but notice an enormous, hairy creature. He mentally calculated that the beast had to be over seven feet tall. It towered over Lucius. The monster watched Constantin, and a constant guttural growl emanated from its jaws.

"We met Maria coming up the driveway." Lucius stood between Maria's mangled corpse and the Strigoi. The Strigoi closely watched Constantin with saliva dripping from its jaws, waiting for Lucius's permission to strike.

"As you may imagine, our presence was a bit of a surprise to your wife."

Still bewildered by the sight of Maria's dead body, Constantin cried out loud, "I didn't even realize that she was gone."

"Constantin," Lucius shook his head, "you need to keep a better eye on your family and the company they keep. She was dialing her phone when we made her acquaintance. After a little persuading, she admitted she had been trying to reach Anne Bishop."

"Anne Bishop?" Constantin squinted. He was clearly perplexed. "Why would she be trying to reach her?"

"Before my friend here lost control of himself," Lucius replied, pointing toward the Strigoi. "Mrs. Antonescu mentioned something about a book."

Lucius asked sternly, "What book is she referring to, Constantin?"

"I don't know," Constantin quickly answered.

Lucius raised his hand and began to clench his fist. Constantin's eyes widened, and he grabbed at his throat, trying to catch his breath.

"Do not lie to me, Constantin," Lucius retorted tersely. "As I am sure you can tell, I have no patience for it."

Lucius slowly opened his hand, allowing Constantin's airway to reopen. Constantin gasped for air.

"The only book I can think of ..." Constantin struggled to speak through his coughing and tried to recover from Lucius's assault. "... is an old journal that has been in my family for centuries."

Constantin hesitated, eyeing the Strigoi, before turning toward the built-in bookshelves on the far wall.

Looking back at Lucius, Constantin's blank stare revealed that he was surprised. "It's gone."

Lucius walked over to where Constantin was standing and demanded, "Tell me about this book."

Constantin put up his hands, fearing what Lucius might do next. "I don't know too much about it. I swear to you. It was in a language that I could not read. My father told me that fathers passed it down to their sons for generations in our family."

Lucius glared at a visibly shaking Constantin. He could sense that Constantin told him everything he knew about the book.

"There is something important about that book," Lucius reasoned. "Bishop would not have kept it otherwise. She and Aitken must be on their way here."

Lucius told the Strigoi. "It is time. Maricela is upstairs."

The Strigoi transformed itself into Reid Bowman. Constantin stared at the doppelganger, mouth ajar.

"I don't understand, Lucius. What's happening?"

"You have not figured it out yet, have you?" Lucius answered glibly. "You humans truly are pathetic. You wanted to know what is going to happen to Maricela?"

Pointing to the Reid Bowman impostor, Lucius continued, "He is here for Maricela. Meet your daughter's paramour."

Constantin shook his head, realizing what Lucius was implying. Sobbing profusely, Constantin begged, "No. Not that. Please, don't do this to my baby."

Lucius replied accusingly, "Under the circumstances, your display of emotion is understandable, Constantin, but do not forget, this is not what I am doing to your daughter. It is what you agreed to all those years ago. You, Constantin, are doing this to your daughter!"

Constantin attempted to shout out a warning to Maricela but found himself unable to speak. He tried to move and discovered his feet could not respond to his thoughts.

Lucius motioned to the phony Reid Bowman, who walked out of the study and headed for the stairs.

Turning back to Constantin, Lucius taunted him, "Stick around. You will want to see how this all ends."

Lucius then muttered, "Aitken and Bishop have tried to interfere with my plans again. This uninvited intrusion will be their last."

***

August 20th
Hall outside Maricela Antonescu's Room, Lake Waccamaw, NC
11:45 p.m.

Reid Bowman stood motionless in the hallway outside the doorway to Maricela's room. The shadow coming up the stairs did not attempt to conceal itself. Reid tightly clutched the fire extinguisher he found in an upstairs closet. While unable to hear the conversation from downstairs, one word was unmistakable, a *demon*. He couldn't place the context in which the thundering voice was using it, but whoever used the phrase *demon* was completely pissed off. If that individual was coming upstairs, Reid wanted to be ready.

At the top of the stairs, the hallway split to the right and the left. Pressed against the wall to stay out of sight, Reid waited to see which option the intruder would choose. He saw the black hair on top of the mysterious male visitor, who had already reached the last step. Every muscle in Reid's body seemed to tense up as the unwelcome guest went to the right, toward Maricela's room. Running out of the shadows, ready to swing the five-pound fire extinguisher, Reid confronted the intruder. What he saw shocked him. It took a moment, but he realized he was looking at himself.

Reid lowered the fire extinguisher to his side, and he and his body double stood face-to-face, but only for a moment. Before Reid could react, he felt a firm hand on his throat. He tried to scream a warning to Maricela but could not make a sound. Reid found himself suspended in mid-air as the person pretending to be him raised him off the ground with one hand. Reid struggled, to no avail, to free himself.

His attacker changed from a human being to something with coarse, long hair from head to toe. At least, that is what he thought had happened. Reid fought to remain conscious and could not be sure of anything at this moment. His eyes bulged from the blocking of his airway and the feeling of terror taking over his body. Everything was fading to black, but before Reid lost consciousness, he saw the beast's razor-sharp fangs and felt the piercing of his jugular vein. Fortunately for Reid Bowman, he never heard the sucking sound resulting from the draining of his lifeblood.

The Strigoi, now fully invigorated by his sixth human victim's blood, again assumed Reid Bowman's identity. Tossing the drained body aside, he promptly remembered the directive, seemingly burned into his brain. The disguised beast reached into its pocket and pulled out the bracelet its tormentor, Lucius, had provided to him. Shapeshifting was an ability he did not understand, but it was an instinct he felt. Something about the object allowed the Strigoi to assume its current form. The Strigoi heard the message in its brain once more.

You will not hurt Maricela. You will complete the act I have described and shown to you. You will gather up Maricela and bring her to me.

The impostor walked across the hall. *Boom-Boom-Boom went its fist on the door.* The lock turned; Maricela opened the door, grabbed the person she knew to be Reid Bowman by the shirt, and pulled him into the room. She locked the door once again.

"Can you be any louder, Reid? I was getting worried. What is going on out there?"

The Strigoi thought for a moment. *How am I supposed to respond to this question?* He wasn't sure how or why, but he verbalized a one-word response: "Nothing."

"That's it?" Maricela asked. "That's all you have to say?"

The Strigoi was unsure what to do next. Instinctively, he felt for the bracelet and presented it to Maricela.

"You found it!" Maricela responded excitedly.

She threw her arms around the person she thought was Reid Bowman.

"I was sure I would never see the bracelet again. Where did you find it?"

All these questions were making the Strigoi anxious. He was relieved when Maricela sat on the edge of her bed and began patting the area next to her.

"Come here, Reid." Maricela smiled. "Come here, silly. Sit next to me."

The Strigoi figured out what Maricela wanted and sat down next to her. She grabbed its arm tightly.

"Earlier, I was telling you more about those dreams," Maricela whispered.

"I just had a feeling of déjà vu—this moment. The two of us are sitting here like this. It was in my dream."

Instinctively, the Strigoi turned toward Maricela. Her smile faded the longer she gazed into the Strigoi's bloodshot eyes.

"Reid, the way you are staring at me is making me uncomfortable." But she was unable to break away.

A blank stare slowly came over Maricela's face, and she felt powerless to resist. The Strigoi leaned into Maricela, who slowly reclined until she lay prone on the bed. Maricela believed that it was Reid Bowman climbing on top of her. As a result, Maricela willingly gave herself and her virginity to the impostor. The trance that came over Maricela turned into a deep sleep, and she was unaware of the beast picking her up and carrying her downstairs.

***

August 21st
Antonescu Residence, Lake Waccamaw, NC
12:15 a.m.

Lucius Rofocale made his way back into the Antonescu study. A self-assured look was on his face as he thought *Jack and Anne would be in for a surprise when they arrived.* Lucius heard a loud thump on the stairs. Turning to a captive, Constantin Antonescu, Lucius beamed.

"Ah, the happy couple has arrived," Lucius taunted Constantin again. "Come in and join us."

The Strigoi, with an unconscious Maricela in its arms, appeared in the doorway. Constantin looked away in disgust, trying not to think about the heinous act perpetrated on his daughter.

"Your daughter is lovely, Constantin. A fetching creature by human standards. Her beauty rivals that of her namesake. Tell me, Constantin, how much do you know about your family tree? Any interest in genealogy?"

Looking every bit the crushed man he was, Constantin did not respond to Lucius's inquiry.

"Cat got your tongue, Constantin?" Lucius asked smugly. "It is okay, partner. I will let you in on a little secret. Our partnership is no accident."

Constantin stared at Lucius with a vacant expression on his face. "What are you talking about, Lucius?"

"More than 250 years ago, in 1737, to be exact, your relatives arrived here through the port of Charleston, South Carolina. I knew a Constantin back then as well."

Lucius continued his taunting, not caring if Constantin wished to hear it or not.

"Anyway, that Constantin had seven daughters," Lucius smirked. "The youngest of which was named ... Care to have a guess, Constantin?"

"Maricela," Constantin answered weakly.

"Give that man a cigar!" Lucius laughed, pointing at Constantin. "That is right! Do you get where I am going with this, Constantin?"

Constantin replied feebly, "I suppose you are going to tell me anyway."

"Right again!" Lucius mocked. "I knew you were smarter than you let on earlier in the evening."

Pointing at the Strigoi still holding a listless Maricela, Lucius went on. "My friend, here, is the result of my relationship with the 1737 Maricela. I want to make sure you are not getting confused. Do you follow me, Constantin?"

Constantin replied despondently, "I understand. All of this is our family curse. You needed my daughter because she was my seventh daughter, whose name is Maricela."

"That is three for three, Constantin!" Lucius affirmed mockingly. "You are so good at this game! I am impressed!"

Constantin grimaced regretfully at Maria's corpse, still lying on the floor at his feet, speechless. Looking back at his violated daughter, he knew his downfall was complete.

"Well, I would love to continue this family reunion, but duty calls. It is time to get our little mother-to-be out of harm's way. I do have a closing thought I want to share with you. I understand the so-called *good book* has a story about giving a man a fish and feeding him for a day. Teach a man to fish, and he can eat for a lifetime. It is something like that, I think."

Constantin interrupted, "What's your point, Lucius?"

"Where I come from, we have a similar but equally appropriate parable. It goes something like this. If you build a man a fire, he will be warm for a night."

Lucius paused to look at Constantin with an evil grin. "Set a man on fire, and he will be warm forever."

The Strigoi, carrying Maricela, exited the study with Lucius. As he went out the front door, Lucius snapped his fingers and yelled, "Burn, baby, burn!"

Constantin Antonescu found himself engulfed in flames, and every resident of Lake Waccamaw most assuredly heard his agonizing screams echoing through the neighborhood.

Chapter 23

August 21st
Catacombs under Antonescu Compound, Lake Waccamaw, NC
12:45 a.m.

Lucius finished replenishing the ceremonial pool with the last drops from his supply of the River Styx's supernatural water. He then checked on Maricela Antonescu and the Strigoi and found them both asleep. Easing into the water, Lucius began floating and soon was in a trance. He instantly felt invigorated, without a moment to spare. The final *'guests'* for the evening would be arriving soon, and Lucius needed to be at full strength to restrain the Strigoi from attacking them. Lucius was looking forward to confronting Mark Desmond's protegee, Anne Bishop, for the first time. But he was reserving the pleasure of slaughtering Jack Aitken for himself.

Reaching out with his mind, Lucius finally connected with his current aide, Tatiana. Lucius had to admit he was a demanding ruler, so he went through assistants regularly. However, Tatiana had managed to last longer than her predecessors.

"Mas-Mas-Master Lucius," a surprised Tatiana stuttered. "It is indeed a pleasure."

"Is it, Tatiana?" Lucius asked sarcastically. "What took you so long to answer me?"

"I apologize, Master Lucius," Tatiana responded nervously. "You have been gone for so long. It was a shock to hear from you."

"I suppose so," Lucius replied dismissively. "Tell me, how has business been in my absence?"

Tatiana gulped. "Slow, Master. Unfortunately, very slow."

"I see. Somehow, I am not surprised. When the cat is away, I guess the mice will play. We will get to the bottom of this soon enough."

"The legions will be very happy to hear from you, Master. There were all kinds of rumors."

"What rumors?" Lucius asked tersely. "Tatiana, I would highly recommend you not hold anything back, for your sake."

Tatiana blurted out, "They're saying you're dead, sir!"

"Oh, are they really?" Lucius sneered. "They should be so lucky! Tatiana, I have a job for you."

"Yes, Master," Tatiana quickly answered. "Anything."

"Take this down," Lucius ordered.

Lucius provided Tatiana with a lengthy list of tasks and gave her one final assignment before he let her go.

"Tatiana. I want to know every demon who repeated the rumor about my so-called demise. When we rendezvous in a week, I expect a complete list. Do we understand one another?"

"Yes, Master Lucius!" Tatiana shouted. "I hear and obey!"

Lucius shut down the mental connection with Tatiana and exited the pool. Bringing along two henchmen, security guards turned into zombies by the Strigoi, Lucius headed up the stairs from the catacombs to the Antonescu's kitchen.

"Time to collect our guests," Lucius told the newly minted zombies.

As Lucius made his way up the stairs, he pronounced, "Let the evening's entertainment begin!"

**

August 21st
Antonescu Residence, Lake Waccamaw, NC
1:15 a.m.

Jack stepped on the corpse, pulled the arrow from its head, and then lingered over the body of what was once a security guard for the Antonescu family. The unfortunate soul seemed to stare up at Jack. As a sign of respect, Jack put down his crossbow and swept his hand across the man's eyes to close them. Anne and Jack had spent nearly an hour making their way to the front door, killing one

Robert Wallace-like zombie after another. The entirety of the carnage left by the Strigoi was enough to make Jack ill; that is, if he could take the time to vomit.

"I wish I had one of these forty-eight hours ago," Jack declared regrettably, raising his crossbow for Anne to see. "I might have saved George a lot of pain and suffering."

"You're getting to be a good shot, Jack, but that makes sense since you've had a lot of on-the-job training tonight."

Jack surveyed the yard and shook his head. "Have you ever seen such carnage?"

"I have," Anne answered thoughtfully. "A lot worse, I'm afraid."

"I'm sorry, Anne," Jack apologized ruefully. "How could I forget Culpeper and all those unburied bodies? I know many of them were your friends."

"It's okay. You gave the victims a decent burial. I don't know that I ever thanked you for that."

"It was the least I could do. Those heroes earned it."

Jack pointed toward the entrance. "Shall we?"

The duo carefully approached the front door. It was ajar, and Anne carefully pushed it open. She examined the hallway and silently waved Jack forward.

"Don't forget to check the corners," Anne whispered. "We'll clear the first floor and meet at the study."

Pointing at a closed door to their right, she said, "The study is that room over there."

Jack cautiously entered the house. An intense odor, like a burnt roast, permeated the air. Anne moved forward while Jack went to his left. Jack held his loaded crossbow before him as he moved from room to room. Anne examined the stairs at the end of the hallway and swept through the kitchen and pantry. While in the kitchen, she noticed a closed door.

"This must be the door to the catacombs," Anne muttered as she reached for the doorknob. She turned the knob but found it would not budge.

She returned to the hallway and found Jack leaning against the wall outside Constantin Antonescu's study.

"I didn't find a sign of Maricela or anyone else." Jack yawned. "I know I haven't slept much, but I feel very drained."

"I struck out too," Anne replied.

Anne rubbed her temple. "I've got a headache."

Shaking it off, she continued. "Let's go into the study."

"Which room is the study?" Jack asked.

Anne had a perplexed look on her face. "Jack, we're standing in front of it."

"I'm sorry." Jack scratched his forehead. "You told me that before, didn't you?"

Standing in front of the door, Jack prepared to shoot if the situation called for it. Anne stayed to the side and gently pushed the door open. Jack rushed forward but ended up stumbling through the doorway and almost fell flat on his face. Anne stepped into the room and scanned the room.

"Clear, Jack," Anne announced loudly, with a slightly irritated tone. "Are you all right? What happened?"

"I don't know." Jack rubbed his eyes. "I'm having trouble focusing."

"Look at this, Jack."

Anne knelt next to a body and placed her fingers on the victim's throat, checking for a pulse. Then the identity of the corpse hit her.

"My God. It's Maria Antonescu!"

Anne squinted and turned away. "Look at the position of her body. I'm betting that the Strigoi broke her neck and back."

Jack pointed at the ceiling. "Do you hear a noise?"

"I think the attic fan just kicked on," Anne answered. "It helps to keep the house cooler."

"Uh-oh. I shouldn't have done that, Anne."

"You shouldn't have done what, Jack?".

"Looking up quickly like that," Jack replied. "I'm prone to bouts of vertigo. Something like looking up at the ceiling too quickly can bring it on. I need to sit here for a minute."

Jack inhaled deeply and rubbed his chest. "I'm having a little trouble catching my breath." Looking down, he asked, "Why is there a pile of ashes in the middle of the room?"

Anne leaned over to inspect the smoldering black pile more closely and saw something shiny among the ashes. Using the tip of one of the arrows, she lifted the object to examine it closely.

"Burnt offerings," Anne pronounced slowly.

"Say again?" Jack asked.

"Burnt offerings." She showed the item to Jack. "I saw this ring on Constantin Antonescu's finger. These ashes are Constantin Antonescu; at least what's left of him."

Anne cringed. "The cremating fire must have been scorching hot."

Instinctively glancing at the fireplace, she thought, *The remains of a recent fire are there, but there is no way a wood fire could create that amount of heat.*

Suddenly, there was a loud thud. Anne turned and saw Jack lying on the floor.

Rolling him over, she shook Jack by the shoulders.

"Wake up, Jack!" Anne yelled anxiously. "Please wake up."

The quiver holding their spare arrows and the Domjen journal fell onto the floor. Anne fought to stay awake, but her head was pounding, and she was nauseous. Slowly she slumped on Jack's chest, and everything faded to black.

***

Several minutes passed. The hum of the attic fan obscured the sounds of Jack and Anne's shallow, labored breathing. Then a door opened in the kitchen, and three figures emerged. One of them inadvertently kicked the shattered pieces of a demolished carbon monoxide detector across the floor. The trio headed into the study and stood over Anne and Jack.

"Ah, sleeping beauty and her beast." Lucius chuckled out loud. "It is so gratifying when a plan comes together as it should. It would be easy to execute the two of you right now but let us have some fun. For old times' sake."

Circling Anne and Jack, Lucius gloated, "Then I will dispatch you both. Very painfully, I might add."

"What is this?" Lucius picked up Anne's quiver from the floor.

Pulling out the arrows, he tossed them in the fireplace, and they immediately ignited. While removing the remaining ammunition from the quiver, a book fell onto the floor.

Lucius picked up the book and opened it to the first page. As he read the first few words, his lips clenched tightly, and his eyes narrowed.

"So, this is what Maria Antonescu gave these two pests in the hospital."

"Interesting. I have seen this journal before, but not for centuries. As I recall, this is where I found summaries of experiments that helped me develop the skills to control the Strigoi. I instructed that fool Domjen to destroy it. I compelled him to throw it into a fire. How and why would Antonescu have it?"

Lucius scratched his chin, deep in thought. Then, examining the journal closely, Lucius noticed something about one of the pages and mumbled to himself, "There are fragments of torn paper still here. A page is missing from this book."

A brief pang of concern entered his mind, but after a few moments, Lucius announced arrogantly, "Well, no matter. Nothing in this journal is going to help Bishop and Aitken now."

Pointing at Jack and Anne, he continued reading the journal while telling the two newly minted underlings, "Take them down the stairs and chain them up next to the sheriff."

Now zombies controlled by Lucius, the former guards obeyed their new master. Each scooped up a body and methodically headed down the stairs to the catacombs.

Lucius pulled the door closed behind him and headed downstairs with a vicious smirk on his face.

***

SINS OF THE FATHERS

August 21st
Lake Waccamaw State Park, Lake Waccamaw, NC
3:15 a.m.

Rabbi Levi parked his Ford Edge in the empty lot and took the key out of the ignition. The Rabbi sat staring at the water, which was easy to see despite the late hour due to the unusually bright moon. While Rabbi Levi studied the beachfront in front of him, his shaky hands found pieces of the now broken mezuzah in his passenger seat. He was at war with himself as he carefully ran his fingers along the jagged edges of the once sacred religious object.

What am I doing here? Having never been to Lake Waccamaw, the surroundings were unfamiliar. He never even knew the lake existed before now. The strange setting fueled the doubts in his troubled mind. When he first read the scroll hidden inside the mezuzah, he knew something was different about the object. The message was unlike any he had ever read before. Its uniqueness caused the Rabbi to lie and tell Anne and her friend it was like any other mezuzah.

The lie was bad enough, but Rabbi Levi also felt guilty for violating the 8th commandment; *thou shalt not steal.* The Rabbi was particularly disturbed at how easily he swiped the mezuzah without a second thought. The only explanation Rabbi Levi had was that it was instinct. Reading the scroll seemingly set off an alarm in his brain, and when the visitor diverted Anne and Jack's attention, he quickly grabbed it from the table and excused himself.

The Rabbi turned on the interior car light and reached to the passenger seat to grab the scroll and read it one more time. Rabbi Levi had already read it at least a dozen times, but he still had difficulty accepting its warning.

משמעות גילוי הקלף הקדום הזה היא שאיתה של צרה ומשפט גדול' עומדת לפנינו

(The discovery of this ancient parchment means a time of trouble, and a great trial is before us.)

הרוע האולטימטיבי בפתח *מלחמה נגד*

(A war against ultimate evil is at the door.)

לא יהיה קל לקבל ולא להאמין למה שאתה קורא
(It will not be easy to accept and believe what you read.)
לרוע המזל, עבור המין האנושי, זו האמת
(Unfortunately, for humanity, this is the truth.)

Rabbi Levi paused and began to ask, out loud, a string of rapid-fire questions. "Trial and tribulation? Is this the precursor to the arrival of the long-anticipated coming of Moshiach? The Messiah?"

While studying to be a Rabbi, he had read Maimonides's *Thirteen Principles of Faith* and prayed for the Messiah to come as part of his daily prayers, but the real Messiah?

"How could this scroll be found in an abandoned building in rural North Carolina?"

"Not exactly a hotbed of Judaism, is it?" The Rabbi added skeptically, as he continued his internal debate about the scroll's authenticity.

While he continued to wrestle with the prophecy in his mind, one detail on the scroll carried great weight with him. It would not be apparent to most people, but Rabbi Levi found it hard to ignore.

The signature. The signature on the scroll read *Judah Loew ben Bezalel*.

Rabbi Loew was a legendary 16th-century Talmudic scholar and philosopher in Prague, a city in the present-day Czech Republic. Rabbi Levi knew that while unfamiliar to most Jews, Rabbi Loew's Torah commentaries were still part of the Yeshiva curriculum. In addition to being called Rabbi, he was also referred to by his flock, in Yiddish, as *Protektor*. The Protector. In the 16th century, Prague was a hotbed of antisemitism, and stories about Rabbi Loew's protecting Jews from persecution and pogroms were numerous.

As far as Rabbi Levi was concerned, anything with Rabbi Loew's signature was serious business. So, when he read the next section of the scroll, Rabbi Levi believed it to be genuine and not the heretical raving of someone who had gone completely mad.

אלוהים הפיח פעם חיים באבק כדי ליצור את אדם
(God once breathed life into the dust to create man.)
לשבור את המזוזה הזו, ותכולתה בשילוב עם המים הלא קלוקלים וחולות וואקמאו יעלו מגן

SINS OF THE FATHERS

(Break this mezuzah, and its contents combined with the unspoiled water will raise a protector from the sands of Waccamaw.)

אזהרה!

(Warning!)

המגן יכול להיות תנודתי כמו הרוע שהוא ינסה להשמיד

(The shield can be as volatile as the evil it will seek to destroy.)

Rabbi Levi understood Judaism considered breaking a mezuzah a terrible sin. The Rabbi cradled the broken pieces of the mezuzah in his hands. *Raise a protector? What does that mean?*

"Is the shield a weapon of the protector, or is it just another name for the protector himself?" Rabbi Levi asked in exasperation while staring out at the lake's still waters.

The scroll's warning made Rabbi Levi hesitate. His thoughts went to the incident in his office. A breeze—no, a wind, blew through the room, causing his most cherished possession, his father's Torah, to fall from its stand on a shelf down to the floor. Then, the pages of the Torah moved as if someone were flipping them in search of something. When the sheets stopped flipping, a letter opener fell from the desk and stuck straight up in the Torah in Deuteronomy Chapter 18, Verse 20:

"But the prophet which shall presume to speak a word in my name, which I have not commanded him to speak, or that shall speak in the name of other gods, that prophet shall die."

"I don't understand, God. What does this all mean?" Rabbi Levi asked with a tone of bewilderment. "Who is the prophet that must die?"

Looking toward the sky, the Rabbi pleaded, "God, what is it that you want me to do?"

Shaking his head, Rabbi Levi leaned back in the seat. He recalled picking up the Torah and sitting back down at his desk, the mezuzah in front of him with a hammer beside it. He sat in the quietness of that office, a similar debate to the one he was having now raging inside of him. *Break only in an emergency* was a phrase that came to mind.

Finally, against his beliefs and better judgment, Rabbi Levi followed the scroll instructions and took a hammer to the mezuzah. Inside he found peculiar items; a second scroll penned on similar paper as the original, a piece of paper with only one word printed on it, אלוהים (God), and strangest of all, two black pebbles.

If this was not confusing enough, the second scroll text was even stranger than the first. The scroll quoted from the *Sefer Yetzirah* known to Jewish Mystics as the Book of Creation. The book is a treatise concerning God's creation of the world. Rabbi Levi personally found the book difficult to understand.

מילים מתוך ספר הבריאה מילים מ- ספ *(Words from the Book of Creation)*

חיוב לאפוטרופוס
(Charge to the guardian)

אלוהים אדירים מצווה שתחזיק את מגן
(Mighty God commands you to hold onto his shield)

כתוב את המילה אלוהים במוחו של המגן
(Write the word of God on the mind of the defender)

אבנים שנוצרו מהכנסת ברק במוח המגינים
(Stones inset in the defender's brain)

מקם אלוהים מוקף אבנים בקצה המים
(Place God surrounded by stones at the edge of the water)

Rabbi Levi put the paper with the word God printed on it and the two pebbles in his pocket. The first scroll mentioned the sands of Waccamaw. Still uncertain why he was at the lake, the Rabbi opened the door to his vehicle and headed for the sand and the water's edge. As he made his way across the parking lot, he prayed.

"Blessed are you, Lord our God, King of the Universe, who has sanctified us with His commandments."

Reaching the end of the parking lot, he continued, "My God, grant me the wisdom of King Solomon so that I may understand the meaning of these scrolls."

Rabbi Levi moved toward the beach. All along the way, he begged, "Lord our God, give me the faith of Father Abraham, who willingly laid his son Isaac on the altar in reverence to your name. Once I discover the meaning behind these scrolls, let me trust in your word, no matter what I might think."

Finally reaching the water's edge, the Rabbi looked out at the moonlit lake. A light breeze raised a ripple on the water's surface. The night was alive with the sound of frogs and crickets. The cry of a Screech Owl broke the air of serenity and startled the Rabbi. He shot a look in the direction from which the sound originated but saw nothing.

"Now what, Shimon?" Rabbi Levi challenged himself out loud. "I made it to the water, so what do I do now?"

The Rabbi thought about the phrase; the second scroll contained; *Place God surrounded by stones at the end of the water.*

"Well, I am sort of at the end of the water. The water ends at the beach, right? It doesn't flow from the beach to the middle of the lake."

God surrounded by stones? Could God mean this piece of parchment with just the name of God printed on it?

Rabbi Levi retrieved the paper from his pocket and examined it again. He moved the sand with his shoe and saw plenty of rocks. So many that he asked aloud, "Which stones?"

Then the Rabbi remembered *the stones in my pocket.*

Pulling the two small pebbles from his pocket Rabbi Levi reminded himself, "God, let me trust in your word."

The Rabbi put the paper with the word "God" on it in the palm of his right hand. He placed a stone on each end of the piece of paper and studied it carefully. Then, Rabbi Levi knelt just where the water met the sand and carefully placed the piece of paper there.

"God surrounded by stones," the Rabbi whispered as he put one stone down. Then he wavered. Closing his eyes, he prayed, "My God, regardless of what happens when I place this last stone down, give me the courage of your servant Moses to face it."

Rabbi Levi put the stone down and stepped back. Nothing happened initially, but the sand under the paper and rocks soon shifted. A small mound formed, spreading out and pushing upward simultaneously.

After several minutes, Rabbi Levi dropped to his knees and cried out. "My God, what have I done?"

Chapter 24

August 21st
Catacombs under Antonescu Compound, Lake Waccamaw, NC
2:30 a.m.

Jack. Wake up, Jack.

Floating on the edge of consciousness, Jack Aitken was unsure if what he heard was authentic or his imagination. However, it was familiar.

Get up, Jack. Please. Before he—

Jack heard the utterance again, but this time more insistent in its tone. Before he, before he what? To whom was the person referring?

Then, a second speaker. A different one, yet recognizable. Masculine sounding and menacing.

Mr. Aitken. Please do wake up now, or I will tear Ms. Bishop's arm from its socket.

Suddenly, Jack was jolted back to reality by a stinging slap across his face.

"Back among the land of the living? Yes, that is better, Mr. Aitken."

Jack's face stung from the hard slap across his cheek, and he blinked as his eyes adjusted to the dim lighting of the catacombs.

"Jack, thank God," the first voice echoed with an unmistakable sound of relief.

Turning toward the sound, Jack saw Anne, covered in blood, but before he could speak, Anne blurted out, "Jack, it's not my blood."

"That is right," Lucius Rofocale interjected while flipping an object in his hand.

Lucius stopped and held the object in front of Jack's face. "It is his blood."

Despite the chains he wore, Jack reeled in horror at the sight of Sheriff Glenn Hill's battered face and with the realization that the head was no longer attached to his body. Lucius started spinning the head on his finger like it was a basketball. After a few rotations, he flipped it up and down in his hand and then tossed the sheriff's decapitated head in the direction of the Strigoi.

"Here, catch," Lucius ordered gleefully. The Strigoi caught the skull as effortlessly as a human might catch a tennis ball. The Sheriff's head disappeared into the beast's massive paw, who tossed it away after sniffing the blood still dripping from it.

"Please forgive my friend." Lucius feigned concern. "He has the brawn, but not the brain, and often acts impetuously. He just discovered that he should have sucked the sheriff dry before he ripped off his head. I am afraid the taste of blood from a dead body is not very appealing."

Jack viewed Lucius's antics with a mix of fear and hate.

"Nervous, Jack?" Lucius gloated. "You should be. Before the sheriff met his end, he revealed everything to me."

Any vestige of the haze that Jack had found himself under was gone. Lucius's taunts carried with them an instantaneous feeling of anxiety. The warning lights were blinking red, and the sirens were screaming in Jack's brain.

What the hell does that mean? The Sheriff revealed everything? Revealed what? Jack thought to himself in rapid succession. He tried to think of how he might bait Lucius into disclosing more details, but Lucius stepped past Jack and stopped in front of Anne. His eyes were now blazing red, and he ogled her unpleasantly. Lucius began to stroke Anne's hair. Anne turned her face away in disgust.

"What is wrong, Anne? Jack is not the only one who knows beauty when he sees it."

Lucius continued to twirl the ends of Anne's hair around his finger as he ogled her. The sight of Lucius fondling Anne ignited a fire deep down in Jack's soul.

"Get your filthy hands off her, you bastard!" Jack yelled through clenched teeth.

Lucius continued touching Anne while reaching out with his left hand and strangling Jack. He held Jack up against the wall and suspended him in the air so that Jack's head touched the ceiling of the catacomb. Jack struggled to breathe.

"Jack, am I going to have problems with you like before?" Lucius asked sternly. "You cannot possibly have forgotten that I do not take orders from anyone, particularly you."

When Lucius finally removed his vise-like fingers from his throat, Jack was almost unconscious. With Lucius's assault seemingly over, Jack hung limply, with the chains from the ceiling attached to his wrists being the only thing preventing him from collapsing to the floor.

"You better be careful with this one," Lucius whispered to Anne. "Did you know that he pulled the proverbial plug on his lovely wife? No telling what he might do to you, my dear."

"Of course I know, you vile piece of filth." Anne was defiant. "You could not possibly understand the anguish of making such a decision. You would have to have a heart and a soul, both of which you lack. You are incapable of grasping the paradox that can exist between love and mercy. These concepts are foreign to every demon and even Lucifer himself."

Lucius grinned smugly while slowly clapping his hands together.

"Bravo, Anne. Bravo. I knew making your acquaintance would not be a disappointment. You remind me of another pious *'warrior'* for humankind. The parallels between you and Mark Desmond are quite striking."

Lucius frowned. "You doubt me? Let me give you one example. After decades of devoted service to JESU, both of you lost faith in and rejected the orthodoxy and methods of your mentors."

Anne countered, "You would do well not to mistake my rejection of JESU as a dismissal of my faith in God. Nor does it alter my feelings for or my relationship with Mark."

Lucius laughed. "It just occurred to me that you have as much in common with Jack as you did with Mark! Both you and Jack ended up killing the one person in the world you loved the most! What a couple you make!"

Before Anne could respond, Lucius resumed his pompous soliloquy. "Anne, now that we have gotten to know each other a little better, I have a question that I am dying to ask. Since you are no longer with JESU, does that mean pre-marital relations are possible?"

Glancing over at Jack, still recovering from his near strangulation, Lucius asked with a raised eyebrow, "How is he, Anne?"

Anne responded coldly, "While nothing that any demon does surprises me, that question is beneath even someone like you. Human or otherwise, no so-called Head of Government is interested in such salacious details."

Jack, still catching his breath, threatened, "Stop it. I swear I will…"

Before he could finish his sentence, Jack felt the back of Lucius's hand across his eye. The impact of the blow sent him flying backward into the wall.

"You are not wearing any armor today, Jack," Lucius declared, picking Jack's head up by his hair. "There is no sword hanging around your waist either. Before this night is over, you will feel pain beyond anything you can imagine. After that, you will experience suffering like you never knew could be possible."

Lucius stepped back. "Anne, you could change his destiny. Mind you, I will still kill Jack, but I could do it swiftly and cleanly."

"Some choice," Anne replied caustically.

"And I will let you go." Lucius paused and studied Anne's face for a reaction.

"Just tell me where Jack has hidden Saint Michael's Sword, and I promise I will keep my word."

"A promise from a demon," Anne proclaimed dismissively, "is no promise at all."

Jack muttered, "She doesn't know."

"What was that, Jack?" Lucius asked.

Jack watched Lucius through his one eye that was not swollen shut.

"Gibbs Secret Number Four," Jack taunted.

Lucius glanced toward Anne. "Tell me, what in the devil he is blathering about now, my dear?"

Anne shook her head and shrugged. "I have no idea."

"You don't watch television, Lucius?" Jack tried to smile despite his split lip.

"*NCIS*? Leroy Jethro Gibbs?" Jack questioned, and after a moment of silence, stated, "I guess not. He is a man who lives by a code. He calls them rules. Not your kind of guy."

"Get to the point, Mr. Aitken," Lucius impatiently tapped his fingernails on the cave wall.

"Rule Four states that the best way to keep a secret is to keep it to yourself."

Staring at Lucius, Jack persisted despite his exhaustion. "Anne does not know. The only one that does is me, and I will never tell you where it is no matter how you torture me, you son of a bitch. Killing me will only ensure that you will never find it."

***

"NO!" The scream echoed through the catacombs. Jack and Anne realized that the Strigoi was gone. Lucius turned around and noticed it as well.

"Damn," Lucius murmured in frustration.

Suddenly, a red-haired teenager appeared at one of the tunnel entrances.

"Help me!" The young woman frantically pointed down the tunnel. "It's after me."

The woman jumped behind Lucius as the Strigoi entered the room.

"What did I tell you?" Lucius rebuked his minion. "You are not to hurt the girl!"

The Strigoi, towering over Lucius, tilted its head to the side as if it could not understand the command. Then it growled and started in the direction of Lucius and the girl. Lucius reached out mentally to connect to the brain of the Strigoi.

"*Remember*," Lucius's order reverberated in the Strigoi's head. "*You are not to hurt Maricela Antonescu.*"

Despite the instinct to kill, the beast froze in its tracks. It snarled with anger and frustration. Its eyes narrowed, glaring at Lucius, but it stepped backward away from his master and the easy meal standing behind him.

"Good." Lucius pointed to a mass of straw in the corner. "Now go lie down until I call for you."

The Strigoi reluctantly complied. The young woman looked up at Lucius with a look of gratitude."

"How did you do that?" the teenager asked. "Thank you."

Lucius smirked at the young woman with an unpleasant grin and, holding her chin in his hand, answered, "You are welcome, young Maricela."

***

Anne viewed Jack with concern. His face and throat were already showing significant bruising. His swollen left eye and the blood oozing from his mouth made him look like a boxer taking a severe beating.

"Jack, are you okay?" she whispered. "It's Maricela Antonescu."

Jack instinctively followed the sound of Anne's voice and subsequently saw a young woman.

Maricela saw Jack, then pointed at the Strigoi. "Did it do that to him?"

Lucius shook his head and answered simply. "No."

Before Maricela could utter another word, Lucius declared bluntly, "I did."

A look of fear came across Maricela's face as she stepped back. Seeing an opening, she dashed past Lucius.

"I'm out of here!" Maricela shouted and fled down the tunnel.

Turning to Jack and Anne, Lucius folded his arms and laughed. "Watch this."

"Get your hands off me!" Maricela screamed. "My father is going to fire your asses!"

Still struggling to free herself, Maricela was ushered back to Lucius by two of her father's former guards. The dim light in the tunnel had shielded her view of the two men, but she now realized, with horror, that the guards were dead. At least, they should have been.

"Be careful with our little mother," Lucius cautioned his zombie henchmen. "She is in a delicate condition."

Maricela began to sob. "I want my mother and father."

Lucius, feigning compassion, spoke softly. "I am sorry to tell you this, my dear, but your parents are no more. They have charged me with your care."

Maricela fell to her knees and cried, "What is happening?"

She shook her head in disbelief. "Where's Reid? He was with me in my room. That is the last thing I remember."

Lucius whistled, then thundered, "Come!"

"Look behind you, Maricela," Lucius suggested.

Still crying intensely, Maricela turned around, and behind her was Reid Bowman. She got to her feet instantly and rushed into Reid's arms.

"Oh, Reid!" Maricela sighed with relief. "I am so glad to see you!"

Jack cried out, "Lucius, stop it! Don't do this!"

"Leave her alone. She is only a child," Anne pleaded.

Lucius held up his hand. Jack and Anne both began to choke, unable to breathe. They watched helplessly as Reid Bowman transformed back into the Strigoi. Saliva from its mouth fell onto Maricela's hair. Maricela's happiness instantaneously transformed into terror.

"OH MY GOD!" Maricela screamed as the Strigoi released her. She slumped to her knees at Lucius's feet.

"Maricela, do not be afraid of the Strigoi. After all, he is the father of your unborn child."

Maricela grimaced a renewed look of horror on her face.

"Yes, dear Maricela." Lucius stared down at her. "He was as gentle as he could be, but I do apologize for the scratches on your arms and legs."

Maricela inspected her arms and legs, seeing the scratches she had not noticed or felt until now. Through her tears, she asked quizzically, "Is this why you called me mother?"

"Precisely. A great honor has been given to you, my dear. You will be the prophet's mother who will proclaim Lucifer's truth to the world."

Lucius put down his hand, allowing Anne and Jack to breathe. As they gasped for air, Lucius reached down to Maricela.

"Come, my dear," Lucius cooed. "You need your rest."

Unable to rise, Maricela fainted and slumped to the floor. Not wanting to stir up the Strigoi further, he motioned to one of the guards to move Maricela to a room at the end of the tunnel.

Lucius sighed. "A lovely creature, but these humans are so flimsy and emotionally fragile."

***

Outwardly, Lucius appeared to be the invincible entity he always was, but the constant need to restrain the Strigoi was draining his strength. He needed a power boost, and he needed it quickly. Lucius retrieved a chalice from the altar against the wall and filled it with water from his ceremonial bath. He quickly downed the contents of the chalice and filled it once more. The water from the River Styx did its job; Lucius felt a rush of energy course through his body. Filling his cup a third time, Lucius returned to Jack and Anne.

"What a pathetic superhero duo you make," Lucius crowed, before taking another gulp of water. "I suppose not being able to smell carbon monoxide put you at a disadvantage, but it was far too easy to capture the two of you. Mark Desmond would surely be disappointed."

Anne could feel the welts rising around her throat from Lucius's agonizing grip. Despite not being anywhere near her, she was sure she felt Lucius's fingers at her throat. It was like he had been standing right before her when the airway became constricted. Yet, after the initial onslaught, the grip loosened to allow her to get just enough air not to lose consciousness. Anne wondered how that could be.

Taking the last gulp of water from the chalice, Lucius returned it to the altar.

"I would offer you some, but I do not believe your mortal body could stand it. It is rather powerful stuff."

"It's only water." In addition to his other injuries, a swollen cheek made it increasingly difficult for Jack to speak.

"But that is where you are wrong, Jack. This water is found only in one place on the planet. As I understand it, water is necessary for humans to survive. This water would do just the opposite. It would kill you."

Jack's gaze met Anne's. Only one box left to check to confirm what they both were thinking.

"Where does it come from?" Anne asked.

"Come, come, Anne," Lucius replied derisively. "You already know the answer to that question."

Lucius reached beneath his cloak and pulled out a book. Anne and Jack instantly knew what it was. It was the Domjen journal that Maria Antonescu had entrusted to them.

"Tsk, tsk, tsk, here are more mistakes you have made."

Lucius held up the journal. "Not only did you clearly not read the diary in its entirety, but you brought it with you as well. So careless. How Domjen was able to hide this from me and why it ended up with the Antonescus is something I am still trying to figure out, but if there ever was a book of secrets, this is it."

Anne felt a knot immediately grow in her stomach. *If only Maria had given us more time with the book. What did I miss?*

"Yes, it is all in here. All those experiments with electricity and the correspondence about them between Domjen and your Founding Father, Doctor Franklin."

Tapping the cover, Lucius declared, "This journal contains vital information on controlling animals through impulses from the brain, which is the key to controlling my friend, the Strigoi. As an aside, in my opinion, Doctor Franklin is every bit the ghoul he appears to be in the journal."

Shaking his head, Lucius went on. "All of those bodies in the basement in London. I am sure he thought no one would ever find them. But, surprisingly, Domjen was the more important contributor of the two. That is why when he offered to be my captive in exchange for keeping Franklin out of the whole affair, well, it was one of the easiest deals I ever made. I guess, as they say, the rest is history."

Jack wondered about the bearded man in the house's basement in Ingold. Was it an apparition or Samuel Domjen himself?

"Do not get me wrong," Lucius resumed, "it was not easy. I drove Domjen mad in the process."

Lucius smiled cruelly. "Sometimes, it can be such a pleasure to do one's job. But I digress."

"Forgive me," Anne spoke politely, hoping it might keep Lucius talking. "Does the water from the River Styx have any medicinal purpose?"

"Well," Lucius exclaimed with surprise, "so you read some of the Domjen's journal after all."

Lucius sneered at Jack. "By the way, you could learn some manners from Anne. Unfortunately, you will not live long enough for any of them to rub off on you."

"Yes, Anne. You are correct that this is water from the River Styx. It has restorative powers and helps maintain my energy level to produce the electrical impulses needed to guide the Strigoi. It is even powerful enough to cure the bite of one. Buried deep in the journal is a description of the rather complicated process involved in curing a Strigoi bite, but I doubt anyone has ever attempted it."

Anne and Jack watched as the journal ignited in Lucius's hand and burned to ashes in seconds. He rubbed the ashes between his talon-like fingers and let them scatter at Jack and Anne's feet.

Lucius gave Anne a devilish grin. "Unfortunately, Detective Wallace did not bite you like he was supposed to; we might have been able to try it."

***

Jack's injuries caused him to fade in and out of consciousness, but his ears perked up when he heard Lucius say something about curing a Strigoi bite. It gave Jack a ray of hope about his brother, although the reality of their current situation tempered any optimism. Simply put, their circumstances were beyond grim; they were hopeless. No one knew where they were, so a rescue was out of the question. Unless Lucius made an unimaginable mistake, the end was near.

"I'm so sorry, Amanda," Jack muttered. "I promised I would protect Louis and David. I failed. My sins just continue to haunt me, and now they will have killed our children. I guess it's true that the sins of the fathers are visited on the sons."

Anne heard Jack's apology and, while Lucius turned his back, whispered, "Jack, I know things don't look good now. I am not a Pollyanna, nor have I ever been, but try not to lose faith. We're not dead yet."

Jack tried to smile, but the pain in his jaw was blinding. He was unsure how much more brutality at the hands of Lucius he could endure but having Anne beside him gave him a much-needed shot of courage.

"I sure wish I had on that armor I wore at Culpeper," Jack joked. "Maybe Lucius would have broken something when he beat me. A hand, a finger, or even a fingernail. The good book says it is better to give than to receive. I'm not holding up my end of things."

"Under the circumstances, your good spirits are admirable," Lucius interrupted. "But hardly appropriate, given the untenable position in which you find yourselves. Need I remind you both that the end is coming soon?"

Anne replied icily, "No, you have made that very clear."

"Lucius, you've got the two of us," Jack added. "Let the girl go. She can't be more than eighteen years old."

"And that matters why?" Lucius asked curtly. "It is a little late to save her now. Or do you think otherwise, Mr. Aitken? Another failure on your part. I suppose your concern for Maricela is noble. After all, her father, Constantin, traded her for wealth and power."

"What?"

"That is right, Anne. Constantin Antonescu sold his soul and daughter's womb for money and influence."

Glancing at Jack, Lucius boasted, "Another father whose sins condemned their child to a terrible end. Just like you, Jack."

Lucius paused and added contemptuously, "And you think we demons are despicable."

Anne shook her head. "How could he sell her to that animal?"

She had barely finished her sentence when Lucius slapped her across the face with the back of his hand. The force of the blow sent Anne sailing backward into the cave wall, knocking her unconscious. Jack moved forward toward Lucius, but the restraint of his shackles and chains prevented him from reaching his target.

"YOU BASTARD!" Jack mumbled furiously through his swollen lips. "If you hurt her, I'll ..."

"You will do what, Jack?" Lucius replied angrily.

Lucius snapped his fingers, and the Strigoi appeared and stood snarling next to him. Lucius glared menacingly at Jack.

"Take his hand. Mr. Aitken requires corrective discipline."

The Strigoi grabbed Jack's hand roughly and watched Lucius. Jack's hand completely disappeared inside its grip. Jack gulped; his mouth was agape. Then watched Lucius with a stunned look on his face.

"Squeeze," Lucius ordered, staring furiously at Jack.

The Strigoi clenched its fist, and Jack began to cry out in agony. The screaming was so loud that it roused Anne from her stupor. She shook her head to regain her senses.

Realizing what was occurring, she yelled, "NO! STOP IT! PLEASE!"

The Strigoi's grip was like a vise, and Jack struggled to free himself, to no avail. The monster appeared to grin at Jack's reaction to the excruciating pain. Crunches and pops echoed through the chamber as the bones in Jack's hand snapped and cracked.

"ENOUGH!" Lucius shouted to the Strigoi, which slowly released its grip. Jack hung limply in his chains, having passed out from the suffering inflicted upon him. Every bone in Jack's hand was beyond broken; the Strigoi had shattered them.

"I warned him." Then, leering at Anne, he continued, "And let that be a cautionary message to you, Ms. Bishop. Be careful who you refer to as an animal."

Lucius pointed at the Strigoi. "You are talking about my progeny, and I assure you he is more human than you realize."

Patting his spawn on its hairy chest, Lucius advised, "We must wake your partner in crime, Anne. I am certain he will want to hear this."

Anne looked regretfully at Jack. "Jack, can you hear me? I am so sorry that I provoked this."

Jack didn't respond.

"Let me try." Lucius kicked Jack's feet which caused Jack to stir. Jack grimaced from the pain and tried to avoid moving his crushed hand as any slight jolt sent waves of pain through his injured extremity.

"Welcome back, Jack." Lucius frowned derisively. "I trust we will have no more outbursts, or I will allow my friend here to remove your arm from your body."

The Strigoi stood just behind Lucius, looking hungrily at Anne and Jack with large canine teeth that were impossible to ignore.

"I will accept your silence as agreement to my terms. Jack, I wanted you to be awake to hear what I was about to tell Anne. I think it is essential you both know the truth about my offspring."

Anne still felt the sting on her face from Lucius's blow. She peeked down at Jack's mangled hand and shot him a look of concern. Jack was conscious but hung limply from his chains.

"This Strigoi is more than three hundred years old, but he is far from being the first of his kind." Lucius paced back and forth with his hands behind his back. "In fact, his origins go back to the beginning of creation itself."

Lucius stopped. "I am saying Adam and Eve and the garden of Eden."

Despite the pain of their injuries, Anne and Jack could not help but be intrigued.

Lucius resumed. "Your holy books, as well as our demon legends, share some similar stories. The classic tale of the formation of the world and all its inhabitants is one of those."

"Naturally, there is your version, and then there is the truth." Lucius sneered. "Lord Lucifer's contributions to the planet as you know it are far more significant, and the results much more consequential than you realize."

Lucius peered over at the growling Strigoi. "Of particular interest to your current situation is God assigning the responsibility of naming all the creatures of the Earth to Adam."

Lucius laughed dismissively. "Let us say Adam was not the sharpest tool in the shed. He required help. Before God, in a fit of rage, turned Lucifer into a serpent, my master was assisting Adam in this regard. Adam asked where the creatures he was naming come from, and Lucifer showed him."

"So, Lucifer created the Strigoi?" Anne asked. "Why am I not surprised."

Lucius shook his head. "Is it not usual for a human child to ask a parent about from where their baby brother or sister originates? Lucifer was doing a good deed. It was Adam who took the next step."

"You expect us to believe this story?" Jack remarked while trying not to annoy Lucius further.

"Whether you believe it or not is your affair," Lucius replied pointedly.

"You need to realize that man, not a demon, created the Strigoi." Lucius let the disclosure sink in for a few moments before continuing.

"A little cloning here and gene-splicing there, and this is the result. This Strigoi can trace its lineage back to the very beginning."

Jack watched Anne, wondering what to believe. Anne held Jack's gaze, which led him to think she might believe at least some of what Lucius was saying.

Lucius added, "For the sake of full disclosure, I have one more detail to reveal."

This part ought to be great. A thought Jack, were it not for his injuries, would have verbalized with sarcasm.

Lucius continued, "The original Strigoi would have been the only one of his kind were it not for the demon, Lilith."

Anne scowled. Her years in JESU had taught her a great deal about Lilith. In Jewish folklore, she was Adam's first wife, not Eve. She refused to be subservient to Adam, and God cast her out of Eden as punishment for her stubbornness. Lilith's revenge for this banishment was to take many forms. To some, Lilith was a witch. In other cultures, she was the killer of infants. Elsewhere, she was a highly fertile, sexually aggressive entity. There were stories of Lilith being the mother of vampires, werewolves, and other similar abominations sent to plague humankind.

"Lilith, in a fit of rage toward God and Adam, bred with the original Strigoi and set in motion the events leading up to today."

Looking down the hallway where Maricela was asleep, Lucius went on. "Since Lilith was initially human, she passed down her fertility to subsequent generations. Lilith's demonic qualities were also passed along, allowing the Strigoi to reproduce."

A stunned Jack and Anne observed the Strigoi transform into Jack! Lucius watched them with a wicked smile.

"I told you earlier that Sheriff Hill revealed everything to me, Jack," Lucius declared. "That includes that your sons Louis and David will be God's supposed prophets. While it was likely so subtle as to escape your attention, the signals initiating their transformation awakened the Strigoi."

Lucius bragged, "Lucifer is thoroughly familiar with the book of Revelation, as am I."

"Chapter 11, Verses 1-14," Lucius affirmed. "Two witnesses to proclaim Christ's second coming. Unfortunately for God, Lucifer has no intention of following the script. Let me share with you how this will go."

Lucius resumed his pacing while Jack's double, the Strigoi, stood at attention with an expressionless look on its face.

"Lucifer has bided his time, waiting for this moment for millennia. The Strigoi has been through five intervals of feeding and hibernating, building the strength required to procreate. Every fifty-four years, our friend would rise, feed on animals for sustenance and then go dormant once more."

Jack recalled what Sheriff Hill told them as he spoke, "Every fifty-four years. The number of times the word demon appears in the Bible."

"Excellent, Jack. I am impressed."

"Over the centuries, the Strigoi fed on animals in different geographic regions, making it easy to hide its presence and avoid detection, even in your modern world. Each region is a point on a pentagram, marking its territory with Lake Waccamaw in the middle."

"And consuming human blood is what gives the Strigoi the ability to procreate," Anne interjected.

"Precisely! And by breeding with a descendant, the offspring of the Strigoi will appear human."

The cave was silent except for the dripping water from the ceiling striking the ground below.

"Lucifer's prophet," Lucius asserted triumphantly, "in the form of Maricela's child, will be a far more effective recruiter for the hearts, minds, and souls of humankind since they will present to the world as a human. Would you not agree?"

Lucius paused and affirmed in a frigid tone, "That will be particularly true when we eliminate the competition."

Jack clenched his teeth, the pain in his face and hand replaced by a burst of adrenaline emanating from that part of his soul that instinctively would protect his children. Now he understood what Lucius meant when he told Jack that Sheriff Hill had told Lucius everything. Through his one open eye, Jack stared hatefully at Lucius.

Lucius, now jubilant, went on. "Anne's membership in JESU is severed, so they are not here to assist your children."

Pointing at the headless body of Sheriff Hill, Lucius emphasized sarcastically, "I am afraid the sheriff will be of no help. With his unfortunate accident, his organization, whatever it calls itself, is now as headless as the sheriff."

Pretending to be sorrowful, Lucius raised his hands as a minister might signal a church congregation to stand.

"Jack, you and Anne are quite obviously tied up at the moment. Even if you were free, judging from how you look, you are not in any physical condition to attempt a rescue of any sort."

Lucius, reveling in his victory, bragged, "Jack, I must say that I now feel like the business I left unfinished in Culpeper is concluding. All the loose ends tied up, and all that. So disastrous for you that you failed to kill me when you had the chance. Tell me, how does it feel to know your children will soon die and that your failure is complete?"

Jack was seething, and his stare was like a laser beam trying to bore a hole through Lucius. His mind urgently searched for a way to free himself and save Louis and David, but he could find no answers to the challenge he was facing. The only way out he could see was the proverbial *Hail Mary pass*. Jack silently began to pray.

Heavenly Father. My sons are in danger. Your future servants are in terrible peril. Only you can save them from the fate my enemy, and yours have planned for them. As much as I love Louis and David, I recognize they belong to you now. Like your servant Abraham, who, in obedience to you, willingly placed his son Isaac on the altar, I am putting my sons in your hands.

As Jack finished his prayer, he heard Lucius speak once more.

"No pithy answers, Jack? No smart-aleck responses? How disappointing. Is this the best you have?"

Before Jack could respond, Lucius went on. "I once offered you a bargain that would save your wife's life, and you refused me. I am going to do something that I have never done before. I am going to bargain with you a second time."

Jack made no effort to speak. He stoically eyed Lucius.

"As prophets, Louis and David are destined to die. Either today at the hands of the Strigoi or, in the future, as described in the book of Revelation, at the hands of the Antichrist. My proposal is quite simple. Jack, your sons are pawns in a high-stakes chess match. Remove Louis and David from the board voluntarily, and I will allow them to live, and you can go home to your children. I promise none of you will ever be disturbed by any demon again. You and your boys can live your lives in peace."

Lucius pointed at Anne. "Anne, if you convince Jack to accept my offer, you can leave with him. You and Jack will be free to go and be a couple or do whatever you wish. You can start life over, free from JESU and demons."

"And if we refuse?" Anne asked.

"It is quite simple. I will send the Strigoi to collect Louis and David. The two of you will watch us slaughter the prophets of God. The Strigoi will bathe in and drink their blood."

"After that, Jack," Lucius continued, "you will witness Anne having the skin peeled slowly from her body. Then, when you plead for death, Jack, we will disfigure you hideously instead and let you see the looks of horror on the faces of the people you encounter. And you will live with the deaths of your loved ones on your conscience, forever."

Lucius watched Jack, awaiting a response. Jack just looked back with a smile on his face. The two of them eyed one another before Lucius finally broke the silence.

"Well, Jack." Lucius exhaled impatiently. "What do you say? Do we have a deal?"

Chapter 25

August 21st
Catacombs under Antonescu Compound, Lake Waccamaw, NC
5:00 a.m.

Jack's gaze did not wander. He just intently watched Lucius through his uninjured eye without saying a word.

"Look at your hand, Jack."

Jack inspected the lump of flesh and bone where there once were fingers.

The veins in Lucius's temples visibly pulsed as he warned, "I would think the consequences of testing my patience further should be clear."

The Strigoi, anticipating Lucius's signal to attack, shifted its weight forward, ready to pounce. It licked the salvia from its lips in expectation.

Anne begged, "Jack, please. Answer him."

Finally, Jack broke his silence.

"It is difficult to have faith in a God you cannot see, and I have wrestled with why God would allow humans to suffer as they do for a significant portion of my life."

"Go on, Jack," Lucius eagerly encouraged his adversary. "Please, continue."

"I want my sons to live, and I want to be there to watch them grow up. I have grave concerns about what being a prophet for God means for their future."

Teardrops fell from Anne's face as she acknowledged his dilemma. "Jack, I understand, and I don't blame you."

Spitting a mix of blood and saliva on the cave floor, Jack cleared his mouth to speak. "I have had enough of making difficult and challenging decisions."

He faced Anne. "Forgive me for saying it, but I am tired of choosing between the lesser of two evils. The difference between bad and worse."

"I see Jack," Lucius spoke reassuringly. "God can be so cruel."

Jack breathed deeply, grimacing in pain. "There are far too many mysteries of faith for my simple mind ever to understand."

He heard the echo of Amanda's plea in his head: *"You must believe, Jack."*

Jack stared at Lucius again; "I guess it is time for me to give up control and submit to what I believe to be inevitable."

"A wise decision, Jack." Lucius beamed in triumph, anticipating Jack's submission to his will. "Shall I draw up the papers for…"

Anne took a deep breath in anticipation of what she was sure she would hear next.

Jack interrupted Lucius and declared, "The Reverend Billy Graham once declared that God does not call his children to a playground, but to a battlefield. My hopes for David and Louis are in God's hands, and it is into those mighty hands that I place their fate. Do with me what you will, but I will never submit to you or Satan."

Anne's heart soared upon hearing Jack's words. She saw Jack in a way that she had never imagined. After Mark Desmond, she thought she would never look at any man again….with love.

On the other hand, Lucius glared at Jack with dagger eyes, realizing he had failed. He had been confident that if the promise of resurrecting his beloved wife were not enough to convert Jack, preserving the lives of his children would be. A raging storm was building inside the demon lord.

Ominously, Lucius announced, "So be it. You will pay the ultimate price for your lack of vision and audacity,"

Lucius motioned to the Strigoi. "Go retrieve God's prophets," he viciously demanded. "Destroy anyone who gets in your way. The time has come that we teach Mr. Aitken a lesson in pain and suffering that he and others will never forget."

Having the directions to George Aitken's home, previously implanted in its brain, the Strigoi once more assumed the identity of Jack Aitken and headed for the cave exit.

Turning his attention back to Jack and Anne, the normally blood-red hue of Lucius's eyes was now nearly black, which foretold the price that Jack and Anne would pay upon the Strigoi's return. There would be nothing to restrain Lucius's fury.

Jack spoke, his speech now slurred, "Anne, I am sorry I dragged you into all of this. I need you to know how grateful I am for your sacrifice on behalf of my family." Blood and saliva dripped from his lips. "And for me too."

While Anne's injuries were painful, she could barely recognize Jack. She could not turn away from his battered face and the imprints of Lucius's fingers around his throat. It was almost as if they had been seared into Jack's flesh, branding him like a cattle baron might label a member of his herd.

"Jack. I have something I need to tell you."

Anne knew the timing of what she was about to say was awkward and irrational under the circumstances, but she felt compelled to verbalize it anyway.

"Jack, I lov—"

***

Anne's sentence was interrupted by a noise sounding like chains dragging across the floor. A loud grunt, such as what a powerlifter might utter as they raised a heavy weight above their head, echoed through the catacombs. Then a large object struck the catacomb's wall, shaking the cave like an earthquake.

Anne, Jack, and Lucius struggled to see through the dust the once intact wall's broken rubble generated. Something was on the ground. It appeared to be stunned as it slowly rose to its feet. The two zombie bodyguards guarding Maricela Antonescu had heard the commotion and arrived at the tunnel entrance.

"GO!" Lucius barked, pointing toward the cave entrance.

The guards instantly obeyed. Briefly, there were some snorts and groans before one after the other; they bounced on the ground, settling back at Lucius's feet. Their eyes were wide open, and their jaws agape. Each guard's upper torso was twisted ninety degrees, and the upper half of their body now faced backward instead of forward; their spinal cords snapped.

Lucius viewed the corpses in disbelief. The dust finally settled, and it was clear that the first object tossed back into the room was the Strigoi! Anne and Jack were shocked!

Jack muttered, "What the hell just happened?"

Lucius glared at the Strigoi and snapped, "Well?"

The Strigoi looked down at Lucius, stunned by what had just happened to it, unsure what to do next.

"Why are you just standing here?" Lucius snarled. " ATTACK! DAMN YOU! DESTROY IT!"

The incensed Strigoi, its vampire-like teeth bared, promptly heeded its master. Never having been repelled in such a manner, its dagger-like claws slashed at the intruder, and it ferociously roared as it attacked in a blind rage. Two beings wrestled with one other, each trying to gain leverage and advantage. At first, the Strigoi dug into the cave's dirt floor using its powerful legs and feet. It pushed its foe backward. But the intruder blunted the attack, and slowly, the Strigoi began to give ground.

"Anne, I am having problems seeing anything right now. Who is that?"

"It looks human, Jack, but there is no human being I know that could go toe to toe with that beast!"

At that moment, the intruder's strength became too great. The Strigoi fell backward. Holding the hairy brute in the air by its wrists, the intruder forcefully drove forward like an offensive lineman at football practice, taking out its frustration on a tackling dummy. Picking up speed, it rammed the Strigoi into the cave wall with such force that Jack and Anne were sure they would be buried alive. Debris fell from the ceiling, filling the cave with a thick dust cloud and making visibility impossible.

They started to choke and fought for air. Each cough caused Jack and Anne great physical suffering due to the severe injuries they had already sustained. While still wheezing, they strained to see anything through the thick cloud of debris. At first, they heard nothing but labored breathing, but then another noise, close to Jack and Anne, could be heard.

"Jack, do you hear that?"

"Yeah," Jack replied. "I think the only thing that isn't hurting is my ears. It sounds like someone is ripping something. Like tearing strips of cloth to make rags."

The tearing noise continued, and as the dust settled, a figure right in front of Anne and Jack emerged. It was a sight they both were familiar with, Jack, in particular, having seen it up close and personal on several occasions. In so doing, Lucius had transformed himself into his pure demon form and had torn the clothes he had been wearing to shreds. Coarse black hair with a blueish hue was everywhere on his body. The fire-red color of his eyes bore through the dust like a laser beam, and his large, protruding canine teeth dominated his facial features. Despite seeing it before, Jack still felt a chill down his spine. A new wave of anxiety engulfed him. *Now the shit is going to hit the fan.*

***

Lucius thundered in a deep, threatening voice, "SHOW YOURSELF!"

A figure stepped forward through the cloud of dust. Jack and Anne could see that the being was more than eight feet tall and every bit as muscular as the Strigoi. It even towered over Lucius. At first glance, its arms and legs appeared human, but looking at the figure more closely, it resembled no human being they had ever seen. It was more like the Incredible Hulk, except that the skin was tan, not green, and looked like the grit from a piece of sandpaper. It dragged a heavy, rusted chain with sizable links behind it.

The arms of the entity were far longer than that of a human being. Its knuckles almost dragged upon the floor, and its forearms were quite prominent. They put Popeye the Sailor to shame. Jack and Anne could see how the being had forced the Strigoi back. The calf muscles in its legs were the size of softballs, and the thighs were as thick as tree trunks. The power of its upper body rivaled that of the Strigoi.

Looking into its face, Jack realized it had no mouth. Its eyes were considerably smaller than a person's, and it had a piece of rock in each eye socket. The overall shape of its skull was more like a child's toy block than a circle. The broad forehead had no creases or wrinkles. The face of the being had no expression on it, nor did it display anything that one might take for emotion.

Lucius sized up his opponent while a steady, guttural growl emanated from his throat. Lucius and the entity circled one another, then Lucius struck! His lightning-fast claw-like hand headed for the temple of his foe's forehead, but the entity blocked the blow. A look of surprise could be seen on Lucius's demonic face when the intruder grabbed Lucius by the throat, pressed him up against the wall, and began to choke him. Jack and Anne were in awe when they saw Lucius begin to flail around, trying to escape his opponent's grip.

Now he knows how it feels, Jack thought.

Jack shouted as best he could at the entity. "Don't let that bastard breathe!"

Out of nowhere, the Strigoi struck the intruder from the side, causing the entity to release Lucius, who fell to the floor gasping for air. Using his telepathic powers, he reached out to assume control over his new enemy. There was no connection. He tried a second time, but there was not even the faintest sign of an electrical current.

"It has no heart," Lucius gasped while still trying to catch his breath. "Or soul."

Lucius struggled to get to his feet. As he did, he wondered if all the months keeping the Strigoi under control had weakened him so severely that he could not defeat the intruder.

Leaning against the wall, he muttered, "Time for me to go," and stumbled down the tunnel toward Maricela's chamber.

***

The Strigoi and his opponent were rolling around on the ground, scratching and clawing at one another. Each tried to get on top, but neither could gain the upper hand. Jack and Anne noticed that with each blow the Strigoi suffered, it seemed to experience significant pain, but its attack on its foe didn't seem to have any similar effect. The being did not bleed, nor did it lose pieces of flesh. It merely seemed to absorb the attack and come back for more.

The primitive brain of the Strigoi and its base instincts tried everything possible to destroy its opponent, but to no avail. The beast almost wished its master would come back to provide guidance or attack the intruder, but it soon realized that no assistance was coming. Growing tired and sensing that the opponent was not showing signs of fatigue, the Strigoi managed to free itself from the grips of the foe and dashed away down the corridor toward the cave entrance. It came across a second figure in the passage, but the Strigoi had lost its appetite for battle and fled.

The expressionless entity stood up and started after the Strigoi.

"No!" the second figure yelled with its hand in front of the entity's chest.

Pointing in the direction Lucius had taken, it demanded, "Go down that corridor and destroy anything you find there."

The entity stopped as it was commanded to do, turned, and lumbered down the corridor after Lucius. The dust from the entity and the Strigoi's wrestling match still hung in the air, but Jack and Anne could now see the second figure, who quickly came to their aid.

"My God!" the man yelled. "We have to get you medical attention right away!"

Anne realized she recognized him.

"Rabbi Levi? What are you doing here?"

The sound of footsteps echoed from the tunnel to Maricela's room. The Rabbi made his way to the tunnel entrance and met the entity.

"Is there anyone down there?"

The entity stood at attention and shook its head back and forth, indicating that it had found no one. The Rabbi pointed toward Anne and Jack.

"Free them."

The entity made its way over to Anne and Jack, then pulled the chains that bound them from the cave ceiling. Both Jack and Anne winced in pain but were grateful to be free. The entity roughly grabbed Jack's arm to remove the shackle around the wrist of Jack's crushed hand. Jack screamed in agony, and the Rabbi quickly intervened.

"Stop it! You are hurting him!"

The entity stopped but showed no expression of remorse. For the first time, the Rabbi saw the headless body of Sheriff Hill and gasped. Placing his hand over his mouth, he turned away and vomited.

"A friend of yours?" The Rabbi asked while cleaning his lips with his shirt sleeve.

Anne replied sadly, "Unfortunately, yes."

"Don't worry." Pointing at the entity, he continued, "He'll take care of transporting the body back to the car."

Jack tried to smile despite his split lip. "Tell us, who is our rescuer?"

"You would not believe me if I told you." Rabbi Levi shook his head.

"Try us," Anne quickly responded, as she struggled to support Jack.

"It's a Golem." Rabbi Levi wrapped his arm around Jack's waist. "An entity mentioned in Jewish historical and mystical books. It is supposed to be a myth."

"Thank God it isn't." Jack winced in pain as the trio slowly made their way toward the cave entrance.

"I have a degree in religious studies," Anne shared. "I remember reading about the Golem of Prague. Now, what was the name of the Rabbi?"

Anne paused for a moment. "Rabbi Judah Loew. I think that is his name."

"You evidently aced the Jewish history exam. I am impressed."

"This isn't the Golem of Prague, is it?" Jack asked, cringing with every step.

"No." Rabbi Levi answered. "I don't believe that it is, but it does beg the question of what is it doing here, right?"

Rabbi Levi shifted his grip to better support Jack's weight.

"The mezuzah," the Rabbi continued. "I must ask your forgiveness, but when I read the mezuzah, I was not upfront with you about it."

Jack and Anne exchanged a look of surprise with one another.

"The mezuzah, in fact, contained a cryptic message that I interpreted to be about the Messiah."

"The Messiah?" Anne questioned.

"Yes. It warned that a time of great tribulation was upon humanity and that a great evil was rising. Were it not for the signature of Rabbi Loew; I would have dismissed it as the ravings of a madman."

Anne interrupted. "Did you see that, that *thing* that ran down the hallway?"

"Only from the back," the Rabbi responded.

"Well, you just had a glimpse of the Prime Minister of Hell who is here to make preparations for the genuine evil yet to come," Anne revealed.

"So, you are telling me everything in that scroll is the truth?" Rabbi Levi asked doubtfully.

"I'm afraid so," Anne replied.

Looking at Jack, she asked, "How are you doing?"

"I've been better."

Glancing down the corridor where Lucius fled, he inquired, "No sign of Maricela Antonescu either?"

"There was a woman back there?"

"Yes, Rabbi," Anne answered ruefully. "An incredibly unfortunate young woman. I'll try to explain it, but it will be hard for you to hear."

"You can tell me on the way to the hospital."

"Wait, before we go, I need to get some water from the baptismal." Jack's eyes met Anne's. "For George."

Anne found a flask, filled it, and slipped it into her pocket.

"Honestly, knowing that Lucius touched this thing creeps me out."

Rabbi Levi stood in front of the Golem, who did not move a muscle and pointed at Sheriff Hill's body.

"Get the linens from the room at the end of the corridor and wrap that body in them. We should try to show the remains of the sheriff some respect."

"Thank you for your compassion, Rabbi,"

Anne bowed her head sadly. "His head is around the corner."

Rabbi Levi felt faint at the mention of retrieving the sheriff's decapitated head.

"Get the head as well, please. " A frightened Rabbi Levi instructed the Golem.

The Golem gathered up Sheriff Hill's remains.

Anne rubbed her forehead. "My car is up the road from the gate, but I think you should drive, Rabbi. I'm feeling a little lightheaded."

"You probably have a concussion," Rabbi Levi replied worriedly.

As the group exited the cave, a figure lumbered toward them.

"It's one of the Antonescu security detail that ran afoul of the Strigoi." Declared Anne.

The Golem dropped Sheriff Hill's remains and went over to the figure who began biting the Golem. Unaffected, it grabbed the zombie's head in its hands and squeezed it like a grape. The Golem's power was on full display as it crushed the zombie's skull and dropped it to the ground. Then it simply picked up the sheriff's body and waited for Rabbi Levi's instructions.

Jack was in awe. "The strength of the Golem is incredible."

**

The sun began to rise as Anne, Jack, Rabbi Levi, and the Golem left behind the carnage in the Antonescu compound and made their way out the front gate. Beads of sweat poured down their backs as the heat and humidity of a late summer morning in North Carolina began to take hold. Progress was slow; Jack needed to lean heavily on Rabbi Levi and Anne, grimacing with every step.

Trying to distract himself from the pain of his injuries, Jack commented, "I noticed something interesting, Rabbi. You did not give any direction to the Golem about taking out that zombie."

Rabbi Levi replied, "While it must obey its creator, it has an instinct about evil. If it were not for the Golem, I never would have found you two. It just started walking in the direction of the cave. It senses evil and seeks it out with the intent to destroy it."

Anne joked. "I recall that only the wisest Rabbi, those purest in heart, could raise a Golem."

"Well, I heard that the Golem only rises from virgin soil." Rabbi Levi chuckled. "And I can't figure out how the sand of Lake Waccamaw qualifies."

"I guess it is hard to separate myth from fact when it comes to this Golem," Jack added.

Anne's car was coming into view, as was a neighborhood resident on an early morning walk with her dog. The dog began to growl and bark as soon as it saw the Golem. Suddenly, the Golem dropped the remains of Sheriff Hill and began to approach the barking animal. Rabbi Levi jarred Jack, causing him to groan as he leaned him against Anne and took off after the Golem.

"NOO! WAIT!" Rabbi Levi shouted at the Golem.

The Golem immediately halted as the barking dog circled it.

"You brute!" The dog's owner shouted, shaking her fist at the Golem. "What are you doing to my Ginger!"

The Golem stared straight ahead, not moving a muscle.

"I am so sorry, miss. He did not mean to scare your dog."

"Can't he apologize for himself?" The woman asked sarcastically, failing to notice that the Golem had no mouth.

"I am afraid he is mute." Rabbi Levi answered. "Again, please accept our apology."

The woman continued walking her dog and was out of sight before Jack and Anne could catch up to the Rabbi.

"Pick up the body." Rabbi Levi demanded. The Golem immediately complied and headed toward the car.

"Why doesn't the Golem speak?" Jack asked.

"The Golem is God's creation." Rabbi Levi explained. "Adam was God's first Golem, I suppose. If you look at it that way, we might all be Golems of some type."

"Lucius's story indicated the Strigoi's origin dates back to Adam too," Anne added. "I guess the Strigoi and the Golem have a connection resulting from their biblical origins. Perhaps this is why it could match the Strigoi's strength."

Rabbi Levi nodded. "One legend says that speech would mean the Golem had a soul and would then become an insult to God. It might also make it susceptible to pain and evil influences."

Arriving at the car, Rabbi Levi helped Anne get Jack into the back seat while the Golem, as instructed, placed Sheriff Hill's remains in the trunk. Rabbi Levi slammed the trunk shut and observed the Golem. Pausing just for a moment, he reached up and removed the parchment containing the word of God from the Golem's forehead. Instantaneously, the Golem collapsed at the Rabbi's feet in a sand pile, and the breeze blew in all directions.

Rabbi Levi reached down and picked up two small stones, the Golem's eyes. He put them in his pocket along with the parchment. The Rabbi got behind the wheel and turned the ignition to begin the forty-five-minute drive to the hospital.

"What happened to the Golem?" Anne asked, as she checked on an exhausted Jack, already asleep in the backseat.

The Rabbi just clutched the steering wheel in silence.

"You destroyed it?"

Rabbi Levi looked out the windshield "Rabbi Loew had to destroy the Golem of Prague because it performed its mission so well, it became difficult to control."

"The Golem is a mixed blessing, Anne. Its sole purpose is to destroy evil. It will do anything to seek it out, including hurting innocent people who might get in its way."

"Didn't Rabbi Lowe hide the Golem in a synagogue in Prague as a precaution against a return of antisemitism?" Anne questioned.

Reaching into his pocket, Rabbi Levi pulled out the scroll that had been in the Golem's forehead along with the two black stones. He showed them to Anne, saying, "That is what the legend says. I have studied Rabbi Loew's epistles quite closely, and I am a cautious man as he was. Let's call these items an insurance policy if the Strigoi returns."

***

August 21st
Aitken Home, N. Myrtle Beach, SC
6:30 a.m.

David Aitken pulled back the sheets of his bed and yawned. Despite turning in early the night before, he did not feel rested. He had several dreams—nightmares, actually. They were as vivid to him now as they were during his slumber. David was surprised that his older brother, Louis, was already awake. He was sitting at the desk with an open book in front of him.

"What are you doing, Louis?" David asked, as he sat down next to him.

"I'm reading," Louis answered. "Someone calling himself Avi Socho told me in a dream that I would find this book on the desk in the morning. I woke up, and it was here."

"Avi Socho?" David questioned. "Who's that?"

"He told me his real name is Moses," Louis responded. "And that Avi Socho means the leader of prophets. I guess he will be a kind of teacher for the two of us."

David did not completely understand what his brother was saying. He shrugged his shoulders and inspected the book that Louis was reading. It had a black cover, and someone had highlighted passages on several of the pages.

"What book is it, Louis?"

"It's called the *Holy Bible*, David. It belongs to Dad. Moses told me it was in Dad's desk drawer and had been there for years."

"Well, how did it get here? Did you pack it?"

"Of course not," Louis replied. "I did not even know it was there. Moses left it for us and wants us to start reading it. He told me that I should begin reading the pages he marked. The book was open on the desk to this chapter called Revelation, and the section is number eleven."

"What does the *Bible* say?" David asked, eager to know more about it.

"It talks about two witnesses. It says some beast kills the two witnesses."

"That sounds scary." David was now a little less excited about the book.

Changing the subject, Louis asked David, "How did you sleep?

"Not so well. I had a nightmare about Dad getting hurt, but he was okay by the end of the dream. I also had a dream about Uncle George."

Louis appeared surprised. "I did too. Dad gave Uncle George a drink, but then I woke up."

"Yeah, I had the same dream, Louis. He poured water on Uncle George's cut, where the monster bit him, and then Dad tried to get Uncle George to take a sip of the water."

"I hope we see Dad soon," David told Louis. "I miss him."

"Me too. Are you hungry, David? I need a bagel."

"Come on, Louis." David grinned. "I'll make us some breakfast."

The two brothers headed downstairs, seemingly cognizant of the events about to unfold at their uncle's bedside but utterly unaware of the outcome.

***

August 21st
Brunswick County Medical Center, Bolivia, NC
8:00 a.m.

"I don't need a wheelchair!" Jack shouted at a hospital orderly.

The adrenaline of the moment enabled him to walk into the hospital, with Anne's assistance, despite his injuries. Clutching the flask containing the water that Lucius Rofocale asserted was from the River Styx, Jack made his way to the elevator. He pressed the button for the third floor, and the elevator started its ascent upward.

Closing his eyes, Jack muttered, "This is going to work. It has to work."

"I hope so, Jack," Anne interjected. "But you know that Lucius told us that the water had not been administered in this way before. We don't know what is going to happen."

"I know, Anne." Jack faced his friend. "But this is my brother we are talking about, and I cannot bear the thought of life without him. Losing him would be like losing half of myself. We are identical twins. I don't know how to explain it any better."

Anne put her hand on Jack's shoulder. "I think I understand."

The elevator reached the third floor, and the doors opened. Jack stumbled into the hallway; it was only with Anne's help that he could gain his balance and not fall to the floor. Josephine saw him from the waiting room and ran down the hall.

"My God, Jack, what happened to you?"

"DOCTOR! WE NEED A DOCTOR HERE!" Josephine yelled.

"It's all right, Jo." Jack waved away the medical staff. "How is George?"

Josephine's eyes dropped. Jack noticed the Pastor in the lounge, sitting with George's children.

"He's still in a coma, Jack." Josephine's voice trembled. "George is on life support. The doctor was discussing our options."

Josephine paused, fell into Jack's arms, and began to sob.

"Jack," Josephine whispered through her tears. "We were just getting ready to say goodbye and turn the machines off."

Jack broke away from Josephine, headed toward George's room, and, filled with resolve, declared, "Not yet, we're not."

Reaching the door to George's room, Jack used every ounce of strength left in his body to push it open. The sight was all too familiar. George was hooked up to every piece of monitoring equipment imaginable, just like Amanda had been, and a respirator moved up and down, breathing for him. Jack moved to George's bedside and removed the bandage covering the bite mark on his neck. By now, the entire family, the pastor, and the doctor had joined Jack in the room.

"What are you doing?" The doctor asked.

Jack ignored the doctor and pulled the cork out of the flask. Anne stood in the doorway as Jack poured the water into George's wound. The instant the water touched the gash, it began to foam, just like when Jack was a child, and his mother would pour hydrogen peroxide into his cuts to clean them. Steam rose from the injured area, and the smell was unworldly. George did not react, but everyone in the room was stunned. The wound healed, and the skin was normal. It was as if no injury had ever taken place.

Jack scanned the room. Josephine and George's children were awestruck, and the doctor blinked in disbelief. Jack opened George's lips and began to pour the rest of the water from the flask into his mouth. When the flask was empty, Jack stepped back from George's bedside, and everyone in the room waited for a response. The room was quiet. All they could hear was the beeping of the machines. A minute passed, but George did not move.

The doctor stepped forward to check George's vital signs, but there was no change in his condition. Josephine looked at Jack hopefully, but Jack just kept staring at George, waiting for a reaction. There was none. The pastor guided George's children from the room while Jack watched for any sign of a change in his brother's condition, but nothing was happening. Josephine slowly made her way to Jack's side and held his hand. She whispered something in Jack's ear, and a single teardrop fell from Jack's eye and slowly rolled down his cheek.

The doctor clicked off the machines, one by one. Josephine hugged her husband and whispered *I love you* in his ear, then started to sob. Anne moved forward to comfort her, and soon Jack was the only one left in the room with his brother. Jack held

George's hand. No beeps from the machines, no respirators, nothing but silence.

***

Jack was at a loss for words. He was so sure that the water would revive his brother that he had not even prepared himself for this contingency. After what seemed like an eternity, Anne returned and put her arm around Jack's shoulder.

"I am so sorry, Jack." Anne's condolence was filled with sorrow. "I thought this was going to work. I wish I knew something profound to say to make you feel better."

"I know, Anne. I appreciate you being here."

Jack reached down and touched George's shoulder. "Goodbye, my brother. Your death was not in vain. Every time I look at Louis and David, I will remember your sacrifice. I will take care of your family."

Looking at Anne, Jack added, "At least George's nightmare is over. I'm afraid mine has just begun."

Jack's voice trailed off, and Anne convinced him to get treatment for his injuries. Before Jack left, he turned the lights off behind him, and the room went dark. George's body lay motionless in the bed. He never moved a muscle.

Epilogue

Three Months Later
Jack Aitken's Home, Bristow, VA

"You know I understand, Anne. I will set a place at the table for you and hope you will be in the chair when I carve the turkey. I'll speak with you soon. Goodbye."

Jack ended the call and put his cell phone down on the counter. He leaned over the sink and looked out the window. It was a breathtakingly beautiful sunny afternoon in Northern Virginia, but the gusts of wind beating against the kitchen window betrayed the chill in the air. Thanksgiving was next week, and Jack felt less than grateful. The last three months had been difficult. The future was uncertain.

The pain in Jack's hand remained intense, and he reached for the pain pills in the kitchen cabinet. He shifted the sling supporting his right hand and managed to open the bottle with his left. Despite multiple surgeries, the physical injuries he suffered at the hands of Lucius Rofocale and the Strigoi lingered. The doctors were pessimistic that he would regain dexterity in his hand, and he still had months of painful rehab ahead. The emotional and spiritual wounds were another matter entirely.

They were raw and angry, with no sign that they would heal soon. It did not help matters that Anne was still in Ocean Isle Beach. After Sheriff Hill's funeral, the mayor had requested that Anne temporarily assume leadership of the sheriff's office until they could name a successor. She agreed to do so out of respect for Sheriff Hill's memory but made it clear that she would be putting in her papers and returning to Northern Virginia. Anne told Jack that she was dedicating herself to protecting Louis and David and supporting Jack in any way possible.

Jack was grateful for Anne's selfless devotion to his boys, but locating a replacement for Sheriff Hill was challenging. Anne's return was long overdue, and now, it was likely that Anne would not be coming for Thanksgiving. It was difficult not having her around every day. She was Jack's sounding board and now, more than ever, his best friend. Jack knew in his heart that something far more significant than Anne's physical presence would be missing on Thanksgiving Day.

***

"Dad, may I have a juice box?" Louis asked with a smile as he entered the kitchen.

"Sure, but I think you will need to get it out of the refrigerator in the basement."

"Okay." Louis darted down the stairs.

Jack was relieved to see a smile on Louis's face. Since their return from the beach, the boys had become even more introverted. In part, Jack believed that the change was a response to the magnitude of the responsibility they would face. They also had questions that Jack felt ill-equipped to answer.

Anne's background in religious studies was an invaluable asset, and she often was able to respond to Louis and David's concerns in a far better way than he could. However, there was one question that Anne and Jack struggled to address: W*hy do God's prophets need to die?*

Jack was struggling with his fears surrounding what the role of being God's prophets truly meant for Louis and David. Trying to explain it all to the boys was beyond difficult. It was impossible. Jack recalled the first time he tried to explain who God was to Louis. Louis's reaction was one of fear. "I don't want somebody looking down at me from the sky all the time!"

Jack knew that dealing with death was something that every person needed to come to terms with, but in Louis and David's case, it led to a host of other concerns that usually came to light in a series of rapid-fire questions.

"Dad, what happens when a person dies?" Louis asked.

Then it was David's turn. "Dad, does it hurt to be killed?"

During the past three years, the boys had lost their grandfather, mother, and, as far as they knew, their uncle.

"Thanks, Dad!" Louis shouted, running upstairs, juice box in hand. "I have more studying to do."

Jack smiled at Louis's enthusiasm as he heard him charge up the stairs and slam the door to his room. David and Louis studied the Bible intensely to prepare for their responsibilities as God's prophets.

Jack's mind wandered back to George. He was constantly on Jack's mind, and losing his brother in the way he did was far worse than Jack could have imagined. It was crueler than death itself. As far as the boys were concerned, their uncle was gone, but Jack could not find a way to tell them the truth. Louis and David struggled to understand the concept of death, and what happened to George would only add to their confusion.

"I watched George die," Jack muttered, thinking back to that night, three months earlier.

***

Despite being given a sedative, Jack could not fall asleep after watching George die. Doctors insisted that Jack's injuries were severe enough to require admission to the hospital. Anne also was being kept overnight for observation due to concussion symptoms. The events of the day were playing over and over in his brain. He was trying to comprehend why the water would heal George's wound, but after pouring the remaining liquid down George's throat, it did not give him back his life. The lack of any reaction made no sense. A response should have been instantaneous. Jack was sure of it!

***

Jack sat at the kitchen table, sipping coffee. He tried to read a magazine, then play solitaire, but any attempt to distract himself was futile. His thoughts continually returned to the same thing—the video. What he saw that night defied logic and reason. Jack was initially elated by what he saw, but it did not take long for that hope to give way to despair.

**

Somehow, Jack had eventually drifted off, only to be awakened when his doctor and the hospital administrator burst into his room. Jack was groggy enough at the time to not comprehend what they were saying, but his jaw dropped when the administrator shoved an iPad in front of Jack's face.

"This video comes from the hospital morgue, Mr. Aitken." The administrator handed Jack the device, her shaking hands betraying her uneasiness.

"You are not going to believe what is on it."

The picture showed a body on a table in the middle of the room with a cloth covering it. Then the administrator hit the play button, and Jack lay agape in his bed, watching the corpse come to life. Robotically, the figure sat up, turned, and hung its legs off the table's edge. It placed its feet on the floor and headed toward the door.

"What the hell." The words slowly fell out of Jack's mouth.

The video next showed the figure walking down the hallway.

"Now, watch this." The administrator hit a button that paused the video, then another that zoomed in on the figure's face.

"George?" Jack whispered incredulously. "It can't be."

"That's what we thought, Mr. Aitken," the doctor interjected.

"Where is he now?" Jack quickly asked.

"The recording from outside the hospital showed him walking through the parking lot, but he eventually steps out of the range of the cameras."

"We've got to call the police," Jack replied.

"We already did that, Mr. Aitken. They can't find him."

"What?" Jack uttered in disbelief.

"Mr. Aitken." The doctor interrupted. "I saw you give him a drink. What was in that flask?"

"Water," Jack answered. "It was water."

***

"Dad, are you okay?" David asked. Jack had not even heard him come down the stairs.

"Sure, buddy," Jack answered, hiding the truth from his son. "I'm fine."

As he left the kitchen, David grabbed a bag of chips. "See you later."

As he watched David go down the hall, Jack poured another cup of coffee. He knew what he gave George was more than just water, but there was no way to expand on the answer without opening himself up to more questions. So, he kept his mouth shut. The police searched for days, but there was no sign of his brother anywhere. Anne even called her friends in JESU, who agreed to look for George, but they had come up empty.

Calling Josephine every few days to update her on the search was hard. He still had no clue where George had gone. No phone calls. No emails or text messages. No letters or postcards. George had disappeared without a trace. Jack put up a good front for her sake, but he was losing hope himself. Every day without any news about his twin's whereabouts was like death by a thousand cuts.

Jack picked up his cup, opened the sliding glass doors, and stepped out onto the deck. The stiff breeze out of the north signaled the colder weather that was on its way. Jack felt a shiver run down his spine and an anxious feeling in his gut. He could not shake the fear that his decision to pour the toxic water down George's throat was ultimately to blame for the predicament they found themselves in, and the answer to only one question would confirm or refute this belief.

Where are you, my brother?

Later That Same Night
The basement of the Bradford House Culpeper, VA

"PLEASE, MASTER LUCIUS!" The voice pleaded. "LET ME EXPLAIN!"

Lucius Rofocale stood with his arms folded, a nasty sneer on his face. The figure in front of him, dressed in rags, was shaking like a leaf.

"Begging is not the behavior I expect from members of my legions," Lucius replied contemptuously. "I also expect one hundred percent loyalty, no matter how infrequently you may see me. You can best judge a demon by what they will not do behind your back."

"Master, I didn't do what you think I did."

"Really? So, Tatiana is a liar?"

"No, sir." The demon quickly interjected. "But—"

"But what?" Lucius interrupted. "Is she, or is she not? It is not a difficult question to answer."

The demon was now terrified, unable to decide what to say next. Lucius swiftly decided for him. Motioning with his hand, an executioner dressed in black stepped forward and, in one swift motion, severed the demon's head from its body. The head struck the floor with a thud, the look of panic now permanently imprinted on its face. There was a knock at the door.

"Come." Lucius uttered tersely.

"Master Lucius, this demon is the last conspirator on the list."

"Good. All of this is becoming tedious."

"The bikers are in the cell down the hall. The knockout pills we used to get them here have worn off, and they are, shall we say, agitated."

"Well done, Tatiana." Lucius nodded approvingly. "Once again, you have demonstrated your value to me."

Tatiana snapped to attention. "Thank you, Master Lucius."

"Tatiana, go check in on our little mother. She is due any time now."

Lucius motioned at the executioner, "You, come with me."

***

Lucius, with a smirk on his face, entered the cell where Tatiana had detained the biker gang.

"Gentlemen, good evening to you."

"Good evening, my ass," one of the bikers protested.

"What the hell is this all about, old man?" Demanded another.

"Charming," Lucius smirked. "Exactly the manners I expected. Tell me, which of you is the leader of your club?"

The tallest member of the gang stepped forward confidently.

"I'm the leader of the Arch Fiends. They call me Prince of Darkness."

"Really?" Lucius expressed with surprise. "I must tell Tatiana that she outdid herself."

"Enough of the bullshit." The leader announced. "We're leaving, now."

Lucius waved his hand, and the gang members all froze in place.

"Prince, I can't move."

"Me too, Prince." Shouted another gang member.

"What's the game, old man?" Prince asked angrily.

"Not a game," Lucius answered gleefully. "A friendly wager."

"I'm listening," Prince replied.

"Simple. My variation on—what do participants call it? Fight club? If you win the fight, you get to leave."

Prince began to laugh. "I have to fight you, old man?"

"Not me." Lucius retorted. Pointing to the executioner, he said, "Him."

Prince sized the executioner up. "He doesn't look like much to me."

"To make it fair, he will fight not just you but the entire gang."

The room erupted with laughter.

"What are you trying to do?" Prince surveyed his gang and chuckled. "Get your man killed?"

"Do we have a wager?" Lucius asked, ignoring the laughter and taunts of the gang. "I will close the door, and whoever walks out is the winner."

"His blood is on your hands, old man."

"One final stipulation." Lucius's lips curled into an evil grin. "Hand-to-hand combat only. Your weapons have been confiscated and will be returned to you if you survive. Agreed?"

Prince punched his open left palm with his right fist several times. "Let's get it on. We don't have all night."

Lucius nodded at the executioner, then shut the door behind him.

"You going to take that thing off your head?" Prince asked the executioner. "I'd like to see the face of the man I am going to kill."

The executioner removed the hood, and the gang burst into laughter once more.

"Look at this guy," one of the bikers remarked. "The old man must be off his nut!"

"And I thought we needed a haircut," chuckled another. "Hey man, if you get hairier, you could be a miniature bigfoot."

The gang slowly began to surround the executioner until they encircled him. The executioner stood still with a stoic look on his face, and after a moment or two, The Prince of Darkness broke the silence.

"Are you just going to stand there?"

Moving closer, the Prince of Darkness towered over the executioner. Looking down, the gang leader stated, "Let's get this over with; it's your funeral, man."

Lucius leaned against the wall outside the room, listening to the cursing and anguished cries of pain emanating from behind the door. All the while, he just stared at the watch on his wrist. Five minutes later, the door opened, and much to Lucius's surprise, the Prince of Darkness, stood in the doorway. Suddenly, a hand burst through his torso, and the dead body fell to the floor. The executioner stepped forward and dropped the Prince of Darkness's still-beating heart from his hand. Lucius peered into the cell and saw nothing but dead bodies everywhere. A perverse smile came over his face.

"I planned to make Jack Aitken my agent of death, but you have done well. Tell me, do you feel any remorse? Any conflicted emotions?"

"No, Master Lucius." The executioner answered with a monotone response.

Lucius viewed his protege approvingly. Three months earlier, he had come painstakingly close to fulfilling one of his ultimate fantasies, killing Jack Aitken. It was true that ensuring the safety of a pregnant Maricela Antonescu was his prime objective, but he had unfinished business with the Aitken family. All three of them. His apprentice, appropriately referred to by his demons as The Executioner, would be the perfect instrument for their destruction. He or perhaps more appropriately, it would succeed where the Strigoi had failed.

"Master Lucius," Tatiana shouted. "Come quickly!"

***

Lucius entered another room in the basement of the Bradford House. Despite the attempts by JESU, their warding spells were no match for him, and he was able to occupy the house and make it his headquarters once more. Lucius saw Maricela Antonescu on a hospital bed in the room. Based on her screams, it was apparent that she was in labor. The epic event was upon them, the prophet's birth, the lord of darkness who will proclaim Lucifer's vision to the world!

Lucius waved to The Executioner to join him. "Come witness the event that will change everything."

The Executioner stepped into the room as Lucius commanded. His brain held no memories of his past. No recollection of what his life had once been. All he could recall was the impulse in his brain that brought him to his master. Lucius had taught him how to kill, and he was an excellent student. Lucius had allowed him to hone his skills by executing thousands of disloyal demons. Destroying the biker gang was his final test. Now, he was ready to fulfill his most important assignment: To kill someone named Jack and his two sons, Louis and David.

Tatiana coached Maricela Antonescu. "One more push, girl."

Not strong enough to escape, Maricela Antonescu had resigned herself to her destiny, her infamous fate. She pushed hard one last time and felt the labor pains suddenly subside. She fell back into the bed, exhausted. Tatiana cleaned up the baby, the false prophet, and handed the child to Lucius.

Lucius beamed with joy, held the baby above his head, and shouted, "IT'S A GIRL!"

Printed in Great Britain
by Amazon